HOLLOW POINT

R.M. RUXTON

Cover design & photography: R.M. Ruxton.

Published by

Rīoghal

ISBN: 978-1-7638577-2-8

DEDICATION

To my wife, whose encouragement, patience, inspiration and support helped
bring this book to life.

<h1 style="text-align:center">CHAPTER 1</h1>

Rex McGregor arrived home and dumped his school bag in the entrance hall, eager to try out the game he downloaded yesterday. It required an old-style modem to get access to the best features and now he had one, stuffed tightly into his bag. He fished out the now slightly less than pristine box and as he stood, he noticed Grandad's old black Bakelite telephone on the corner of the sideboard. *Thanks Grandad, I might need that,* he thought. He grabbed it from the table and clomped down the hall to his bedroom. He located the old telephone point under his desk and folded his tall lanky frame beneath to plug in Grandad's phone. When Rex asked him about the phone line last night, Grandad said it should still work and would call a technician friend to check it. Sitting cross-legged and bent over awkwardly under his desk, Rex picked up the heavy black handset to check for a dial tone but instead heard a ringing tone, as if he had dialled a number. He hung up quickly. That wasn't supposed to happen.

Rex was about to try again when the phone's bells rang loudly, a long continuous ring. Rex banged his head on the underside of the desk in surprise and ran his hand through fine sandy blonde hair, searching for a bump. The phone kept ringing. Tentatively, Rex lifted the handset again.

'Who is this?' asked Rex, sure it would be the phone technician.

'Mister Potato Head,' said a man. He didn't sound much like a technician. Much too old. Too old to be making prank calls.

'Yeah, right, and I'm Rex.' A memory from a movie popped into Rex's head.

'Good,' said the voice. 'Glad you contacted us. This is a secure line. We're reactivating Point Cruise and you will assume command of operations from the base once you get it up and running. This will be your operation from head to toe. Recruit as you see fit, report to no-one, and above all, keep it black.'

'Sure,' said Rex, playing along with the joke.

'Oh, and one other thing. Leave the hotel operating as cover. The owners are rich enough to buy Miami, and it will keep the locals from poking around.'

'Got it. Then what?' asked Rex. This joker was surely going to come to the punchline soon.

'You'll know when you're needed. As I said, this is your show. Good luck.' The phone clicked and went silent.

Rex held the heavy black handset away from his head and looked at it, not quite understanding what just happened. He listened again to the silent line and tapped the hook button a few times. The receiver crackled and was silent again.

Rex replayed the conversation in his mind. His dad's new hotel was at Point Cruise, and it was already being 'reactivated'. The place was a rundown wreck until his mum and dad bought it off the government and redeveloped it into a hotel. He was due to go there at the end of school term, not that he wanted to. His parents' hotels were always the same. Polished marble and suited up drones with too much gel in their hair. This one was a bit different at least — it was supposed to be haunted. Not actually haunted, but his dad said there was a growing demand for haunted hotels. It couldn't be reactivated any more than it already was, and Rex couldn't close it because it wasn't his to close, let alone command. He couldn't figure this one out right now - if there was anything to figure out. Just some random prank call. Maybe some crossed wires. He lifted the handset again to check. Normal dial tone. He clacked the hook buttons a few times. Still normal. Rex used the old rotary dial to dial the technician's number to see if he had any idea. The tech answered on the third ring.

'Hi, it's Rex McGregor here. Grandad said I should check with you to make sure this line is okay to use?'

'G'day, Rex. Yes, it's all working again. There was something weird about it though and it took a while to figure out which phone line to use. Your apartment block backs onto the old spook building, and I think they had a few special lines installed. They were all dead though. Why? Any problems?'

'Not anymore,' said Rex. 'I think I got a crossed line for a minute, but it seems to be working now.'

'Yeah, I suppose that could happen. The old exchange equipment hasn't been active for years now. Should be fine now though.'

'Cool. Um ... you said, 'spook building'?'

'Oh, yeah, ah ... Airlie House I think it's called. Used to be ASIO headquarters or something. The police own it now but like I said, all the old lines to that place are dead. Your building used to be a tennis court last time I worked in that area.'

'Huh,' said Rex. 'Well, anyway it seems to be working now. Thanks.'

'No worries. Good luck.' The tech hung up. His last words reminded Rex of his previous phone conversation. Maybe there was some connection between Mister Potato Head and Airlie House.

Rex extracted himself from underneath the table and rubbed his head again. Lost in thoughts about bases and how to activate them, he began removing the old modem from the packaging, dropping quick start leaflets on the floor. Point Cruise wasn't his operation anyway, it was his father's new hotel, and only the major investors knew all the details about that. Leave it running ... pfft. He shrugged and finished hooking the modem up to his laptop.

Someone at school, he couldn't remember who, mentioned something about a retro-style game called Stealth Ops Experience that was available for free on an obscure site he'd never heard of before. When he found the site and read about the game it didn't really sound very enthralling, but it required an old-style modem to get access to the best features. There were some good reviews of the game, so he decided to give it a try. He logged into the game and selected the special mode. The modem sprang to life and made weird buzzing sounds before falling silent, with just a few blinking lights to show it was active. A progress bar appeared on the laptop screen showing the special features were downloading. After a few minutes of watching the bar edge slowly along, Rex decided there was nothing to do but wait. A perfect opportunity for one of his favourites; microwave pizza.

Rex's parents would have a fit if they knew he was stuffing his face with prefab, tasteless, snap frozen, garlic laden garbage. The cheese was possibly even worse than the plastic-coated slices they served up at school. Whether it was the guilty pleasure of defying the culinary palate his parents had acquired over generations, or the simple fact that it was instant pizza cooked with minimal effort, it tasted bloody good. Well, to a starving teenager it did, and he polished it all off in a few minutes.

He dumped the plastic packaging in the bin, slotted his plate in the dishwasher, swung the dishwasher door shut with his heel and headed back to his room. The game was still downloading special stuff, the modem lights blinking rapidly. Rex turned his thoughts to homework. Some reading for English, an assignment for Geometry, and a Computing Studies test first thing in the morning. The English text was boring and predictable; not one of Steinbeck's finest. Rex could run rings around what the Computing Studies teacher knew, and the Geometry assignment was about stuff Rex had figured out years ago.

Rex opted instead to investigate what the technician had said about the phone lines and started searching for information on 'Airlie House'. The first thing he found was that as well as being a police training facility, it once belonged to the Health Department as a tuberculosis clinic and was for a small time a girls' school. Nowadays you could hire it out for functions. Hardly spooky. He clicked on another link to the history of the house and found that it was once used as the headquarters of Special Operations Australia during the Second World War. This was more like it. Reading further, he found that SOA planned and carried out some daring raids on Japanese held harbours. *But*, Rex thought, *that all happened years ago. Even if it was just a crossed line, why would someone be calling an organisation that didn't exist anymore?*

The download window popped up bringing Rex back to the present. The game had finally finished downloading. Rex looked at the time. Almost ten and he had a test in the morning. The game would have to wait until tomorrow. Rex saved his searches about SOA and went to bed.

The test took Rex less than half an hour to complete. He spent the remaining half hour doodling a cartoon he dubbed 'Do Computing Teachers Dream of Electric Students'. Hardly a work of art, and not likely to be any competition to Phillip K. Dick's universe. After the test, Rex pinned it up on the school noticeboard while no one was looking. He'd pinned many other of his musings on this board. Some were thinly veiled digs at teachers and got quite a laugh before being removed, usually by the teacher depicted. Others were quietly moved to the glassed-in section to be protected, usually the ones pointing out some teacher's sleazy attempts at pushing their political views. Rex wasn't sure which teacher saved them, but they obviously agreed with him. Hopefully by the end of term exams he would have a whole series.

After the break, Rex made his way to the Geometry classroom, avoiding the usual bullies on his way. Every school he attended had bullies, some of them teachers and Rex always tried to stand up to them. They were all unique in the way they operated, but the personalities were all the same. Each one of them had something going on at home that they couldn't or wouldn't deal with, but none of them had the guts to stand up to their own individual oppressors. Instead, they took their frustrations out on everyone else. Sometimes, they found themselves again to be victims. Rex was big enough and smart enough to fight back now, but after being expelled twice from different schools just for defending himself he learned that it was easier to avoid them. These days he left them to their own insecurities. Except for Mr Turnbull. There was no avoiding him. Rex wondered if the cartoon he just posted was such a good idea after all.

The classroom was still emptying its previous fill of students when Rex arrived. He slipped in amongst the tail end of confused students dejectedly filing out. The teacher noticed Rex as he sat at his usual seat.

'Morning, Rex. How did your Computing Studies test go?' asked Mr Babbage.

'Pretty good, I think,' said Rex, knowing that he had got all the exam questions correct. Mr Babbage was Rex's Computing Studies teacher last year and was one of his favourites.

'Pretty good? Aced it more like. You're already a year ahead of the syllabus. Anyway, I've just got to go and get some more notes. You'll be alright if I leave you in here until I get back?'

'Yeah, no problem.'

Mr Babbage slid the door shut behind him and Rex was alone for a few minutes until the rest of the class arrived. Rex took out his laptop and opened the school website, then logged in to the teacher portal using the administrator account and password he'd guessed. He'd never used this access to change his results, just to find out before anyone else did. He checked if Mr Turnbull had scored his test from earlier. The results had just been uploaded — 100%. Rex took a screenshot of the results. The door lock clicked signalling the return of Mr Babbage. Rex quickly shut down the teacher portal and went back to the school home page. Mr Babbage came back in with a grin on his face. As he passed Rex, he leaned down and said quietly, 'Turnbull isn't happy with your latest artwork, Rex.'

'What? It's not even about him.'

'Yeah, I know, and thanks for not making me look like an idiot, but Turnbull thinks it's about him. Just a heads up.' He moved to the front of the classroom as the rest of the class moved into seats around Rex.

Near the end of the class, Rex decided he better check his test score again, just in case Turnbull had figured out who drew the cartoon. Obviously he had, because his score was now 74%, changed just a few minutes ago by Mr Turnbull. Rex clenched his jaw tightly as he fumed. That was a 'B'. Rex had never got a 'B' at this school, and he wasn't about to get one now – certainly not in Computer Studies, and definitely not because of Turnbull. The smarmy git was just jealous that a student was smarter than him. But if he simply changed the score back with the administrator account they'd know it was him. Still, he couldn't let Turnbull get away with it, and there was another way. First, he took a screenshot of Turnbull's alteration, then opened his database management system and connected to the student score database. He found the transaction that altered the score and reverted it, then erased the record of Turnbull downgrading his score. Now there was no trace of Turnbull ever having altered Rex's score in the first place, no record of Rex doing anything, and his grade was back to 100%. He logged out just as the class was wrapping up.

On the way to his next class, Rex passed by the noticeboard. His cartoon was gone. *That figures*, thought Rex. He got to his locker, dumped his bag down and was about to open it when Turnbull came out of the staff room and spotted Rex. He started walking toward Rex, a smarmy smirk on his face. As he passed Rex he said, 'You're not as smart as you think you are, McGregor.'

'Neither are you,' said Rex under his breath.

Turnbull stopped and turned back to Rex. 'What did you just say?'

Rex had had enough and turned to face Turnbull. Out loud and slowly, he repeated, 'Neither. Are. You.'

Turnbull took a step towards Rex, raising his finger to poke into Rex's chest. 'Now you listen to me. Scribbling stupid cartoons about me doesn't make you smart.'

Rex stepped back to stay out of Turnbull's reach. 'They're not about you, and it's not what I was talking about. How smart do you feel now?'

Again, Turnbull stepped closer to Rex. A lot closer. With each word, he poked Rex in the chest. 'Smarter. Than. You.'

Rex could feel his anger rising and being prodded edged him close to hitting back. If he did, though, he'd be expelled – again – but he wouldn't let Turnbull think he could push him around either. 'Back off!' he shouted.

Turnbull stepped backwards in surprise, caught his foot in the straps of Rex's bag and fell sprawling on the floor. Other students laughed and cheered as Turnbull struggled to his feet. He pointed first at Rex, then at a security camera behind and above Rex. 'I'll have you for this.' He turned and walked hurriedly back to the staff room.

At the end of the next class, Rex checked the student portal to see if the official test results had been posted. Still 100%. Too late for Turnbull to change them back now. He closed his laptop and was about to enter the next classroom when from behind, someone called out.

'McGregor!'

It was Turnbull. He looked almost happy, smirking like a career criminal that had just bribed a judge.

'Principal wants to see you. Something about assaulting a teacher, and hacking your test score.'

'I didn't change my test score, and you assaulted me,' replied Rex with an air of innocence. That wiped the smirk off his face.

'Principal! Now!'

On his way to the principal's office, Rex reflected on what had happened. Turnbull was obviously setting him up and would never leave him alone from now on. Was it worth even trying to defend himself? He only had half a term left here anyway.

Time to face the music.

'I didn't push him, he tripped. And I only yelled at him because he was poking me in the chest.'

'Yes, Rex, I saw the video. I'll deal with Mr Turnbull later.' The principal took off his glasses and placed them on his desk. 'Now, about your test score.'

'I got 100%,' replied Rex.

'Mr Turnbull says he gave you 74%.'

Rex stayed silent, thinking fast. Technically, he didn't actually change the score.

The principal sighed. 'Look. I know Mr Turnbull gave you 74% because he showed me a screen shot.' Rex opened his mouth to retaliate, but the principal continued. 'However, I did see the modification time stamp, so I know he changed it to that. I also know there's no way you would have such a low mark, so ... I believe you got 100%, and I'll be reviewing your test myself later to check.' The principal tapped his fingers on the desk, thinking. 'Unfortunately, whatever you did to reverse Mr Turnbull's change means that you had to have accessed something you shouldn't have, and as you know, that means I have to take disciplinary action.'

'But Turnbull changed my score,' protested Rex. 'What's going to happen to him?'

'I said I'd deal with *Mr* Turnbull later, but yes, he will also be disciplined.'

'What about him poking me?'

'Ah, well, I'm sorry Rex, but the camera didn't pick that up. It does show that you never touched Mr Turnbull though, so it's pointless either of you pressing charges for assault. As for the other matter, I will speak to your parents later, but it is likely, given your past experiences and the conditions for your enrolment here, that you will no longer have a place at this college. I'm sorry Rex, but rules are rules.'

CHAPTER 2

'Incoming torpedo! Eight-hundred metres, bearing two three seven at sixty knots, Captain.'
'Helm, steer eight zero. Fire Control, standby to deploy decoy,' said Rex.
'Aye, Captain,' came simultaneously from the two stations.

The voice recognition on this game was amazing. No wonder the special features took so long to download. Rex's view of the sub's status showed various panels indicating what was happening. There were no fancy 3D views showing the incoming torpedo, no realistic explosions. It might have been real but for the fact that Rex was viewing it through a screen.

Rex waited until the torpedo had closed to within five hundred metres. 'Deploy decoy,' Rex said into his headphone-mounted microphone.

'Deploy Decoy. Aye, Captain.' A pause, and then, *'Decoy deployed. Tracking to intercept torpedo.'*

Rex figured the trick with these decoys was to swing them around right in front of the torpedo to confuse its guidance system, then run them away from the sub until the torpedo detonates or runs out of fuel.

'Decoy is in contact ... tracking away.'

Rex watched the blips on the radar-like screen showing echoes from sonar receivers arrayed along the hull of the sub. The two dots indicating the torpedo and decoy disappeared without a sound.

'Torpedo detonated, Captain. Decoy lost.'

A moment later the screen image shook to indicate the shockwave from the explosion, and a low boom and echoing rumble in Rex's headphones confirmed the hit. The game wouldn't allow him to pass training mode because the decoy was not supposed to be destroyed. It was either re-read the briefing and pass a test or wait three hours before trying again. The laptop battery wouldn't last through all that. Rex shut down the game and thought about what he was going to tell his parents.

Matt noticed that Rex no longer had his headphones on and ventured a conversation. 'Kicked out again?' he asked.

8

'Um, sort of. I would have quit anyway. How did you know?'

'School term hasn't finished, and I'm driving you down to Lenzie Bay. Wasn't that hard to work out really.' Matt changed lanes to avoid a truck struggling up the outbound slope of the Westgate Bridge, the driver gave a wave and a thumbs-up as they passed. 'Plus, your dad told me.'

Rex caught Matt's grin in the rear-view mirror. 'Ha ha,' he said, and couldn't help cracking a smile himself.

'So, what's the game then?' asked Matt. 'My nephew is into them, and I need a present for his birthday.'

'Stealth Ops Experience,' said Rex, relieved not to have to think about what his parents were going to say. 'It's a submarine-based simulation. No fancy graphics, but you can tell it what to do through voice commands. Not bad so far, but it forces you to learn all the theory before you can start missions.'

'Mmm, sounds a bit too complicated for my nephew. And he mumbles too much. Probably wouldn't be able to play it.'

'I only got it yesterday. This is the first chance I've had to play, but now it wants me to do more theoretical stuff or wait for ages.'

'Ah, right,' said Matt, understanding. 'I supposed you were busy packing ... and a few phone calls, I imagine.'

Rex stared out of the window, recalling the dread laden phone calls to his mum and dad last night. In the end, it was settled; he would go to the hotel and help out while other arrangements were made. His dad didn't say much, so Rex couldn't tell how angry he was. He just said to pack up and be ready at nine in the morning for the car he'd organised. Matt, from Matt's Luxury Transport, was an ex-army, or air force ... or something. Rex couldn't remember what Dad had said exactly. Matt did work for his dad all over the world, but any trips for the family Matt handled personally. Rex was still fuming about being expelled and worried about what his dad would say when Matt picked him up, so he wasn't in the mood for small talk. As soon as he was in the car, he started the game and put on headphones to avoid conversation.

Matt changed lanes again to pass a slow-moving bus full of bored school kids. Rex looked up at them, their faces pressed against the windows. Eyes in both vehicles seemed to join in fellowship of boredom. Or dread.

'Isn't that your school?' asked Matt. Rex didn't even notice they were wearing the uniforms of the latest school to expel him.

Rex turned to look back as they passed. 'Yeah, I think so.'

'Is Turnbull still there?'

'Yeah. He was the one who got me booted,' said Rex, failing to disguise the utter dislike for Turnbull in his voice.

'Figures,' said Matt. 'My three boys went there too. None of them liked him and I don't blame them. He always was a sneaky git. Vindictive, too.' He shook his head, remembering. 'Bloody Turnbull. Screws up all the time but they haven't fired him.'

Rex lapsed into silence, brooding over the injustice of being punished for Turnbull's corruption.

It was about forty kilometres before reaching Point Cruise that Rex's brooding about being kicked out reached a head and he could keep his silence no more. Between pauses while he went through the whole situation in his head, he complained to Matt.

'It's not fair that I was kicked out for something Turnbull did.

'Technically, I didn't change anything. I just corrected an injustice.

'It wasn't incompetence it was just plain wrong.

'Turnbull should have got kicked out for altering my score, not me.

'It wasn't as if I broke a bully's nose like at the last school. Being expelled for that I can understand.'

Matt looked in the rear-view mirror occasionally as Rex went over the entire episode, interspersing solutions of how the schools IT department should be run with rants about how useless Turnbull and the principal were. He thought Matt wasn't really listening, just concentrating on negotiating the twisting mountain road that led down from the hinterland to the coast.

By the time the limousine approached the main street of Lenzie Bay, Rex's rant had run out of steam. They pulled up at a pedestrian crossing to allow a bus load of tourists to shuffle past, blinking in the strong sunlight. Matt took the opportunity to turn in his seat and face Rex directly for the first time in the journey.

'Look, mate, I know you didn't really do anything wrong, but you know what some people are like. They all work for someone else and have to impress them in order to make themselves look good. They have no sense of duty, and don't even try to do what they know is the right thing.' Matt turned back to face the wheel and moved the car gently forward when the crossing was clear.

Rex considered this in silence. At least someone agreed with him. Maybe his parents would too.

Minutes later they turned onto the road that snaked around the headland to the Hotel. Rex started to pack his laptop and headgear back into a bag. A few turns later, the hotel was in sight. A portico came into view extending over the driveway attached to a tall brick building that looked as though it belonged in a *Midsomer Murder* mystery. The facade facing the driveway blocked in and out to accommodate different sized rooms. A moss encrusted slate roof curved backwards from stone-pillared balustrades and over windows that seemed to be too small for rooms of any useful size. When Rex first saw the hotel about a year ago, he thought it was rather shabby and a little bit creepy, like an English manor house abandoned after a gruesome murder. Now it seemed somehow more welcoming. The only reason he wasn't living here already is because his parents wanted him to finish at least one whole year at a single school. So much for that.

Matt pulled the car up at the entrance and killed the engine. 'At least your mum, dad and grandad won't have to travel back and forth to Melbourne so much. You'll all be here together.' Rex didn't seem to notice, instead thinking about what his parents were going to say.

'Time to face the music then, I suppose,' said Rex, staring at the door.

Matt turned to face him again. 'Look, I'm sure you're right, it really didn't warrant expulsion, but the principal was always going to back the teacher before you. Don't worry. Your mum and dad will understand. So will your grandfather.'

'I guess there's no point in arguing is there.'

'No, not really. You didn't really want to stay there anyway, did you?'

Rex didn't really know what the alternative would be. Did Lenzie Bay even have a school? He climbed out of the car and Matt loaded his bags on to a porter's trolley. There was no one to be seen, no one to march out and grab him by the earlobe and drag him to his room. Not even a porter hoping for a tip. The place could have been deserted but for a small dog trotting toward him.

'Tom seems pleased to see you,' said Matt as he closed Rex's door and walked around the car. Tom was a battle-scarred Pembroke Welsh Corgi that seemed to come with the hotel. Defined muscles, deep red fur, a wide, wise looking face and a thick black scar across the top of his nose made him look like he could take on anything. Nobody was quite sure who owned him or how old he was. He sniffed at Rex's shoes and looked Rex in the eyes as if to welcome him back to the hotel, wagging what was left of his tail. Rex crouched down to scratch him under the chin, and Tom repaid the favour by licking Rex's wrist with a tongue that had the very end missing.

'He must like you,' said Matt, one leg halfway into the driver's seat. 'He'd take your hand off if he didn't.' He waved a sort of half salute. 'See you next time Rex,' he said. He swung into the limo and closed the door behind him.

Rex stood as the limo pulled away and disappeared down the ramp that led to the basement car park. Tom ambled off in the opposite direction leaving Rex to push the trolley and his luggage into the hotel entrance.

Last time he was here, the interior was a work site and just about everything was covered up with sheets of plastic but now, despite its appearance on the outside, the inside of the hotel was the five-star finish Rex had become used to in his father's hotels. Although this one had a distinctly Old English feel to it, you could tell all the wood was newly varnished and polished. The floors were large slabs of mirror-like white marble. Even though there seemed only to be dim wall sconces for lights, the high ceiling of the foyer was well lit by hidden indirect lights. There was a bright outline of sunshine angling down one wall highlighting a very shiny full suit of armour, though it wasn't clear from where the light was coming, since the foyer appeared to have no windows. Opposite, a staircase swept up from the right side of the reception desk, curving back over the foyer. On the wall behind the landing was a large oil painting of a four masted barque in full sail, struggling against an obstreperous sea. To the side of the staircase, a grandfather clock at least eight feet tall stood marking off time with a calming steady beat.

Rex maneuvered the trolley over to the left of reception and looked around, expecting his mother or father to burst from the door behind the desk and lecture him about being expelled ... again. He reached out his hand to tap the bell on the desk.

'Ah, Rex! You're here,' said a voice behind him, causing Rex to jump and whirl around. Towering over him was a man — tall, muscular, hawkish dark-blue eyes, short dark hair, and dressed in dark camouflage. Rex's panic subsided a little as he realised it was Grandad.

'Where did you come from?' asked Rex.

'France, originally, but just now from that door there.' He pointed behind where Rex had left his trolley.

'You've got to stop sneaking up on me,' said Rex. 'You nearly gave me a heart attack.'

'Good!' replied Grandad. 'This is supposed to be a scary hotel after all.' He reached out both arms and gripped Rex by the shoulders. 'It's good to see you here. We need all the help we can get right now.'

Rex glanced over his shoulder. 'What about Mum and Dad? Are they going to kill me, or what?'

'Ha!' Grandad's bellowing laugh echoed for a moment. 'Don't you worry about them. They've got too much other stuff to be worried about before opening night. You might want to offer to pitch in though. You know, smooth the waters?'

'But ... aren't they mad?'

'Well, yes ... and, no.' Grandad released Rex and lifted a section of the reception desk so he could walk behind. 'I certainly never expected you to last long at that dreary school, and I know they've already organised for you to start earlier than expected at a new school.' He reached under the desk and took out a plastic card and a key attached together on the end of a lanyard. 'Not telling you which one though,' he said with a grin. 'Although I think you might actually enjoy this one.' He dangled the lanyard over the desk. 'Here's your room key, thirty-seven. Grab your stuff. Lift's over there.' He pointed to the back corner of the lobby. 'Porter doesn't start until Monday. Your mum and dad are interviewing now actually, so settle in and we'll see you for dinner.' He disappeared through the door behind the desk and Rex was left alone with just the slow ticking of the grandfather clock behind him.

Realising he was off the hook, at least for now, Rex wheeled the luggage trolley over to the lift. The doors sensed his approach and slid open allowing him to push the trolley straight in. As he turned to locate the lift buttons, another door at the end of the lobby opened. Rex heard his father saying his goodbyes to an interviewee. Before Rex could press the third-floor button, he saw a teenage boy about his own age but taller and thicker emerge nervously, close the door behind him and let out a lungful of air as if he'd just surfaced from a deep dive under water. He ran his hands up through short brown hair disturbing its previously neat appearance. He noticed Rex just as the doors began to close, and the two of them exchanged understanding smiles before the door closed. The lift took Rex upstairs with barely any indication that it was moving.

CHAPTER 3

Rex knew he could roll over and sleep in, but his mind had other ideas. His mum and dad had been unreasonably reasonable last night as he told them his version of events at school. Weirdly, they didn't seem angry at all - disappointed that this was the third school he'd been kicked out of, but they didn't seem surprised. At one stage in the discussion over dinner, Rex even thought he detected some respect. Then they ruined it by pointing out that he could have just gone to the principal in the first place. Rex knew they were probably right, but when they told him that Turnbull still hadn't been given the sack, he figured the outcome would have been the same anyway. There was just enough disappointment in their voices for Rex to offer to help out with the hotel without being asked. He must remember to thank Grandad for the tip. They finished up the interrogation by telling him the new school was the local High School, and thought he could do with a less competitive atmosphere. Did they even know what school was like? At least while he was here, he would be able to figure out what that phone call was about.

He lay awake in his new room, still getting used to the lack of city background noise and the way the light leaked around the still new curtains. This room was temporarily his while renovations on the private section of the hotel were completed. He looked around in the dim light. It was decorated in the same style as all the other hotel rooms, but without the cardboard no-smoking signs and room service menu. The thought of food convinced Rex to give up on sleep and go in search of breakfast. He pulled on jeans and a T-shirt, closed the door behind him and headed downstairs.

He arrived in the kitchen to find it deserted. Wondering if there was any food in the hotel at all, he navigated his way around the islands of stainless-steel cookers and worktops to the huge door of the cold store. Yanking sideways on the heavy handle, he slid the door open to find the racks almost empty. The only evidence of food was stacked neatly on one side, close to the door. Rex had never seen a hotel cold store this empty before and took the opportunity to wander in and look around. He walked to the far end of the room where cooling units were arrayed overhead. Large fans behind wire grills circulated cold air over the storage racks. Tubes ran from each unit to a gap above a metal door at the end of the central walkway. A sign on the door said, *Restricted Space — No Unauthorised Entry*. Rex went back to the crates near the door and selected some ingredients.

Rex had been in enough of his father's hotels to know the basic layout of a large kitchen. Cold store: bacon, eggs, sausages, tomatoes, juice; Freezer: hash browns; Herbs: kitchen garden. The last was dreamed up by Grandad and was now in most of his dad's hotels. He balanced the makings of a basic hot breakfast on one arm as he slammed the heavy door shut behind him with his free arm. Someone had obviously been supervising the kitchen setup very closely. Everything Rex needed was just where a junior chef doing the graveyard shift room service would expect to find it.

Breakfast was one of the few meals Rex was good at. He prepped, cooked, and cleaned up after himself leaving the dishwasher to take care of the pan. Holding a plate in one hand and a large glass of orange juice in the other, he backed his way through one of the swing doors into the hotel dining room and chose the table farthest from the window. The only other person in the room was a rotund man sipping coffee and writing in a small notebook at a table with a view out to the lake.

Rex picked up a piece of crispy bacon, chomped half of it off and wiped his fingers on his napkin before attacking the eggs with knife and fork. He almost finished off the whole plate before he noticed the man by the window had moved to the coffee machine. The man took two cups and quickly produced cappuccinos with the expertise of a city barista. He set the cups down in saucers, tucked a couple of books under his arm and came over to Rex, a coffee in each hand.

'Thought you might like a coffee,' he said, setting one down beside Rex, and the books in front of himself.

'Thanks,' said Rex.

'I'm Thomas Limbick, an investor in Roy's …, uh, your father's business. It's Rex, isn't it?'

'Pleased to meet you,' said Rex. He leaned over his breakfast, and they shook hands. 'Enjoying your book?' Rex could see the title on the spine - *A Drizzly Tuesday in Holland Park*.

'Not really, but a friend of mine wrote it. I felt obliged.' He regarded the book a moment as if still making up his mind. He turned back to Rex. 'Are you here on work experience before end of term?'

'Sort of,' said Rex. No one had to know the real reason he was not in school.

'Hmmm.' Mr Limbick didn't seem convinced. 'Well, you couldn't ask for a better placing. Beautiful scenery, a well-run organisation, plenty of things to explore. This place has a long history. Do you know much about it?'

'Not really,' replied Rex. 'I think it used to be some kind of military training base, then a mental hospital.'

Limbick smiled. 'Some might say the two are the same thing.'

Rex didn't think much of the joke. Grandad used to be in the forces, and he certainly wasn't mental.

After a pause, Limbick continued. 'I was in the army once. Intelligence. That certainly was crazy at times.'

'Were you a spy?'

'I suppose you could call it that, although it's nothing like the movies, you know. Very few people actually go undercover these days, but there was a lot of it during the war.'

'Australians?' Rex was doubtful.

'Oh yes. We were rather good at it too.'

Rex considered this while stirring the foam into his coffee. Limbick eyed Rex carefully for a moment. He seemed to be weighing something up in his mind.

'In fact'—Limbick leaned forward and lowered his voice conspiratorially—'I used to work here.' He sat back to watch the reaction on Rex's face. Rex raised his cup to drink, made the connection with the mysterious phone call and almost spluttered coffee all over the table.

'This was a secret base?'

Limbick raised his eyebrows and nodded slowly. Possibilities formed in Rex's mind for a moment before Limbick brought him back to reality. 'It's all but gone now though. I believe a basement level is being used by your father, but the rest ...' He waved his hand in dismissal. 'Anyway, the place was mostly gutted before we left. I believe some of the original navel stuff is still there, but I doubt anyone knows where it is anymore.'

'What sort of stuff?'

'Oh, ahh, well ...' Limbick looked at the ceiling as he tried to remember. 'When the navy built the place the power supply was prone to failure, so they put a tube system in place to communicate. Like they used to have on ships. I think they just covered them over instead of pulling them out.'

'Is that why you invested in this hotel?' asked Rex.

'Partly that. A bit of nostalgia I suppose, and I've known Roy and Sylvie for years, but mainly because I like the idea of a haunted hotel.' He paused, an anxious look developing on his face. 'I only hope the other investors don't pull out. It's a risky prospect this one, you see? Nobody else has put so much into an untested market. I got involved because I didn't want to see this lovely setting turned into a towering resort with no genuine landscape left.' He sipped his coffee and stared across the room and out the window.

'Who would do that?' asked Rex.

Limbick replaced his cup in the saucer and looked over at Rex. 'Oh, I don't know, Arabs, Asians ... it wouldn't be the first time they've ruined an idyllic hotel. It happened in the Seychelles. Then there are the so-called conservationists who want it for a wind farm or some nonsense. There are some locals with grand plans as well. At least your father wants to keep it largely as it is.' He picked up his notebook and waved it in the air as he said, 'Perseverance is the key, Rex. Perseverance. Remember that.'

Rex gave a weak smile and a nod, not totally convinced of this man's sanity.

Limbick went on. 'There have already been people creeping about at night, shadows in the black. Of course, that could just be just your grandfather's theatrics. Or poachers.' He finished his coffee and clattered the cup down on the saucer. 'So. Kicked out of school, eh? Which one?'

'Ah ...' Rex forced his brain to focus on the new subject. 'Domain Grammar,' he said, wondering where this was going.

'Hmmm, figures. I know a few people there. Some of them are more suited to the public system, but they're mostly pretty good. Still, getting kicked out for blowing the whistle on a teacher ... that's a bit rough.'

'That's what I thought,' said Rex. Finally, someone was on his side.

'I assume you had proof?'

Rex didn't even realise what a weird question this was coming from a complete stranger. He was glad to be able to rant to someone. Anyone. 'Of course I did, I had a screenshot. The principal just latched on to the fact that I had to have been hacking to get the evidence in the first place and ignored the fact that the teacher altered my score. They just assumed I was trying to hack my grades.' He paused and added, 'As if I need to anyway.'

'A good point. Did you raise that with the principal?'

'I didn't have to, he knew I would have got a high mark, but it didn't matter.' Rex imitated the principal's weasely voice. 'Rules are rules, Rex.' He pushed his plate away in disgust.

Limbick remained impassive and waited for Rex to cool down a little. He seemed satisfied with something.

'Well, Rex. I don't think you'll have any problems at your new school. I hear their setup is like Swiss cheese and very relaxed.' He stood, picked up his books and clapped Rex on the shoulder. 'I have to arrange some things, but I look forward to catching up later.' He smiled at Rex and headed for the doors to the lobby. He waved his notebook over his shoulder and repeated, 'Perseverance!'

The doors swung silently shut behind him, leaving Rex alone.

Nice bloke, thought Rex. A bit weird. He seemed vaguely familiar, like he'd seen him before somewhere.

Everything seemed connected lately.

Over the weekend, Rex got to know the hotel pretty well. Filling in for staff that hadn't started yet meant lugging bags out of cars and into rooms, answering calls for room service and when no one was looking, parking cars in the basement garage underneath the hotel. It only took a minute to drive the car down the ramp, find a spot, mark its number on a card and return via the lift to the lobby. If the lift was busy, Rex climbed the stairs up from the garage. Even though it was right underneath the hotel, there seemed to be an awful lot of stairs.

Grandad took Rex on a tour of the non-public areas of the hotel, starting with the storeroom that Rex thought must be on the same basement level as the garage. There was a service lift for the hotel staff that was separate from the guest and garage lifts, and ran from this level to the top floor. Leading off from the storeroom through a bolted door was an area left over from the days when the building was a mental hospital. With all white tiles and harsh fluorescent lights, the space now had workbenches with all sorts of machines for working with wood and steel, a rack of electronic gear in one corner, and a strange circular well near the end of the room. The well stood about waist height and was brimming over with water. Around the base of the well was a grate to drain the overflowing water away. Thick rubber-clad cables came out of the well and snaked over to an electronics rack where they divided and plugged into various complicated looking modules.

'What the heck is that?' asked Rex, pointing to the well.

'That's our opening night act,' replied Grandad. 'A bit of a light and sound show. All controlled from here.'

'Where does this go?' said Rex, peering into the depths of the water.

'To the lake. I'm not exactly sure why it was built like that, but it has certainly proven to be handy.'

'What happens when it rains?'

'Well normally we'd have the lid shut'—Rex noticed the heavy iron hatch folded back behind the well for the first time—'but apparently the lid isn't for keeping the water out. It drains over the sides and through the grate. I'm not exactly sure where it goes after that.'

'What's the show?'

'Hah! You'll find out. Just make sure you're in the dining room at seven tomorrow night.' A chirping noise came from Grandad's pocket. He extracted a phone and read the message. 'I'll leave you to it. Don't touch anything for now, I'll show you how it all works after the show. Just pull the door locked behind you.'

Alone, Rex wandered around looking at each machine and carefully examining the racks of blinking lights, buttons and displays. Cryptic mnemonics surrounded switches and knobs that looked too complicated to touch. After a few minutes, he pulled the door of the well room closed behind him and wandered around the storeroom. An open space allowed access to towels and bed linen stacked on racks built so high they almost touched the ceiling. There was another door next to the well room. Rex tried to open it, but it was locked. Looking around, Rex noticed a grill in the ceiling near the corner. *Must be an air vent*, thought Rex. Now standing underneath the grill, Rex listened and heard faint voices and a car door slam shut. The garage must be on the other side of that wall. *There should be a door here*, he thought. Seems an obvious place to put one for loading supplies. Rex gave up on speculation and headed back to his room. School tomorrow. He had better get his books together.

The stares from the few kids that turned up to school early made Rex think the limo was not such a good idea. He clamoured from the back seat to the front seat, long limbs bending in impossible ways much to Matt's amusement and exited the car from the front door. He hooked his bag over his shoulder and avoided any eye contact as he headed for what he presumed was the office. There was no sign, but it seemed the best bet. It was the only entrance bracketed by pillars copied from an ambiguous ancient era. Tentatively, he pushed his way through the door, part of him hoping no one would be there so he'd have to return home. *Wow*, he thought, *I'm already calling the hotel home.*

A bespectacled, middle aged, miniature matron bustled out of a door and almost rammed Rex back out into the yard.

'Oh! I didn't see you there.' She stepped back and removed her glasses to let them hang around her neck. 'You must be the newbie! Rick, isn't it?'

'Rex. Rex McGregor.'

'Well, Double-Rex McGregor, come with me and we'll get you settled.' She was still tittering to herself about her little joke as she led Rex into a corridor and around a corner. 'I'll show you where your home room and the lockers are. Then we'll see if Miss Lally is around. She's normally in early. I'm Mrs Mansfield, the principal. Most of the kids just call me Mrs M. Now, a few house rules you need to know. No mobile phones are to be used on the school grounds or we crush them. Uniforms are not optional, but ties are. No smoking, no canoodling, no drugs or alcohol, blah, blah, I'm sure you know the rest.' After walking down an endlessly long corridor flanked by prefab, cloned classrooms, she pulled up at a group of lockers indistinguishable from all the others but for the numbers stenciled on the doors.

'You can have two-four-seven, one-zero-one or three-five-seven. Don't ask why they aren't painted in consecutive numbers. I think the painter was from Venice.'

'Um ... three-five-seven thanks.'

'Good choice. All primes.' She reached up to the electronic lock, keyed in 357#3233* and turned the handle to open the metal door. 'Now, think of a four-digit number, key it in and turn the handle back to close. That will be your combination. If you ever forget, come and see me and I'll reset it for you.'

Rex keyed in eight-zero-zero-eight and turned the handle.

'That's right. Now key it in again and open the door to test it.'

Rex did so with predictable success, pushed his bag inside the locker and closed it again. He turned to find Mrs M gone. Puzzled, Rex moved down to the next doorway to see if she'd gone into the nearest classroom, but it was deserted.

'I can't find Miss Lally.' Mrs M's voice came from right behind him, making him jump. 'Not to worry, I know who can show you around.' She marched off further down the corridor to another door and disappeared inside. By the time Rex had caught up she was coming back out of the door again. A girl followed behind her who looked Rex up and down and smiled.

'This is Penelope, and this is your home room, number ten. Penelope is in your home group. She'll show you where the timetables are. Miss Lally can fill you in on the rest.' She headed back up the corridor towards the office, calling out as she went. 'If you need anything, let me know.'

'Mrs M's not one to stick around with students,' said Penelope. She was shorter than Rex by about half a foot, with dark brown straight hair cut just above her shoulders, striking green eyes that poked out a little too much, and eyebrows like caterpillars. Rex felt doubly out of place dressed in his crisply pressed uniform compared to Penelope's slightly dull and frayed school dress. 'Come this way. Miss Lally will be getting her morning cup of tea.'

She led Rex up the corridor after Mrs M, who had disappeared in a crowd of other students filtering in from the school yard. Penelope and Rex pushed through the crowd, drawing a few interested looks and some whispered chatter and laughter. They came to a door where the adjacent windows were plastered over with notices and newsprint that looked older than the school itself.

Penelope followed his gaze. 'Yeah, some of that is really old. They found it under the lino when they demolished the old school buildings.' Rex tried to read some of the words, but most of the stuff lower down that he could see was obscured by small children's pictures of dogs chasing cats. Penelope entered the staff room to fetch Miss Lally. Rex waited outside and looked higher up the window trying to make out headlines: *War! — Drought Ends — Earthquake: Smugglers Cove Sealed — Panther Sighted.* Rex had seen something about a panther in the weekend papers. Grandad laughed when he read it, shook his head slowly and muttered something along the lines of 'some things never change'. Penelope returned with a short woman with thick, black-rimmed spectacles.

'Ahh, you must be the new lad,' she said with a thick Scottish accent. 'I'm Miss Lally.'

'This is Rex,' said Penelope.

'Good, good. Well, your first class is with me, and it's almost time. Come along, then.'

They approached the door of their home room where more students were talking outside. Another girl with long wavy blonde hair, blue eyes and a cheeky face noticed Rex. She smiled at him and introduced herself. 'Hi, I'm Amy. You're new here?'

'Yeah. Hi, I'm Rex.'

'I see you've already met Penelope,' said Amy with feigned sweetness.

'Ah, yeah,' said Rex, noticing Amy added a bit more emphasis on the last syllable of Penelope than was necessary. Obviously some animosity between these two.

Penelope piped up, eager not to be sidelined. 'Yes, this is Rex McGregor. His parents own the new hotel.' She looked pleased to be able to reveal this information. The look Rex gave her might have set her hair on fire had she been standing any closer. He didn't want people to know he was from a rich family. People treated you differently. Rex was suddenly conscious of his brand-new shirt and his tie, which no other boy seemed to be wearing.

'It doesn't matter what his parents own, Penelope. He's a student here like all the rest of you.' Miss Lally continued to Rex. 'Have ye got your locker yet?' Rex nodded.

The bell rang interrupting any further comment. As Rex entered the door, he heard Penelope sniping at Amy. 'First it's Scott, and now you're after fresh meat.'

'You would jump to that conclusion wouldn't you,' said Amy, before following on behind Rex.

Miss Lally brought the class to attention. 'Alright everybody, settle down, settle down.' The class quieted; some had noticed the new student. 'I'd like you all to make welcome our newest student, Rex McGregor. As some of you may already know'—she directed her gaze at Penelope, sitting on her own near the front—'Rex's family are the new proprietors of the hotel on Point Cruise, opening tonight.' A few of the students who were not clued in to this information pricked up their ears. 'Rex joins us after leaving a very good school in Melbourne, so try not to embarrass yourselves. I'm sure you all realise that it is very daunting to join a new school mid-term, so please do your best to make him feel welcome.' The class sat in silence; stunned or bored, Rex could not tell.

Miss Lally scanned the room. 'Alright, everybody appears to be here. Those of you with different classes, off you go. Rex your first class is here with me, I have your timetable here.'

Two thirds of the students rose out of their seats to leave. Rex was relieved that Penelope was one of them.

At the end of Rex's first English class with Miss Lally, she handed him his timetable with his classes already highlighted in yellow.

'Your next class is Computer Studies. I hear you're quite a wiz.'

Rex didn't remember anyone asking him what classes he wanted to take, but since everybody already knew everything about him, he figured it was pointless to argue.

'Amy can show you where to go. You have Computing now, Amy, don't you?'

'Yeah, sure.' Amy gathered her books. 'Room nineteen.'

Rex glanced down at his timetable. On the bottom, there was a badly photocopied map of the school. It was difficult to tell which of the rooms was which, so he was glad he had a guide. He followed Amy out of the classroom and walked with her back up the corridor towards the staff room.

'I don't suppose you have your Computing textbook?'

'In my locker,' he replied, thinking he wouldn't need it anyway.

Amy seemed to expect his answer and asked, 'Your locker is just up here? I think I saw you here earlier.'

Rex scanned the locker numbers, found number 357, and punched in his number to open it. He took his bag out and turned to find Amy grinning to herself.

'What?' asked Rex, not sure what could possibly have amused her.

'Nothing,' said Amy. 'It's just that I had a bet with myself what your locker combination would be.'

Rex gaped. 'You saw my combo?' he asked. What's wrong with it?'

'Nothing, nothing ... it's just ...' she hesitated. 'Well, it's the same combination just about any boy who has messed about with making up words on a calculator would use.'

Rex still had no idea what she was on about. Amy must have sensed Rex was clueless and dropped the subject. Rex rummaged around in his bag, pulling items out and stacking them on the floor. He took out his mobile phone and sat it on the pile of books only to have Amy snatch it up and hide it under folded arms.

'Didn't anyone tell you about the phone crushing?' Amy asked Rex. She looked around to see if anyone else had seen it.

'Yeah, but seriously? They crush your phone?'

'Hell yeah. I lost my old one doing just what you did. They're dead serious. They've even got a special crushing machine.'

'Even if it's off?'

'Yep. Something about them rotting your brain ... or privacy ... or something. When they first started it, they got dozens.' Amy looked around the corridor furtively, then slipped Rex's phone back into his bag. 'Don't even bring it to school. It's not worth the risk.'

Rex found his Computing book, put the rest back in the locker with his bag and closed the door. Amy was leaning against the lockers watching Rex, her eyes almost level with his.

'Thanks for warning me,' he said to Amy. 'Are they strict about anything else?'

'Nope, just phones. Weird, I know. And don't worry, I won't tell anyone your locker code. Come on.' She walked on, smiling over her shoulder to see if Rex was following.

Through habit, Rex began to walk to the front of the Computing classroom, but Amy grabbed him by the arm and yanked him into the back row. 'No one can look over your shoulder here,' she explained as she sat at the seat second from the end. Another boy slid past behind them to take the end seat, exchanging greetings with Amy as he went. Rex recognised the boy from the hotel the day he arrived.

'This is Scott,' said Amy. 'His dad knows your Grandad. Scott, this is Rex.' Scott reached across Amy to shake Rex's hand causing Amy to lean back uncomfortably.

'Hi. Did you get the job?' asked Rex.

'Oh,' said Scott. 'That's where I've seen you before. Dunno yet, your mum and dad will let me know. They're training someone up at the moment and didn't want me to start too soon.'

'Congratulations. It didn't look like the interview went well, though.'

'First one I've ever done, and I don't think I've ever been that nervous. Anyway, I don't know how much you know about computers, but this class is pretty easy,' said Scott.

'Right,' said Rex, remembering his last computer class. 'What happens if you know more than the teachers?'

Scott and Amy both laughed. 'Nothing,' said Scott. 'They know we all learn this stuff a lot earlier these days. We wanted to start next year's lessons, but they said they're changing.'

Amy continued. 'We're allowed to do anything computer related if we're ahead. They take the view that we can do what we want at home, so there's no point in restricting us at school ... apart from phones. It's a trust thing.'

'Yeah, as long as you don't expect anything to download quickly,' said Scott. 'Seriously, it's like they're using a couple of cans with string between them as their internet connection.'

The teacher began the lesson. This was easy stuff for Rex, and he was finished within fifteen minutes. He sat back in his chair to see both Scott and Amy finishing off their work as well. When they were done, they noticed Rex was also finished and exchanged glances.

Rex asked Amy, 'What do we do now?'

'Normally I would just surf the internet, but it's too slow here, so I catch up on homework or read a book.'

Rex could see Scott trying to view some aviation site, the images slowly appearing one by one.

'Do they know why it's slow?' asked Rex.

'No, they haven't got a clue. It is supposed to be fast, but they can't figure it out.'

Rex turned to his laptop and released a diagnostic program into the school's network. It soon began to scroll information up the screen. Rex examined the information carefully, nodded to no-one in particular, then clicked a few options. He ran the diagnostic again, smiling at the result.

'Bloody hell!' said Scott, his eyes wide open staring at his screen. 'It just got really fast.'

Amy looked from Scott's to Rex's screen. 'What did you do?' she asked Rex.

'Throttling was applied to everyone as a whole instead of individual connections, so everyone was limited to the speed of one connection. Easy fix.'

Scott and Amy looked impressed and began testing out the faster connection.

After a few minutes, Amy leaned back in her seat. 'So, did you get kicked out of your last school?' Rex studied her expression. He had been asked this question before by other students in other schools, mostly for them to gain ammunition for rumour attacks later on, but from Amy the question seemed to be asked out of genuine interest.

'Technically, I left. Although they were going to expel me anyway.'

'How come?'

'They said I was hacking.' Rex smiled at the irony.

'No way!' Amy looked incredulous.

'Well, sort of. I got 100% in a test. A teacher changed my test result to 74% and I ... unchanged it. They booted me for accessing what I wasn't supposed to, not for correcting my result.'

Scott chimed in. 'You're not serious?'

'Yep. The teacher didn't like me. I even had proof he did it.'

'Unbelievable,' replied Scott, shaking his head.

'That really sucks,' said Amy. 'Oh well, at least you get to use your powers for good instead of evil here.'

Rex laughed, relieved that he wasn't immediately being accused of showing off. This was the friendliest school he'd ever been to.

'Hey?' Scott leaned forward on his desk to talk directly to Rex. 'You're living at the hotel, right?'

'Yeah,' said Rex. 'My dad bought it last year. Tonight's opening night, actually.'

'Yeah, I know. My dad got an order of fish this morning. He runs a fishing boat from the marina. So ... do you stay in a guest room, or is there a like a family residence kind of thing?'

'Scott! You can't ask him that,' said Amy.

' 'Course he can,' said Rex. 'And yeah, there is a private area, but it isn't finished yet, so, yeah, I am in a guest room.'

Amy gaped; at Scott's directness or the reply, Rex couldn't be sure.

'Cool,' said Scott.

'I suppose,' replied Rex. 'I don't think I've ever lived in a normal home.'

'What about in Melbourne?' asked Amy.

'Yeah, well. I guess. That was probably the closest I suppose. But Mum and Dad were hardly ever there.'

'Cool,' said Scott again. 'Complete freedom. How many parties did you have?'

'None,' said Rex. 'I guess that's how it's always been.' He paused. 'I don't think I ever had enough friends for a party anyway.'

'Well, I'm sure you'll make plenty here,' said Amy. She ventured a question of her own. 'Is it true that the hotel is haunted?'

'Ha!' laughed Rex. 'Yeah, that's the legend, but really it's only artificially haunted. It's a kind of theme, the haunted bit. Dad and Grandad have been working on it for ages. There's some sort of show going on tonight for the opening, something to do with the lake, but I don't know what exactly. I've seen all the gear that works it though.'

'Cool,' repeated Scott. 'What about the smugglers?'

Rex was surprised at the question. 'What smugglers?'

'I heard there used to be a smuggling racket going on there.' Scott's eyes drifted upwards. 'Or was that the pub?'

The bell rang prompting everyone to start packing up their laptops and books as the teacher gave instructions for homework.

Outside the room, Rex was about to ask Scott about the smugglers when Penelope marched around a corner and walked straight into Amy.

'Watch where you're going, ditzy,' said Penelope.

Amy's face began to redden. She was in the process of dropping her bag and facing up to the insult when Scott went on the defensive, moving his large frame in between the two.

'What's your problem?' he said, straight to Penelope's face.

Penelope backed off, flustered at the unexpected resistance.

'Well?' insisted Scott.

Penelope struggled to get words out through tight angry lips. 'She's not your type!' She turned on her heels and marched off back around the corner.

Scott looked around at Rex and Amy. 'What the ...?'

'She's mental,' said Amy. 'Come on, Rex, we've got maths next.' Amy stalked off down the corridor.

Rex muttered a 'see you later' to Scott and hurried to catch up. Amy didn't seem to be in any mood to discuss what just happened. As Rex walked beside Amy to the next class in silence, he thought back over the day so far. He decided that Penelope was not someone he wanted to hang out with.

CHAPTER 4

At seven that evening, Rex pushed the doors of the kitchen open slightly so he could see the opening night show. He was expecting some fancy smoke, projection effects and cheesy sound effects, but all he could see was a dining room filled with the first guests the hotel had managed to attract. Some had come in fancy dress for the opening night; a woman in a roaring twenties dress and hairpiece, a couple of skeletons, Mr Limbick looking a little like Alfred Hitchcock, a Poirot seated next to an Egyptian mummy, and a cloaked Grim Reaper, rather appropriately seated on his own.

The dining room lights flickered and dimmed. At first, Rex could not see anything. Then, something silvery white began to rise from the centre of the lake visible through the dining room windows. A ghostly woman in flowing robes emerged, her hair waving slowly in tendrils about her head as if she was still underwater.

Some of the diners noticed the apparition and their gasps alerted the others. The sound of scraping chairs preceded a second round of gasps.

Rex peeked through the gap in the kitchen doors, captivated with the show and the reaction of the diners.

Mr Limbick was watching the scene with rapt attention, absentmindedly twisting his red cravat while other guests sat frozen in their seats or clutched at their partners for support.

The woman rose fully out of the water, hovering just above its surface. She held a sword by its jeweled handle with both hands, swinging it warily from side to side, as if expecting to be attacked. Unlike the woman, the sword was solid, not a ghostly echo from the past, and it flashed light back at the dining room windows. The woman ceased swinging the sword and held it before her, ready for attack. She began to speak, though soundlessly, her words lost to the cool night air.

'What's she saying?' the man closest to the window murmured to his wife.

Rex turned his attention back to the woman in the lake. She raised the sword and swung it over her right shoulder, then soundlessly hurled the sword towards the diners. One or two flinched before realising it would fall well short of them. It speared into the lawn and swayed back and forth as the woman dissolved back into the lake. Ripples subsided to form a mirror of the night sky.

The man's wife broke the silence. 'She said something about avenging her killer and protecting all others.'

'How could you tell?' asked a guest at another table.

'She reads lips,' said the husband.

'Did she say anything else?'

Rex and other guests followed the exchange keenly.

'It was hard to see her clearly,' said the wife. 'But I think she said something like, 'The worthy one shall take the sword and slay my downfall'. She was difficult to read from here, though. I could be wrong.'

The lights flickered again and came back on at their normal intensity. Many of the guests took this as their cue to retire for the night. They left the dining room amid a cloud of whispered speculation, some a little shocked, others smiling as if they were leaving a cinema after a funny movie. Mr Limbick remained at his table, writing in the notebook he carried everywhere.

Rex hung back in the kitchen until the dining room was empty enough to talk to Limbick without others overhearing. Limbick looked up as Rex approached.

'Ah, Rex! How are you?'

'Good thanks. What did you think of the show?'

'Marvelous,' replied Limbick. 'The sword was a brilliant touch. Without that it could just have been a movie, but that touch of realism gave it that extra bit of spookiness.' He gazed out the window, thinking back on the show. 'Were the words she spoke significant?'

'No, they're from a video game. Grandad rang me a while ago asking about creepy phrases. I wondered what he was on about. I told him the first thing that came to mind, and he got all excited.'

'What about that sword?' Limbick nodded toward the sword, still swaying gently in the lawn between the hotel and the lake, the jewels in its guard and pommel flashing.

'Just a prop, I think. It normally hangs on the wall behind reception,' said Rex.

'Just as well.' Limbick's voice was suddenly low and serious, his eyes staring out the window. 'Because someone's trying to steal it!'

Rex snapped his head around to see. Sure enough, there was a hooded figure straining to pull the sword out of the ground.

'If that's not part of the act, you'd better get your dad.' Limbick rose from his seat and headed for the doors to the lawn while Rex ran out the dining room door to the lobby. He found his dad talking to one of the chefs from the kitchen.

'Someone's stealing the sword!'

Roy cut his conversation off and said to the chef, 'You go through the dining room. I'll go out the front to head him off.' The chef ran out of the lobby through the dining room doors. 'Rex, find Grandad. He'll be in the storeroom.'

Rex ran to the stairs that led to the basement level.

CHAPTER 5

Rex and Grandad burst out of the service corridor to find Roy coming into the lobby from the dining room. 'Did you see where they went?' asked Roy.

'Well, not from the basement I didn't,' said Grandad. He headed for the door next to reception. 'Let's check the video.'

Rex and Roy followed Grandad through the door. 'Woah!' said Rex. It was his first time in this room, and it was totally at odds with the rest of the hotel. The walls were a checkerboard of video images, with scenes of around and throughout the hotel cast by projectors on the ceiling. A console inlaid with buttons, screens and controls lit softly by down-lights was set back from three of the walls, with one of the sections showing a radar sweep. The other wall had racks of equipment like the ones Rex saw in the basement to control the light show.

'Wow! Mission control, or what? Do you launch rockets from here?' asked Rex.

Grandad smiled and pushed a swivel chair towards Rex. 'Not anymore.' Rex wasn't quite sure he was joking.

Grandad brought a replay of the show up on a screen. Pressing a few buttons, the image expanded to take up most of one wall. He found the view from a camera facing the lake and skipped through the show. Water erupting from the lake, a woman jumping up and throwing a sword all in a matter of seconds. The scene was static for a moment then a figure appeared at the sword. Grandad froze the image and enlarged it.

'Can't see his face,' said Grandad.

'It's the Grim Reaper,' said Rex. 'He was in the dining room during the show.'

Grandad rolled the video slowly, trying to catch a glimpse of face. The hooded figure tried to pull the sword out of the lawn by its wet, slippery handle, struggling to keep his feet sliding out from under him.

'Looks like a man,' said Roy.

'How come he can't pull it out?' asked Rex.

'It's held in by electromagnets,' said Grandad.

Rex was about to ask about how it worked when Mr Limbick entered the scene, running as fast as his large frame would carry him. Shortly after, the chef followed. Limbick reached the Grim Reaper first and tried to tackle him to the ground but slipped on the Grim Reaper's scythe that was lying on the ground. He glanced off the Grim Reaper and fell, his momentum sliding him further toward the lake. The hooded figure saw the chef coming at him and snatched his scythe up off the ground, bringing it up in an arc that met the chef's neck and knocked him off his feet. The chef's feet flew forward, his neck still pinioned in the air by the blade of the scythe. He fell to the ground motionless. The figure pulled his scythe back and stood over the body for a moment before turning and advancing toward Limbick.

'No!' said Rex, in horror at what was surely about to happen next. The handle was raised, but instead of slashing the blade down, the figure stabbed the handle down on Limbick's head.

Limbick stopped moving. The attacker looked around as if he heard something, then ran from the scene.

'You better check him,' said Grandad, the urgency clear upon his face.

Roy steered Rex toward the door and turned back to Grandad. 'You'll call the Police?'

Grandad was already on the phone, his back to the screens. 'Calling them now.'

Roy pulled the heavy security room door open and started heading toward the dining room doors, Rex following close behind.

Neither Rex, his father, or Grandad saw the image still projecting onto the wall when the Grim Reaper returned to the lifeless figure of Mr Limbick. He reached down and took something from Limbick's hand, straightened, and tucked it somewhere in the folds of his cloak.

Outside of the security room, Roy turned and stopped Rex in his tracks. Guests congregated at the foot of the stairs in a coven of curiousness. Roy leaned close to Rex. 'Go out front and meet the police when they arrive,' he said in a low voice.

'Ok,' said Rex. 'What about this lot?' he said, inclining his head toward the excited guests.

'They're harmless enough, ignore them for now. They'll be enjoying it anyway. Just make sure you get to the police before they do and try not to get in any more trouble.' Roy strode off through the dining room doors. Rex made as if to follow his father but at the last moment turned towards the front door and hoped none of the guests noticed his hasty exit.

Outside the front door, Rex paused to listen for police sirens. Nothing. Before they arrived, he could check out the area at the rear of the hotel between the main building and the other run-down building that was still being landscaped. He ran away from the front of the hotel to the rear corner and rounded it at speed, coming to a halt when the security lights came on. Small piles of sand and aggregate, a pile of rocks for retaining walls, and a cement mixer all cast long shadows back to the trees and bushland behind the hotel. Rex paused before slowly moving among the building materials, eyes wide and listening for any movement, taking care to stay well away from anything someone could hide behind.

The sound of a twig snapping made him freeze, straining to see and hear the source. As his eyes adjusted to the dark among the trees, two bright eyes blinked and stared back from an overhanging branch. A possum looked down at Rex, decided he was no threat and continued his tightrope walk along the limb.

Rex could hear a siren in the distance. After a long look into the shadows of the trees, he turned and retraced his steps, trying to force himself to relax. Before he reached the corner of the building he was nearly bowled over by something big and black. Rex reeled backwards in fright, trying to see what it was. From folds of darkness, a hand reached forward and grabbed Rex by the throat, propelling him backwards until he felt the sharp jab of the cement mixer handle in his back. Rex grasped his attacker's arm to try to pull it away, but every attempt was met with a tightening grip on his neck. Realising his struggling was making things worse, Rex relaxed his grip on the arm but kept his hands on it while he thought of his next move. He couldn't see the face of his attacker in the shadows of the hood; the security light shone in his eyes making it impossible to discern any features.

'What do you want?' asked Rex, his words strangled. If he couldn't identify this bastard by sight, he might be able to by his voice.

'Get out!' It was a strained whispered hiss that didn't give Rex anything to identify other than a bad case of halitosis.

'Why?' ventured Rex. 'What's the problem?' Rex struggled to get the words out with the hand around his throat.

'The Point is mine!'

Rex could hear the sirens getting closer, but he didn't think it would be long before Mr Grim-Face realised that too.

Options flitted through Rex's brain: kick this guy between the legs and try to run for it — unlikely to succeed but well worth the pleasure of inflicting pain on him; bluff and say he knew who he was — likely to get himself killed; keep him talking until the cops arrived — become a hostage for hours while the local cops called in reinforcements; feign death — yeah, that would do.

Rex rolled his eyes up without closing them and relaxed his body, becoming a dead weight. The hand holding his throat relaxed and allowed him to fall to the ground. The black figure glanced around and, realising the sirens were close, ran towards the forest track. Rex jumped up to try to see where he was going, but shadows engulfed the receding figure. He was about to head off back to the front of the hotel when Tom raced around the corner, saw Rex, and came skidding to a halt. Rex pointed toward the track. 'That way!' he commanded.

Tom took off in pursuit of a scent trail only a dog could follow in the dark.

Rex ran back to the front of the hotel in time to meet the police pulling up under the portico and Grandad coming out of the hotel entrance. Rex slowed to a fast walk before the police were out of the car. Grandad raised his eyebrows and made a suggestive look to where Rex had come from.

'He got away,' said Rex, hurriedly. The police were releasing their seatbelts. 'Tom's after him.'

'Right,' said Grandad quietly. The police climbed out of their car, adjusting their heavy belts laden with various pieces of equipment, and checking the position of their pistols. Grandad addressed the police. 'Rex will show you round to the lawn where it happened. Suspect fled into the hills, long gone now. Probably knows the caves.' The junior officer made as if to start asking about caves, but Rex cut him off. 'This way,' he said.

Rex started running around to the lake side of the hotel. The two police officers slammed the doors of the car and ran after Rex, their hands automatically reaching for their radios, pistols and other equipment to verify they were in place for whatever situation might confront them next. Rex turned to check if they were following and saw Grandad slip around the back of the building.

Rex led the police to the lawn area between the lake and the dining room. A few of the more curious hotel guests gathered outside the dining room doors and took the opportunity to tag along. They reached the lifeless body of the chef.

'This one's dead,' said an elderly lady. Her matter-of-fact tone suggested it wasn't the first time she'd seen a body.

The senior police officer squatted down and placed her fingers on the chef's neck, avoiding the obvious damage inflicted by the Grim Reaper's scythe and looked away with despair, nodding in confirmation. She stood and turned to her colleague.

'You'd better call this in,' she said. 'Don't use radio. Phone command requesting Homicide and Ambulance.'

With a solemn face, the elderly lady removed the thick knitted scarf from her neck and draped it over the chef's head.

Rex didn't wait to hear the rest and ran over to Mr Limbick. He placed his fingers on Mr Limbick's neck, feeling for a pulse just as the policewoman had done moments before. He didn't exactly know what he was feeling for until he felt it, the faint throbbing of blood through the carotid artery.

'He's alive!' said Rex over his shoulder. The sound of his voice must have awoken Mr Limbick. His eyelids opened lazily, and wide-open pupils slowly came back to life. The other police officer came over to Rex, closely followed by the old woman. The torchlight on Mr Limbick's face caused his pupils to close sharply. Rex remembered this as a good sign from medical television shows. Mr Limbick began to speak.

'Ahh good, you're here,' he said in a faint, laboured voice. His eyes seemed unfocussed, casting around at the dark shapes above him. 'Look after things for me.' His head turned from the old lady to Rex revealing a bleeding gash on his head. Rex resisted the urge to wince. 'Rex'—he paused to take a few shallow gulps of air—'this is Mrs Birch.' Some more shallow breaths, the colour draining from his face. 'She's an associate of mine ... you can ... trust her.' Rex looked up at the old lady. She nodded a silent acknowledgment. Mr Limbick's head relaxed so he was staring at the stars. He moved one hand to his jacket pocket, feeling for something. 'Find the diary ...' He seemed out of breath but continued. 'And remember ...' another breath, '... perseverance ... is the key.'

Rex thought for an instant he was talking to Mrs Birch, but then he remembered Limbick had said that word to him before: *Perseverance*. It had to mean something, though he could not for the life of him think what it was.

The ambulance crew running down the lawn towards him brought Rex back to the present. He looked down to see Mr Limbick looking directly into his eyes.

'Don't worry Mr Limbick, help is here,' said Rex. Limbick nodded slowly and closed his eyes.

Rex stood to let the medics do their work. One was asking Mrs Birch questions, writing the answers on the back of her hand. 'What is his name?' she asked.

'Thomas Limbick, born 30 October 1936, no allergies, no medication, no conditions, blood type oh positive.' Mrs Birch waited between each fact to make sure it was understood.

'And you are?'

'Birch, B-I-R-C-H, Maureen. Close friend and colleague.'

'What happened?'

Rex chimed in. 'He tripped and fell, then was bashed on the head with the end of a wooden pole.'

'Ouch.' The medic squatted next to her colleague. 'You get all that?'

'Yes,' he replied. 'He's unconscious now, but his BP and rate are okay. Let's get him on the cart.'

It was almost two in the morning by the time Rex pushed open the door to his room and let it close after him. He slumped into one of the armchairs in the room, exhausted from wrangling guests and giving a statement to the police. He was going to tell them about his encounter with the Grim Reaper around the back of the hotel, but as he described running out of the hotel, he saw Grandad give an almost imperceptible shake of his head. He picked up the story again from when the police arrived. Grandad gave his statement next and backed up Rex's version of events. He also failed to mention his own detour behind the hotel. Come to think of it, Grandad never did say where he went.

The police had asked for a copy of the surveillance footage. Grandad said he would deliver it first thing; something about backups running and not wanting to disturb them. Rex knew that was probably not true, guessing Grandad wanted to be selective about what was handed over. Rex would ask him tomorrow. Well, today now.

He realised he was drifting off to sleep and dragged himself out of the chair to get ready for bed. Thinking about the Grim Reaper's threat would have to wait. So would *perseverance*.

CHAPTER 6

Rex slept in past his alarm and had to rush to be ready for school. He grabbed an apple from a bowl on the reception desk on his way through the lobby and headed outside to the hotel guest bikes. He grabbed the first one out of the rack and rode furiously down the hill towards the town, munching on the apple as he went. Fortunately, it was mostly downhill, only a five-minute ride.

Approaching the gate to the school he saw Penelope, coming the other way. 'Not in the limo today, Rex?' she said with a sneer. Rex ignored her and flipped his apple core neatly into the bin at the front gate before riding across the forecourt to the bike racks. As he dismounted, he sneaked a sideways look back to see Penelope huffing off towards the front door of the school.

Rex entered the school from the rear, in part to avoid Penelope, but mostly to get to his locker by the shortest route possible. No doubt the whole town had heard about what happened last night and would be all over him for the details.

He stepped into the corridor but before he had a chance to get to his locker, Mrs M bailed him up.

'Rex!' She beckoned from an office door. 'In here please.'

Rex was partly glad he didn't have to face the other students, but equally worried about what would happen next. Being called into offices at school had not usually gone well for him in the past.

'Have a seat,' said Mrs M with a smile. She closed the door behind her. 'Don't worry, you're not in trouble.' Rex sat at one of the chairs in front of the desk. It was a standard issue teacher desk with plastic laminate surfaces. Everything on it was ordered and neatly aligned with the edges. The surface gleamed as if it was highly polished glass. Mrs M took the other seat on the same side of the desk as Rex. *This was new*, thought Rex. He relaxed a little.

'I've been briefed by the police on what happened last night. I just wanted to let you know that the school sent an email out to all students and parents asking for them to respect your privacy. We don't want anyone to jeopardise the police investigation by gossiping and speculating about what might or might not have happened. Not strictly the truth, but with a bit of luck you won't be bothered too much.'

'Thanks,' said Rex. No teacher at his previous schools had ever gone in to bat for him like this, let alone the principal.

'I've also told Penelope to knock it off. I saw her on the way in.' She indicated her view from the window to the front gate. 'A smart girl, but she has trouble finding the right way to make friends.'

'Mmm,' said Rex. He wasn't so sure about the smart bit.

'If you need anything, or need someone to talk to, I'm always around and available.'

'Thanks,' said Rex. 'I haven't really had time to think about it all yet.'

'Well, talk it over with your friends, but'—she waited until Rex looked directly at her—'choose which friends carefully, eh?'

Rex nodded.

'Anyway, that's all I had to tell you. I told Miss Lally you'd be late, so off to maths first up.' She stood and opened the door again.

Rex headed for his locker and grabbed his maths textbook, glad that the rest of the students were still being accounted for in their home rooms. On his way to the classroom, he passed his own home room. The door opened and students began filtering out. The suppressed longing to ask him all about what happened was written all over their faces, but thankfully they heeded Mrs M's request.

He stifled a yawn with his fist as he sat down at the back of the maths classroom. He was overcome by a huge yawn and didn't notice for a second that Amy had pulled out the chair next to him. She sat down, leaned on the tabletop facing him with her arm propping her head up, holding back her hair.

'Are you going to make me ask, sleepy head?' she said, her eyebrows raised.

Rex was glad it was Amy. She seemed to be the most sympathetic person he had met so far. He opened his mouth to speak when Scott plonked down on the chair on the other side of Amy and leaned around her to face him.

"Oodunnit then?' said Scott.

'Oi!' Amy dug Scott in the ribs with her elbow. 'You're not supposed to ask.'

'You just did,' replied Scott, rubbing where Amy had jabbed him.

'No, I didn't ... alright yes, I did.' She turned back to Rex. 'So? Spill then.'

Rex wasn't quite sure he wanted to tell anyone else but Amy yet, but figured Amy would probably tell Scott anyway. He looked around the room. Miss Lally was organising her lesson at the front of the class while waiting for the rest of the students to arrive. A few other students were chatting quietly on the other side of the room, including Penelope, who was watching Rex, Scott and Amy from the corner of her eye. Rex turned back to his eager audience and began to tell them about the events of the night before.

Rex continued his story in hushed tones whenever the rest of the class was making enough noise to cover his voice. On the other side of the central aisle,

Penelope seemed to be engrossed in her textbook, but Rex could tell she was straining to listen in. Occasionally, the frustration of not being able to hear would get the better of her and she'd glare in their direction.

'What happened to Mr Limbick?' asked Amy.

'Airlifted to Melbourne,' Rex replied. 'The chopper landed on that flat bit on the bluff right near the hotel.'

Scott whistled in appreciation, earning another glare from Penelope.

'Any idea who the Grim Reaper is?' asked Amy.

'No, but when ...' Rex's reply was cut off by Miss Lally who was now standing over them. Rex hadn't even seen her coming.

'Alright you three, you've been talking for the last half an hour. I think you'd better get back to work before Penelope has an aneurysm. The three of you can do all of the optional problems from the first three chapters for homework.'

The three of them looked across the aisle to see a satisfied smirk on Penelope's face, a look that quickly faded to guilty shame under the death stares from her accused. She buried her head in her book and pretended to be working.

At the end of the class, Amy seemed ready to tackle Penelope to the ground, but Scott stood in her way and wouldn't let her pass until Penelope had safely exited the room. She opened her mouth to protest Scott's blocking maneuver. Scott preempted her. 'You've already got extra homework; you want to add a suspension too?'

Amy's shoulders sagged as she realised he was right. She turned to Rex. 'Meet us in the milk-bar after school?'

'Yeah, right-oh,' said Rex. Amy shoved past Scott and left.

'Bit of fight in her, that one,' said Scott. Rex raised his eyebrows and nodded.

Both Scott and Amy went home for lunch. It was one of the perks of living and going to school in a small town. Rex, unwilling to pedal back up the hill to the hotel, bought a bucket of chips from the local fish 'n' chip shop. The sun came out giving an unseasonal warmth. He headed across the road to the beach and sat on the sand before a stadium of adoring seagulls, each squabbling over the best position to receive the crumbs Rex would occasionally flick into the pack.

Quite an eventful few hours, he thought to himself as the waves rumbled in further down the shore. Scott and Amy seemed alright, Penelope was obviously a pain, and the teachers seemed reasonably fair given the situation. *And now, I'm sitting on a beach in the sun*, he thought. A smile grew on his face as he lifted his gaze from the ever-encroaching birds to look out to the horizon. *I could live with this*, he thought. *Beats the city any day.*

When his chips were mostly gone, he began to flick bits to the birds he felt most deserving, avoiding the bullies, and favouring the ones that hadn't yet learned to assert themselves. He reserved a large, blighted chip until last, and made sure the dominant bird caught it. It took flight with the flock of hungry contenders in hot pursuit. All that effort and it would be lucky to get any food in the end.

Rex stood, brushed himself off and headed back to school. Some dark clouds were gathering behind the hinterland hills threatening to roll over the coast and out to sea. He hoped they'd hold off until he got home, then changed his mind. A bit of rain wouldn't hurt him, it's only water. He didn't have classes with Scott or Amy for the rest of the day, so he looked forward to seeing them at the milk-bar.

CHAPTER 7

After school, Rex grabbed his bike and rode to the milk bar. The clouds looming over the inland hills had darkened and concentrated but not yet pushed over to reach the town. He parked his bike in a rack outside *The Breakers Milk Bar* next to another hotel bike. It had no lock keeping it in place, so Rex didn't bother to tether his own bike.

Entering the shop, he was greeted by an approachable woman with a kind face who looked about sixty. 'You must be Rex,' she said. 'I'm the owner, Mrs Reynard. I was wondering when you'd show up. Can I get you a milkshake?'

'Maybe later, thanks,' replied Rex. 'I'm meeting friends.'

'Not a problem, dear. Take a seat in one of the booths and I'll let them know when they come in.'

Rex didn't question how exactly how she knew who he was waiting for, but this was a small town; she probably knew what he had for breakfast.

'Oh, and if you feel like something a bit healthier than chips for lunch, I can have a ham and salad sandwich ready for you at lunchtime tomorrow,' said Mrs Reynard with a wink. She disappeared through the door to the back room. *The woman's a mind reader*, thought Rex. He found a booth near the back of the shop that was secluded from view of the front door and sat down to wait, listening to the somehow soothing strains of Caribbean reggae and wondering if he was kidding himself to think anyone was interested enough to meet him.

Within a minute, Scott and Amy burst through the streamers hanging in the doorway and headed straight for his booth.

'Figured you'd be back here,' said Amy.

'Not like you to keep a low profile in this town,' said Scott with a grin. Amy sat opposite Rex and shifted along the seat to let Scott sit next to her, facing Rex.

'I'm surprised you want to hear more,' said Rex. 'I laid it on a bit thick this morning. That and the school sending out emails.'

'Yeah, well, just because you're rich, doesn't make you obnoxious,' said

Scott.

'We'll let you know when you are, don't worry,' added Amy.

Rex felt himself relax a bit.

'Anyway. you didn't tell Limbick to go after the Grim Reaper,' said Scott. 'If you'd gone it could have been you who got it in the neck!'

Rex contemplated that for a moment and came to a decision.

'Listen,' he said. He leaned onto the table. 'Before all this started, back in Melbourne I mean, I got this weird phone call.' Rex replayed the conversation verbatim, including the bit where he banged his head, much to Scott's amusement. He went on to tell them what the phone technician had said.

'Freaky,' said Amy.

'I know,' said Rex. 'And then I get booted out of school and end up here.'

'Sounds like the call was meant for you then. Who else would be able to keep the hotel going?'

'Yeah,' said Scott, 'and with all that bother last night, I'd say you're the man. What was that he said? Reactivate the base? That means there must have been one there before.'

'Hmmm,' nodded Rex. 'That's a possibility. I mean, there are tunnels all through the bluff apparently. My grandad knows about them. But surely if it was a secret base, there'd be more than just a couple of buildings on a cliff?'

'Well, mate,' said Scott leaning forward and clapping Rex on the shoulder. 'That's your job: to find out. It's your mission.' Rex thought for a moment Scott was joking, but there was no smile on his face, nor on Amy's.

'So that's two things on your list to find,' said Amy. She looked at Scott, then back to Rex. 'The diary? Come on, you must remember that?'

'Right,' said Scott, attempting to cover the fact that he'd forgotten completely about the diary Mr Limbick asked Rex to find. 'You have your orders, what's your plan?' Scott looked at Rex expectantly.

'No idea,' said Rex.

'Right then,' said Scott, placing his hands flat on the table in front of him. 'Maybe some food will help. Any orders?'

'A pink Neenish please,' said Amy.

This appeared to be a thing Scott and Amy did regularly. 'Umm, I dunno, anything. A Neenish?' said Rex reaching for his wallet.

'My shout.' Scott waved Rex back into his seat. 'Perhaps not a pink one though, eh?' he said, and headed for the counter.

'So, anyway, how come Grim Face couldn't pull the sword out of the stone?' asked Amy.

'Well, he's obviously not descended from King Arthur for a start,' said Rex.

Amy's jaw dropped and her eyes widened.

'I'm kidding, I'm kidding.' Rex laughed, then looked thoughtful. 'Although, it has been in the family for years. We have a matching set of them along with some other old stuff. You know, crowns, tiaras, sceptres, that kind of stuff.' Rex was getting into the swing of it now and enjoying Amy's reaction. She was quietly giggling along at each outlandish claim. Rex continued. 'It was specially made from a ferrous alloy and hardened by Grandad's ninja minions.' Rex remembered Amy's initial question. 'That's why it was ideal for the show actually. Magnets in the ground held it in place after the moistened bint chucked the sword. That took a bit of practice apparently. There are holes all over the lawn where it didn't line up. Lucky there was no wind last night, or we might have lost it.' An idea occurred to Rex. 'Hey, why don't you come up to the hotel on Saturday and I'll show you the set up?'

Scott appeared at the table with white paper bags wafting out a delicious smell of pastry and icing. 'Yeah, I'll be in that,' said Scott, as he sat and distributed the packages. To Rex he said, 'I get them takeaway in case we don't finish them.' He leaned into the table and gestured the others to do the same. 'Penelope is right next door,' he whispered, thumbing over his shoulder. They all leaned back. Rex figured it was best to continue the previous conversation.

'So now the sword is locked up with the rest of the treasure,' said Rex. Scott was about to open his mouth to ask what treasure, but Amy jabbed him in the ribs with her elbow and put a finger to her lips.

Rex was really hoping only Amy would come to the hotel. Still, Scott had warned them about Penelope, and he could use all the friends he could get right now.

'So, is nine o'clock alright?' asked Rex.

'Shouldn't we make it earlier?' asked Amy. 'It might take a while to find the … sword.' She looked Scott and Rex in the eye in turn. They both nodded their understanding. There was more than a sword to look for.

'Any time's fine by me,' said Scott. 'Dad usually wakes me up at six anyway.'

'Alright, seven then,' said Rex.

'Great,' said Amy.

The plastic strips hanging in the doorway being swept aside to bang on the glass of the open door caused Scott and Amy to look around. Rex half stood to look over the partition between booths. A man with a bald head and a pink shirt pushed into the cafe ranting to a meek looking middle-aged woman following close behind.

'Bloody kids!' he said. He didn't wait for the woman to clear the door before letting the strips fall back slapping into her. 'Always leaving their bloody bikes in the way.'

He ordered two small coffees. Rex watched from the booth in the corner as Mrs Reynard took the order. The smile she had when serving Rex with was noticeably absent.

'Who is that?' Rex asked, not shifting his eyes from the man. 'And why is he wearing a pink shirt?'

'Nelson Garrett,' replied Amy and Scott together.

'He's the local real estate 'mogul',' Amy said, doing inverted commas with her fingers and rolling her eyes.

'That's why the pink shirt,' said Scott. 'All real estate moguls wear them, didn't you know? It says, 'Oh look at me I'm thoooo thuccethful!' What a tosser.'

'And another thing,' Garrett said, waggling his finger in the woman's face. 'Those thieving frogs and their fancy hotel have to go. I didn't slog my guts out all these years in this hole of a town to let the biggest deal of a lifetime go to some cashed up Frenchies and their brat kid. My family owned that land long before the bloody government stole it off us. They forced us out, and now I want it back.' He paused. 'Whatever it takes!'

The woman nodded along with every jab of his finger.

Garrett finished with, 'I'll show those bloody clowns how to do a deal, and they won't know what hit them.'

He slapped some coins down on the counter as Mrs Reynard pushed the coffees towards him. He picked one up and was about to continue ranting when Penelope sneezed loudly in her booth.

Garrett glared in her direction with a scowl. Rex ducked down to avoid being seen. 'Dirty disease carrying Ebola monkeys,' he muttered, heading for the table on the other side of the door near the front window.

'I honestly don't know why Beryl puts up with him,' said Amy. 'She's Garrett's receptionist.'

'Well, that's my cue to go,' said Scott. 'Heaps of homework. You're lucky you didn't start last week, or you'd be doing it too.' He slid the uneaten half of his custard tart into a white paper bag and carefully folded the paper closed.

'Yeah, I'm off too,' said Amy. 'Wouldn't want to give anyone Ebola.'

'Or catch it,' said Scott with a glance over his shoulder towards Penelope.

They said their goodbyes without mentioning their plans for the weekend, leaving Rex alone to finish his Neenish tart.

After casting dirty looks at Scott and Amy as they left, Garrett continued his diatribe to Beryl, Rex straining to hear.

'... I heard it was a stunt. Nobody was really injured, and they took that old guy away so we couldn't tell if he was faking it.'

Beryl nodded along in obedient agreement.

'That'll teach them for starting a bloody haunted hotel. I'll make damn sure it goes down the drain. This deal I've got set up is just the start.'

Knowing that sooner or later Penelope would decide to corner him, Rex screwed up his empty paper bag and slipped out the side door to avoid Penelope and the still raving Garrett.

Sitting alone in the next booth, Penelope heard the plastic door flaps of the side door slap back into place as Rex left. *He could have talked to me,* she thought sulkily. She gazed over at Garrett and thought, maybe finding out what Garrett's up to would get Rex to talk to her. She stood, tugged her school jumper straight, put on her best butter-wouldn't-melt-in-my-mouth smile, and strode confidently towards Garrett.

After exiting Breakers and collecting the hotel bike from the rack, Rex cycled around the corner to the supermarket. Tomorrow's expedition might be hungry work, so he bought some muesli bars and other snacks he couldn't get from the hotel kitchen. After paying and stuffing everything in his school bag, he cycled out of the carpark to head home. It was getting cooler now. A breeze had picked up blowing in off the bay, further concentrating the clouds looming over the coastal hills. *Still time to explore*, thought Rex, and did a U-turn after checking for traffic.

He rode back down to the main street, the expanse of the bay widening before him. As he approached an intersection, a small car roared around the corner and headed straight for him. Just when Rex was about to take evasive action, the car jerked back into the corner and sped up the street. Rex thought he saw a thumb and finger mimicking a revolver being fired at him. He caught a flash of the sign on the car door; something Real Estate. *Had to have been Garrett*, Rex thought. Unperturbed, he signaled and turned through the intersection. He headed along the esplanade that ran almost the entire foreshore from the north to the pub below the bluff in the south.

It was the quiet time between school getting out and locals finishing work. With the sound of the waves on his left and caroling magpies marking out their territory from the rooftops of the shops on his right, Rex was beginning to like this place.

He followed the road around to the marina. A few weekender yachts rocking lazily in the calm waters, protected from the swell of waves on the other side of the rocky breakwater. Projecting into the marina near where the breakwater wall met the foreshore was an old and abandoned pier still resisting the ravages of time, and slowly being restored when public funds permitted. Rex navigated around a dilapidated old ute and an array of lobster pots stacked along a wall holding back the sand dunes above. The smell of stale fish assaulted his nostrils before being carried away by the breeze. He dismounted and propped the bike against the handrail of the pier. Looking down, Rex realised that the pier didn't actually end right at the edge of the land but continued back further before it was covered with sand from the encroaching dunes. Further up the slope was the old fisherman's pub *Scales*, its large iridescent windows offering a panoramic view over the bay, bested only by his dad's hotel further up and around the bluff. This part of the pier had been fully restored. The thick decking timbers were closer together unlike those on the pier proper which had a wider gap between each one. Rex walked the short distance to the construction fence carrying signs that warned of imminent death to all those that passed. He leaned over the railing. The shallow water lapped gently against the sand some three metres below. The tide was just beginning to creep back in, slowly measuring its way back up the massive old wooden piles driven deep into the sand. Rex could make out something carved into the girder. 'DISA,' it said in dark, deep capitals. It looked like only half a word; perhaps an incomplete job, or maybe a malicious slur about someone named 'Di'. It was close to the sea wall, but not so close that remaining letters would have been obscured had they been there. Rex wondered if it was the original builder signing his work. He leaned over further trying to see how far back the pier went before running into rock, but the failing light and gloom beneath the pier made it too dark to see.

A few spots of rain fell on the back of Rex's neck. He looked up to see that the clouds had pushed over the hinterland hills and were slowly descending towards the town. Time to go. Mounting his bike, he cycled back out of the marina, past the pub carpark and back to the road that led to the hotel, headed for home.

CHAPTER 8

Two men trudged in silence one behind the other in the dark along a poorly formed track, pushing wet ferns out of the way ahead of them. The first, skinny and bent over like an old man, lit the way with the feeble glow of a battered old torch. His other hand gripped a thick hessian sack slung over his shoulder. The second man, short with a large beer-gut, carried a large spotlight slung from a strap over one arm and a shotgun broken and cradled on the other. The first man killed the light and stopped. The second man slithered into him almost knocking him over.

'Oi! Watch where you're poking that thing, Eddie. You'll have me giblets,' said the first man.

'Sorry Ken. Wotcha stop for then?'

'Thought I heard something. Shhh!' They remained silent in the dark for a few seconds. 'Nothing,' Ken muttered. He switched the torch back on. 'Only three tonight. The boss ain't gonna be happy with that. Complete waste of time.'

'Yeah, probably spooked by the storm. We'll tell him we'll go for lobsters next week instead.'

'I'm not taking my boat around that coast,' Ken protested. 'Bloody treacherous!'

'No, not with the boat. We'll hump the tanks right to the beach down that tunnel he told us about. We can stash a fair bit of stuff and come back for it later.'

'Well, we're going to have to get on to it then or we'll lose the moonlight for a few weeks. I got bills to pay, ya know. I can't afford to be cooling me heels in Scales all week.'

'Alright, alright, I'll get the tanks filled tomorrow,' said Eddie.

They rounded the spur and were heading into a valley. Confident that nobody could see their light from the shore now, Eddie turned on the spotlight.

'Did you see that?' Eddie steadied the bright beam, pointing to where the valley ended with a steep climb.

'No, what?' Ken rolled his eyes. 'There's not going to be any more birds on this side of the hill Eddie, I've told you that.'

'Nah, nah, too big to be a bird. I never seen green eyes like that either.'

'Come off it, Eddie. Not another bloody puma.' Ken dissolved into laughter which gave way to a hacking cough.

'Get stuffed, Ken. You know I was joking when I told that story.'

'Yeah, right-oh.' Ken recovered from his coughing fit. 'Probably just reflection off the wet bushes. Let's just get back to the ute. That's if we don't get lost in these bloody caves again.'

The entrance to the tunnel was invisible, covered with thick ferns and bushes the two men couldn't name. Ken thrust his torch into the middle of a wall of dripping growth and pulled the greenery aside, revealing a dark space within. He stood aside, holding the way open allowing Eddie to sidle his way past with the shotgun and spotlight. Ken followed, careful to allow the ferns to overlap naturally. Once inside, Eddie killed the spotlight and slid it around on its strap to his back. He reached into a pocket on his leg and retrieved a modern LED torch with a lantern down one side. He turned it on bathing the tunnel in sterile white light. Ken's old torch was useless in comparison, so he turned if off and hung it on his belt.

'This way,' said Eddie, and headed off up the gently sloping tunnel.

'Never would have guessed,' said Ken to himself, following.

The rough walls of the tunnel were dry in some parts, and shiny, hard and slick with seeping water in others. Their footsteps echoed back irregularly from down the tunnel as if miners worked around them, heard but unseen.

The two men passed several off-shoot tunnels, ignoring them as they were two small to use or headed in the wrong direction. The tunnel had flattened out and began getting larger until they walked into a cavern, about ten metres across and fifteen metres high. The choice of route from here wasn't so obvious. There were a dozen openings to choose from, but no tracks on the hard rock floor to follow.

'Two o'clock in, ten o'clock out,' said Eddie. He headed for the tunnel to the left of the one directly in front. Ken followed, believing that Eddie knew what he was doing.

Another fifty metres further, the tunnel took a sharp right, the result of the tunnelers avoiding a seam of hard rock. Eddie didn't break stride as he rounded the corner and continued clomping along confidently.

'You sure this is the right way?' asked Ken.

'Everything looks different coming from the other direction, especially after rain. We've been here before. Look, see? Footprints.'

Eddie pointed to a drift of damp sand. A clearly defined boot print pointed the way. He marched on.

Ken was about to protest that the boot print was facing the same direction as they were going, but then he remembered they'd been lost in here before. He shrugged and followed, trusting Eddie. The tunnel turned back to the left, having cleared the mass of rock that caused its path change. Eddie swung around the corner to find a pair of boots blocking his path. He halted suddenly, causing Ken to crash into his back. Both looked up at the same time. Standing there in front of them was a large man dressed in black combat gear with glowing green goggles raised above a mirrored helmet visor. Before they could react, the soldier had snatched the shotgun from Eddie's arm and swung it around to knock his torch flying. It smashed against the wall and went dark, leaving Eddie and Ken shouting in surprise and confusion.

Eventually, Ken found his feeble torch. He switched it on to find Eddie facing the tunnel wall, arms outstretched sweeping back and forth grabbing at thin air. Ken swung the beam around frantically searching for the huge black beast.

'He's gone,' said Eddie. 'Where the hell did he go?'

Ken swung the torch back the way they'd come. Nothing but empty tunnel. 'What the hell was that anyway?' said Ken.

'I don't bloody know, but he's got my shotgun.' He pushed past Ken, heading back the way they'd come. 'Let's get the hell out of here.' Ken began following, then stopped.

'Hang on,' he said and swung the beam back behind them. 'He's got the bloody birds too!'

'Come on!' Eddie pleaded.

A minute later they were back in the multi-tunnel chamber. Eddie led them towards the tunnel next to the one they just exited.

'You sure about this one?' asked Ken.

'Nope,' said Eddie. 'But I'm not hanging around.'

BANG!

A deafening blast shattered the rock on the ground behind them. The pair ran screaming down the tunnel, away from the blast.

<h1 style="text-align:center">CHAPTER 9</h1>

Rex's mum and dad were busy when he got home, so he didn't get a chance to ask if Scott and Amy could stay next Saturday. His dad was in a meeting with the police going over the events of opening night and his mum was busy on reception, snacking between customers in lieu of dinner. Rex helped himself to a chicken breast and salad from the kitchen and went to his room. He pulled back the curtain to find that the rain had started in earnest, falling almost straight down with the lack of wind. Only a few drops made it past the eaves to trickle lazily down his window.

Rex fired up *Stealth Ops Experience* on his laptop. He finished his dinner while reading the briefing and completing the quiz that allowed him to start the mission. He paused the game to cleanup his meal tray and take it back to the kitchen. It was a condition of him having his own room that he serviced it himself, even the cleaning.

As he headed back from the kitchen Rex detoured through the lobby to see if his mum, Sylvie, was free. She was on the phone, her thick reddish-brown shoulder length hair hooked back over one ear, talking about a booking. Rex was about to head up the stairs past the painting of the ship when the conference room door opened and a short bald man with a large, hooked nose and an ill-fitting, shiny suit came out, his face looking like thunder. Rex's heart leapt for a moment thinking it might be about the car incident, but then Roy followed him out of the room finishing a sentence, '... there's really no need for you to be here. If I thought I needed legal advice over a simple police statement I would have called you, Nick.'

'Make sure you get a copy of the statement. I'll want to see what they have,' said Nick. The door to the conference room opened again. A uniformed policeman and a detective stood in the doorway.

'Everything okay?' asked the detective.

'Yes, Nick was just leaving.'

Nick was already strutting toward the main door, avoiding looking at the police as Roy ushered them back into the conference room. Rex heard the detective ask, 'Do you think it could have been ...' before Roy closed the door with a solid *thunk*. Sylvie was just finishing up the call, so Rex decided to seize his chance.

'Mum, can I have some friends stay on the weekend?'

'Which friends are we talking about, love?'

'Scott and Amy. You know Scott's dad, and Amy's family have lived in town forever. She'll have to have her own room, but Scott can stay in mine, and I'll clean Amy's room afterwards.'

'Alright, but only if their parents agree. I'll see Scott's dad tomorrow, but you'll have to ask Amy to get her parents to call me. Give her my mobile number.'

'Thanks, mum!' Rex ran up the stairs in case she changed her mind or found more chores for him to do, only slowing at the top. He made his way back to his room, trying to think of a plan for the weekend. The faint sound of wind howling outside gave the corridors an eerie atmosphere. Rex smiled at the prospect of this scaring the guests. He pushed his door open and closed the curtains to the dying light of the day. The rainstorm had passed, and all was calm outside. Rex sat back down at his desk to continue playing his game. *Weird*, he thought. *It sounded windy a second ago.*

Rex awoke to the sound of wind whistling in the eaves. Lazily he turned in bed to see what time it was. A quarter to eight. 'Oh hell!' he said, before jumping out of bed and heading for the bathroom. By the time he made it to school for roll call, it was just on eight thirty. On the way to his first class, Mrs M bailed him up near the staff room.

'Rex!' She waved a note in the air at him. 'Your mum rang,' she said, and handed a note to Rex. It was a sticky-note folded together to keep the contents semi-private. Rex peeled it open and read: 'You are needed at the hotel at lunchtime — Rex's mother'. Rex looked up to ask Mrs M when this had arrived, but she was gone. *Great*, Rex thought. *That's all I need.*

Rex's classes were full-on this morning, and the teachers were making sure everyone was working instead of chatting. Rex barely got a chance to say a word to Scott and Amy. By the time lunch time arrived Rex felt like he'd done a whole day's work already. He left his school bag stuffed in his locker and grabbed his hotel bike from the bike shed and pedaled home. He wondered why they needed him at the hotel. He didn't have any chores that morning, so he hadn't forgotten to do anything.

He rolled up to the bike racks near the side door, dismounting before reaching them and slotted the bike into the end slot for a quick getaway later on. He unfastened his helmet on the way in the door, hung it on a coat hook and headed to reception. Sylvie looked up as he came in. 'Sorry, Rex, our dish-pig didn't turn up today and we really need you to help out. Help yourself to lunch in the kitchen and try to get through whatever you can before heading back to school.'

'Okay. Wasn't there anyone else?'

'No sweetie, we've had staff calling in sick all morning. I'll need you back here straight after school too.' The phone rang, and she blew him a kiss as she picked it up.

Antonio the chef handed Rex a hat as soon as he entered the kitchen and pointed him to the washing station where the dishes were piling up. Rex put on the hat and filled a deep tray with soapy water for the cutlery to soak in, then began filling racks with whatever there was most of on the bench. Antonio's pasta primavera had been popular for lunch, judging by the amount of pasta dishes. Funny how people often went for the only Italian dish on a French menu. When the dishwasher tray was full, he rinsed it off with the sprayer hanging overhead. The tray sat on slides that led into the dishwasher. Underneath was a sink with a disposal unit for grinding up food scraps. He pushed the tray into the dishwasher until the conveyor took hold and dragged the tray into the unit. The automatic washer was a great time saver, but you had to be careful of lighter dishes being pushed out of the rack and fouling the spinning sprayers under the trays.

As the last rack was pushed out the other side of the machine with the cutlery still steaming hot, Antonio called out to him. 'Hey, Rex, leave the rest. I can get that later. I've got some lunch for you.' Rex washed up and put the last of the glass racks back on their shelf. He sat down at the staff table and wolfed down a plate of pasta primavera.

Glancing at his watch, he realised he had to leave. 'Sorry Tony, gotta go. Thank for lunch, it was delicious.' He wiped his mouth on his hat and flopped it down on the empty plate. 'No, Rex. Thank you! Go, go! I'll clean it up!'

Rex ran for his bike. He was back at school just in time for the first afternoon class.

It felt like no time at all had passed when he next rolled through the hotel gates. Bicycles already filled the racks by the side door, so Rex followed the driveway around to the ramp that led to the underground carpark. He coasted down the ramp and parked the bike in a rack by the sporting equipment store. As he headed for the lift, he noticed one of the cupboard doors was ajar. He pushed on the door to close it on his way past, but something was stopping it from closing. He opened the door to investigate and found a tennis racquet handle had fallen. He opened the door and found a stack of old canvas tarpaulins stuffed in behind it, so he gave them a push to make room for the racquet. An open tube of balls fell and rolled off the shelf, hitting the floor and bouncing balls out. A few balls rolled down to one of the drain grates spaced up the middle of the floor. Rex snatched the tube off the ground, put it upright on the shelf and went after the loose balls. As he straightened up from grabbing a ball, he noticed the blank wall at the end of the carpark. On the right-hand side was the lift and emergency stairs, but the rest of the wall was blank other than a sign, *Lift*, with another arrow sign screwed into the wall underneath pointing right. A blank wall, ball in hand, and not really wanting to start whatever chores were awaiting him upstairs, Rex did what any teenager would do.

His first shot hit close to the stairway door making a solid 'thuck!' noise before rebounding off the floor and back into his hand. Rex aimed for the sign next but missed to the left. This time the ball sounded like it was bouncing off a regular stud wall instead of concrete. He moved up to the wall. It was rendered with smooth concrete. He gave it a hard tap with his knuckles and was rewarded with a hollow sound like knocking on a door — and sore knuckles. He used his fingertips to tap on the wall, slowly moving across the wall towards the stairwell door. Bonk, bonk, bonk, bonk, thuck! He tapped left and right, pinpointing where the change in sound occurred — about a metre from the door. The surface looked identical, but for some reason had been built to blend in with the concrete wall of the lift and stairs. Rex put his ear to the hollow side. It was like listening to a seashell where you can always hear the sea. The lift chimed and the door opened. Rex stood back from the wall and turned to see Nick standing half in the lift, his arm holding back the closing doors. 'What are you doing here?' Nick asked.

'Tidying up,' replied Rex. Then he realised he didn't need to justify himself and added, 'And, I live here. What are you doing here?'

'Ah ... pressed the wrong button.' Nick stepped into the lift and the doors closed. The floor indicator above the doors showed the lift going up.

Rex returned the balls to the equipment cupboard, closing the door firmly. *That was a bit dodgy*, Rex thought. *Nobody gets out of the lift if they know they've hit the wrong button and anyway, that lift only goes from the ground floor to the carpark. The lawyer wouldn't need to be down here anyway.*

Upstairs, Rex passed his mother, still on the phone, and went to the door beside the reception desk. His mum must have pressed a button under the reception desk counter, because the door clicked as he reached it and a light near the handle turned from red to green. Rex pushed the door and went in. He scanned the images arrayed around the walls, searching for any sign of Nick the Shifty. One of the images was divided into many smaller images from different cameras around the hotel. Whenever any movement was detected that camera feed was transferred to one of the other larger areas in full size. Rex could see the basement he'd just come from, empty, the carpark lift, empty, and still on the Ground floor, and the driveway. A car in the driveway started moving back from its parking place. The image jumped to a larger screen and Rex saw Nick's unmistakable profile in the driver seat clearly, phone tucked between ear and shoulder. *Idiot*, thought Rex. *Should be using hands-free*. The car moved off towards the hotel gates. Rex could make out the numberplate. *INNOXIUS*. He scoffed. 'Yeah, right. Not guilty my foot.'

The door from reception opened and Rex's mother poked her head in, her dark red hair hanging free from one side of her head. 'Rex, sorry I've got people cancelling all over the place, and another kitchen hand has just called in to say they've quit. Could you help out in the kitchen? You can have the weekend off. Not many guests here anyway the way it's going.'

'Yeah, right-oh,' said Rex.

'Thanks honey.' Her head disappeared and the door closed behind her.

Rex turned his attention to the screens. On one of them he could see a waiter outside the laundry door talking on a mobile phone. He couldn't hear what was being said, but the waiter didn't look happy. He was shaking his head, looking exasperated. After a few seconds he held the phone in front of his face and very deliberately stabbed his thumb on the screen to end the call. He mouthed a soundless word, still shaking his head, opened the laundry door and disappeared through it. Rex could probably catch him on the way to the kitchen if he hurried. He exited the room and went through the porter's door to a corridor that went past the laundry and looped back around to the kitchen.

As he passed the laundry door, it was shoved open and the waiter he had just seen on the monitor came out still holding his phone, nearly colliding with Rex. 'Oh, sorry. Wasn't watching where I was going.'

'No, you're alright,' said Rex. He glanced at the phone. 'Bad news?'

'What?'

Rex pointed to the phone.

'Oh, no. Just some wan ... ah, idiot wanting to pay me *not* to work here. What a nut case.'

'What, like another job?'

'No, no. Just to not show up. I think he was a scam artist. Anyway, got to go.' He waved with his phone and strutted off up the corridor, pocketing his phone as he went.

Weird, thought Rex. He continued to the kitchen to start work.

CHAPTER 10

It was a busy evening in the kitchen, despite the lack of guests staying at the hotel. Word had spread about the opening night, and clearly Antonio's culinary skills were getting attention around town. Tonight's special was a grilled sea perch with local olive oil and semi-preserved melon, stuffed zucchini flower and green olives macerated in a lemon syrup with laurel, served with a barquette of morel mushrooms flavoured with Rutherglen Muscat wine. Judging by the number of fish Rex had to scale, it was a best seller. He scaled them meticulously, making sure each fish was completely scale-free. One time he was served a fish with the scales left on at a hotel in Canberra by a lazy and dangerous chef who thought it was trendy. Those things are indigestible.

After most of the mains had been served, Antonio told Rex to take a break. Rex pulled the gloves off his hands, washed up and went out the kitchen back door. A single bulb in a glass dome fitting that was obviously original to the hotel cast a soothing dim light. It was half full of insects and had stains from where it had filled with water and dried off again with the heat of the globe. Rex sat down on the bench seat by the door and breathed in the fresh ocean air, free of the smell of fish scales and guts. The kitchen was at the back of the ground floor and partly dug into the slope of the land. The floors above extended further back and ended up level with the area at the back of the hotel, where Rex had met the Grim Reaper. The other direction flattened out to form the lawn area before the lake. He leaned his head back against the wall, allowing the stars to slowly develop as his eyes became accustomed to the gloom. Rex couldn't remember the last time he had looked at the stars, probably when he was much younger and camping with his mum and dad before they got too busy running hotels. Cities had too much light around to see anything in the sky other than the moon and the blinking lights of aircraft. It was peaceful and quiet out here. Well, almost. Rex could hear two people talking, though faintly. *None of my business*, he thought. He tried to estimate where the southern cross would be, even though it was out of view on the other side of the hotel. The voices continued and eventually curiosity got the better of him. He stood and walked to the corner of the building to try and hear better.

As he edged closer, he could hear two people talking; one trying to convince the other. Only parts of the conversation carried around the corner.

'... take it from me, this place is finished ... get you other jobs in town, better jobs ...'

'... pretty full tonight ... I haven't heard of any openings ...'

'These jobs aren't advertised ... they're that good.'

Rex couldn't believe it. It sounded like someone was trying to poach staff, just like that phone call earlier. He crouched down and chanced a look around the corner, pulling his head back before anyone could see him. Just outside the dining room, two waiters stood before a third person who was speaking to them. The unseen person was hidden behind a pencil cypress tree trimmed into a tall, tapering cone. The waiters had their back to Rex, so he eased his head around the corner once more to listen better.

'All I'm saying' —the hidden voice went on—'is that it would be in your best interests to leave. Before you get hurt.'

'What's that supposed to mean?' asked one of the waiters.

'Well, you saw what happened to that other guy.' Then the voice took on a nasty tone. 'Make sure it doesn't happen to you!' The door slammed leaving the two waiters alone. The voice sounded a lot like Shifty Nick, but Rex couldn't be sure. He glanced at his watch and realised his break time was almost over.

He headed back to the kitchen, thinking. Someone is definitely trying to sabotage the hotel. First it was the Grim Reaper, then mysterious phone calls, and now outright intimidation. Rex made a mental note to ask the waiters about the hidden man after service.

Rex finished up the rest of the night being the dish-pig. Near the end of service, he noticed the waiters hovering around the service area. Rex saw his chance to ask them about what happened earlier but as he approached them, Antonio placed four desserts on the serving bench. The waiter Rex had spoken to earlier in the day said something about impatient covers, loaded up with plates and backed out of the service door to the dining room. Rex didn't get another chance to talk to any of them.

At the end of the night, he fell into bed exhausted. So much for the easy country life. A few days ago, he was relaxing with friends and a Neenish, and now ... hang on. The thought reminded him of that afternoon in The Breakers Milk Bar with Scott and Amy. Garrett said he wanted to take back the hotel. He had to be behind all this. Nick must be working for Garrett to get the staff to leave. Rex went over his thoughts again putting the pieces together. His parents would have to hear about this. Otherwise, Nick could be giving all sorts of dodgy legal advice and reporting back to Garrett. Dad wouldn't believe him without proof, probably. His eyes drooped closed. It would have to wait until the morning.

CHAPTER 11

Rex awoke early the next morning. He got ready for school, planning in his head what to do the following day when Scott and Amy stayed. Rex wanted to check out the rest of the hotel and the bushland on the hill behind the hotel, maybe even find the caves everyone kept mentioning. He made his way to the kitchen hoping to avoid his parents. Partly because he didn't know how to tell them about Nick, and partly because he didn't want to get roped into more work. Most of the staff had not arrived to relieve the night shift yet, so the hotel was quiet. He found some Bircher muesli in the hotel kitchen cold store, so he grabbed a bowl and spoon from the service area, scooped out a large dollop and began eating. As he was chewing, he wandered up and down in the confined space of the cool room. The racks were almost full now that the kitchen was fully operational. He peered into the gloom behind the grill above the door at the end of the room. It seemed to go on forever. *Must go somewhere though*, he thought. The cooling units were like a split system air-conditioner, so the other half had to be somewhere. He didn't remember seeing any near the kitchen door.

Rex mentally put it on his list of things to explore on the weekend, finished his muesli and slid the door back in place behind him, shivering from the chill. He placed his cutlery in the soaking tray and put the bowl on a washing rack, the action becoming automatic after the last few days. He slipped out the door to the service corridor unnoticed, grabbed a hotel bike and cycled down the road into town.

It was another busy day at school. The teachers all seemed to have colluded to keep any casual conversations to a minimum. The first time Rex was able to get a few words to Scott and Amy was the morning recess.

'What's up with the teachers today?' said Scott.

'Yeah, I know. Always hanging around pretending to help,' said Amy. 'You can't even scratch yourself without one turning up to watch you.'

'Definitely creepy,' agreed Rex. 'Hey, I wanted to tell you about last night.'

Amy cut him off. 'Well, it will have to wait. Speaking of creeps ...' She nodded towards the nearby corner of the building. Rex and Scott looked around just in time to see Penelope's head being pulled out of sight.

'Yes,' said Rex. 'Walls apparently weren't content just having ears, they've started growing heads now too.' Scott grinned, but Amy was quietly fuming and staring daggers at the corner in case Penelope's unfortunate head reappeared.

'Anyway,' said Rex. 'I've got to work at lunch time again and be home straight after school, so it will have to wait until tomorrow now.'

'They're killing you, mate,' said Scott.

'It's the price to pay for having the whole weekend off,' said Rex. 'Speaking of which, bring some sturdy shoes tomorrow. We'll go exploring up the hill.' The bell rang signalling the end of the break. 'Come on, better get going. Teachers on the war path and all that.' They gathered up their books and headed their separate ways.

When Rex arrived at the hotel just after midday, he approached the reception desk ready to tell his mother about Shifty Nick and Garrett. As she looked up, the phone started ringing. Rex started talking before she could answer it. 'Mum, I need to tell you something. I heard someone talking to some waiters last night.' Sylvie's eyebrows raised with interest. 'It sounded like ...' Before he could get any more out, another phone chimed in to compete for attention. Sylvie sighed. 'Hang on a tick ...' She lifted one receiver and connected the call. 'Point Cruise Hotel, would you mind holding please? Thankyou.' She pressed another button and the ringing stopped. 'Point Cruise Hotel, would you mind holding please?'

Rex was grateful that she was putting him above the customers for a change. Might at least be able to get a few minutes to tell her about last night. His hopes soon faded though, as his mother continued talking on the phone. 'No, I'm sorry I can't comment on that ... no ... ' Rex could hear the tinny sound of a whiny female voice firing questions without drawing a breath. Sylvie made a sorry face at Rex mouthed the question, 'later?'.

Rex was about to dig in and say he'd wait, but Antonio opened the dining room door. 'Rex, good. You're here. Give us a hand, will you?' He disappeared back into the dining room. Rex continued to wait, hoping his mother would end the call. The dining room door opened again. 'Come on, haven't got all day,' said Antonio. He disappeared again. Rex abandoned his quest and followed Antonio through the door.

Inside the dining room was a cart loaded with small vases, each containing a single yellow rose with just one leaf left artfully on the stem, and some larger vases with native Australian wildflower arrangements. 'I need you to put one of the smaller ones on all the tables please, Rex,' said Antonio. 'Then the larger ones on the side tables around the room. There will be one left over; that's for your dinner tonight. Your mother's friend, Vivienne, is coming.'

Rex liked Vivienne. She and Mum had been friends for as long as he could remember, and she always gave him her full attention whenever they talked. Kind of like a cross between a doting grandmother and cool auntie, but much younger and way more attractive. Rex always felt he could tell her anything knowing that it would be kept in confidence and not be reported back to his parents.

He distributed the large vases around the room before wheeling the cart around, weaving between tables and placing the table vases at the centre of each one. He reserved the best one for last and took it upstairs to the family dining room; one of the few rooms completed in the private section of the hotel. When he entered, he could hear Grandad banging about in the small kitchen, humming quietly to himself as he prepared the evening meal.

'That you, Rex?' asked Grandad from the kitchen.

'Yeah,' said Rex.

'Come and have a taste of this.'

Rex went into the kitchen where a large pot of simmering stew was bubbling away quietly on the gas range. Grandad dipped a spoon into the thick broth and lifted it out carefully, holding his other hand underneath to catch the drips. Rex leaned over and took a sip.

'Mmmm, not bad …' said Rex, recognising Grandad's unmistakable rabbit stew. '... For chicken stew.' He grinned.

'Ha ha,' said Grandad. 'A touch more salt though?'

'Yeah, not too much though. It's right on the edge.'

'Good man,' replied Grandad. Grandad didn't agree with saltless diets. Salt was needed for proper brain function he always said. He threw a pinch of salt in the pot.

'I didn't know you went shooting last night,' said Rex.

'Hmm. Sort of,' replied Grandad. 'I only fired one shot and end ended up with these three,' he said, indicating the three skins rolled up on the end of the bench. 'You'd better take them down to the cellar before your mother sees them though. She'd go crook at me for doing that up here.'

Rex moved to take the skins, but Grandad thrust a plate with a thick sandwich into his hands. 'Lunch,' he said. 'Corned beef and pickle.' One of Rex's favourites, especially as Grandad prepared the beef himself. He tucked into the sandwich leaning against the bench, watching as Grandad speared a rotisserie skewer through another rabbit which had already been tied up with culinary string. Rex thought it was quite weird to be eating a corned beef sandwich and have his mouth start watering at the prospect of roast rabbit.

He finished his sandwich and slid the plate into the dishwasher. 'Antonio's got you trained,' said Grandad. 'Tell you what, after you've taken those skins downstairs, why don't you just head off back to school?'

'Nah, I want to make sure I get the weekend free. Scott and Amy are coming to stay.'

'Ah right,' said Grandad. 'I'll make you some lunch for tomorrow then.'

'See ya later then,' said Rex, and headed back through the dining room.

'Hey, Rex?' said Grandad, appearing around the kitchen door slinging a tea-towel over his shoulder. 'If you see Scott, ask him to tell his dad there might be some uninvited guests poking around his favourite spot in the next week. His dad will know what I mean.'

Rex passed on the message to Scott in whispers during English class. Scott looked at Rex with one eyebrow raised. Rex shrugged his shoulders. The teacher paced back towards them, so Scott gave Rex a surreptitious thumbs up to indicate he'd pass the message on, even though he had no idea what it was about. After school, Rex saw Scott and Amy briefly as he was heading out of the schoolyard on his bike.

'See you tomorrow,' he said. 'I want get home early so I can finish up prep quickly and get everything ready.'

'Yeah, no worries,' said Amy. 'Want us to bring anything?'

'Apart from hobnail boots?' added Scott.

'Maybe a backpack. Grandad's making us lunch. Probably half a kangaroo or something. See ya!' He rode out of the school grounds leaving Scott and Amy to wonder if he was serious.

Rex was just finishing setting the dining room table. He heard Vivienne and his mother's voices as they came in the private apartment's front door.

'Oh, this is lovely!' she said as she entered the room. Vivienne looked more like a modern version of Grace Kelly than her namesake. She wore a pink floral sleeveless dress which fitted perfectly and, though simple, gave the impression that it was straight off a designer's catwalk.

'Hello, Rexxy,' she said. She leaned into Rex, one hand on his right shoulder the other on his left forearm and kissed his cheek. She moved to the other side for another kiss, then back to the other side again for another.

'Hi Viv,' said Rex.

'You're almost as tall as your father now, what is that? Six feet?'

Rex nodded bashfully. 'You look like your father did when he was seventeen. Way more handsome though,' she teased. 'You've got a girlfriend coming tomorrow I understand?'

If Rex wasn't already embarrassed enough from Vivienne kissing his cheeks, the thought of Amy being called his girlfriend finished the job.

'Amy, *and* Scott,' he said, feeling his ears get hot as blood ran to them.

Vivienne chuckled. 'I'm sure you'll have a lot of fun exploring tomorrow,' she said. 'Who knows what you might find?' Rex didn't quite understand what she meant but knew it would become clear later. Everything Vivienne said usually turned out to be exactly as she said, even if it wasn't obvious at the time.

'Ah Vivienne, you're here.' Rex's dad entered the room, shook off his suit jacket and hung it over the back of a chair.

'Hello Roy,' replied Vivienne giving him a well-practiced two cheek kiss. 'You haven't been working Rex too hard, have you?'

'All self-inflicted I assure you. He's earned the weekend off alright, even though we are short staffed.' Roy saw Rex's growing look of dismay at the prospect of being asked to work on the weekend. 'Don't worry, Rex, we'll manage.'

'Bookings are down anyway so we'll be fine,' said Sylvie, seating herself next to his dad's favourite seat. Roy pulled out a chair for Vivienne, seating her opposite his own place. For as long as Rex could remember his dad had always sat to the right of his mother, choosing not to sit at the head of the table. Rex sat next to Vivienne leaving the end place for Grandad, who was still in the kitchen.

Grandad shouted from the kitchen. 'Bonsoir, Vivi!'

'Bonsoir, Sydney,' said Vivienne. Their mutual greeting in French was another thing Rex could never remember being different.

'What are we having?' asked Vivienne.

'Roast bunny!' said Grandad. He entered the room with a silver platter laden with roast potatoes, carrots, pumpkin, and shallots surrounding a golden, juicy rabbit.

'Oooh, smells lovely,' said Vivienne. 'One of yours?'

Grandad smiled. 'Don't worry, there's no shot in it.' He leaned in between Vivienne and Rex to place the platter at the centre of the table. Aside to Rex, he winked and said, 'I used a metal detector this time.' He moved back toward the kitchen.

Roy metered out wine to each place, including a small amount for Rex. 'For all the hard work,' he said to Rex.

Rex said his thanks. It was traditional for the whole family to have wine, even the older children in small amounts but even so, Rex wasn't a fan. *Perhaps that was the idea*, he thought.

Grandad returned with a serving dish of steaming broccoli and beans. 'Well, dig in everyone!' He handed a carving knife and fork to Roy and took his place at the end of the table nearest the kitchen.

The next hour was taken up with eating, sips of wine and general conversation about what other people in the town were doing. Rex recognised a few of the names, but hadn't really been paying attention, preferring instead to concentrate on the deliciously moist meat that he knew was hard to perfect. Grandad had a way with game, and there was no beating his roast veggies. Even Antonio badgered Grandad for his recipes and suppliers, but Grandad would just smile, tap his nose, and wink or give some other cryptic reply.

After a dessert of ice cream and fresh fruits, the evening was coming to an end. The conversation moved from discussing the renovations in the private apartment to the hotel and how difficult it was to get staff. Rex pricked up his ears at this and decided the time was right to put forward his theory.

'Actually, I think someone might be trying to poach our staff,' said Rex.

'What makes you think that?' asked his father.

'Well, last night I saw a couple of waiters outside on their break talking to someone. It sounded like he was trying to convince them to work for him.'

'Did you see who?' asked his mother.

'No, I couldn't see without him seeing me.' Roy and Sylvie glanced at each other.

'Probably just an over enthusiastic diner,' said his father. He drained the last of his wine.

'The voice sounded familiar, though,' Rex continued. 'And I saw your lawyer poking around the carpark. Said he hit the wrong button on the lift.'

'Oh, I hardly think Nick would be doing anything underhand. He's a lawyer after all,' said his mother.

'It just didn't smell right,' said Rex. 'I don't trust him.'

'Now, now, Rex. We're just having trouble getting staff because of what happened on opening night, that's all.'

Rex was about to protest, when Grandad stood and said, 'Come on, Rex, give me a hand in the kitchen.' Rex left the table reluctantly and followed Grandad into the kitchen.

When he emerged after helping Grandad stack the dishwasher, everyone was standing, his father had his jacket back on ready to leave. 'Rex? Would you walk Vivienne to her car please?'

'Ah, yeah okay,' replied Rex.

'Bye, Sylvie, see you soon,' said Vivienne, then to Rex, 'Come on,' and headed for the door. Rex followed; a bit miffed that he hadn't had the opportunity to push his point. 'Night, Mum, Grandad,' he said on his way out.

As Rex and Vivienne emerged from the lift on the ground floor, Vivienne slid her hand into the crook of Rex's arm. They passed Roy at reception who already had a phone held between shoulder and ear as he tapped on the computer keyboard. He looked up as they passed and waved before turning his attention back to the caller.

Outside the hotel entrance the night air was getting a chill to it. The stars were out, and they both walked in silence for a bit, Vivienne staring up at the stars.

She stopped and turned towards Rex. 'You're quite sure something's up, aren't you?' It sounded more like a statement than a question.

'Yes,' said Rex, probably a little more vehemently than he intended. 'They never listen to me.'

'Well, I do.' She still had her hand in his arm and reached over with the other to give him a reassuring squeeze. 'They still see you as their child. But ...' she followed on quickly seeing Rex about to protest. '... like most parents, they don't realise that they're raising an adult, not a child.'

She let that sink in a bit while they resumed walking slowly towards Vivienne's bright red Mustang. 'You can't tell them you're not a child. They need to see it.'

Rex slumped a little, realising she was right.

'Don't lose heart, Rexxy. You'll find a way to convince them but keep an open mind. The truth has a way proving to be different to what we expect.'

She gave him a hug, then retrieved the keys from her bag and got in her car. The car growled to life, and her window slid down.

'Nice car,' said Rex.

'Custom build,' she said with a wink. 'Persevere, Rexxy. You'll find what you're looking for, I know it.' She smiled at him and drove slowly through the gates of the hotel and out of sight leaving Rex under the cool canopy of stars twinkling with settling dew, the deep note of the Mustang purring off in the distance.

CHAPTER 12

Despite everything that happened that night, Rex slept soundly. Maybe it was all the hard work catching up on him, or maybe it was the calming influence of Vivienne. He rolled over in bed to check the time. A minute to six. He lay back waiting for the alarm to sound while he organised his thoughts. He'd tell Amy and Scott about Nick and the person trying to steal staff. Maybe they'd have an idea about what to do. Scott would probably remind him that he wasn't sent here for that; he was sent to open the base. He wasn't quite sure what Amy would say. Would she be like Scott, or more like Vivienne? He was imagining talking to Amy, picturing her smile and lovely blue eyes when the alarm started beeping. He leaned over, hit the off button, swung out of bed, and started getting things ready for the day.

He put together a backpack with a few things in it. They would be climbing the hill behind the hotel later and, having never been up there before, thought he'd better pack a few essentials. A compass, a printed-out map of the area with contour lines to show the hills, a small first-aid kit and a small pair of binoculars. He dressed for walking—jeans, long sleeved shirt, sturdy boots—and stuffed a thick wooly jumper in the backpack just in case they found a cave. The only torches he could find in a hurry were three tiny keyring torches. The police were giving them away at a careers expo he'd gone to in the city. He left the backpack just inside the door of his room, pulled the door locked behind him and headed for the lift.

Rex stepped out of the lift on the ground floor to see Amy walking in through the entrance, a car parked just outside the door. As she saw Rex, her face lit up with the same smile Rex had pictured earlier. She turned and waved to the car as it drove off.

'That was my mum,' said Amy. 'She has a conference call at seven, so she dropped me off early. She said to say hi.'

'Hi, Mrs Amy.' Rex waved over Amy's shoulder, but the car was already gone. He turned back to Amy to catch an embarrassed look on her face which she tried to hide by putting her bag down and fussing with the handles.

'Here, let me get that,' said Rex. He bent down take Amy's bag, their hands touching before Amy relinquished control of the handles and stood brushing hair from her face. As Rex stood up with the deceptively heavy bag, Amy was smiling.

'Do I have to check in?' she asked.

'Oh, ah ... no,' said Rex. 'I just have to get some keys.' He led the way to the desk where his dad was, as usual, tapping on a keyboard with a phone to his ear.

Roy looked up as Rex approached and pressed a hand over the mouthpiece. 'Hello, Amy. I've got some keys for you. He handed over a folded card with a keycard in it. 'Next to your room, Rex.'

'Thanks for letting me stay, Mr. McGregor,' said Amy.

'My pleasure. Anything you need, just dial nine.' He turned to Rex. 'Here's one for Scott too. The adjoining room to yours.' He handed him another card. 'Grandad turned the lift security on last night, so you'll need your pass to go anywhere other than ground floor.' He turned back to the screen and returned to discussing booking dates on the phone.

Rex took the key cards and turned to Amy. 'The lift is this way.'

'Extra security after opening night?' asked Amy.

'Yeah. Probably doesn't want anyone unwanted poking around.'

In the lift, Amy held her card to the reader. It beeped and a light turned from red to green. Rex pressed the button for the third floor and the doors slid shut silently.

'Who's been poking around?' asked Amy.

'I saw our hotel lawyer in the underground garage. There was no need for him to be down there, or anywhere else in the hotel, really, except meeting rooms. I told Mum and Dad that last night. I guess Grandad must have been listening at least.'

Amy picked up on the cue. 'At least?' she asked.

Rex realised he hadn't yet told Amy about last night's dinner. 'Oh yeah. Last night'— the lift doors opened and Rex led Amy towards their rooms—'I tried to tell Mum and Dad that someone has been poaching staff.'

'What? Really?'

'Yeah, I saw someone outside the dining room trying to convince the waiters that they should leave and work somewhere else.' He paused as he realised something else. 'Of course! That's why we're so short staffed. Someone's been paying them extra *not* to work here.'

'How do you know that?'

They reached the door to Amy's room. She tried swiping the door card across the unit above the door handle, but nothing happened.

'You'll have to put it in the slot. It's some extra-secure card Grandad ordered. Even he can't pick these locks.' Amy slid the card in the slot at the top of the lock and a light turned green with a soft click. Rex opened the door to let Amy pass.

'Wow! Nice room,' said Amy looking around. Rex put her bag on the luggage trestle.

'Yeah. Mine's the same but a mirror image,' said Rex. It was weird looking around at a room so similar to his but so different at the same time.

Amy sat on the bed. 'So, someone's been paying staff to stay away?'

'I think so yeah. That's what one of the porters said. He got phone call.'

'What did your mum and dad say?'

'They thought it was probably another guest. I didn't really get a chance to tell them about the porter's phone call.'

'Well, if they don't start listening, they'll lose all their staff. You just have to persevere.'

'Oh, not you too. Everybody's been saying that to me lately. You're not going to hug me as well, are you?'

Amy gave a nervous laugh. 'No, I don't think so.' Rex began to laugh as well. As Amy looked away to hide the look on her face, the bedside phone rang. With a look of 'who could that be?', Amy picked up the phone and offered a tentative, 'Hello?' She listened for second. 'No, er ... he's gone to his room, he'll be out in a sec.' Amy blushed a bit as Rex's eyes widened. He wasn't supposed to be in Amy's room alone with her. 'Okay, tell him we're on our way.' She hung up. 'Scott has arrived.'

'Oh cool. We better go get him.' Rex opened the door for Amy. 'Quick thinking about me not being here. Thanks for that.' Amy smiled as she walked past him through the door.

Rex and Amy collected Scott from reception and took him to his room. After testing the connecting door and marveling at Rex's computer setup, they headed back to reception. Rex grabbed his backpack on the way.

'Let's take the stairs,' said Amy. 'I've always wanted to make a grand entrance.'

Rex and Scott both rolled their eyes but went along with the idea anyway. On the way to the grand staircase, Rex filled Scott in about his theory of the staff being poached. As Rex predicted, Scott thought this must be confirmation that Rex had to open the base before someone else finds it.

'It's obvious, isn't it? Some one's trying to get the place shut down so they can take it for themselves. We have to find the base. Who knows what could happen if it falls into the hands of evil.'

'Bit dramatic, don't you think?' said Amy.

'Maybe so, but until we find the base, we don't know what's at stake,' said Scott.

'Or who's trying to stop us,' Rex finished.

They continued down the plush carpeted corridor to the head of the stairs. Rex was starting to think Scott had a point. If the hotel closed, they'd never find the base.

They descended the first flight in silence. Amy slid her hand down the handrail to steady herself as she looked around at the paintings and game trophies hung all around. 'Speaking of dramatic,' she said pointing to the huge frame hung above the main landing.

'Bloody hell,' said Scott. 'I bet that took a while to paint.'

They stood on the landing staring up at the vast expanse of canvas. Beams of sunlight breaking through clouds lit a vessel by being chased by a foreboding, dark storm. The barque was pitched up in the swell, waves breaking over its deck. Up close, you could make out some of the crew lashed to their stations, a lookout in danger of being tossed from his nest, and the captain struggling to stay on his feet with his arms linked through the wheel. Just as the ticking of the clock by the stairs made its way into Rex's conscience thoughts, he saw that Amy was looking not up at the battling barque, but at the title plate at the bottom of the frame. Amy noticed Rex looking at her. She pointed at the frame, a grin on her face.

Rex read the title. *Perseverance.* 'Oh, for crying out loud,' he said.

Scott saw what the other two were looking at and read the title. 'Ha! It's like it's trying to tell you something.'

Rex rolled his eyes and made his way down the remaining flight to the lobby floor. Scott and Amy followed, suppressing their mirth.

'Back in a sec,' said Rex as he disappeared into the dining room. Amy gazed around the vast foyer while Scott strolled over to examine the clock. 'You could get buried in this,' he said.

'Yeah,' replied Amy. 'And if it chimes, you'd be a dead ringer.'

They were both still giggling about this when Rex pushed through the dining room door backwards, stuffing a package into his backpack.

'I got some food,' he said, answering their unasked question. 'Let's go.'

Rex led them back up to the first floor and used his keycard to unlock an unmarked door opposite the lift. Beyond was an unfinished short corridor lit only by a single bare bulb. It was suspended from the roof by a twisted cable that looked like it was an original fitting. The only other feature was a door at the other end with several heavy bolts securing it. Rex unlocked each of them, using both hands to slide the last heavy bolt aside. He shoved at the door. It opened outwards, sudden bright sunlight momentarily blinding them. They stepped down a few bluestone steps, the treads worn in the middle from countless boots in the past. Rex shoved the heavy door shut behind them.

'This is where the Grim Reaper got me,' said Rex. Around them were the abandoned landscaping supplies and building materials. 'This was supposed to be finished by now.'

'So, not only are they poaching staff, they're poaching your tradies as well?' asked Amy.

'Yeah, probably,' replied Rex. 'Anyway, that's where we're going.' He pointed up the hill behind the hotel. 'And that's what we're looking at first,' he said, pointing to the run-down building beyond the work site.

The bluestone building rose three floors high, capped with a slate roof and short eaves. From this angle, the top of the roof wasn't visible. A builder's crane stood beside the building, its boom indicating the direction of the slight breeze. Rex, Scott and Amy picked their way through the piles of masonry, sand and weeds to a temporary builders' door secured shut by a twisted piece of fencing wire. Rex untwisted the wire and pulled the door open, trampling down weeds to allow it to swing open all the way. Inside, there was nothing but bare walls and a smell of something mouldy.

Amy wrinkled her nose. 'Clearly this hasn't been opened in a while.'

'No, I don't think it has,' said Rex. They wandered further into the space. Most of the inside walls had been removed which made it seem bigger inside. 'The architect is still coming up with ideas. He said he was having some trouble because of some interesting features … whatever that means.' Rex doubted that this place had anything remotely interesting about it.

Scott walked over to the iron framed windows that faced out over the side of the bluff. The waves at high tide thrashed the rocks below. 'Nice view,' he said.

'How big is this place?' asked Amy from the back of the room. She was standing by a temporary railing that fenced off a large section cut out of the floor. She leaned over the railing without touching it. Rex joined her at the rail and looked up.

'Two floors above this one'—Rex looked down—'and at least three down, but it's too dark to see.'

'That can't be right,' said Scott, who was still at the windows. 'From here it looks like we're only one floor up. It must go underground.'

'That would explain the smell,' said Amy. 'But by the breeze coming from down there you'd think it would have aired out.'

'Yeah, but we just opened the door,' said Rex.

'True,' said Amy. 'Though that breeze is stronger than an open window on the floor below, unless they're all open.'

'They're not,' said Scott. 'Come and look.' Scott had a window open and was leaning out of it. They were the type that are hinged near the top and swing out to open. Rex and Amy joined him. All the windows on the floor below were flush with the walls of the building. Rex leaned out and looked down, then up.

'Nothing else open either,' said Rex. He noticed Amy still wriggling her nose and turned to Scott. 'Maybe leave it open a crack, eh?' Scott nodded and secured the window in a slightly open position.

'Well then,' said Amy through her hand as she covered her nose. 'Nothing to see here. Let's go.' She was halfway to the open door when whatever it was that Amy had smelled from the depths of the building reached Rex and Scott. Both of them did a fair impression of Amy and ran to catch up to her.

Outside with the door firmly wired shut again, they took in deep lungsful of fresh air. Tom was sitting on a pile of sand at the work site watching with amusement, sniffing the tainted air enthusiastically.

'Can't be anything too bad in there,' said Rex. 'Tom would be all over it.'

'Maybe it's his secret bone stash,' said Scott.

'Or the bodies of his victims,' said Amy.

'What?' asked Rex.

'Oh yeah, he's got quite the reputation. There's not a dog in town that will take him on. Or human.'

'Not twice anyway,' added Scott. 'He's a legend around town. He seems to have the ability to sniff out trouble. Sometimes the cops just follow him around.'

'Not much crime in this town, you see,' said Amy.

The flow of interesting smells must have ended when the door closed. Tom yawned, jumped down from the sand and trotted away around the hotel.

'Let's head up the hill, shall we?' said Rex.

'Lead on, Macduff!' said Scott, misquoting Shakespeare.

Rex approached the gap in the bushes that Tom disappeared through when he chased the Grim Reaper. There was a rough track that headed up the hill and out of sight through bushes. They followed the track in single file, stepping over fallen branches and pushing through dense undergrowth. After about thirty minutes, the track ceased its upward path and traversed the contour of the hill. The dull roar of moving water could be heard, and they soon came across a deep rocky creek. There was a steady torrent of water flowing, but it looked like the creek could handle much more. The path ended at the foot of a tree trunk fallen across the creek, broken near the other end and caving into the water.

'That's recent by the look of it,' said Scott, pointing at the end of the trunk on the other side of the creek. Although rotted, the break was clearly quite new.

'Probably done by the Grim Reaper,' said Rex. He pulled out his contour map and pinpointed their position. 'If we're here'—he said pointing to the intersection of a dashed blue line and a dashed brown line—'then this track goes around the hill and back down to the golf club. Clearly we're not playing golf today.'

'Lucky, 'cause I forgot to pack my clubs,' said Scott.

Rex ignored the joke. 'I really thought this might be one of the tracks that just ends. I was hoping we might find some caves.'

'Oh well,' said Scott. 'Where does the creek start?' Rex traced the blue line of the creek uphill until it branched out to several feeders. Halfway along the dashed blue line of the main creek there was a larger blue spot.

'Is that a pool?' asked Scott.

'Could be,' said Rex.

'Let's follow the creek up and have a look then,' said Amy. Rex hoped she was right, or the day would be a bit of a disappointment.

After another half an hour of climbing over and under trees, pushing through fronds of tree fern and avoiding the largest spider webs, the creek widened out.

'Do you think this is it?' asked Amy.

'Must be,' said Rex. The creek ended in a wall of water, ferns and hanging ivy. The roar of the water flowing over the falls drowned out the pings of bellbirds and background hum of insects.

Scott squeezed past them on the narrow track and approached the waterfall. 'Hang on a minute.' He pulled aside a curtain of vines beside the torrent of water. He cried out. 'Whoa! Have a look at this!'

Amy and Rex joined Scott to look behind the curtain.

'Crikey!' said Amy.

'Pay no attention to that dam behind the curtain,' said Rex. He pushed his way through the vines and onto a flat concrete ledge wide enough to walk along.

Rising from the ledge was a tall concrete wall capped with an overhang that kept the undergrowth and water away from the wall. The wall was about ten metres wide and slightly concave. At the centre bottom of the wall was a large iron pipe you could almost crawl into. A small steady stream of water flowed out of it from behind the wall.

Amy had to nearly shout to be heard. 'It's a dam spillway,' she said with a grin.

'Dam it, you're right,' said Scott.

Rex carefully walked along the moss and slime covered ledge that was slick with spray and algae, stepped around the end of the pipe and over the stream of water. He reached the other end of the wall and held aside the vines. 'Guys? I think we might have found the base.' He disappeared through the vines. Scott and Amy followed across the slippery surface using the dam wall to steady themselves. On the other side of the vines the wall continued, but without the overhanging growth and water. The wall was much taller here. It didn't continue the curve of the dam wall but changed to a convex wall curving out then back into the hill. Rex was already disappearing around the other side. They pushed through thick bracken, walking further around and up the hill as they followed the wall. The sound of waterfall died away and they soon came to a flight of steps set into concrete that led up to an opening in the wall. They climbed the steps and pushed a heavy steel door open.

Inside was one carefully constructed straight stone wall that looked out of place; all the other walls were smooth concrete curves. A long horizontal opening in the curved wall gave a view over the hill they had just climbed and out to the sea. Sunlight cut through the opening at an angle, lighting motes of swirling dust stirred up by the new arrivals.

'It looks like some kind of bunker,' said Amy.

'A bit strange though,' said Scott. 'Wouldn't there be a canon or something here? And at least another door?'

'Bricked up maybe?' Rex stared at the wall, moving across its face looking for signs of new work or the crack of a door. 'I can't believe it,' he said.

'What? Did you find something?' asked Scott, hopefully. He leaned against the wall, testing to see if it moved.

'No. That's the thing. Nothing. It's like I've been sent on a wild goose chase.' He spread his arms out indicating everything around him. 'And yet there's all this! It's clearly some kind of bunker. There's a well-engineered, constant fresh water supply, and someone trying to get us out of the hotel.' He dropped his arms to his side. 'Even my own parents don't believe me!' Rex kicked the wall in frustration.

'Stop!' said Amy.

'Sorry,' said Rex. 'I know I'm harping on about this, but ...'

'No,' said Amy. 'Look.' She pointed at Scott's hand.

Scott recoiled from the wall shaking his hand. 'What is it? Is it on me?'

'No, it's not anything creepy. Look.' Amy was still pointing at where Scott's hand had been.

'What?' said Rex. 'I don't see anything.'

'It moved,' said Amy moving forward to the wall keeping her eyes on the rock. She reached up and pressed inward on the stone. It didn't move.

'It pushed in before. I saw it move.'

Rex and Scott exchanged a glance. Amy caught their expressions. 'I'm telling you, it moved. What else were you touching?' She directed her question at Scott.

'Er ... I dunno,' said Scott.

'He wasn't,' said Rex. 'His other hand was in his pocket.'

'Then what were you doing?' Amy asked Rex.

'Nothing, I just kicked the wall.' Rex demonstrated by prodding a stone one row up from the floor.

'That's it. It did it.' The stone under Amy's hand receded half an inch into the face of the wall.

'Ow, wow!' said Scott. 'It's got to be a secret door.'

Rex started pushing the stones in the wall one by one, working toward Amy. 'Nothing,' he said, then ducked under her arm still pressed to the key stone and continued testing. Just two stones further on, and Rex found what Scott had predicted. Part of the wall swung inward at Rex's touch. Amy and Scott crowded around Rex to look inside.

'Wait,' said Rex. He swung his backpack off his shoulders and rummaged in the top pocket, stopping the door from closing again with his foot. He produced some flat metallic rectangles attached to keychains.

'I got these from a careers expo. I thought they might come in handy.' He handed one each to Amy and Scott. 'Test them. One's a bit dodgy.'

'What are they?' asked Scott. Amy pressed the button on her rectangle and the light on the end shone in Scott's face.

'Oh. Right,' said Scott. 'Cool.' He tested his torch, and it gave an erratic mostly feeble glow.

'Here, try this one,' said Rex. He swapped Scott's keychain with another which lit up brightly.

'Lucky I brought spares,' said Rex. 'Come on, let's see what's in here.'

'Wait,' said Amy. 'How do we know we can get out again?'

'Good point,' said Rex. 'Hold the door, Scott, I'll check it out.'

He disappeared into darkness, a tiny keychain torch in each hand as his only illumination. The door began swinging shut again. Scott put his foot against the door before it was halfway closed.

'Can you see anything?' Scott said into darkness.

'Yeah,' said Rex. 'I can see the lock mechanism. You must have to press that stone up top while kicking the one near the floor.'

'But can you open it from the inside?' asked Amy.

'Dunno,' said Rex. 'I think so. Let the door shut, Scott. If I can't open it in a minute, do what we just did to get me out.'

Scott removed his foot from the door. It swung shut and locked with a barely audible click.

'You can't even tell it's there,' said Scott. He examined the edges of the now closed doorway.

'Shhh!' Amy hissed him to silence. She was checking her watch, counting down the seconds to a minute. Scott fell silent, still peering at the wall for tell-tale signs of a door.

'That's a minute,' said Amy. 'Press that stone.'

Scott leaned against the stone as he had done a few minutes ago. Amy pushed the lower stone with her foot. Scott's stone didn't move.

'Are you sure that's the one?' asked Scott.

'Yeah, it has a mark like a sideways rocket on it. I checked. What about yours?'

'Yeah, it feels like a …'—his eyes glanced at her chest—'erm … like a melon.'

Scott heard shouting, then thumping from within the wall. He could barely make out Rex's cries for help.

'Help! I can't get out! Heeelp!'

Scott and Amy started pummeling and kicking the trigger stones, their faces masks of horror. In their desperate attempts to rescue Rex, they failed to notice the door open and see Rex stick his head sideways through it to look up at them.

'Only kidding,' said Rex.

Scott and Amy's faces turned from desperate fright to disbelief, to relief, then to indignation.

'I'm sorry, I'm sorry!' said Rex. 'I couldn't resist.' He smiled in attempt to disarm their rising anger. 'Come in, it's easy to open from the inside. You can lock it so the trigger won't work too.'

Scott and Amy stepped through the door a little uncertainly. They thumbed their keychain torches illuminating the concrete chamber within. The door clicked shut behind them, and they both whirled around to face Rex at the door.

'Relax,' said Rex. He played his torch over the wall. There were complicated looking levers, pipes and metal rods linking the two trigger stones to the door latches. 'You can open it from the inside with this lever,' he said, indicating a handle on the door with his torch. He demonstrated by pulling the handle. The door swung open easily, light flooding in over Scott and Amy like a river of relief.

They all turned to look at the room they were in and played their torches around. It was small and empty but surprisingly clean. Smooth concrete made up the walls, ceiling and floor. There was another doorway with a thick steel door covered in large rivets and set in a steel frame. It looked like it would stop anything. It swung open easily, leading to a corridor.

'Did you try the light switch?' Amy had her torch pointed at an old black switch on the back wall. A steel conduit led from the box it was mounted on to the ceiling where it branched, leading back through the wall and across the ceiling to a weatherproof light enclosure like the ones found on ships.

'Yeah, tried that,' said Rex. 'No good.'

'Can't you just chock the entrance door open while we look around?' said Scott.

'Ahhh ...' Rex looked around for a rock.

'There,' said Amy pointing. 'On the wall behind the door. There's a latch.'

Rex swung the door all the way open until its handle clicked into the latch.

'Okay. Let's go,' said Rex. He took the lead and started down the passageway out of the entrance room. Amy followed closely. Scott glanced back anxiously at the latched open door before also following.

The first door down the corridor was open. Rex shone his light inside checking the floor for obstacles.

'What's in there?' asked Scott, who couldn't see in past Amy and Rex.

'Just some pipes and big taps,' replied Rex. He advanced into the small brick-walled room.

'I think they're called stop cocks when they're that big,' said Amy as she played her torch over two large pipes. Scott stifled a snigger. The pipes came through the back wall at waist height to the left of the chamber, turned and ran horizontally across the wall, then turned again downward and disappeared through the concrete floor. A smaller pipe came through the right-hand wall and joined the top pipe, and a third pipe rose out of the floor terminating in a strange, box shaped grill at head height. There was a lever attached to another valve just underneath it.

'Look, there's a sign,' said Scott. He shone his torch beam on the left-hand wall and edged around Rex and Amy to reach up and wipe the enameled plate metal sign with his hand. Once clear of dusty grime, they could see a diagram that looked like it was of the pipes in the room. The top pipe was labeled 'Water In', and the lower pipe was labeled 'Water Out'. The word *Trompe* in large letters was underneath where the pipes went into the floor.

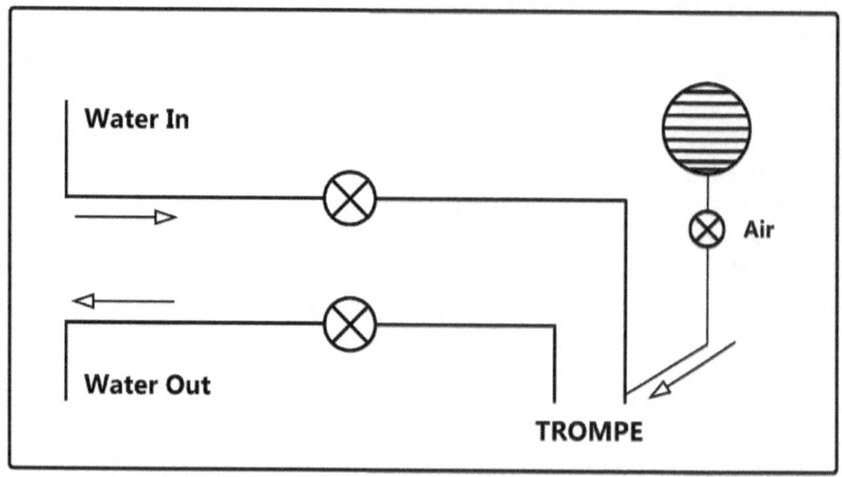

'Not much of an artist this Trompe guy,' said Scott. Rex and Amy laughed.

'Yeah,' said Amy. 'And judging by the amount of water he needs, he's thirsty too!' The three of them doubled over with laughter, the sound amplified by the smooth concrete walls.

Rex was holding on to the top water valve handle with one hand, and his stomach with the other. As his mirth subsided, he noticed the handle in his hand. He stopped laughing. 'Hey, shut up. Listen!'

Scott and Amy stifled their laughter with difficulty.

'What is it?' asked Amy. She was still giggling at her own joke.

'I think it's running.' Rex placed his ear against the wheel of the valve and listened for a second or two. 'Yep. It's running alright, but not much by the sound of it.'

Amy bent her head to the other side of the wheel facing Rex and listened with her eyes closed. She heard a faint hissing sound like a tap turned on to a trickle. She opened her eyes to see Rex's face close to her own. His eyes were closed as he listened. She watched him for a second or two, forgetting Scott was in the room with them. Rex opened his eyes. Suddenly realising they were so close to each other caused them both to stand away from the pipes. They both looked back to see if Scott had noticed but he had moved around them while their eyes were closed and was now staring intently at the box on the end of the smaller pipe. Rex turned away to join Scott.

'It looks like the air filter on my dad's boat,' said Scott. He reached up and turned the lever before Rex could stop him.

'Doesn't seem to have done anything,' said Scott with a shrug, unaware of Rex's momentary fright.

'I'll try this,' said Amy, getting a grip on the lower wheel. She strained to turn it anti-clockwise and was rewarded with a loud squeak as the wheel moved ninety degrees. She repositioned her hands for another turn, but this time only managed move it slightly. 'That's as far as I can turn it,' she said, sweeping her wavy blonde hair back behind her ears.

'I'll try,' said Rex. Amy stepped away and he moved in to take her place.

Rex strained to turn the wheel with his legs braced wide apart. After a few seconds the wheel began to turn, slowly at first, then easier as it loosened up. After several turns it stopped suddenly, as if it had reached the end of its travel.

'Well done,' said Amy.

'You loosened it,' said Rex. He grinned at Amy.

'Doesn't sound like the water's running though,' said Scott. Rex turned back to Scott and shone his torch at him. Scott was leaning over with his ear to the top water pipe.

'I'll try the other one,' said Rex.

He clamped the tiny torch in his teeth and grasped the top wheel. He tried to turn it, but it wouldn't budge.

'Mate, you look like something from Dr Who,' said Scott.

Rex grinned around the torch in his teeth, then stuck his hands straight out in front of his body, his fingers clawed. He chanted ... 'You - will - com - ply. Help - me - turn - the - wheel.'

They all laughed. Scott handed his torch to Amy. She held the two torches aloft to give Rex and Scott plenty of light. The boys grabbed the wheel and heaved momentarily before Rex stopped.

' 'Ang on ... pluh!' He dropped the torch in his mouth to his hands, wiped it on his shirt then stowed it in his jeans pocket. 'Let's try that again,' he said. He repositioned himself at the wheel.

They heaved again, and this time the wheel slowly turned. They only managed a quarter of a turn before they could do no more.

'Well, that was a big success,' said Scott.

'It's running though,' said Amy.

They could all now hear a faint rushing sound of water. Scott moved back to the box and cocked an ear to it. 'Sounds like this thing is sucking air too.'

'I wonder what it does,' said Amy.

'Dunno,' said Rex. 'Maybe it's for a fountain or something.' Rex was about to make another suggestion when there came a loud *gloop-gloop*, gurgling sound from outside the room.

'What the hell was that?' asked Scott. He turned on the spot and backed up against the pipes.

'Dunno,' said Rex. He fished his torch out of his jeans pocket. 'Let's check it out.'

Amy handed Scott his torch back and followed Rex into the corridor. Scott followed warily.

The next door along was slightly ajar. Rex stood at the hinge side of the door and reached out to push the door open while holding his torch with his other hand. *Gloop-Gloop-Gloop!*

This time they all took a backward step. Amy hit the wall opposite the creepy door with her back, and Rex flattened himself against the wall beside the door.

Gloop-Gloop-Gurgle.

'Wait a minute,' said Scott. He was back in the pipe room. He swung his head around the door frame and said, 'I know what it is.' He stepped back into the corridor, put his hand on the door, and with a flourish of his torch pushed the door open ... 'The Dunny!'

Sure enough, at the end of the narrow room was an old toilet, its iron cistern high up on the wall dangling a chain with a brown porcelain handle. The toilet *glooped* again in greeting.

'How did you? ...' said Rex.

'There's one of these outside the back of Scales. Sometimes it's cleaner than the ones inside.'

Amy grimaced. 'Ew.'

'This one's pretty clean,' said Scott. He pushed the door open all the way. 'No T.P. though. These old dunnies make some funny noises when they're filling up. I guess the echoes make it sound pretty creepy.'

The cistern finished filling and stopped its gurgling.

'I'll see if it flushes.' Scott stepped into the cubicle to reach for the chain hanging from the side of the cistern.

'No!' Amy and Rex said together.

'Leave it 'till later,' said Amy. 'It makes too much noise.'

'Oh. Okay then,' said Scott.

They continued slowly edging along the concrete corridor, playing their torches over the walls, floor and ceiling looking for any more pipes or levers. A short way along, it took a turn to the left and about four metres later another turn, this time to the right. Shortly after the second turn they came to a heavily barred gate that ran from ceiling to floor. It hung on huge, solid looking hinges and the lock was surrounded by a large thick metal plate. Engraved into the plate beside the lock was a letter **X** with a dagger overlaid on top of it, the word **UNIT** in capitals below. There was no door handle, just a hole for a large key. Rex gave the gate a tentative rattle, but it barely moved at all.

'Looks like this is as far as we go,' said Rex.

'What's down there?' asked Amy. She slid her arm through the bars and held her torch as far forward as she could reach. 'There's a sign, but I can't make it out. It's covered in too much dust.'

'Anything else?' asked Rex. He craned his head as far as he could without squashing Amy

against the wall.

'Just more doorways. Can you make out the sign on the wall there?'

'Not really,' said Rex, disappointed.

Rex and Amy withdrew from between the bars of the gate and turned reluctantly back the way they came. Scott pushed around them to get a better look beyond the gate but was equally disappointed. He turned to follow Rex and Amy back to the secret door.

They passed the toilet door wrinkling their noses at the newly disturbed stench. As they passed the pipe room door, Rex stopped suddenly. Amy ran into the back of him, then Scott ran into Amy.

'What the ...' began Scott.

'Shhh!' said Rex. 'The door's closed.'

'I thought you latched it open,' said Scott.

'I did,' said Rex defensively. 'It mustn't have latched properly.'

Amy voiced their fear. 'You don't think someone else is here, do you?'

'Nahhh,' said Rex, his voice almost a whisper. 'This place is old. The latch is probably broken.' Even so, he still moved cautiously along the corridor until he could illuminate the door with the narrow beam of light from his torch. Amy stayed safely within an arm's length behind Rex. Scott quickly scanned the pipe room with his torch on his way past, just to make sure there were no surprises waiting to corner them. He finished his reconnaissance and re-entered the corridor to find Rex and Amy had reached the door. Rex was examining the latch on the wall.

'The latch is stuck open now,' said Rex. 'I think it might be controlled remotely. See this pipe?' He played his torch beam over the latch and followed a narrow tube that went down the wall and into the floor.

'Whatever. Just open the door,' said Scott, irritated by the delay.

Rex pulled the door lever and fresh forest air flooded in to greet them. They pushed each other through the door in their haste to get out and hurried to the horizontal slot overlooking the forest beyond. Behind them, the secret door quietly clicked shut.

Each of them leaned on the ledge taking in the fresh air without speaking. They were all glad to be out of the confined space of the bunker. After a few minutes, Amy broke the silence.

'There must be another way in.'

Rex and Scott turned to Amy. They were both thinking the same thing. You can't have a bunker on the side of a steep hill with only one entrance.

'But where?' asked Scott. He thumped his hand on the ledge. 'I know! The smugglers caves!'

'Yeah, maybe,' said Rex sceptically. 'But a bunker would have to be secure against anyone just walking in from the beach.' He stared out at the view, thinking. He could see the top of the flagpole on the old part of the hotel in the distance below them, the Australian Red Ensign gently flopping in the slight breeze. Below it, Grandad's radar beacon rotated at a hypnotic pace, relentlessly sweeping the horizon for vessels, friend or foe. With a start, Rex realised the purpose of the bunker he was now standing in.

'It's a lookout,' said Rex. 'I can't believe I didn't figure it out before. Look down there. See the radar?' He pointed down at the hotel. 'Grandad said he had it replaced after dad bought the hotel because it wasn't working. That's the new lookout, this is the old one.'

'Bit of a stretch, isn't it?' said Scott. 'They already had radar during World War Two. Not nearly as advanced as that one, but still, why would they need this place?'

Amy rolled her eyes. 'It was a gun emplacement.' She crossed her arms on the ledge, rested her chin on them and gazed out at the view. Rex turned to her.

'What makes you say that?' he asked.

'The shape.' She looked at Rex, then Scott, but they showed no hint that they knew what she was talking about. 'The position,' she went on. 'The blast door.'

'It can't be,' said Scott, turning to take in the room. 'There's not enough room.' He looked down at the rough concrete floor. 'And there's no bolts or tracks ... or anything.'

Amy shrugged. She was sure she was right, but couldn't really put her finger on why, and Scott did have a good point.

'Anyone else hungry?' asked Scott.

'Good idea,' replied Rex. He handed out packages from his backpack. Each one had a six-inch-long baguette of crusty French bread with mustard, pastrami, tomato, basil and camembert, a bottle of water with a dash of lemon juice in it, and a small container of fruit salad.

They ate gazing out over the view. Were it not for the trees that must have grown since the bunker was built, the entire point would be clearly visible. They hid the coastline and, but for the roof tops of the hotel buildings, the view would be solely trees and ocean.

'What's the pattern on the roof by the radar?' asked Amy. The others gazed down on the old hotel. On the roof just beyond the turning radar was a series of parallel white lines painted on the flat roof. They looked like someone had tested out painting a short pedestrian crossing in different sizes, arranged ninety degrees to each other.

'No idea,' said Rex. 'Looks freshly painted though.'

'Hmmm,' said Scott. The others looked at him expectantly while Scott continued to gaze out into the view.

Eventually, Amy prompted him. 'Come on then. Spill.'

'Huh?' Scott's thoughts were broken. 'Oh, um yeah. The thing on the roof is a camera calibration target.'

'Oh, right! Well, that clears that up then,' said Amy, her voice dripping with sarcasm.

'And what'—asked Rex—'is a camera calibration target doing on the roof of a hotel where nobody can see it?'

'Oh, I've seen it heaps of times,' replied Scott. Rex and Amy looked at each other, then back at Scott, expectantly.

He continued. 'Yeah, I've flown over it heaps of times. It's for calibrating cameras on aircraft. The smaller the lines it can see clearly, the better the lenses are set up. I asked my instructor.'

Rex realised he didn't really know much about Scott, other than his father was one of the local fishermen.

Amy's jaw hit the floor. 'Your instructor?' she asked. 'You never told me you were learning to fly.'

'Yeah, well,' Scott looked a bit sheepish. 'Didn't know if I'd like it or not. Someone gave me a gift voucher — don't know who, the card was missing. I thought it was a stupid gift.' He noticed the questioning looks on Rex and Amy's faces. 'I thought you knew ... I'm not good with heights.'

'Right.' Amy continued with a sarcastic voice. 'So, you're scared of heights, and you not only actually go up in a plane, but you like it so much you learn how to fly one.' She finished with an eyeroll.

'Um, yeah. Pretty much,' said Scott. He shrugged. 'Doesn't bother me at all. Go figure.'

Rex watched the exchange with a mixture of amusement, both at Scott's unlikely hobby and Amy's indignation at only finding this out now.

'But that's not the weird part,' Scott continued.

Amy started up again. 'There's more? What? You, you ... help your dad on his fishing boat but can't swim?'

'Well ...' said Scott.

'Oh, I don't believe it!' Amy threw her hands in the air and retreated to the other end of the bunker.

Scott continued. 'I can, but I'm not going to win any Olympics, if you know what I mean.'

Rex ignored the latest exchange, and asked, 'So, what *is* the weird part?'

'Well, those things are usually only used by military aircraft and satellites. So, if there's one on the hotel, that must mean ...'

Rex finished the sentence. '... that the hotel must really be the base.'

From the other side of the room Amy said, 'Well, derrr!' Seeing the expectant looks on the boys faces, she continued. 'Add it all up.' She held up her hand and ticked the points off on her fingers as she said them, 'Weird phone call says, 'open the base' and mentions the hotel. Rex gets kicked out of school and moves here. Someone creepy git nearly kills the one guy, an ex-spy, who might have answers. Creepy git then threatens Rex. Radar. Military doohickey on the roof.' She dropped her hands. 'To me, that all equals, wait for it ... Secret Base!'

Rex and Scott nodded in unison, adding it all up in their heads.

'Hey, that reminds me,' said Rex. 'Remember what Limbick said before he conked out?'

'Perseverance?' asked Amy with a cheeky smile.

'Yeah, but before that. He said, 'Find the diary'. He had a little black book with him when I saw him in the restaurant. Maybe he meant that.'

'He must have lost it chasing after the creepy thief,' said Amy.

'Yeah.' Rex thought to himself a moment. 'We'll have a look tomorrow.'

'We should check out around the outside of this thing while we're up here,' suggested Scott.

They all agreed, exited the bunker to explore outside and continued to discuss everything that had happened up to this point. After they had established there were no other entrances, and since none of them was willing to get wet finding a way in under the water in the dam, they returned to the bunker for a rest, water, and another look at the view.

'We should be getting back,' said Rex. 'It will get dark pretty quickly once the sun goes over the hill.'

They went back down the steep narrow steps on the side wall and followed the wall back around to the curtain of vines next to the waterfall. Behind the waterfall, the pipe they stepped over earlier was now flowing a little faster. Rex wondered if it had anything to do with the pipes in the bunker.

Carefully they edged along the side of the dam wall and made their way back down the hill to the narrow, barely defined path by the collapsed tree bridge. Rex turned to look back. He couldn't tell the bunker was there at all and could barely hear the waterfall over the sounds of trees rustling, birds chattering and the bubbling of the creek. They continued back down the hill to where another track joined theirs. Rex reached down and picked up a forked stick that had fallen from a tree, then took four large careful steps into the scrub beside the track to the bunker. He stretched up over his head and hooked the stick over the lowest tree branch of a young mountain ash that would one day grow to be over a hundred and twenty metres tall.

'Good thinking,' said Scott.

Amy led the way back down the hill at a brisk pace leaving the boys behind at times. They arrived at the hotel just to find the shadow of the hill climbing up the walls of the hotel, and Tom sitting on the doorstep of the disused entrance. He gave a woof as a greeting and trotted off again. Rex fancied the old dog was heading off to report their return.

CHAPTER 13

That evening, Rex's parents were working the hotel. A waiter had called in sick, so Sylvie covered for him while Rex's dad looked after reception. Rex showed Amy and Scott into the dining room in the private residence. Grandad was in the kitchen.

'Hi, Grandad, this is Amy and Scott.' said Rex, introducing his friends.

'G'day you two,' he replied.

'What's for dinner?' Rex asked.

'Roast Bounty!' Grandad announced. 'Have a seat, dinner is served.'

He brought out two plates with a small, dressed bird, golden and crisp surrounded by steamed fresh vegetables and roast potatoes, and sat them before Amy and Scott. He went back for two more dishes for Rex and himself. Sitting at the table he noticed them all waiting. 'Well, dig in!'

They all ate hungrily, slicing into the perfectly cooked bird, and piling up veggies on their forks.

'Delicious pheasant, Grandad,' said Scott. Rex was a bit taken aback that Scott called him Grandad before he remembered everyone already knew who Grandad was, and that Grandad knew everyone in town.

Grandad smiled, and leaned over to Rex to say quietly, 'It might be pheasant.' He winked at Rex. Rex nearly choked as he stifled a laugh.

'So, what have you lot been up to today?' Grandad asked.

Scott started off, talking around a cheek full of roast potato. 'We hiked up the hill behind the hotel.'

Amy continued. 'Yeah, and found a fantastic waterfall.'

If Grandad knew what they were talking about, Rex didn't see any hint of recognition in his face.

'Really? Well, I expect that comes from the spring that feeds the hotel,' said Grandad. 'Find anything else?'

The three of them looked at each other, trying to decide how much to tell. They hadn't really discussed what they would say to anyone who asked.

'Just an old lookout,' Rex ventured.

'Oh, right,' said Grandad as he speared another piece of pumpkin with his fork. 'Probably part of the old government buildings.'

Grandad kept his eyes on his food. 'Must be a good view from up there.'

'Yeah, awesome view,' said Amy. She laid down her knife and fork on her plate. 'Grandad? Do you know what the ...'

Rex coughed as if choking on his food in an attempt to stop Amy talking about the base, but she continued anyway.

'... painted lines are on the hotel roof?' she continued, giving a 'did you think I was that stupid?' look to Rex.

'Something to do with camera calibration I think,' replied Grandad. 'They were there when I installed the radar, so I repainted them. Don't know if anyone uses them though.' Rex thought that Grandad knew full well they would have seen the calibration target, so there was no sense in hiding it. 'You would have seen them from the air wouldn't you, Scott?'

'Yeah, a few times,' replied Scott. 'We don't really fly up this way much when I'm learning. There's no beaches to land on in an emergency.' Scott thought a second and added, 'There's no air force base near here though, so I don't know who uses them. They don't look big enough for satellites to use.'

'Mmmm,' said Grandad. 'It's another mystery.' He forked another mouthful of juicy meat into his mouth and chewed.

Figuring they'd got all the information out of Grandad that they were going to get, they dropped the subject.

Dessert was fresh strawberries and cream with melted dark chocolate drizzled over the top. They finished up, well fed and eager to head back to their rooms to talk about what Grandad had, or hadn't, said.

Back in Rex's room, they went over what they discussed with Grandad.

'Do you get the impression your grandad knows more than he's letting on?' asked Amy.

'Yeah,' said Scott. 'No way was that pheasant.' He caught the looks of the other two. 'Really delicious though.' He flopped into the chair in the corner, flung a leg over one arm and burped.

Amy was about to continue but Scott got in first. 'He knows full well what that calibration target is for. Otherwise, why would he bother repainting it?'

'Good point,' said Rex.

'And,' said Amy. 'Governments don't build fortified bunkers with fantastic views and abandon them. They'd charge people money to use them rather than sell them off.'

'Yes,' said Rex. He thought back over the exchange. 'You know, he was the one that brought it up in the first place, remember?

'I reckon he wanted to see if we'd found it.'

'I told you,' said Amy. 'It all adds up. Spooky call, dead guy, ex-spy ...'

'Unnecessarily powerful beast of a radar,' interjected Scott. Amy pointed at

Scott, acknowledging his point.

'... exactly,' said Amy. 'And a zebra crossing on a roof that Grandad repainted just for the hell of it?' She noticed a bottle of complimentary water on Rex's desk and absentmindedly screwed the top off and took a swig. 'He knows.'

They fell silent for a minute, digesting this information as well as their meals.

Rex broke the silence. 'Well, if he's not telling us, it'll be for a good reason. He's ex-special forces. We might need him.'

'Actually, we do need him,' said Amy. 'He can show us the video of Mr Limbick being attacked. Maybe we can see what happened to the diary.'

'We'll ask him tomorrow,' said Rex.

'Maybe he'll know what that logo was on the door,' said Scott.

'Yeah, he might,' said Rex. 'But then we'd be letting on we found the base ... well, part of it anyway.'

'Internet search?' asked Scott.

'Oh yeah, why didn't I think of that?' Rex turned on his desktop computer, while Scott and Amy pulled up chairs to sit either side of him.

'Try 'logo of an X with a dagger',' said Scott, pointing at the search engine page.

Rex typed in Scott's request verbatim and flipped to the images tab. Scrolling through, there was nothing that looked close to what they had seen on the bunker gate.

'Add 'special forces',' said Amy.

Rex added the words 'special forces' on the end of Scott's request and hit the Enter key.

Still nothing. 'I'll try Z instead of X,' said Rex.

'Bingo!' Scott pointed at an image very similar to what they had seen, but with a 'Z' instead of an 'X'. There were many similar images, all mentioning 'SOA' and 'Z Special Unit'.

They spent the next hour going through all the pages they could find, each calling out interesting bits.

'No mention of X Unit, and too much info for one night,' said Rex. They gave up.

'No,' agreed Amy, stifling another yawn. 'Maybe it was extra, *extra* secret'.

'Try again tomorrow,' said Scott, getting up and heading for the adjoining room door. 'I'm off to bed. Call me in the morning.'

Amy also headed off to her room, leaving Rex alone. He looked back at the computer screen with a strange feeling that he'd missed something. It could wait.

It was almost midnight. Rex was awakened for the second time that night by a strange noise, and this time it wasn't Scott's snoring. A low-pitched moaning kind of sound that seemed to be coming straight through the soundproofed door. Rex sat up in bed to try to hear better but the sound of him moving in the quiet room pushed the other sound into the background. He got up and pulled on jeans and a t-shirt, then held his ear to the door of his room to see if he could pick it up again. There it was again; a mournful sigh that seemed almost to be grieving. *Ridiculous*, Rex thought. *It's just the wind.* He turned back from the door and was going back to his bed when ... *tap, tap, tap!* He nearly jumped out of his skin before he heard Scott on the other side of the adjoining room door say 'Rex! Did you hear that?'

'Yeah,' said Rex. 'It's just the wind.'

'No, it isn't, I looked outside. Dead calm.'

Rex's phone rang. 'Hang on, Scott.' He picked up the phone but before he could say anything, Amy said, 'Did you hear that? It's not the wind, I checked. And it wasn't Scott snoring.'

'Hang on a tick.' Rex opened his desk drawer and rummaged around inside, retrieving a sheet of paper, slightly crumpled. 'I've got a list of all of Grandad's haunting events.' He scanned the list. 'Nothing scheduled for tonight though.'

'Let's check it out.' The line clicked, and Rex replaced the phone back on its base. He walked back to the front door, knocking on the adjoining door. 'We're going to check it out.'

'Right-oh,' Scott replied.

Rex emerged from his room to find Amy waiting for him, and Scott coming out of his door. Scott's hair was even more frightful than usual while Amy's looked freshly brushed. Rex ran a hand through his own hair hoping Amy wouldn't notice he hadn't combed it.

'Let's try the quiet end first,' said Rex pointing up the corridor past Amy's room. 'There's less people in rooms that way, and it's in the oldest part of the hotel.'

They all began walking slowly in the direction Rex pointed, not speaking, trying to move as quietly as they could. About halfway along, they heard a noise like an echoing bell, and what could have been low voices.

They all stopped in their tracks. Amy pointed to a room door, then moved closer to it. As Rex and Scott started to move the moaning, groaning noise started again, seemingly coming from all directions at once. Rex didn't notice Scott had stopped. He collided with him, standing on his foot. 'Ow! Watch it!' Scott complained.

'Sorry! And, shhh!' The noise continued, rising and falling. They all slowly rotated on the spot, trying to determine which direction the noise was coming from. As they turned around to face the door again, the door opened. They all jumped back in surprise. It was Mrs Birch.

'You heard it too?' she asked.

'Y ... yes,' said Amy. 'But we thought it was coming from your room.'

'What?' Mrs Birch gave a puzzled look, then said, 'Oh, no. I've got the TV on in the background. Some old Bond movie I think. Sean Connery. Submarines.' The three outside the room relaxed slightly. 'Not what I heard though. Some sort of groaning. Wasn't you three, was it?'

'No,' said Rex. 'Wasn't us. We were checking it out ourselves, actually.' Scott nodded in agreement.

'Oh, alright then. Well, I'll leave you to it. Goodnight then.'

'Goodnight, Mrs Birch.' Her door clicked shut.

'Let's try further on,' said Rex.

They crept further along the corridor. Passing between room doors, the groaning started again, louder this time. Amy was closest to the wall. 'I think it's coming from in here,' she whispered, pointing to the service hatch between rooms.

'What are those doors for anyway?' asked Scott.

'For access to the plumbing,' said Rex. He fished in his jeans pocket and produced some keys on a ring. He selected a complicated looking key and inserted it into an unmarked hole on one side of the door hatch. As he slowly opened the door, Scott and Amy edged back out of the way. The noise started again, much louder this time. Rex reached inside the door and flicked on a light switch. On the roof of the narrow space, a single fluorescent tube flickered and hummed a few times before blinking to life, making shadows dance in the confined space. There was nobody in there, just pipes, dust, and cobwebs. Relieved, the three of them edged closer to have a good look inside.

'There! At the back.' Amy was pointing deep inside the narrow space. She pushed Rex forward into the service room, following close behind. Scott hung back, just inside the door. Rex edged forward a few paces trying to avoid getting covered in spider webs. 'Keep going,' said Amy. 'At the back on the right.'

A group of brass tubes rose through the floor, joined near the top by some kind of tap, with another tube arising from there that bent away from the wall near the end, with an oval shaped cone on its end. A plug was loosely inserted into the tube, attached to the oval shape with an old-style brass linked chain.

'What is it?' asked Amy.

'Looks like a ship's speaking tube,' said Rex.

Amy reached up and pulled the plug from the end of the tube. The noise stopped.

'Thank goodness for that,' said Scott. He had edged closer into the space to get a better look.

'Try putting it back in,' said Rex.

Amy replaced the plug, clicking it in place. A loud piercing high pitched whistle made them cringe until Amy quickly pulled the plug out again.

Rex turned the tap lever below the mouthpiece. Amy replaced the plug, no whistle this time. 'Cool,' said Scott. 'Job done, let's go.' He was already stepping out of the hatch.

'Wait!' said Amy. Scott rolled his eyes and stepped back in the hatch. Amy was leaning with her ear up to the end of the tube. She straightened up and plucked the plug out of the tube, letting it swing from its chain. 'I think I hear voices.' Rex was about to ask her what they were saying, but Amy held up a finger to warn him to silence. She whispered. 'One man, and ... a woman. I think.' She pressed her ear to the opening, her eyes moving about as if searching for them while she concentrated on listening. About half a minute later, she straightened up and replaced the stopper. 'They faded out. But I thought I heard the man say, 'The place is riddled with caves' — I couldn't make out what the woman was saying.'

'Does that mean they are in the hotel grounds somewhere?' asked Scott.

'We need to check out the security monitors,' said Rex.

'Let's go then,' said Scott, already out the door.

Amy and Rex shuffled out. Rex closed and locked the door.

'Why would there be a ship's speaking tube in the middle of a hotel?' asked Scott.

'Good question,' said Rex. 'I know this was used by the army or something, but I didn't think it was a naval base. Actually, Mr Limbick mentioned something about them the morning of when he ... you know.'

'What made it start moaning now?' asked Scott.

'No idea,' said Rex. 'But we should grab torches just in case. There's some in the supply room. It's on the way.'

Rex disappeared into the supply room and returned a few seconds later with torches for each of them.

'These aren't supposed to leave the building. Come on, we'll take the stairs, it'll be quicker,' said Rex as he headed off up the corridor and past the lifts.

They reached the wide-open area of the stairwell to the lobby. It was almost completely dark at this time of night, but with enough light to descend the stairs without using the torches. As they turned to traverse the landing at the halfway point, Scott ran into the frame of the giant picture hanging on the wall. It shifted slightly and Scott grabbed the frame to steady it. 'Oops! Sorry,' he said, and tugged it back into place. As he did so, there was a clank. They all froze on the spot, waiting to see if they were about to be squashed by a giant canvas. The frame remained steady. Scott backed away; his hands ready for a pointless attempt to stop the behemoth from falling. Amy flicked on her torch and looked up at the massive painting and its elaborate gilt frame.

'Come on,' said Rex. He and Scott started moving again. Rex looked back to see Amy still staring at the picture, her head cocked slightly to the side as if trying to hear the raging storm tossing the ship. 'It's fine, let's go,' said Rex. She joined them as they descended the last string and headed toward the security room.

Rex used his access card to unlock the security room door and the three friends entered to find Grandad watching the images arrayed around the walls.

'Ah, here you are,' said Grandad without looking up. He pointed to a screen showing one of the hotel corridors. 'Saw you coming,' he said.

'See anything?' asked Rex.

'Yeah. Caught a shadow on the rear external number three. I'm going to have to reposition that camera. Or add another.' He manipulated some buttons on the console and the vision on one of the screens juddered slightly as it backed up. Rex thought he saw a flicker before Grandad pressed the play button and the juddering stopped. 'Top left corner,' he said. As they watched, the shadow of a figure was cast across the corner of the frame, moving slowly. 'That's all I got.'

'Well, it wasn't us,' said Rex. 'We were checking out some weird noises near Mrs Birch's room.'

'I know,' said Grandad. He indicated another screen. 'Find anything?'

Amy spoke. 'Yeah. An old ship's speaking tube. The call tube wasn't turned off properly. It was making some really weird noises.'

'Ah. That explains the reports I've been getting,' said Grandad. He turned and smiled at them. 'I told them it must have been a ghost.'

Scott was watching the radar monitor, the beam line sweeping around relentlessly, showing a single vessel off the coast. 'That's my dad's boat,' he said. 'Maybe he could see something.'

Grandad indicated the marine radio set into the console. 'Give him a call then,' said Grandad.

Scott lifted the microphone and dialled up the coastal station frequency for shore to ship communications. 'Saint Helena this is Lenzie Coast, Lenzie Coast on Channel 71 for position report ... you there, Dad? Over.' He released the button on the side of the microphone.

A few seconds passed before the speaker came to life. 'Lenzie Coast this is Saint Helena, Saint Helena. I'm one mile south of the point and heading back to harbour. You're up late, Scott. What's up? Over.'

'Someone's been prowling around outside the hotel. Have you seen any lights up here behind the hotel? Over.' The radio squelched quiet for a few seconds.

'I haven't seen anything so far, and nothing up there now. If I see something, I'll let you know. Over.'

'Right-oh, thanks. Worth a try. Lenzie Coast out.'

'Have a good night. Saint Helena out.' The radio fell silent.

The three friends looked at each other dejectedly.

'Right, you three, back to your rooms. I'll keep an eye on things for a while,' said Grandad in his serious voice. 'And don't go creeping about outside tonight. Whoever it is has already killed one, injured another and had a go at you Rex. You're safer inside at night.' The three hesitated. 'Go on. Nothing more you can do tonight. Get some sleep.'

They headed back to their rooms, taking the lift this time. By the time they reached their rooms they were yawning almost constantly. Saying their goodnights, they went to bed after agreeing when to meet in the morning.

CHAPTER 14

Rex woke early despite the late night and yawned his way downstairs to find Grandad. He took the back stairs to keep the lift free for guests to use. Not that there were many these days. He just passed the kitchen when he heard, 'In here, Rex'. It was Grandad. *Seriously the man had a sixth sense*, thought Rex.

'I figured you'd be looking for me,' he said. He was tucking in to scrambled eggs and bacon.

The last of the early morning in-room breakfasts had been sent upstairs and just the chef and a dish-pig were in the kitchen. The smell of oven roasted tomatoes, chipolatas and bacon made Rex's stomach growl.

'Any more on the monitors?' Rex asked.

'Not a sausage,' replied Grandad. 'Having breakfast?'

'No, not yet. I'll wait for the others.'

Grandad kept eating, watching Rex stare into space, waiting for him to come out with whatever he had on his mind.

Rex seemed to come to a realisation. 'We've got to catch this creep.' He looked at Grandad, who nodded while chewing on a delicious strip of fried crispy bacon. Rex stared off into space again.

Grandad prompted, 'Perhaps a trap?'

Rex was still staring into space, but answered as if he himself had asked the question, 'Yeah, but where to set it up?'

Grandad loaded a fork with fluffy yellow egg. 'Somewhere confined with limited entrances and exits, perhaps?' He took the last mouthful and waited for Rex to digest his suggestion.

'Yeah ...' said Rex vaguely, still staring into space. *Somewhere like a cave,* thought Rex. *So, Grandad definitely knew about the caves.* His attention snapped back to the kitchen. 'Any suggestions?' he asked, watching Grandad carefully.

Grandad just shrugged his shoulders still chewing, but his eyes crinkled at the edges like he was smiling. He swallowed and lined his knife and fork up on the plate. 'Well, that's enough for me,' he said. He wiped his mouth with a napkin, headed over to the dish-pig and handed him the plate. As he came back past Rex on his way out, he gave Rex a good luck pat on the shoulder. 'Be careful,' he said, before pushing through the swing doors to the dining room. Rex was left to his thoughts.

He knows there are caves, and he wants to catch this guy as well, thought Rex. *If only he'd just admit he knows and tell us how to get into them.* The smell of hot scrambled eggs steaming under Rex's nose overpowered any semblance of reasoned thought and reminded him how hungry he was. He headed back upstairs to get Scott and Amy for breakfast.

After the weekend, the three friends met after school in the milk bar.

'Yeah, he must know about the caves,' said Scott. 'Anyone who's lived in this town for that long must know.'

'Well, he's not letting on if he does,' said Amy. 'The fewer people who know the better if you ask me.' Rex shot her a look. Amy countered, 'Well, obviously we need to know. I'm just saying, those caves probably go all the way under the point, and I'll bet they connect up to your hotel as well.'

'Yeah, they must. We heard those people through the speaking tube, didn't we?' said Rex.

'Probably connect up to ... the base,' added Scott, using fingers like bunny ears to emphasise 'the base'. 'If they get into that, we're finished.'

'But if we don't know where any of the entrances are, how are we going to trap them?' asked Rex.

'Where did you say the Grim Reaper grabbed you?' asked Amy.

'Out the back by the building works, why?'

'Did you see where he went?'

'Yeah, up the track.'

'So ...' prompted Amy. She looked back and forth between the two of them. 'Honestly, boys can be so thick sometimes.'

'So ... there must be an entrance up the hill somewhere,' finished Rex. 'We know that, already.'

'Probably down by the sea as well,' added Scott. Rex and Amy looked at Scott, wondering why he hadn't volunteered this information sooner.

'Well, you know.' Scott returned their looks. 'All the smuggler stories? You could probably get into them from Scales as well, but I asked Dad once and he reckoned nobody has ever found the entrance. I'll ask him again though.'

'And I'll poke around the hotel a bit more. There are still rooms I haven't been in on the ground floor.'

Amy looked at her watch. 'I've got to go.' She grabbed her school bag from the floor under the table. 'I promised Mum I'd pick up some steaks from the butcher. I'll be back in a minute.' She hurried out, almost knocking someone over who was coming in.

Scott polished off the rest of his Neenish tart. In between mouthfuls he asked, 'How are we going to trap him anyway?'

'I don't know. We don't know where any entrances are, and a camera isn't enough. He'll probably have that disguise on again anyway. We need to catch him in the act.'

'What about along the track? A rack of sharpened sticks suspended from a tree?'

'Tempting.' Rex smiled. 'But we can't kill him. Some kind of cage maybe?'

'With a trip wire? That could work.'

'What about Tom? He might set it off.'

'He's a corgi. He's only a foot and a half high including his ears. We'll just set the trip wire a bit higher.'

They sat, mulling over possible problems before Scott said, 'How do we get him to go that way though?'

'Hmmm,' said Rex. 'If we knew where any of the caves were, we could flush him out by yelling out we're coming to get him.'

'Yeah,' said Scott. 'And accidently let slip the only way he could get away is by going through the trap.'

Rex slapped the table. 'Of course! The speaking tube. We know he goes past wherever it comes out. As soon as we hear him in there, we could use that!'

'Brilliant!' said Scott. 'Bags not going in that room again.'

'What room?' Amy said as she slid into the booth beside Scott.

'The service room where we found the speaking ...' Scott was cut off by Amy.

'Shoosh!' She pointed toward the booth closer to the door behind Rex. 'P-e-n-e-l-o-p-e,' she mouthed.

Rex and Scott exchanged looks, thinking about what Penelope might have heard.

'Why is she always listening in to our conversations?' said Scott out loud.

'Because she has no friends,' said Amy, equally as loud.

'Come on, let's go,' said Rex.

Gathering their bags, they left without even acknowledging Penelope's presence. They headed across the road to the beach foreshore, found a free picnic table without too much seagull poo on it, and reconvened.

'What exactly were you two talking about while I was gone? How much did she hear?' asked Amy.

'I didn't know she came in,' said Scott, answering Amy's second question first.

'We reckon we can set a trap on the track with a trip wire and flush El-Grimmo out by shouting through the speaking tube,' said Rex.

'Did you mention the caves again?'

'Yeah,' said Rex, thinking back on the conversation. 'But only that we didn't know where they were.'

'Well,' said Amy pensively. 'We can only hope she didn't hear much or know what you were going to trap. What sort of trap, anyway?'

'Not sure,' replied Rex. 'Can't be anything lethal though.'

'Pity,' muttered Scott.

They sat for a while discussing options for a trap, the background roar of the rising tide surf covering their conversation from curious colleagues. A few seagulls approached from the air, riding the onshore breeze before touching down on the soft sandy grass nearby, hoping for a crust or a chip.

'It sounds like something from Gilligan's Island before it was filmed in colour,' said Amy after hearing about Scott's idea. 'Do you even have a colour TV?' She laughed.

'Oh, yes!' said Scott, imitating the voice of an old man. 'One of Pye's finest, the Pye Series 14. On Pye, you can rely!' Seeing Amy's blank look, Scott finished in his normal voice. 'Of course I've got a colour TV, and yes, it is more modern than 1977 and if you don't like my ideas for a trap, how about you come up with something?'

'Alright. Sorry.'

Rex watched them arguing, staying out of it. *Must be a history there*, he thought. After a few minutes silence, Rex sought to smooth things over.

'Ahh, do you really have a fifty-year-old TV?'

'Yeah. Still works,' replied Scott. 'Useless now, of course, since digital came in, but works like a charm. Australian built and built to last. Dad used to work for them before they went out of business and he started fishing.'

'I didn't know your dad did that,' said Amy. 'Oh!' Amy's face lit up.

'What?' asked Rex and Scott together.

'Your dad has fishing nets, doesn't he?' she asked Scott.

'Yeah, of course he ... oh, right! Why didn't I think of that?'

'What?' asked Rex.

'We can use a bit of old netting for the trap. Dad keeps all the old bits for emergencies, I'll check if there's a bit big enough. And some rope too.'

'Worth a try,' said Rex.

'I still don't reckon it'll work, though,' said Amy. 'Anyway, I better go before these steaks grow legs and carry me home.'

Scott said to Rex, 'We can go and look now if you like. The boat's on your way home and I need to help Dad out anyway.'

Across the street, Penelope watched her three rivals. She had a feeling Mr. Garrett would want to know about what she just heard. He was always interested to hear what she had to say about her schoolmates, and especially anything to do with the hotel. She watched them arise from the picnic table, Amy heading in one direction and Scott and Rex towards the Marina. Rex seemed nice when he wasn't around the other two. Getting him away from the other two was tricky though. She sighed, gathered her own belongings, and left the milk bar headed for home, wondering what it would be like to live in a hotel instead of a crowded feller's cottage.

CHAPTER 15

The following Friday, Scott stayed over at the hotel with Rex. They spent the evening in Scott's room making plans and rigging up the net Scott scrounged from the Saint Helena. After a few failed attempts, they had a net that would lay flat and close reliably when the ropes were pulled up.

The following morning after breakfast, they returned to their rooms to gather the makings of the trap. When they were ready, they met outside Rex's room.

'Okay what's the plan?' said Scott.

Standing in the passage, the old fish net had the chance to permeate another space with the smell of stale fish guts. Rex considered for a moment, his nose wrinkling at the now apparent stench. 'Down to the first floor. Better take the back stairs with all ... this,' he waved his hands at Scott's backpack, and then the air around it. 'Then out through the back passage'.

Scott sniggered. 'Kind of appropriate considering how bad this net smells.'

'You're telling me.'

They made their way down the stairs trying not to make too much noise as ropes, metal hooks and loose bits of net clanged against the metal fire escape handrail, Scott still chuckling. 'It's like we're in the guts of the hotel, headed for ...' Rex was pretty sure what was coming next. They exited the stairs on the first floor and again entered the old passageway to the back door. As Rex opened it, Scott proclaimed, 'The Back Passage!' and added a sound effect to accompany their exit into the bright sunshine.

'Be free, foul stench,' said Rex theatrically, adding a Shakespearean flourish to send the putrid aroma on its way. Both were still laughing as they made their way to the start of the track.

The intersection of the first fork in the track seemed like a good place to set their trap; the loose, sandy ground providing the perfect covering over the net. Ropes were positioned and covered in sand and bracken, hiding them completely from view. A thin, dirty cord was set across the track at waist height leading to a rig made of rope and steel rings that would be the trigger. Scott expertly throwing several ropes over high branches in nearby trees, along with a rope rig to work like a block and tackle. Together they hoisted a massive log into the tree canopy, the leverage of Scott's rig making it slow but easy work. When it was in position, the main rope was secured to the trigger rig and tied off until later. Scott tugged the other rope free and retrieved the lifting rig leaving the heavy log swinging gently, ready to haul the netted prey off the ground.

By the time they had finished, the sun had long since disappeared over the hill behind the hotel. They used some fronds of bracken to sweep away any evidence that they had been there and removed the safety rope from the trigger. The trap was now set. Anything touching that thin cord would pull a pin out of the trigger allowing the heavy log to drop and pull the carefully laid net around their victim and up into the air.

'I can't even tell it's there,' said Scott when they stepped back to admire their handiwork.

They gathered their now empty backpacks and headed back to the hotel to clean up and eat.

When twilight had finally given up its last sparkle, Rex and Scott took positions at the bottom of the track. They hid themselves among scrubby bushes and bracken, surrounded by a fog of mosquito repellant. After the hard day's work and stuffing themselves with fish and chips at dinner, it was all they could do to stay awake. As the time finally crept past eight, their post-meal stupor had worn off and been replaced by rising excitement. They didn't have long to wait before they heard footfalls further up the track, accompanied by twigs cracking and the rustling of undergrowth being pushed aside. Presently, they heard a muffled shout, quickly followed by the sound of thick rope sliding over a branch, then the dull thud-thud of the log falling on its end and then to its side as the trap was sprung. 'Go, go, go!' Rex shouted to Scott. The pair of them leapt up from their hiding places torches blazing, and shot off up the track, their tired muscles protesting with the sudden effort.

Scott reached the trap first and skidded to a stop, casting the beam of his torch around the scene. Rex gasped up behind him and took in the scene. There was no struggling foe swinging in a gently spinning net; no moustached menace cursing them as meddlesome kids; no trapped transgressor ... nothing! Even the trip wire was still intact.

'Stand back,' said Scott. Rex backed off a few paces, and Scott carefully made his way around the edge of the hidden net to the taught trigger cord. He reached out a finger and gently pushed the cord until, with a *snick*, it suddenly slackened and fell to the ground. The net stayed hidden in the sand.

Rex joined Scott by the side of the track and played his torch beam up the tree by the trigger. The log was no longer suspended in the air. It had fallen, digging a divot out of the ground before falling to its side and rolling a short way down the hill wrapping the rope around itself.

'How could that happen?' asked Scott. 'We double checked everything.'

'Twice,' added Rex.

Scott waded into the undergrowth toward the trigger, leaving Rex beside the track holding his torch aloft to better light the way. Scott disappeared behind the tree with the trigger rig tied to it. 'The rope gave way!' Scott called out. 'Hang on ... it's been cut!'

He stormed out from behind the tree and returned to the track. 'Well, that's that then.'

'Yeah, at least for tonight,' said Rex. 'We might as well go. He isn't going to come back tonight. He knows we're on to him.'

The pair of them returned to the hotel in silence, each trying to figure out what could have alerted the intruder and silently fuming over a wasted exercise. Maybe Amy was right; it was too obvious. At least they tried.

Rex and Scott stumped dejectedly into Scott's room and dumped their bags on the floor of the bathroom.

'Phew, they stink a bit!' said Rex.

'Yeah, maybe that's what gave the trap away,' replied Scott. 'New netting would have been better, but as it is Dad'll kill me if he knows I took one of his good towlines.'

They slumped into chairs and flicked the TV on to see if there was anything worth watching. Scott flicked through the free-to-air channels, barely pausing at each scene before saying 'nope' and going to the next. The usual re-runs of tired talent shows, fake marriages, renovation dramas and some guy crawling through what looked like a factory with his finger on the trigger of a pistol. 'Nope.' The next channel was an old war movie and Scott, having gone through all the channels, gave up and settled for turning the volume down low. Both of them stared blankly at the screen not really taking it in. A telephone was ringing, but the actors seemed to be ignoring it. Even when the scene changed to outdoors, the ringing continued.

'You'd reckon they'd answer that phone,' said Rex.

'Mmmm,' agreed Scott. He pointed the remote at the screen and pressed mute. The sound stopped. He pressed mute again. Background music playing a jaunty military march. No telephone.

'You killed it,' said Rex. 'See if you can get it back,' he said, with a smile on his face.

'Mmmm hmmm.'

Scott again pointed and clicked. Silence. Point and click again. Jaunty music. And a telephone ringing. The pair of them looked at each other not believing what just happened. Then it dawned on them.

'The phone!' they both said together. Scott reached over the back of his chair for the desk phone and picked it up, while muting the TV again.

'Hello?'

'Could you two come down to security, please?' It was Grandad.

'Yeah, sure,' replied Scott. 'Be there in a few minutes.' He rang off.

'That was your Grandad. He wants us in the security room.'

'Ruh, row. Ret's ro, Raggy.'

They entered the security room to find Grandad finishing up a phone call. 'Thanks for letting us know, we'll check it out, bye.' He turned to the boys.

'More reports of shadowy figures with knives outside looking in windows. Funny how they all seem to be walking around in thin air outside the second floor though.' He waited for the boys to understand what he was saying. Rex got there first.

'Right. Levitating larcenists,' said Rex.

Grandad smiled.

Rex continued. 'Not one your special effects, then?'

'No, the place is supposed to be haunted, not under siege,' said Grandad. 'Here.' He handed Rex a heavy semi cylindrical gadget that looked like half a pair of binoculars. 'It's a thermal monocular. We normally use it for checking for fires and wiring faults in walls, but it will also tell us if someone's lurking around outside.'

Rex turned the gadget on and scanned the room. 'Wow, cool!' He handed it to Scott to try.

Grandad continued. 'Head out the front and make a circuit around the back. Scan the bush. If you see something, just come back in. I don't want you tackling anyone. They've already killed once, remember?'

As soon as they exited the front door of the hotel, Scott was scanning the area beyond the forecourt.

'Nothing human sized,' said Scott.

'Right, let's try around the back,' said Rex.

They headed around corner of the building, stopping every now and then to scan the undergrowth at the edge of the forest and the hill behind.

'Nothing,' said Scott, scanning slowly. 'Wait!' He stopped scanning and manipulated some buttons on the device. 'Something really hot up the hill a bit. Not big enough to be human, but too hot to be an animal.' He lowered the scanner. 'We need to get closer.'

They continued around the rear of the hotel until they got to the landscaping works that still lay abandoned after the fateful opening night.

'Try again,' said Rex. Scott began scanning the tree covered hillside.

'There!' Scott pointed with his free hand at something only he could see. 'And there's a line going to it. Really faint, though.' Holding the device to his eye he slowly moved it downwards, tracing the line until he was pointed almost directly down at his own feet. He lowered the eyepiece. 'What the?' He swept a foot through the sandy ground and snagged something. Rex squatted down and raked his fingers where Scott's foot had caught.

'Got it.' Rex pulled up a power cord that was mostly hidden in the sand. It was coming from the direction of the hot thing in the trees and led behind them towards the building. The two of them turned. Then they saw it.

Up on the wall of the hotel's second floor were the shadowy figures the guests had been complaining about. Crude two-dimensional figures moving about jerkily like a primitive cartoon.

'It's a projection,' said Rex.

'And that'—Scott pointed over his shoulder—'must be the projector!'

'Right,' said Rex. He walked toward the hotel, running the cable through his hands to trace it to its source. He arrived at a power outlet on the wall hidden behind a shrub. He pulled the plug out of the socket.

'That did it,' said Scott looking up at the wall. 'No more creep show.'

Rex started winding the cord using his forearm as a spool, the cable crooked between his thumb and pointer finger on one end and his elbow on the other. 'Let's trace it up the hill,' he said.

'Wait, what's that?' asked Scott pointing at the cable. Along the cable there was something written in black marker, barely visible now since it had been buried in dirt. Scott read aloud what he could make out. '... rett Real ... something ... tate.'

They didn't have time to figure it out. The cable suddenly stretched tight from the bushes to Rex's elbow, yanking him toward the trees. 'Hey!' Rex yelled. 'Quick, grab it!' Before Scott could register what was happening, the cable had been yanked off Rex's arm and started slithering toward the trees. 'Let's go!'

Scott shouted. 'No wait!'

Rex stopped in his tracks and looked back at Scott in exasperation. Scott continued. 'Remember what your Grandad said? Just scanning, no tackling?'

Rex looked as if he might ignore Scott for a second, then reached out for the scanner. 'We can at least see where it goes.' He peered through the eyepiece at the bush until he saw the plume of heat Scott had seen earlier. 'There!' He pointed away up the hill. 'There's someone there with it ... it's moving.' The pair of them followed the progress of the blob of heat through the bush, Rex through the scanner and Scott by following where Rex was pointing. 'Gone now. Just disappeared.' He remained motionless. 'Hey, see if there's a record button on this thing, I don't want to move from where it disappeared.'

Scott came closer to Rex, standing on tiptoes to look on top of the scanner while Rex held it still. 'Yep, there.' He carefully pressed the button while cradling the bottom of the scanner so as not to push it off course. 'I should have thought of that earlier,' said Scott admonishing himself.

Rex lowered the scanner and turned it off. 'Yeah, me too. But we got something anyway.'

'What though?' asked Scott. 'He was gone by the time we started recording.'

'Have another go.' Rex handed Scott the scanner.

Scott took it, turned it on and held it up to his eye. 'What?'

'See those numbers at the bottom of the viewfinder?'

'Yeah, so?'

Rex reached out and gently moved the scanner sideways while Scott was still looking through it. 'Notice anything?'

'Oh.' Scott lowered the scanner. 'The coordinates and heading. That means—'

'That means we know where he disappeared. That means we found a cave entrance.'

The pair of them broke out into grins.

'We better get back,' said Rex.

'Yeah. Can't wait to tell Amy.'

Back with Grandad in the security room, they went over what happened.

'Well at least that solves that mystery,' said Grandad after Rex and Scott had explained about the projection.

'Yeah, but we should have recorded it,' said Scott.

'We only got something at the end. Can you download it?' Rex asked.

Grandad took the scanner and plugged a cable in the side of it. A few minutes later, they were watching a colorful blob on the screens of the security room.

Scott was puzzled. 'But we didn't hit record until the end.'

'It automatically records the few minutes before you start recording just in case. So you don't miss anything.'

'Cool,' said Rex.

They watched as the image showed the thin line from when Scott was tracing the cable. The only indication was the image moving was some numbers changing at the bottom of the screen. Two big yellow blobs pushed up from the bottom of the screen. 'My feet,' said Scott.

The next minute or so showed shaky blobs of Scott's legs and feet until the image steadied to show a large blob carrying a hot blob that got smaller and smaller until it winked out to black.

'Pause it there,' said Rex. He grabbed a bit of notepaper and a pen and wrote down the numbers displayed on the bottom of the screen.

'Right, you two, off to bed,' said Grandad. 'I've got guests to contact.'

Lying in bed with no chance of sleep happening soon, Rex couldn't help but go over everything again in his head.

Someone was definitely trying to sabotage the hotel. But who was it? He thought back over everything he'd seen. Shifty Nick creeping about where he shouldn't be. Someone in a pink shirt nearly running him down in the street. Someone getting staff to quit. The projector. Something on the cable ... Wait, what did Scott say it was? '... rett Real something tate.'

Rex suddenly sat up in bed. 'Garrett Real Estate!'

It all started fitting together. The pink shirt in the car — he didn't even realise he'd noticed that before. Nick was the only lawyer in town, so no doubt he worked for Garrett as well. And the name on the cable ... which was gone. Rex slumped back on the bed. He had nothing he could really tie to Garrett, but it was a start. At least now they could find a cave entrance, and he could tell Dad now. This had to convince him, surely. He drifted off to sleep wondering about how Garrett knew about the trap.

Rex wasn't looking forward to meeting Scott and Amy at school on Monday, even though he had good news for Amy. After the telling off Rex got from his dad about setting the trap he was certain Scott's dad would find out. Sure enough, when he found the two of them in the corridor by their lockers, Scott did not look happy.

'What happened? I got a right dressing down yesterday. What the hell did you tell your dad?' said Scott.

'Everything,' said Rex, but with the widening eyes of both Scott and Amy he continued. 'Well, not everything, obviously. Just everything about the trap and Garrett.'

'Garrett?' said Scott and Amy simultaneously.

'Yeah, remember? 'Rett Real Something Tate'?' He looked at both of them, waiting for them to understand. 'Gar-rett Real Es-tate,' he said sounding out the syllables. Amy still looked at him as though he was mental, but Scott got it.

'Oh yeah. The cable.'

'What bloody cable? What are you two on about?' said Amy.

As they headed toward their first class of the week, Rex and Scott took it in turns telling Amy about the trap and the projector.

'Told you it wouldn't work,' said Amy with a smug look on her face. 'Garrett probably smelled the thing a mile away.' Rex and Scott looked at each other as if to say, 'oh yeah, of course'. They wouldn't give Amy the satisfaction of hearing that, though.

'Doesn't matter anyway,' said Scott. 'We found the cave entrance.'

'You did?' Amy's face lit up.

'Ahhh, about that,' said Rex. 'You know how I wrote down the details on that bit of paper?' he said to Scott. 'Well, Dad made me steam clean our carpets because of the smell, and ... well, I accidentally steamed it. Can't read a thing.'

'What about the recording?' asked Scott.

'Dad banned me from the security room for a week. Right before he took all the trap gear back to your dad.' He winced slightly, knowing that would remind Scott about getting him in trouble. 'So, I can't get the details until next week.'

'Yeah, well I'm grounded too. I have to help Dad out on the boat all week.'

'And I have to be dish-pig every night,' replied Rex. 'Dad said it was for 'endangering the public' or something.'

'Mine said it was for not telling him I'd taken his stuff.'

'What? Not that you had taken it, just that you didn't tell him?' asked Amy.

'Yeah. He said he would have let me take it if I asked. Oh yeah, Rex. Apparently, Grandad wants to keep the net?'

'That'll be for one of his haunting gimmicks,' said Rex. 'It stinks to high heaven.'

'Is that what the smell is?' asked Amy. She took hold of Rex's sleeve and leaned in to sniff it. 'You smell fishy, Dishy!'

Rex jerked his sleeve out of her fingers. 'Get off.' He would have looked offended, but Amy was smiling ... and close to him.

'Oi! You lot!' Mrs Mansfield called from up the corridor. 'Move it, or you'll be late for class.'

Scott began to protest. 'The bell hasn't even ...' but his last word was drowned out by the sound of the bell signalling the start of class. Mrs M just raised an eyebrow. 'Yeah, right-oh,' finished Scott. Mrs M retreated with a smirk, and the three of them headed off to class.

CHAPTER 16

The next day, Rex waited by the gate for Amy to emerge from school. Scott was already well on his way to his dad's boat, and Rex thought he should pay him a visit. As she approached him, Rex said,' Have you got time to come and see Scott?'

'Sure. I'm not grounded for setting mantraps. Still feeling guilty?'

'A bit. But it had to be done, even if they didn't believe me.'

They walked from school to the main street and crossed to the foreshore path opposite The Breakers Milk Bar, Rex wheeling one of the hotel bikes beside him.

'You told your parents about the man carrying the projector?'

'Yes,' said Rex patiently, having gone over this several times in the last two days.

'And the cable?'

'Yes. 'Nothing conclusive, no real proof,' they said.' Rex hoped that would put an end to it. Apparently not.

'But why tell them about the trap?'

'Well, like you said. The smell was kind of obvious, and that rope was cut. It didn't break on its own. I thought that would sway them, but Dad just got angry knowing we were creeping about at night with a dangerous killer on the loose.'

'He's got a point,' said Amy.

'Yeah, I know. But they're not doing anything. They know someone's got it in for the hotel but won't believe it's Garrett.'

They walked in silence for a few minutes, both turning over the available facts in their minds. The tide was out, so they walked out on to the beach headed for the marina, Rex pushing the wheels through the deep dry sand.

'You know I almost got grounded too?' Amy had to raise her voice to be heard over the surf and the stiff breeze blowing in from the bay.

'What? Why? You didn't do anything,' replied Rex.

'Yeah, I know. But it took a bit to convince Mum. She caught me out. Asked me why I didn't stop you. I said I told you it wouldn't work … then she had me.' Amy imitated her mother's voice. 'You knew about it? You knew about it and didn't stop them?' She reverted to her own voice. 'I just used the excuse that boys don't listen to girls, and I wasn't there anyway. She backed down after that.'

They headed back up the beach to join the foreshore path before it got to the marina and headed for the commercial fishing area beyond the derelict pier. They found Scott and his dad stacking lobster pots on to the Saint Helena.

'I thought you two were grounded,' said Scott's dad as they approached. Scott's dad reminded Rex of a stereotypical pirate with his bushy tangled red beard. All he needed was a tricorn hat, an eyepatch, and a parrot on his shoulder.

'I have to work evenings,' said Rex. 'Amy used her feminine wiles and got away with it.'

'Oi!' Amy whacked Rex on the arm. 'I had nothing to do with it.' She saw an opportunity for revenge. 'And Rex has something he wants to say to you.'

'What?' said Rex. Amy glared at him. 'Oh. Aahh … yeah. Sorry, Mr Lawson. For getting Scott into trouble. We should have just asked for help. Won't happen again.'

Scott's dad considered this for a moment while Scott continued to stack the round wire and netting baskets, wisely staying out of this exchange.

'Yeah, it will. And call me Charlie. No need for formalities.' He stacked another pot, then sat on the gunwale. 'That'll do Scott, we've got enough.' He turned to Rex. 'How'd you set up the trap anyway?'

Rex and Scott took turns in describing the net, trigger rope and counterweight. Rex finished with, 'We couldn't have lifted that log without Scott's block and tackle rope rig. That was some fancy knot-work.' Charlie raised his eyebrows and looked at Scott, as if seeing him in a new light.

'Impressive.' He scratched his beard with thick calloused fingers. 'Maybe I've been a bit hard on you.'

'Does … that mean I'm not grounded?' said Scott hopefully.

'No,' replied Charlie. Scott's shoulders slumped. 'But I might consider an early release, given, you know, your excellent character references.' He indicated Rex and Amy. 'In any case, we're done for today, so you can go for now.' Scott grinned and jumped from the boat to the deck of the marina.

'Thanks, Dad.'

'Oh, don't thank me,' he said. 'I want you back before dark. If you want to go to your lesson tomorrow, you're still going to have to work for it.'

'Right-oh,' he said as he joined Rex and Amy.

The three headed back to where the old pier joined the marina.

'We'll never find those caves at this rate,' said Rex. 'With us grounded and the inquest on Saturday.'

'Oh yeah I forgot about that,' said Amy. 'Will you have to give evidence?'

'Probably. I was there.'

'Do you think Garrett will show up?' asked Scott.

'Maybe,' said Rex. 'I think it might be a closed court though.'

'Maybe that's why your dad went off at you. A bit too close to the inquest to be stirring up trouble,' said Amy.

Rex nodded. 'Probably.'

'Do you reckon your dad will get off?' asked Scott.

'It's not a trial, but yeah, he'll be alright. He's been over it all with a barrister. He's just worried someone might get hurt. Hopefully more guests don't leave. He's already offering them refunds.'

'Any takers?'

'No, not yet. Most of them are actually enjoying it. Mrs Birch is staying. She said she's not letting anybody tell her what to do.'

'When that's all done and dusted, we can get back to searching for caves,' said Scott, hoping to change the subject to something cheerier.

Out of the blue, Amy said, 'I don't suppose your plane can take photos of the hill behind the hotel?'

'No, not easily. I wouldn't be allowed to anyway. The owner of the plane doesn't like things being attached to it. Something about insurance. Nice idea though,' said Scott, seeing Amy's disappointment.

A thought occurred to Rex. 'Does your instructor have detailed topographical maps?'

Scott thought for a moment. 'Yeah, sort of. Doesn't your dad already have them?'

'No, I've asked him. And Grandad.'

'Well, that's strange.' Scott drifted off in thought.

After a few moments, Rex and Amy looked at each other, then back at Scott.

'What is?' they prompted together.

'Well, my instructor does the mapping for local council. Land survey stuff. He told me he did a close pattern over the whole point a few weeks back. Someone requested it apparently. And if it wasn't your dad, who was it?'

Rex had a good idea who it was and was pretty sure Scott and Amy were thinking the same thing. Garrett.

'Can you get a copy?' asked Amy.

'No, he just supplies the data from the radio altimeter, someone else does the mapping.'

'Can you get me a copy of the data?' asked Amy.

'Maybe. I'll see what I can do.'

'Cool,' Amy looked at her watch. 'Oops, gotta go. Seeya tomorrow.' She headed off around the marina.

'Yeah, I better go too,' said Rex. 'I'll try to get some extra Brownie points by turning up early.' He mounted the bike and cycled off past Scales towards the road that led to the hotel.

Scott wandered back to the boat, wondering why Amy wanted the altimeter data. He found his dad securing the lobster pots to the deck.

'Thinking about world peace again?' It was Charlie's little joke he used when he saw his son lost in thought.

'Have you heard anything about caves under the point?' Scott asked.

Charlie crooked an eyebrow and examined the sky for a moment. 'Well, there are rumours about smugglers using Scales to fence their stuff. But people have searched for an entrance in that pub and never found anything.'

Scott sighed. His dad went on. 'Doesn't mean there never was one. And rumours have a habit of getting crucial details wrong.'

'But do you think they're true?' asked Scott.

'Oh yeah. There are loads of stories. How do you think that old pier got its name?' Scott didn't quite know what he meant by that, but his dad hadn't finished. 'The stories dried up after the war. I guess smugglers didn't want to go anywhere near a mental asylum.'

'Have you found an entrance?'

'Nope. Bloody dangerous, caves are.' He regarded Scott for a second. 'And if you find one, be bloody careful. I know you're looking for them, but ...' he shook his head slowly. 'Just ... be careful.'

'Yep,' said Scott, grateful that his dad wasn't going to outright ban him from trying to find them.

'Right then.' He tightened up the last of the lines holding the cray pots, stretching out his back. 'Come on, let's get some food in us.' He slapped Scott on the back and disembarked, heading for Scales.

CHAPTER 17

Nearly all the locals turned up outside the town's tiny courtroom on Monday for the inquest. Rex, his family, several hotel staff, and some guests were already inside. The coroner arrived late and had to edge his car around all the people waiting patiently outside. The bailiff met him as he was getting out and had a hurried conversation. The bailiff climbed the steps to the front door.

'Okay everybody, can I have your attention please?' he called out. The chatter and murmured conversations died away.

'I know you're as eager as I am to find out what happened, but as time is short the hearing will be closed to the public.'

A murmuration of protest began to rise in the crowd. 'But ... the coroner has said he will make a public announcement at the town hall at the conclusion of the hearing.' The crowd grumbled in disappointment and started to disperse. The coroner took advantage of the distraction to enter the courtroom via the chambers door at the side of the building. When most of the crowd had walked off down the street to go back to their daily business, the bailiff entered the front door and was about to close and lock it when a foot blocked the door from closing. Garret pushed his way in.

'This is a closed court Mr. Garrett,' the bailiff said, blocking Garrett's path with outstretched arms.

'I'm a witness,' said Garrett, shortly.

The bailiff relented and let him take a seat just as the coroner entered. 'All rise,' he called out ceremoniously.

The coroner waved everyone back down. 'Yes, yes, let's get on with it shall we.' He sat and spread the contents of a folder over the desk.

'Right, are all the witnesses here?'

'Yes, Your Honour, plus one *not* on the list. A Mr. Nelson Garrett?' The coroner rolled his eyes. The other witnesses whipped their heads around to see Garrett scowling at the back of the room.

'Mr. Garrett? You are not on the witness list. Were you at the hotel on the night?' The bailiff motioned his hand at Garrett to stand up. Garrett hesitated then got to his feet.

'Ah ... n ... no, Your Worship,' he stammered. 'But that hotel is a death trap and I want to ...'

The coroner cut him off. 'I am not interested in rants about the hotel Mr. Garrett. If you were not there to witness the event, you cannot have seen anything. Now, unless you know the identity of the assailant?' He raised his eyebrows expectantly.

'Ah ...' Garrett looked shiftily around the room taking in the other witnesses faces. Rex was sitting next to Mrs Birch, and both were scowling at Garrett. 'Ahh, how could I if I wasn't there?' he answered evasively.

'Right. Then you are not required as a witness. Bailiff, will you please show Mr. Garrett out.'

Garrett was ushered out of the door and the door locked quickly behind him. He stumped off, heading for his agency.

Inside, the coroner heard all the witnesses and sat stony faced as he watched Grandad's security vision of the chef being brutally cut down by the hooded figure. When there was nothing more to be heard and no more questions asked, the room fell silent as the coroner shuffled paper and made notes. Presently he looked up and addressed the court.

'Well, I think it is pretty clear what happened here. Murder by persons unknown. Mr. McGregor, I find that you were in no way responsible for the death of your employee.' A wave of relief swept over the gathered witnesses. The coroner continued. 'I'll take a one-hour recess to formalise my findings and, given the interest shown by the crowd outside, we will reconvene in the town hall for the verdict. I would ask you all to not announce the verdict until the official ... er ... announcement. Thank you for your attendance.'

The bailiff stood and called out, 'All rise.'

Everyone stood. A mixture of relief and the recognition that someone had died tempered any celebration. The coroner disappeared through the door at the back of the courtroom and everyone else started shuffling towards the door to the street.

On the steps outside, Mrs Birch nudged Rex with her elbow. 'Told you so. Mind you if we didn't have that video, it might have been a different matter.' Mrs Birch seemed to be treating the whole affair as a personal affront to her own interests. 'A picture tells a thousand words.' She smiled to herself and added, 'Or, just the one.' She stepped off of the wooden steps and headed towards Rex's dad leaving Rex to wonder what she meant.

A few of the townsfolk had returned to see what they could find out, but apart from some mentions of 'quietly confident' and 'the coroner will make the right decision', nobody was letting on. Even Penelope turned up, lurking across the road trying to catch Rex's attention. *She'd have to wait*, thought Rex. He suddenly realised how hungry he was, and since his parents seemed to be busy in conversations with other witnesses, he headed toward the hotel bus to get home quickly.

CHAPTER 18

Rex rode back into town on a hotel bike, battling a head wind and hoping to beat the ominous looking clouds pushing over the hills behind town. He dropped the bike off at school, which was still in lunch break, and ran to the town hall making it just in time for the announcement. A middle-aged man dressed like an old-time salesman with a top hat was setting up some public address speakers on either side of the town hall steps, before which a crowd was gathering. Rex found Scott and Amy in the crowd and joined them, still catching his breath from the run.

'What did I miss?' he asked.

'Nothing yet,' said Amy. 'Idiot coroner should have found out if the hall was being used before commandeering it for his big moment, though.'

'Yeah,' added Scott. 'You should have seen his face when the Antique Society president told him to bugger off.' He started chuckling. 'Looked like his head was going to explode.'

'Looks like Garrett's trying to get in on the act too,' said Amy.

Garrett was fussing about on the side of the makeshift podium with something covered in black fabric.

'He tried to muscle in on the inquest as well,' said Rex. 'He got thrown out.' At that moment, Penelope appeared from behind the black draped display.

'What the hell is she doing there?' asked Scott.

A burst of feedback screeched from the steps as the microphone was handed to the coroner.

'Ah ... hello?' A short burst of feedback brought everyone's conversations to an end. 'Um, sorry for the delay. Bit of a mix-up, heh heh.'

Seeing the crowd's stony response, he pressed on. 'Right, well. Firstly, I'd like to acknowledge the trad ...' he was cut off by someone in the crowd yelling out, 'Get on with it!'.

The coroner, seeing his welcome was quickly running out, continued. 'Ah ... right. Since you all know what this is about, I'll cut to the chase.' He realised too late his poor choice of words and cringed to himself. 'Ah, right. I find that Mr Baldwin was killed by persons unknown, and that the hotel managers were not in any way responsible. I understand from the police that they are making enquiries to find the perpetrator. Also, I understand the other man injured in the attack is recovering well. My official notice will be published in the local and city newspapers next Monday. Ah, thank you all for your, ah ... patience.'

He clicked the microphone off and passed it to an outstretched hand before making a hasty exit.

Rex turned to Scott and Amy. 'Come on then, lunchtime's nearly over.'

'Hang on,' said Amy. She grabbed Rex's arm and wheeled him back around, pointing towards the makeshift stage. 'What's he up to?'

Garrett had grabbed the microphone and clicked it on with another burst of feedback that made everyone cringe.

'Yes, ah, thank you Mr ... ah ... Coroner.' The coroner had already disappeared around the corner headed for his car.

Garrett continued. 'Since you are all here, I have an announcement to make.' He turned to Penelope. 'Pennellope, if you wouldn't mind?' He motioned for Penelope to remove the black draping from an easel. Penelope scowled at him for pronouncing her name wrong and jerked the covering off revealing a picture of a multi-story hotel perched on a rocky bluff.

'Despite the findings of the coroner, I think it is clear that the owners of the *current* hotel on the cape should be held responsible for this young man's tragic death.' Groans issued from the crowd and people began to leave. 'We all know there has been a lot of unrest at the hotel of late, and I for one am sick of it! The place is an eyesore, and these gimmicks cooked up by the hotel management *directly* led to people getting hurt and are scaring people to death! But I have a plan to end all that and rejuvenate the area, providing a world class resort experience and all you people jobs, jobs, jobs!' He was getting quite worked up and turned to the artist's impression of a glittering glass-clad tower surrounded by palm trees. He went on, describing various attributes of the hotel without noticing that most of the crowd had walked away leaving Rex, Scott, Amy, and a few others milling about talking amongst themselves and to Rex's parents. Garrett turned back to a now severely depleted crowd and got even more agitated.

'It's only a matter of time before someone else dies, you mark my words!' He jabbed his own chest, almost yelling now. 'I am the rightful owner of that hotel, and I own half this town!' He glared out at what was left of his audience. A bored local news photographer raised his camera and took a half-hearted snap. Garrett finally got the message that nobody was interested, shoved the microphone into the chest of the man in the top hat with a *thump* and pushed his way past him, calling out over his shoulder. 'Clear that up will you Pennellope.' Enraged by this second mispronunciation, she yelled after him. 'IT'S PENELOPE, YOU BEETROOT BUFFOON!' Her shout boomed out over the PA speakers and echoed back from nearby buildings. Startled, she glared at the remaining crowd before she too stormed off, abandoning the easel.

Amy could barely control her mirth, until Scott shot her a look. Rex was still looking at Garrett's hotel mock-up. 'Let's get a closer look at that.'

They all climbed the steps and gathered around the easel. 'Urgh, it's hideous,' said Amy.

'Yep,' agreed Scott. 'Garrett's taste in architecture is as good as his taste in shirts.'

Rex picked at the side of the poster. 'There's a few of these things here. You think he'll notice one missing?'

'Probably got thousands of them printed,' said Scott, and reached up to grab one of the clips holding them in.

'You can't do that!' Amy scolded. She looked around guiltily and seeing nobody was watching, relented. 'Go on then, hurry up. We're late for class.'

Rex folded the poster up and stuffed it under his jumper while Scott and Amy were trying not to look suspicious and failing. They took off around the corner of the building at a run, heading back to school.

'You think anyone saw us?' asked Amy as they slowed to a normal walking pace.

'Not anybody that cares,' said Scott. 'Everyone knows Garrett is an idiot. The only reason he gets any business in this town is because he's the only real-estate agent here.'

'Why would anyone use him then?' asked Rex.

'He runs all the rentals in town. That's what he meant when he said he owns half the town. He doesn't own the houses; he can just make life miserable for anyone renting that crosses him.'

'Nasty piece of work,' added Amy.

'Well, I know damn well he doesn't own the hotel,' said Rex. 'But if he thinks he does, how dangerous is he going to be?' He thought that over for a moment. 'Enough to kill? Enough to evict all the renters?'

'Bloody man's a menace,' said Scott. 'And I don't think he'll stop if he doesn't get the hotel.'

'What do you mean?' asked Rex.

Scott stopped and said, 'Give me the poster.' Rex handed it over and Scott refolded it back over itself, so the lower half of the picture was visible. 'Notice anything?'

Amy got there first. 'Where's Scales?'

Scott nodded. 'The pub will be his next target.' He turned to Rex. 'We've got to find that base. The other day Dad said something about there being a tunnel under Scales. If Garrett gets hold of the pub, he might get easy access to the hotel.' He refolded the poster and the three resumed walking in silence. *He's right*, thought Rex. *If Garrett acquires any large amount of property, he'll ruin the whole town out of spite.*

CHAPTER 19

That afternoon, Rex stowed his bike in the rack amongst the other hotel bikes. As he was walking back to the front door, a black car with dark windows drove in the front gate at a brisk pace. Rex couldn't see in through the front window because the afternoon sun was reflecting from it into his eyes. As it approached Rex, the rear side window opened, and a hand emerged holding an envelope. Rex stood to the side ready to talk to whoever it was, but the car didn't stop. The envelope was flipped towards Rex as the car drove past him. Rex recoiled and caught the letter, more from reflex than skill. The car wheeled around the outside of the portico, tyres squealing slightly on the new asphalt surface and disappeared back through the hotel gates.

Rex stood for a second watching the gates until he realised the car had no number plates. He looked at the envelope. Across the top were the letters 'O.H.M.S.'. It was addressed simply to Mr Rex McGregor. He turned it over, no return address. Rex looked around and, seeing the hotel cameras aimed directly at him, hastily stowed the envelope in his school backpack and entered the building.

Inside, Rex found his grandad leaning against the reception desk talking on a phone handset, its cord stretched over from the other side. Rex's dad was busy on a computer terminal and his mum had her back turned pressing buttons on the printer's touch screen. Rex made for the lift and pressed the door close button before anyone noticed him. With any luck, nobody would bother checking the security footage to see the delivery.

Back in his room, he slit the envelope open with his pocketknife and withdrew two folded pages.

Dear Rex,
If you haven't realised by now, I am the man to whom you spoke on the phone, and it was
I that asked you to reactivate the base. I trust you are making progress and am grateful that

you are fending off the attacks being made against you and your family. I would also like to thank you for coming to my aid on your opening night. You very likely saved my life.

Unfortunately, my recovery is taking longer than expected. To that end, I feel I can no longer continue to be relied upon as your mentor. As such, I am stepping back from 'the business' and wish you the best of luck. To help you on your way, I offer to you my shares in the hotel.

I have quite enough money to live out my days very comfortably, and I believe it only fitting that you should have a stake in the hotel given the commitment I have asked of you.

Enclosed you will find a document. Although it looks like a commitment to the Official Secrets Act, there is no such thing in Australia. It is a pledge to defend Australia and it's people from all who may seek to harm it, by whatever means. By signing it, you will receive certain privileges and have access to a great deal of information, support, and resources. It also signifies that you agree to obtain the same pledge from others before disclosing privileged information. Your friends, Amy and Scott, will become a part of your team, of that I am certain. Since they already know as much as you, they should also sign the enclosed document before you return it.

You will need to find others, but be careful. Be certain of their loyalty, and value those that join you, even if they make the occasional mistake.

I must warn you that few know of our mission and, that what we do is not seen as legal by most. Let me reassure you that what we are and do has been sanctioned by Australia's highest authority.

I have great faith in you, Rex. I believe you will choose to make this your life, and that you will support everything for which we stand — when you find out what that is, of course.

When you are ready, your response will be collected in the same way it was delivered.

Good Luck.

> *Yours Faithfully,*
> *Thomas Limbick.*

Rex re-read the letter then set it aside to read the pledge. Across the top was the name of the organisation: 'Excalibur'. Rex lowered the page and stared at the ceiling, trying to remember where he'd come across that before. Of course! The sword on opening night. But there was something else ... another sword. Rex raised the page again and read through it. By the time he finished, he was starting to get an idea how serious this was. Stuff about not being subject to any civil or criminal liability for any act, about not identifying other members or disclosing information. It finished with the scariest part — penalties for offences against the Crimes Act 1914 apply, up to and including capital punishment. Death.

Rex sat on his bed and thought. If he signs this, then technically, he can't tell Scott and Amy — at least not about Mr Limbick. He looked at the space for his signature. Above were the words 'Signed with and/or in the presence of ...' and space for three signatures. *We all have to sign it at the same time; that way I can tell them about Mr Limbick and see if they are willing to sign it*, he thought.

He moved to his computer and searched for Official Secrets Act. Limbick was right; there was no such thing for Australia. But also, the Crimes Act 1914 had been repealed, and Rex was pretty sure the Death Penalty had been abolished as well, so why would that apply? *Anyway, it made no difference*, thought Rex. *If it didn't apply, there was no legal harm in agreeing to it.*

He brought up his scanning utility and fed the agreement through the scanner, which converted it to text. He removed the bits with the name of the organisation and anything else that would mean anything to someone intercepting it and sent it on to Scott and Amy with the subject: *Read this! Talk tomorrow.*

He sat back, his mind reeling. This was quite a commitment. He never thought he'd end up being a spy.

The next day in class, Rex waited until Miss Lally was keeping Penelope occupied before showing the letter and pledge to Amy and Scott.

When they had both read it through a few times, Amy turned to Rex.

'You haven't signed it,' she said.

'Not yet, but I will. But only if you two do.'

'Well, I will,' said Scott.

'Me too,' said Amy. 'But you should be first.'

'You never even met Mr Limbick. Are you sure you want to do this?' asked Rex.

'Yeah, I'm sure,' said Amy. 'I looked him up. He owns 51% of the hotel. If he's willing to bet that much on you, then so am I.'

'And if it helps to stop Garrett, I'm all in,' said Scott.

Amy pushed the document to Rex and handed him her pen. Rex took it and quickly signed in the first space. Amy slid the document in front of her and signed as well, then pushed it to Scott, whose pen was on the paper to sign as soon as it slid before him.

'That's that then,' said Scott. 'We're now officially part of X Unit.'

Rex's jaw dropped. 'That's where I've seen it before.' He lowered his voice. 'On the gate inside the you-know-what.'

'Yeah,' said Scott. 'Thought it was obvious.'

'Quick put it away,' said Amy urgently. Miss Lally was finishing up with Penelope and looking if anyone else needed help. She walked over to their table.

'Everyone all right here?' she asked.

'All good, thanks,' said Amy. Miss Lally smiled and returned to the front of the room.

At home after school, Rex took a fresh envelope from reception and sealed the pledge inside. He made sure nobody was in the security room before he went back out the front door of the hotel. He stood in the same place he was when he was given the letter and raised the envelope to the camera so the address 'Mr

Limbick' would be visible. He half expected a car to instantly zoom through the gates and snatch it out of his hands, but there was no sound of a car coming up the hill. He waited about five minutes, leaning against the doorway and trying to keep the envelope out of sight. He was about to give up and go inside when he heard Tom bark from near the gate. Rex watched him trot into the hotel grounds, tongue lolling to one side. He came up to Rex, sniffed at the envelope and disappeared inside the hotel. Rex was about to follow him when the car with no plates slid through the gates and came to a stop beside him. The back window opened a crack. Rex waited, trying to peer inside, but it was too dark to see anything. The car just waited, idling. Presently the back window slid down a bit more, then back up to leave the same slim opening. Rex figured he was to post the letter. He slid the envelope halfway into the open part of the window and it was tugged quickly from his hand like a fifty dollar note into a poker machine. The window closed again, but the car remained stationary. The window opened again, and a bigger envelope slid out halfway. Rex noticed his name on it, so reached out and withdrew it from the window. The window immediately closed, and the car accelerated around the outside of the portico and out of the gates.

Back in his room, Rex again used his pocketknife to open the larger envelope. This one didn't have O.H.M.S. on the top and contained a piece of heavy, embossed paper, and a letter.

Rex's jaw dropped. The embossed page was a share certificate for five hundred and ten thousand shares, and in his name! Rex quickly multiplied 510,000 by the price per share and his knees went weak. He half lowered himself, half fell into the armchair. He knew the hotel chain was worth a lot but had no idea it was *this* much. He took out the letter. It was from Mr Limbick, explaining that Rex was now the majority shareholder in the hotel, and would be represented on the board of directors. Limbick offered to represent Rex in this role while he was busy with school, Excalibur, and the base.

Rex wondered how his dad would react knowing he now owned most of the hotel. *He'll find out soon enough*, thought Rex. *And anyway, it's just this hotel, not the whole chain. Still, it was nice to know he owned a hotel.*

CHAPTER 20

Rex woke early the next day and couldn't get back to sleep. Eventually he gave up, deciding he might as well get to school early and poke around in the library for information on old caves on the point. Less than an hour later he entered the library and found Amy already there, flipping through a heavy book.

She looked up. 'Oh hi! How did it go?'

Rex sat down opposite her at the table. 'Well, we're now operatives of the mysterious organisation called Excalibur, and I own more than half of the hotel.'

'So, you're rich then. Well, rich-*er*.'

'Yeah, but only on paper. And since I'm not selling, I'm not really rich.'

'Well, you are really. Or your family is at any rate. At least now nothing can be done to the hotel without your approval. Can you hire and fire people?'

'I don't know, probably. I might leave that to Dad though, I have no idea how to run a hotel, and I don't think he even knows about this yet. Plus, we've got other things to worry about at the moment.'

'True. Let it sink in for a while. It doesn't really change anything.'

'Yeah, it does. Now whoever's trying to ruin the hotel ...'

Amy interjected. 'Your hotel.'

'... *my* hotel, is messing with *my* future.' He looked down at the book Amy was leafing through. 'What's that anyway?'

'A History of Lenzie Bay,' said Amy. 'Nothing about caves'—The first bell rang out warning of classes starting soon—'but I've got some more digging to do.'

'Ha ha,' said Rex, smiling. Amy's face lit up her bright blue eyes sparkling, equally pleased with her own unintended joke and, that Rex liked it.

'We should go to the town library at lunch time. They'll have more local history books than here. Meet at the gates?'

Rex agreed and they headed out to the lockers to get their books for the first class.

At lunch time, Scott and Rex waited by the school gates for Amy but she was nowhere to be seen. After ten minutes of waiting and chomping down sandwiches, they decided to go without her. It was a fruitless exercise. After many searches of the computerised catalogue at the library they found nothing related to any caves, or anything to do with the base at all. It was as though the place never existed. They resorted to picking random local history books from the small collection on the shelves and flipping through them, hoping to find a glimpse of a photograph or a phrase that would give them a clue. There were a few vague references to the smuggling trade, but nothing specific. Eventually, Rex called time.

'I've got nothing. You?'

'Not a sausage,' said Scott.

'We've got to get back. We should come back here with Amy. I bet she'll find something.'

'I can't. I'm grounded until the end of Sunday, remember?'

'Oh yeah. Sorry. Well, if you see Amy let her know I'll be coming back here.'

The three met at the end of the school day before Scott headed off to his dad's boat. Rex and Amy began walking to the library, Rex again wheeling one of the hotel bikes. As they walked, the front wheel began to squeak.

'We couldn't find anything at lunch time. Where were you anyway?' asked Rex.

'Yeah, sorry about that, but I had a thought. Remember your opening night?'

'Yeah, what about it?'

'People dressed up in costumes, didn't they?' Rex nodded. 'Yeah, well that got me thinking. There's only one place around Lenzie Bay that rents out costumes. So, I called them.'

Rex's eyes lit up. 'You're brilliant! Is that what you did at lunch time?'

Amy nodded and continued. 'I went to *Breakers* to use the payphone there. Anyway, I made out I was planning an event for Hallowe'en and wondered if they had any grim reaper outfits. They did. One. But it was out at the moment being cleaned.'

'I bet it was,' said Rex.

'I asked who had it, but they wouldn't tell me.'

'So, another dead end then.' The bike squeaked again, louder and longer this time.

'Well, this is where it gets interesting. While I was there, that creepy lawyer came in with Henny Penny'—Rex had to choke back a laugh—'and she handed over what looked suspiciously like a long, hooded robe to him. It was wrapped in that dry-cleaner's plastic.'

'What happened then?'

'She said to him, 'That'll be twenty-seven dollars. And Whatsisname said to her ...'

'Nick.'

'Yeah, Nick said to her, 'I've only got a fifty.' Then she started getting uppity and he said 'Here take it. It all goes on Garrett's account anyway,' and left.'

'So that means Garrett must have hired the suit.'

'And,' continued Amy. 'Pennellope is being paid to do Garrett's dirty work,' she finished, satisfied that she'd nailed Penelope by pronouncing her name the way Garrett had.

'But it also means that Nick is being paid by Garrett.'

At this point the squeaky wheel developed into continuous squeal.

'Sounds like your front wheel is seizing up,' said Amy.

'Yeah, and it sounds like a long walk home.' Rex lifted the front wheel up off the ground by the handlebars and pulled the bike up to the town library bike racks.

Rex and Amy spent the next hour going through more history books in the library and having whispered conversations about Amy's information.

'You won't find what you're looking for by talking you know.' The librarian was standing over their table.

'Sorry,' they both said.

Amy saw an opportunity. 'It's just that we're doing a school project on local geography and wanted information on the caves at the point.' The librarian raised an eyebrow. 'Or, or, smugglers?' Amy finished, not feeling very convincing.

The librarian furrowed her brow for a few moments. 'Well, you won't find anything about caves. The government cleaned all that out when the point was used as by the military. But you might find something about smugglers in our ... er ... other records. You'll need special access though. Come with me and I'll set you up.'

The librarian led Rex and Amy back to the front desk and into a side room. Most of the room was filled with large sliding shelf units with what looked like steering wheels on the end of each one. On the only free wall was a table with a couple of computer terminals.

'Take a seat,' she commanded. 'Here's your access cards.' She handed them each a plastic card, like a micro-chipped credit card but with many more contacts on one end. It already had their first and middle names printed on them, but not their surname. Rex thought maybe that was for security reasons and tried to get a look at Amy's middle name, but she flipped it over before he could see.

'You put the card in here,' the librarian indicated a slot on the top edge of the keyboard. 'Then you can type in your password. I've made it your birthdays, but you will need to change it after you first log in. You'll figure the rest out. Let me know when you're leaving. Good luck.' She went out of the room allowing the automatic door closer to click the door shut behind her.

Amy turned to Rex. 'What just happened?'

Rex did a gallic shrug. 'Must be perks of the job.' He held the card in the air under the bright glare of the ceiling lights, slowly turning the card. 'There's an 'X' on this card if you hold it the right way in the light.'

Amy continued. 'You don't think it's strange that she had cards made specifically for us with our names on them, *and* knew our birthdays?'

Rex turned back to Amy. 'A few weeks ago I would have, but Limbick did say we'd have resources when we joined Excalibur. This must be a part of it.'

'Hmmm,' replied Amy. She turned back to the terminal, plugged her card in and entered her birth date. After entering a new password, a complicated search screen appeared. 'I'm in. Right then, 'Lenzie Bay, Caves, Tunnels, Smugglers, Court Records'.' She finished typing and hit the enter key.

The screen went mostly blank, then results started appearing one line at a time down the screen in fits and starts, like it was putting up each topic as soon as it found it.

'That will be every mention of Lenzie Bay in the world,' said Rex.

'No, look, it isn't.' Amy pointed at the results. 'It's taken all the words together to figure out what we want. These are all court records for offences in Lenzie Bay with a mention of caves or tunnels.'

She clicked on one of the links and they both scanned the text, Rex leaning in close to Amy. Each document they read mentioned various people being fined for poaching or accessing private property by way of underground access.

Rex pointed at the screen. 'There!'

Amy found where Rex was pointing and saw what caught his attention.

'Scales!' they both said together. Amy read the next part aloud.

'The tunnel entrance through the cellar at the public house known as Scales is ordered to be sealed.'

'So, there are definitely tunnels near Scales,' said Rex. 'There must be another entrance.'

'Yeah, and I bet that's how Garrett's getting to the hotel without anyone seeing him.'

There was a knock at the door before it opened. Amy's screen went back to the log in page automatically. It was the librarian.

'We're closing now, but you can come back any time. Just bring your cards.' Rex and Amy followed her out of the room and headed for the front door of the library.

The librarian held the door open for them and handed Rex another card. 'This one's for Scott. Oh, and ah, best not to mention this to anyone else.' She tapped the side of her nose with her index finger.

CHAPTER 21

Every few hundred metres on the trip home Rex had to dismount, run the bike backwards for a few turns of the front wheel before lifting it up and giving it a good backwards spin. He found that this would give a little more squeak-free travel. He arrived through the gates of the hotel, performed the de-squeak maneuver for what he hoped was the last time, and rode directly around to the underground carpark. After locking the bike in the maintenance room, he took the carpark lift up to the lobby level.

As he came out of the corridor to the carpark lift, Rex saw Shifty Nick loitering around the dining room doors. Rex pulled back into the corridor to watch. Nick glanced around, failed to spot Rex, and gave a tentative push on the dining room door. It was locked and didn't budge. Nick looked around again and Rex ducked his head back just in time. When he dared look again, he saw Nick withdraw something from the jacket pocket of his badly fitting shiny suit. He hid it behind his back. After another quick glance around he dropped it on the floor next to the doors and casually wandered off in the direction of the main desk. Rex left his concealed position and headed towards the dining room, but before he could retrieve what Nick had dropped, Mrs Birch appeared and scooped it up off the floor. She took the glasses that were hanging around her neck and put them on to examine her find. It was a small black book, a diary. She opened the cover to the first page just as Rex reached her. 'Oh!'

She closed the diary and noticed Rex. 'Ah, just the man I want,' she said removing her glasses and letting them hang around her neck.

'Good afternoon, Mrs Birch. What have you found?'

'It's Limbick's diary.' She handed it to Rex. 'Yours now, I believe.'

Rex took the diary. 'Ah, thanks.'

'I'd keep that safe if I were you.' She gave Rex a wink and headed for the lift. Rex looked around. Nick was at the front desk facing away from Rex and talking to Roy. Rex was in half a mind to go up to him, confront him about the diary and tell him to get out and never come back. He even took a few steps in their direction but remembered that his dad might not know about the shares yet. He turned back and headed up the stairs instead. Nick could wait. There wasn't anything he could do now anyway, not without Rex's approval.

Climbing the stairs, he passed the huge painting of the *Perseverance*. It reminded him of something. He just couldn't put his finger on it. At the top of the stairs, Rex made sure there was nobody about before opening the diary. He flipped past the first few pages of calendars, yearly planners, unit conversions and maps to the first page of Mr Limbick's flowing cursive script.

The time has come to act. I can no longer stand by and allow good people to be dominated by those with evil in their hearts.

There was a blank space, then ...

V funyy pnyy hcba gur byq grnz naq svaq n arj trarengvba bs gubfr jvyyvat gb svtug sbe gurve serrqbz, naq gung bs bguref. Guebhtu uneq jbex, oenirel, yblnygl naq crefrirenapr, jr funyy evq bhefryirf bs gubfr jub frrx gb qrfgebl hf.

Gibberish!

Rex flipped through the rest of the diary. All of it was in the same weird, perfectly hand-written gibberish. He let his arms flop to his sides and looked up at the ceiling. Why the hell was this so important? He went on to his room, flipping open pages at random and trying to make sense of it. Before he knew it, he was sitting at his desk, the diary opened in front of him.

Scanning through the pages, he noticed some of the nonsense words were repeated. Maybe some kind of code.

He grabbed a pen and wrote out the alphabet, then went back and wrote the number of each letter underneath. 1 for A, 2 for B, and so on. Flipping to the first page of the diary again, he picked out a word at random and wrote the letters down, then wrote its number underneath. Then he grabbed his old calculator, punched in the numbers and turned it upside down. Hmmmm, not calculator code then.

He looked again at the first few lines of gibberish. There was punctuation. He picked the first word after the first comma. Three letters - 'naq' - 14, 1, 17. He gazed at the result for a moment, then it hit him. 14 is 13 letters - half of the alphabet - away from 1, and 1 is 13 letters away from ... He added more letters and numbers to the end of the alphabet starting from the start again. He rewrote the alphabet on a line, then underneath wrote the encoded letters:

A B C D E F G H I J K L M N O P Q R S T U V W X Y Z
N O P Q R S T U V W X Y Z A B C D E F G H I J K L M

Okay Let's see, he thought. N = A, A = N, Q = D. 'And'. *That's it! All the letters are rotated by half of the alphabet.* He picked out a random word of gibberish from the second sentence and applied his new theory. CREFRI...

P, E, R, S, E, V ... Oh, for heaven's sake. Perseverance!

Rex started from the start and translated the first two sentences of code into normal letters.

I shall call upon the old team and find a new generation of those willing to fight for their freedom, and that of others. Through hard work, bravery, loyalty and perseverance, we shall rid ourselves of those who seek to destroy us.

Sounds like a mission, thought Rex. He flipped the page and translated a few words to check the code was the same. It seemed to make sense. *This could take all night*, he thought. *Hang on, I can automate this.* He fired up his computer and scanned the pages in one at a time, checking each page was converted to text correctly and fixing anything wrong before scanning the next page. Then he wrote a quick little program to rotate the letters thirteen places. He was confronted with all of Mr Limbick's diary in plain text. He fired up his printer, printed it all out and sat down to read.

CHAPTER 22

Rex woke to find himself on his bed with pages of Limbick's diary strewn all about and spilled onto the floor. He glanced at his clock — a quarter to nine — and leapt out of bed. He was halfway to the bathroom before remembering it was Saturday. Relieved he gathered up the pages and stacked them on his desk. Quickly, he emailed Scott and Amy telling them he'd got the diary and to meet him at the hotel as soon as they could make it. When he returned from the bathroom, Amy had replied saying she was on her way, and Scott had replied that he was still grounded, but would talk to his dad. Rex punched holes in the pages of Limbick's diary and clipped them into a folder so they wouldn't fall all over the place again. He locked the diary in the room safe. Just enough time for breakfast before Scott and Amy got here.

Rex pushed through the kitchen doors, lured by the smell of crispy bacon to find Antonio sliding an omelette onto a plate and placing a sprig of parsley on top. He held it out to Rex but just as Rex was about to take it, he took it back. 'Wait, wait ...' He took some tongs and transferred some still sizzling bacon from a skillet to the plate and held it out again. 'Breakfast is served,' he said with a wink. Rex took the plate gratefully and headed to the staff table where there was a place set ready. He barely noticed the hint of truffle and trace of dill as he virtually inhaled the contents of the plate. When he was finished and the world came back into focus, he noticed Antonio leaning against a bench regarding him with amusement. '*Faim?* Hungry?'

Rex let out a small burp. 'Not anymore. That was delicious.'

'I'm glad to hear it,' Antonio smiled. 'Your friends are waiting for you in the lobby.'

'Oh! Thanks.' He scrambled out of the chair and left the swing doors to the corridor flapping back and forth in his wake. Antonio chuckled and picked up the almost completely clean plate. The flapping door suddenly stopped, and

Rex's head appeared. 'And thanks, Antonio. Just what I needed.' Antonio performed a slight bow and Rex's head disappeared again.

When Rex walked into the lobby, Scott and Amy were sitting on the dark leather chesterfield gazing up at the stairwell and the picture of the *Perseverance*. He plonked down next to them. 'Not grounded then?' he asked Scott.

'No, well sort of. I still have to be home by sundown.'

Amy was impatient. 'Yes, yes, come on. The diary? Where did you find it?'

'Just over there when I got home yesterday.' Rex pointed to the dining room doors, now stood open for breakfast. 'Actually, Mrs Birch beat me to it.'

'That's ridiculous. Someone would have noticed it there before then, surely,' said Amy.

'They would have,' agreed Rex. 'But seeing as how Shifty Nick only just dropped it there, you can understand how they didn't.'

Amy and Scott's jaws dropped. Rex went on. 'Mrs Birch picked it up first, but as soon as she saw whose it was, she gave it to me.'

Scott fumed. 'Bloody Nick. Did you kick him out?'

'Of course he didn't,' said Amy. 'What was in it?'

'Gibberish. Doesn't make sense at all.'

'What?' Scott and Amy replied together.

'All of it written in code,' Rex teased. Amy and Scott's faces fell. 'Which is why I spent last night deciphering and reading it. It's upstairs in my safe.'

'And? What did it say?' asked Amy.

'Well, to tell the truth, I kind of fell asleep reading it so I didn't get very far. It's funny though, the first long word I deciphered was Perseverance.'

The three were so engrossed in talk of the diary that they didn't notice Mrs Birch was passing by on her way from the dining room, fussing in her handbag to the sound of jangling keys.

'Yes, a lovely old vessel, the Perseverance,' she said absent-mindedly.

Distracted, they all gazed up at the giant canvas as Mrs Birch continued towards the reception desk.

'Perseverance is the key,' said Amy, distantly.

'That's what Limbick said, yeah,' said Rex.

Amy continued to stare at the picture. 'Are you sure? It couldn't have been 'Perseverance *has* the key' by any chance?'

Rex cast his mind back. Limbick, half conscious, blood over his face, breathless. 'I suppose, yeah.'

Scott sat upright. 'It is! I mean, it has! It does!' With no further explanation he walked quickly to the stairs and climbed them two steps at a time. Rex and Amy caught up to him on the landing.

'Remember when I nearly knocked it off?' asked Scott. 'It clanked.'

Rex realised what Scott meant. 'The key's inside the frame,' said Rex urgently. 'You both check each end; I'll check the middle.' Scott and Amy went to each side of the picture carefully examining the frame while Rex got down on his knees and examined the name plate attached to a box at the bottom.

He felt his way around the edge, gently pushing any imperfection he found. When he got to the right-hand end, he felt something raised. There was a faint cross, like an 'X' that looked like it had been painted over. 'I think I found it!' As the others stopped looking and joined him, he leaned his head under the bottom edge to try and see the mechanism. He pressed the end with the X. There was a click and the bottom edge of the box swung down and a heavy key fell out on Rex's head. 'Ow!' The key thudded down onto the carpet. 'Why does that keep happening to me?'

Amy picked up the thick, old lever-style key. The handle end was a plain flat circle with a hole for hanging it on a hook. From that, a stout round rod of black iron led to a thick square tab on one side of the rod. The slots in it were X shaped with complicated additional cuts. Some of the parts within the pattern were thinner than others.

'This is it,' said Amy quietly. 'We've found the key to the base.'

'Up for another hike?' asked Rex.

Before heading up the hill, Rex, Scott and Amy stopped off at Rex's room.

'After all that's been happening, I thought I'd better get organised,' said Rex. He reached into his cupboard and pulled out some backpacks and handed one each to Scott and Amy. 'I found these online. This kit has everything we need.'

Amy unzipped hers and started rummaging through it. 'Torch, headlamp, first-aid kit, water bottle, rope ... fishing line?' She looked up at Rex. 'How long do you think we're going to be up there?' she asked.

'It's a bug-out survival bag. There's food for two days as well. Apparently if you add a few extras you can live in the bush indefinitely, if you know what you're doing.'

'Yeah, well,' replied Scott. 'I hope it doesn't come to that. I've got be home this afternoon.'

'I'm sure it won't take that long,' said Amy. 'How big can this base be anyway?'

On their way back downstairs, they stopped off to fill the water bottles and grab some fruit and sandwiches from the kitchen. They made their way out through the back passage — Scott repeating the joke and sniggered to himself while Amy rolled her eyes — and headed off up the hill. They came up to the first fork in the track. Amy wrinkled her nose.

'This is where you set the trap, isn't it?'

'Yeah. How did you know?' asked Scott.

'I can still smell the fish,' said Amy.

'Hey, that reminds me,' said Rex. 'Tell Scott about Garrett.'

'Yeah, let's keep moving though.' They headed off in the direction of the bunker while Amy retold what she found out about Garrett hiring the Grim Reaper costume via Nick, and Penelope helping them. By the time she finished they were at the fork in the track where Rex hung the branch up as a marker.

'I told you. You should have thrown Nick out,' said Scott, before taking a swig from his water bottle.

'He couldn't,' said Amy. 'Then he'd know we're on to him.' Rex hadn't thought of that but didn't let on. 'Come on or we'll never get there.' She went on ahead of the two boys. They followed, both impressed that Amy was taking the lead.

This time, they knew the point to leave the track and head for the creek. They soon reached the pool below the bunker. 'You can hardly tell it's there,' said Amy, looking up at where the bunker was.

'I think that's the idea,' said Rex. 'Come on.' He gave her a playful push.

'Oi, watch it!' She made out she was going to push back but turned and ran up to the curtain of ivy, pushed it aside and disappeared. By the time Rex and Scott caught up, she was past the waterfall and disappearing around the corner of the bunker.

<h1 style="text-align:center">CHAPTER 23</h1>

When they reached the lookout, they dug into their backpacks and pulled out torches and headlamps. After putting them on, Rex said to Scott, 'Would you like to do the honours?'

'With pleasure,' replied Scott. He reached up and grasped the melon shaped stone and poked the rocket stone near the ground. There was a faint click and again the secret door swung open to Rex's push.

The interior of the bunker looked way less scary with a bit more light. Rex led them into the first room where the water valves were. 'I had an idea,' he said, reaching into his backpack. He pulled out a small hammer.

'You're going to cave our heads in and leave us here to rot?' asked Scott.

'What? No!' said Rex. 'I thought we could loosen up that valve a bit with some percussive persuasion.' He motioned Scott over to the valve. 'Give me a hand, sicko.'

Amy giggled.

Rex continued. 'I looked up what a Trompe is. It uses water to compress air. It might be for the ventilation system and since we're going inside, a bit of fresh air might come in handy.'

'Oh, right,' said Scott. He grabbed hold of the stuck valve wheel and braced himself against one of the pipes going down through the floor. 'Give it a whack.'

Rex started tapping all around the shaft of the valve. 'It's working, keep going,' said Scott. The valve was turning a little each time Rex tapped it until it suddenly came free, and Scott nearly fell over backwards. 'Got it!'

Rex grabbed the wheel and turned it back and forth a few times. 'Yep, that's loosened it.' He turned the tap all the way in the open direction until it would turn no more.

'It's flowing now,' said Scott. 'Listen.' They fell silent and listened. There was a rush of water going through the pipe labeled 'Water In'. Then, the small pipe with the grill on the end started to hiss softly. A few moments later, the sound of rushing water increased. Rex put his hand on the 'Water Out' pipe.

'Yep, definitely working,' he confirmed. 'Let's go unlock the base.'

They exited the room, followed the dog-leg corridor, and approached the big steel gate. Rex stowed the hammer in his backpack and dug out the heavy key. Scott and Amy stood back to let him get close to the door. Rex slotted the key into the lock. 'Here goes,' he said. He turned the key slowly, sensing for any resistance. At first, he needed quite a bit of pressure to turn it, but at a certain point the resistance eased off and the lock clicked open. Rex carefully pulled the key out and gave the gate a tentative push.

A loud squealing noise like a hundred fingernails scratching down a blackboard made all three of them cringe. Rex pushed faster. The extra speed stopped the squealing and the gate swung open, thumping the wall with a thud.

'We've done it,' he said.

They advanced through the gate and locked it behind them. On the right hand-side of the corridor were three doors. A dusty sign on the first one said 'Battery Commander' and underneath in smaller letters, 'Communications'. Rex turned the doorknob and pushed the door open. Motes of dust swirled in the light of their torches as they played them around the room. Inside was an old desk missing its chair, a rusty old filing cabinet, and what looked a bit like a small old fashioned telephone switchboard mounted on the wall.

'I wonder what that connects to,' said Amy.

'Probably the hotel,' said Rex.

They backed out of the room and made their way along to the second door. This one was as wide as the corridor and made of solid steel with a vault style, three-handled lever set in the middle. The sign said 'Magazine — NO SMOKING'. Scott grabbed two of the levers and turned anti-clockwise. The levers rotated ninety degrees and stopped with a clunk. Scott had to push hard against the door to start it opening. It eased open to reveal that it was set into a very thick steel doorframe. The large room inside was empty but for a steel wheeled hand cart and bare steel walls. Shells for a cannon must have once been stored here. Everything now seemed more serious.

'That explains the weird corridor,' said Scott. The others looked at him waiting for him to explain. 'It's a blast deflector? So the ammo store doesn't blow up if something hits the cannon? Apparently, explosions don't go around corners very well.'

'You're kidding,' said Amy.

'Nup. Absolutely true.'

Amy looked sceptical. Scott shrugged and pulled the big heavy door closed again.

They moved on to the third door. The sign said, 'Stairs', and below that, 'Paternoster'.

'What's a paternoster?' asked Scott.

'Latin for 'Our Father',' replied Rex. 'Or maybe it just means 'Stairs' in military speak, I don't know.'

'How do you know these things?' asked Amy.

'I did Latin at my last school,' replied Rex. 'Not by choice, though.'

Amy rolled her eyes and turned back to the door. She turned the knob and pushed it open. It tried to spring back, but Amy quickly chocked it open with her foot.

The three of them cast the beams of their torches around the interior. To the left was a wide staircase made from a spiderweb of metal beams and mesh suspended in a concrete shaft. They could only make out the first landing below before it turned back on itself and continued down, zig zagging its way into darkness. Rex gave the guard rail a tentative rattle to test its strength. It barely moved and looked as solid as the day it was built.

'That's a lot of steps,' said Scott. He was craning over the top of the rail, being careful not to get too close.

Amy pushed him aside to get a look, grabbing the rail and angling her headlamp and torch down the gap between the strings of stairs.

'I can't see the bottom,' she said. She leaned back briefly to retrieve a coin from her pocket then leaned back over, positioning the coin in the centre of the shaft. She let go and the coin flashed in the torchlight as it fell out of sight. No one moved or spoke, waiting to hear the telltale sound of the coin either hitting the handrails or the bottom of the shaft.

They heard nothing.

'That's ten cents I'm never getting back,' said Amy.

All three straightened up and looked at each other, each understanding what the other was thinking. It was very, very, deep.

'I'm not going down there,' said Scott.

'Me neither,' added Rex. 'I once had to walk down forty-two floors when there was a fire drill in a skyscraper. It's murder on your legs, and you sure as hell won't want to climb back up them.'

'There must be a lift then,' said Amy. She continued deeper into the room, Rex and Scott following behind.

The ceiling opened up to an even taller space. Amy turned her torch slowly around the room. In one corner was a tarp covering something. Legs of what looked like furniture and equipment was visible where the tarp didn't meet the floor.

In the other corner was the top of some giant lift mechanism. A huge structure of iron girders and beams carried what looked like a set of wheels from a steam locomotive only much, much larger. They were suspended diagonally offset from each other in the upper half of the room over the front and back of another wide shaft. Between them, suspended by super-sized bike chains looping over each wheel, was a large box shaped room open at the front and back. On either side of the shaft at floor level were two openings in a wood paneled wall, each with boxes slightly larger than a telephone booth in them. By the left opening, a large arrow pointed up, and a corresponding down arrow was on the right. The wooden walls looked out of place amid the otherwise bare steel and machinery. Between the two openings was a lever and some indicator lights labelled in gold lettering — 'Stopped', 'Out of service', and 'Running'. All were dark. The lever was slanted to the right, under the 'Running' label.

'That looks dangerous,' said Scott. 'Such a shame it isn't working.'

'Looks like it's the stairs then,' said Amy.

'Good. I hate lifts.'

'Let's eat first,' said Rex. He grabbed the tarp in the other corner with both hands and carefully started dragging it from the pile of equipment. Amongst the strange looking cabinets and wooden cases were some chairs and a table. Rex disentangled the chairs from the various legs of other furniture and cables and handed them to Scott and Amy, then dragged the table to the middle of the room. They each sat on a chair around the table and ate sandwiches, their headlamps casting huge shadows of each other on the walls behind.

In between mouthfuls, Scott asked, 'How many stories high do you reckon we are?'

'Dunno,' said Rex. 'We climbed nearly three hundred metres up the hill, so at least that much.'

'What's that compared to a building though?'

Rex thought for a moment. 'The Eiffel Tower maybe.'

Scott looked at his watch. 'I'm not sure I'm going to have time to go all the way down the stairs and back then get all the way back down the hill to the boat before sundown.'

Amy looked at him, one eyebrow raised.

'What?' said Scott. 'It's true, and we have no idea what's down there.'

'Are you going out on the boat?' asked Rex.

'Yeah, for a while. Dad's trying out a new pot hauler and wants me to help. A couple of hours.'

'Well, take your backpack. There's a UHF radio in it. If we find a cave to the beach, we might need you pick us up.'

Amy shot Rex a look. 'I'm kidding!' he said. Amy relaxed.

'We'll be going around the point, so I'll keep an eye out,' said Scott.

'Good idea,' said Rex, before biting into an apple.

They finished their lunch and stowed everything back in their backpacks. Rex and Amy went with Scott to the heavy gate, letting him through before locking it from the inside.

'Is that absolutely necessary?' asked Amy.

'No,' said Rex. 'But this might be the same key to another door out of here, so we might not be coming back this way.'

Amy nodded in reluctant agreement, retrieved the key and stowed it in her backpack.

'I'll be off, then,' said Scott.

'Right-oh,' said Rex. 'Turn your radio on. Channel 55. If you don't hear from us by the time you're back from the boat, you'd better raise the alarm.'

'Okay. But I'm probably not going to be able to hear you from under a mountain. You'll need to be near an entrance.'

Rex and Amy went back to the stair room. As they entered, they heard a soft hissing sound coming from the strange lift. As they approached, they could hear creaking noises as well.

Amy put her ear close to the lever. 'It's coming from here.'

Rex grabbed the lever and rotated it to the 'Stopped' position. The creaking subsided and the hissing stopped after a few seconds.

'Maybe it runs on compressed air,' said Amy.

'Of course,' said Rex. 'The trompe must be building up the pressure.'

A loud hissing noise filled the room. Amy and Rex jumped back from the machinery expecting it to explode, but then the noise stopped again.

'It's the radios,' said Amy with relief. She reached into her backpack and pulled hers out. 'It's on full blast,' she said turning the volume knob down.

Rex retrieved his own radio to check the volume level. 'He must have tried to call us.'

Amy held her radio up to her face and pressed the transmit button. 'Scott? You there?' The radio gave a brief burst of static before going silent.

There was a pause while Rex and Amy waited.

Amy tried again. 'Scott. Repeat please.' Rex nodded in approval.

Another pause. The radio burst into life. 'Yeah, I'm here ... Hey you know that pipe under the waterfall? It's flowing full blast now, so whatever we did worked.'

Amy again pressed the transmit button. 'Yeah, it sure did. We're going in now, so ... talk to you later.'

'Ten-four good buddy. Scotty out.'

Amy put the radio back in her backpack.

'We're going in?' asked Rex.

'Yeah. It's why we're here isn't it?' She motioned to the lever. 'Give it a try now.'

Rex pulled the lever over to the 'Running' position again. The mechanism behind the lever gave a short, sharp hiss. From the depths came a series of clunks and clanks, echoing up from the lift shaft. The huge wheels above them began to turn, drawing the box suspended between them around the radius of the wheels as the box below it descended the shaft. The box on the left rose to meet the wheels as it followed the others. The lift came up to speed settling into a rhythmic clunk, clunk, clunk, as the chains suspending the lift cars passed over the cogs of the pulleys.

Rex and Amy looked at each other, a look of excitement mixed with concern, or outright terror, as they realised what they were about to do.

'You ready?' asked Amy.

'As ready as I'll ever be.'

They waited until the next car came down almost level with the floor and stepped into the box, each grabbing a handrail inside and holding on tight. Surprisingly, the car didn't shake around and felt quite stable.

'This is definitely freaky,' said Amy. There was no door on the car, and no back wall either, so on two sides the walls were slowly but steadily moving upwards as they descended. There was no indication of how far down they were going. Rex looked at his watch and made a note of the time. Then he leaned down and put a finger on the moving wall, his hand moving upwards as they descended. When his hand was about a metre from the floor, he lowered his hand.

'That's about half a metre per second,' he said.

'How deep do you think this place is?' asked Amy.

'No idea. Keep an eye out for signs though. Looks like this lift can load from both sides.' Amy nodded and they rode further down in silence.

After a while, Rex glanced at his watch. 'That's about six minutes. We're still above the hotel.' A sign came into view on Amy's side. 'Level 3 Approaching' it said in bold red letters.

'Should we get off here?' asked Amy.

'Let's wait until ground level.'

The wall on Amy's side opened up as the lift lowered into the room. As the opening passed them, they played their torches around trying to take in as much as they could before the floor rose above eye level. It was another room much like the one at the top of the shaft, with hard concrete walls and equipment stacked under tarpaulins in the corners. There were closed doors and signs they couldn't make out in the short time they had to look.

Another sign, *Level 2 Approaching*, slid up the wall, on both sides this time. Amy's side was an empty room with some large doors leading out of it. Rex's was similar.

The first level rolled past them revealing more closed doors and shrouded equipment.

At last, the *Level 0 Approaching* sign rolled past on both sides of the shaft.

'Let's get out my side,' said Rex. They prepared to step off the lift into the room. The floor of the level rose to meet the floor of the lift. 'Now!'

They both leapt out of the lift and walked clear of it, turning to watch their car descend below the level of the floor. There was a control handle on the panel between lift openings the same as the one at the top.

'Let's stop it for now,' said Amy. She turned the handle over to the 'Stopped' position and the lift slowed to a stop with a final shudder, both the up and down cars lined up with the lift openings. The room fell silent. Shining their torches around the room, it was much like the others they had seen. Amy walked closer to the wall and examined it carefully, especially in the corners. She reached out and touched the wall, feeling the concrete then rubbing her fingers together.

'There's no mould in here,' she said.

'Yeah. Must be fresh air getting in somewhere. Let's try some doors.'

'Okay, but let's try to head back towards the hotel.' Amy pointed at the door opposite the lift. 'We'll start with that one. It's directly opposite the down car of the lift, so we'll remember which one we took.' She looked around at the other doors. 'And it's the only sliding door.'

'Good thinking,' replied Rex.

He grabbed the lever on the side of the door and yanked it to the right. The lever pivoted on the bottom and the heavy door began to slide open. A breeze of fresh air swept through the doorway and momentarily blew Amy's hair away from her neck and over her shoulder. It was a moment before Rex realised that Amy had spoken to him.

'What?' he said, not quite sure why he hadn't heard her.

'Let's go,' she said, and stepped through the doorway out of Rex's sight. She smiled to herself and started walking slowly down a long passageway.

Rex let go of the door lever, keeping his hand ready in case the door started to close again automatically. It remained still so he scooted around the doorway and caught up with Amy, falling into step beside her.

'What do you think?' Amy asked.

'Ah ...' Rex wondered what exactly he was supposed to be thinking about. 'It's ... long?'

Amy turned and smiled at him. 'Ha ha. How far do you think it goes?' She pointed down the passageway.

Rex followed her gaze. 'Oh, ah ... probably a few hundred metres?' he said, unsure really, but not wanting to sound like an idiot.

'That would take us roughly back to the hotel then, do you think?'

'Probably, yeah. Let's pick up the pace a bit.' They walked faster, only slowing down when some doors into the passage approached. They tried each one, but none of them would budge.

Finally, they arrived at a junction. There were lighter patches on the wall from signage that had either been removed or had fallen off.

'That's helpful,' remarked Amy.

'Hmmmm,' said Rex. Rex shone his torch down the corridor to the right. It looked the same, but with less doorways. 'If we've been heading for the hotel, then going right would take us to the new wing. We know that's empty so going left might take us to the hotel.'

'Let's give it a shot.'

They turned left and began to walk again. The breeze seemed stronger from this direction. Rex resisted the urge to see if Amy's hair was being swept back, concentrating instead on what looked like another junction. Another corridor went right, but only for a short distance. Rex held his hand up to the breeze coming from the short passage, then moved it around to the passage they were in.

'It's warmer from this way,' he said, indicating the short passage. At the end of the passage on the left-hand side was a gate made of heavy steel bars set into a steel doorframe. Rex put his torch through the bars and played it down the walls of the passage beyond. There were some metal box shapes on the floor that were about waist high. Pipes and cables led from them to the wall, travelled up and along it away from Rex, then disappeared around a corner to the right.

'I think I know where this is,' he said.

Amy faced him. 'The hotel?'

'Yeah. The cool room in the kitchen. At the back there's a metal door, but where the coolant pipes go through you can see rough walls.' He withdrew his torch from between the bars. 'I reckon that's our way back to the hotel.'

'Can we unlock it?' Amy played her torch beam around the door and frame. There was no lock like the base door, but there was a keypad set into the wall beside the door. It was black and almost invisible against the black of the doorframe. She gave the digits a few presses. There were no beeps or flashing lights. 'It's dead.'

'Let's keep going then.'

They returned to the main passage and continued walking. After a short distance another passage branched to the right. It was the same length as the previous one, but with a gate on the right-hand side.

'It's the other end of the last one,' said Rex.

'Hey look!' said Amy. Her torch beam was shining on a large keyhole. Above it was the same symbol as on the door to the base. She hurried to slide off her backpack and retrieved the key. It slid into the lock with ease, and she clicked it open. Rex pushed the door. It swung open without a sound.

Rex turned to Amy and whispered. 'There might be someone in the cool room.' Amy nodded in understanding. They both crept along the passage, edging past the cooling units that pushed warm air at their legs. They reached the door to the cool room. Amy pointed to the lock. It had two keyholes, but one was shaped the same as the X key. Amy was about to put the key in the lock, but Rex put his hand on hers. 'Let's look first. I'll lift you up.' Amy nodded. Rex reached up and turned off Amy's head lamp. He turned his back to the door and linked his fingers together, palms upwards for Amy to stand on. She put her foot into his hands and held on to Rex's shoulders while she hoisted herself up. Amy's leg felt warm against his cheek. He looked up to see her face lit from the cool room. She looked down at him and gave a thumbs up sign. Rex let her down again.

'It's a cool room alright,' she said in a normal voice. 'Nobody in there.' She flicked her headlamp back on and turned the key in the lock. It opened and the door swung into the passageway, a draft of cold air spilling out over their feet. Rex peered around the door then signaled for Amy to lock it again. Amy locked the door, and they retreated back to the main passage.

'Well, that could have saved us some time,' said Rex, referring to the trip up the hill. 'At least we can get back quickly.'

They were about to continue walking along the passage when Rex noticed a small door set into the wall of the passage. They both stopped to check it out. There was a small knob on one side. Amy reached out and pulled it. The door opened to reveal another speaking tube, this one on a short, flexible hose.

'Have a listen,' urged Rex.

Amy lifted the brass earpiece, removed the bung, and held it to her ear. Her eyes immediately widened. 'I can hear someone,' she whispered urgently. She closed her eyes and listened intently. Rex remained stock still so as not to make a sound. Amy opened her eyes again, replaced the bung and set the earpiece back on its cradle. 'They've gone.'

'There were two of them?'

'I think so. I'm not sure, but I think one of them was a woman.'

'Could have been some people in the hotel?' suggested Rex.

'Yeah, maybe,' said Amy slowly. 'They didn't sound happy though.'

'We better keep going,' said Rex.

After a few minutes of walking and testing locked doors, the passageway widened and began to slope downwards. It was a while before either of them noticed. Eventually, Amy said, 'We're going downhill.'

'Yeah,' said Rex, just realising the change in direction himself. 'And there are no more doors.'

'Huh,' said Amy. 'Which way does the cool room door face?'

Rex figured out what Amy was getting at. 'We must be heading towards town.'

'This could take a while then.'

Rex was about to agree when he noticed something in the distance, far down the passage. 'Look, I think it flattens out down there.'

'I'll race you!' said Amy. She ran ahead of Rex before he could react. Rex bolted after her. He struggled to catch her even though it was downhill and he was slightly taller than Amy.

Amy reached the flat before Rex, but only just. They slowed to a stop to catch their breath, Amy smiling at Rex. 'I win!'

'You can run alright,' said Rex. 'Jolly well done,' he said in fairly passable English accent. Amy seemed satisfied.

Looking around, they saw that they were no longer in a passage but another room, much wider than the passageway. There was a large heavy door on the left-hand side, with large metal wheels running on tracks, and what looked like a crank handle to open it. Beside it was another door of normal width but as heavy and thick as the other one, with a smaller crank handle.

Rex approached the smaller door and examined it. He turned to Amy. 'If we go out this way, we might not be able to come back in.'

'Let's have a look anyway,' said Amy.

Rex grabbed the crank handle and started winding it anti-clockwise. For an old door it turned remarkably easy. The crank wound large bolts in from the doorframe and soon the door was free. Amy joined him hauling the door open. The other side of the door looked like a rocky cave wall. The only way to tell it was a door was the small slot for a key, and even that looked just like a crack in the rock. They peered out. There was a wide cave running parallel to the corridor that curved away in both directions. Cautiously, they edged out of the door, scanning for any sign of life. Nothing. Rex shone his torch back at the cave side of the larger door. 'Hey look,' he said.

'What? I don't see anything,' replied Amy.

'That's what I mean. There's a great big door there, and we can't even see it from this side.'

'Cool,' agreed Amy. 'Okay. Which way?'

'Probably the same direction we were headed.' Rex indicated down the cave. 'It's still heading downhill.'

'Well, let's not go too far. Not with the door open.'

Rex nodded and led off down the cave. As they followed a curve around to the right, they could see a light in the distance. Amy put out her arm to stop Rex. 'Look,' she said. 'Daylight.'

They walked toward the light and could soon turn off their headlamps and torches. Near the end of the tunnel, they could hear the sounds and smells of saltwater and seaweed. Emerging from the rough rock walls of the cave, they found themselves on sand underneath a wooden structure. Peering out from the shadows Rex recognised where they were.

'It's that old pier in the harbour,' whispered Rex.

Amy dropped her head backwards and closed her eyes. 'Ohhh, now I get it.'

'Get what?'

'Have you seen what's carved into one of the pylons?'

'Yeah. 'Dissa' or something.'

Amy just looked at Rex, smiling and waiting for the penny to drop. Rex's shoulders dropped and he broke out into a smile.

'Well, that explains that then,' he said.

Both said together, 'Disappear!'

Rex was still smiling when he looked at his watch. 'We better head back.'

They reentered the cave and headed back up to the hidden door. They were about to go in when from deeper in the cave came a metallic clacking sound. Rex and Amy stopped dead still. Rex turned off his torches. 'I'll go and have a quick look. Wait here so I can see the way back without a torch.'

Amy nodded, and Rex crept carefully towards the source of the sound.

There was another bend in the cave and soon Rex could no longer see Amy's torch. Ahead, a light was moving around, casting shadows on the walls of the cave and there were sounds of someone moving about. Rex edged forward being careful not to trip on anything in the darkness. As he rounded the corner, not ten metres away was a man with his back to Rex holding something long. Beside him was a large wooden crate and some large canvas duffle bags. The man leaned down and lifted the lid of the crate, leaning it back against the rock wall of the cave. It was then that Rex saw what the man was holding — a rifle. The man took the rifle by the barrel and lowered it gently, stock first, into the crate. It was as though there was something in there that he didn't want to touch, because he let go of the barrel without even putting his hand in the crate.

He replaced the lid and reached down to pull a dusty old canvas over the whole crate. He stood, arching his back as though stretching it after lifting heavy weights, then turned towards Rex with a lamp held out in front. Rex saw him at the same time as the man saw Rex.

It was Garrett!

Thinking quickly, Rex turned on his torch and aimed it right at Garrett's face. Garrett recoiled from the sudden bright light shielding his eyes before turning and running, headed away from Rex. Rex bolted the other way.

Amy heard footsteps first, then saw Rex coming around the corner of the cave running full tilt, his torch beam swinging wildly around the walls.

'Get in,' said Rex. Amy jumped back through the doorway, quickly followed by Rex. He turned off his torch again and poked his head around the doorframe to see if he was followed.

'It was Garrett!' said Rex. 'He ran the other way, so there must be another exit somewhere.'

'We could follow him. Find out where the other exit is?' said Amy.

'No. I think we better find Grandad. If these caves go all the way to the hotel, he might pop up there somewhere.'

Rex started to push the door shut, but Amy stopped him.

'Wait, I'll get Grandad. I'll use the cool room exit. You go after Garrett.' Rex wasn't too sure of this idea after seeing Garrett with firearms. Amy continued. 'If you can't find him, come back and go out under the pier. I'll lock this door once you've gone.'

Rex nodded. 'Alright but keep your radio on. Hurry!'

Amy pushed Rex through the door and leaned on it to shove it shut. Rex turned on his torch and was gone before she could get the door fully locked. She bolted back up the long wide corridor, headed back to the cool room entrance.

Rex moved up the cave much faster now. He knew Garrett was only holding a lamp when he bolted away, but he might have doubled back to get the rifle. Rex had to get there before he did. He arrived at the crate and stopped, listening. Some strange clicking noises came from under the canvas. Rex pulled the canvas off and lifted the lid.

Shining his torch inside he gave out a short yelp of surprise. It was full of lobsters. They were very much alive and crawling over each other, their spiny legs snapping against the sides of the crate as they tried to climb out. Peering through the spindly legs and bug-like bodies, Rex could see the rifle underneath them. But there wasn't just one rifle, there were lots of them stacked in a rack at the bottom of the crate, each held in its own wooden support. Rex checked there were no empty slots before replacing the lid and dragging the canvas back over the crate. He headed off in pursuit of Garrett.

The cave went deep, skirting the contours of harder rock. Many smaller branches led off from the main tunnel. Rex figured Garrett would try to get out as soon as he could, so he stuck to the main cave. Soon it began to head downhill again, and Rex picked up speed. He raced past an offshoot and felt a blast of cool air. Skidding to a stop, he backtracked and headed cautiously down the tunnel, a salty breeze in his face. *This must head to the coast.* Sure enough, a few bends later Rex emerged into bright daylight.

Garrett was nowhere to be seen.

CHAPTER 24

Amy emerged into the cool room, quietly stowing her torches in her backpack, and locking the door behind her. She was about to venture out into the kitchen when the cool room door opened. It was Antonio.

'Ah, Amy! I didn't see you come in. Helping your mother do deliveries?' He indicated several boxes of fresh produce on the racks of the cool room.

'Y-yeah,' Amy stammered. She had totally forgotten that her mother was supplying the hotel now. 'Bit of extra pocket money,' she added as she slid around Antonio.

'Gotta go,' she said, and headed for the kitchen door in search of Grandad.

Antonio stood in the cool room and looked around with a slight smile on his face then went back into the kitchen, slamming the door shut behind him.

Amy found her way back to the hotel lobby and knocked on the security room door. No answer. She went back to the reception desk and asked Rex's mum even though she was still on the phone. She gave a shrug and went back to her conversation. Amy walked as quickly as she could outside to see if she could find Grandad.

Off the coast, Scott was standing in the pilothouse of the Saint Helena, his hips braced against the control console while he peered through binoculars. The upper half of his body swayed in opposition to the rocking of the boat as it rode the swells of the sea. 'There he is,' said Scott to no one in particular. Rex had appeared from behind a rock halfway up the bluff near the hotel. He looked around for bit, then started scaling his way up.

Scott's dad appeared in the doorway wiping his hands on a rag. 'There's who?'

'Huh?' Scott was surprised. Charlie gestured to Scott to hand over the binoculars, and held them up to his eyes, training them on the distant coast.

'I can't make out who that is,' he said. 'But they're on the hotel property, and that bloody killer's still on the loose.' Charlie took the binoculars outside for a better look. 'Turn us into shore, will you? Don't go too close though or we won't be able to see anything.'

Scott took the wheel and turned it. The boat followed slowly around and headed towards the bluff. Charlie was on the bow peering through binoculars.

A burst of static came from Scott's backpack hanging on a hook at the back of the cabin. Scott remembered the UHF Radio. He opened the bag and fished it out. When he turned back to the wheel, he saw his dad speaking on the phone. 'Oh no,' he said, and raced out of the cabin headed for the bow.

As he reached his dad he heard, '… yeah, I can't make out who it is, but they're not supposed to be there. Right-oh. Yep. I'll let you know if I see anything else.' He rang off and turned to see Scott before him with a horrified look on his face.

'Cops are on their way'—He saw Scott's expression—'and that wasn't the killer was it.' Scott shook his head slowly. 'Oops.'

Scott held up the UHF radio and spoke into it. 'Rex, you there?' He let go of the transmit button with a short burst of static.

A few seconds passed before the radio burst into life.

'Yeah, I'm here.' Rex sounded breathless. 'Did you see Garrett? I think he came out this way.'

'No, we only saw you.' He looked at his dad. 'And ah, you should know. The cops are on their way.'

Scott was expecting Rex to explode, but instead there was a moment of silence before the radio burst into life again.

'Okay thanks for the heads up. I'll call you later.'

'Roger that,' said Scott.

Charlie handed Scott the binoculars. 'Sorry about that. I could call them back.'

'No, it's alright,' replied Scott. He had the binoculars trained on the top of the bluff. 'He's made it to the top; he'll be back at the hotel soon anyway. They might even find Garrett along the way.'

At the top of the bluff, Rex struggled through tea trees grown thick and dense to stand up to the unrelenting sea breeze. He knew the hotel had to be in the direction away from the cliffs, but couldn't tell if he was even near or if he was going in circles. He broke out of thick undergrowth onto a narrow, barely discernable path only to find Tom standing before him with his abbreviated tongue lolling out the side of his mouth. Tom turned and trotted along the path in a direction Rex was sure would lead back to the cliffs, then stopped and turned his head back, waiting for Rex to follow. *Okay*, thought Rex. *He knows this place better than I do.*

Tom led Rex along the winding, overgrown path for a few minutes before emerging near the hotel gates. Rex brushed tea tree leaves from his shirt. Mrs Birch was near the hotel entrance admiring the flowers planted in beds along the walls of the hotel. Tom gave a single loud bark. Mrs Birch looked up and saw Rex just as a police car swung through the gates of the hotel, it's lights flashing wildly. Rex ducked back into the trees. Tom ran after the police car to join Mrs Birch. The police car stopped at the entrance and the same two officers that attended opening night got out. Mrs Birch glanced towards Rex before confronting them.

'Why haven't you caught him yet?' she demanded.

'We only just got here,' replied one.

'Caught who?' asked the other one suspiciously.

'Garrett of course, who else?' Mrs Birch was edging backwards placing the police between her and Rex, keeping them facing her. She was wearing a large hold-all bag over one shoulder and clutched it to herself a little nervously. Tom helped by eyeing the police aggressively and occasionally letting out a low growl.

Rex realised what she was doing and made a break for the hotel entrance. The police continued their argument with Mrs Birch.

'Mrs Birch, we don't even know if it's him. And anyway, that's not why we're here.' He made to turn back to the entrance and would have caught Rex almost at the door.

Mrs Birch intervened. 'Of course it's him.' The policeman turned back to Mrs Birch. 'Who else do you know with an obsession about this place?'

The distraction was enough to let Rex slip in the doorway unseen.

'Mrs Birch, listen,' said the officer. 'We've had a report of someone hanging around on the point.' He turned to where Rex had emerged from the bush. 'You haven't seen anyone have you?'

'No, of course not. But if they were seen near the bluff, they'll be using the caves. I doubt you'll find him now though; the whole point is like Swiss cheese. He'll be long gone.'

The officers looked at each other, knowing Mrs Birch was right.

'Well, if you see anything, let us know, will you?'

'Of course.' She smiled at them each in turn. 'Now, since my taxi hasn't turned up you won't mind driving me into town, will you? I fancy a pint at Scales.'

Inside, Rex found Amy in the lobby still looking for Grandad.

'What are they doing here?' asked Amy, nodding toward the entrance. The flashing lights through the door made the entrance hall look like a nightclub.

'Looking for me, actually.'

'What?'

'They think they're looking for an intruder. Garrett got away though. I couldn't find him.'

'You obviously found another entrance though,' said Amy.

'Yeah, but that's not all. Come on, we need to go back in.'

Rex led the way back to the kitchen and they went into the cool room unseen. On the way back down the corridor to the *Dissa-pier*, Rex filled Amy in with what he saw.

When they arrived back at the crate the canvas was gone. The crate lid was propped up inside the crate allowing lobsters to climb out where they crawled down the tunnel towards the water, navigating by instinct. The guns were gone. So were the empty bags.

'He must have doubled back and taken them,' said Rex.

'How many were there?' asked Amy. Rex counted the empty gun holders.

'A dozen.'

Amy watched the last lobster flop over the edge of the crate onto the sand to begin the laborious journey towards water. 'They won't make it,' she said.

'Well, I'm not giving them a piggyback ride,' said Rex.

'No, but we'll have to clean them out sooner or later or they'll stink as bad as Scott's net.'

Rex was looking in the crate. 'Wait, what's this?' He leaned into the lobster free crate and pulled out a heavy egg-shaped metal object. 'Uh oh.'

'That's a hand grenade!' said Amy.

'I know,' said Rex. He rotated it, examining it closely. 'Pin is still in. It's safe.' Amy rolled her eyes. 'Well, as safe as a live hand grenade can be.'

'What will we do with it?'

'Give it to Grandad. He'll know what to do.'

CHAPTER 25

Rex and Amy carefully opened the cool room door to see if anyone was in the kitchen. There was still some time before the preparation for the evening meals started, so the kitchen was dim and quiet. They made their way out of the kitchen. Rex was holding the grenade in his backpack so it wouldn't jiggle around and accidently knock the pin loose. Arriving at the security room, Rex used his keycard to enter. Grandad swiveled around on his seat.

'Ah! There you are. I've been looking for you,' said Grandad. 'Amy, your mother called wondering if you'd like to stay for dinner?'

Amy seemed taken aback by the sudden invitation, and that her mother would suggest it. 'Ah ...'

'I'm cooking,' said Grandad enticingly. 'And your mum and dad won't be home until late. They had to go somewhere to pick up some supplies, or something. I'm doing fresh lobsters.'

'Okay then,' agreed Amy. She looked at Rex, panicking for a second about the mention of lobsters.

'Um, actually Grandad, we wanted to talk to you about something.' Rex wasn't quite sure how to broach the subject. 'We found something today.'

Grandad raised his eyebrows and smiled. 'Did you now? Well done.'

'Um no, well, you see, it's quite dangerous.'

Amy helped him out. 'We thought you'd know what to do with it.' She nudged Rex with her elbow and made him jump slightly. 'Show him.'

Grandad nodded to show that he wanted to see.

Rex slowly relaxed his grip on the hand grenade from outside of his backpack, then reached inside. He gingerly extracted the heavy metal ball being careful not to snag the safety pin on the sides of the bag.

Grandad's eyes opened wide. 'Oh ho! That's a beauty!' He shuffled forward on his chair and plucked the grenade from Rex's hand and rolled back to the desk. 'Safety clip's still on, nothing to worry about.' As if to reinforce this claim, he tossed the grenade from hand to hand. Rex and Amy both fought the urge to rush forward and grab it. Grandad saw their reaction and chuckled. 'Relax, it's fairly new. Which is still a bit of a worry, but it's not going to go off unexpectedly.' He thumped it down on the desk beside a coffee mug.

'Anyway, dinner's at six upstairs. Afterwards I'll drive you home, Amy ... and drop that pineapple off at the police station afterwards. I'll have to tell your dad, Rex, he'll need to know. So, you found it in the building works out the back, didn't you? In the part not covered by the old cameras?'

Amy and Rex glanced at each other. 'Yeah. Yeah, that's where we found it,' said Rex.

'Good lad. Anyway, I've just had some new cameras installed. I'm going to configure them to record before dinner, so ... see you at six.'

Grandad obviously wanted them to leave so he could get on with the job. Rex and Amy took the hint and headed back to Rex's room.

When the door of Rex's room closed behind them, Rex and Amy both let out a breath as though they'd been holding it since seeing Grandad.

'Do you think he knows?' asked Amy.

'Yeah, I reckon he does. He practically told us not to tell him where we really found it.'

Amy nodded. 'Then he knows we've found the base as well then.'

'Really?'

'Yeah,' said Amy. 'Did you see his face when you said we'd found something? I think he was expecting us to come clean about the base.'

'Hmmm, maybe. Plus, where did he get the lobsters from?'

Amy pointed at Rex. 'Exactly. He must have been down there and picked up a few.'

Rex considered this for a moment. 'But why doesn't he just come out and tell us?'

Amy shrugged. 'Don't know. Maybe he can't say anything until you do? What was it that Limbick said on the phone? 'It's your operation.''

Rex looked at his watch. 'Nearly six. Time for dinner — Oh!'

'What?'

'We haven't told Scott we're okay.' He fished into his backpack and drew out the UHF radio and keyed the transmit button. 'Scott, you there?'

He waited for a reply and was about to try again when Scott's faint voice came in.

'Yep, I'm here. So, you made it okay?'

'Yeah, we're all good. Did you see anyone?'

'Just you.' There was a pause, then 'Did, ah, anyone else catch up with you?'

Rex knew he was talking about the police. 'No, all sorted.' He paused. 'Any chance you can come for dinner?'

'No, not tonight. The hauler we were testing needs to be moved, so I'll be down at the harbour for a while yet.'

'Okay. I'll fill you in tomorrow. See you then.'

'Okie-Dokie, see ya.' The radio went silent.

Rex looked at his watch again. 'Better get cleaned up. There are fresh towels in the bathroom.'

As they entered the family dining room, Grandad poked his head around the kitchen doorway.

'Good! Right on time. Have a seat, it's just us tonight.'

Amy chose the seat next to the end of the table. Rex darted around and pulled her chair out for her, holding it for her as she sat down.

'Thanks,' she said, watching Rex as he sat down next to her. Rex looked up and saw her looking at him, smiling.

'What?' he asked.

'Nothing,' said Amy and turned her head away just as Grandad swept into the room with three plates. He placed them down before Amy and Rex with a flourish, announcing, 'Lobster Thermidor. Freshly caught. *Bon appetit!*' He sat opposite them.

Rex and Amy looked at each other, each wondering if they were the lobsters from the cave.

'Looks delicious,' said Amy to cover her expression.

'Thank you. Dig in. Don't want it to go cold,' he said. He reached for a bottle of Chardonnay and poured them each a small glass. 'Your mother said it was okay,' he added with a wink to Amy. He replaced the bottle in an ice bucket and raised his glass, waiting for Rex and Amy to raise theirs. 'Thermidor,' he toasted. They clinked their glasses together and sipped before turning their attention to the meals.

On each plate before them were two halves of a lobster shell stuffed with steaming succulent meat spiced with herbs, tomatoes, English mustard and topped with a gratin of Gruyere cheese. A delicious salad complimented the rich red colours of the Lobster, drizzled with a French mustard vinaigrette.

After all the running around today both Rex and Amy dug in and ate heartily. Their plates were clean in no time, leaving just the shell of the Lobster halves. Grandad smiled with approval.

When Grandad finished, he took a sip of wine, pausing as he replaced the glass on the table as if he was deciding something.

He looked up at Rex. 'Mrs Birch tells me you found Mr Limbick's diary.'

Rex and Amy briefly glanced at each other before Rex replied.

'Um, yeah. Well, she got to it before I did.'

Grandad nodded. 'Good reading?' he asked.

'Not really sure yet. I haven't had time to go through it all, just the start.'

Grandad smiled and nodded. Under the table, Amy nudged Rex with her elbow and gave him a meaningful look. Rex was in two minds whether or not to bring up *how* they found it, but clearly Amy thought he should.

'Ah, actually, we only found it because ...' he paused. Another glance at Amy. She nodded. 'Well ... I saw Nick pull it out of his pocket and drop it.'

Grandad's eyes widened. He sat back in his seat, thinking.

'You think he's the one in the costume?' he asked.

'No. We still think it's Garrett. Amy did some detective work.' Rex looked at Amy inviting her to continue.

'Yes,' said Amy. 'Sure of it. Nick is just working for Garrett. I saw him paying off Penelope for some dry cleaning.'

'Penelope?' said Grandad, one eyebrow raised.

'Yes. She's been doing jobs for Garrett. I don't know how she can stand working for him really, the way he treats her. It's like she's his slave or something, it's just disgust ...' Grandad raised a hand to stem the head of steam Amy was building up.

'Wait, how does that make it Garrett?' Grandad asked.

Amy reset herself. 'Nick was paying Penelope for some dry cleaning, a big black robe. Penelope is working for Garrett.' She paused to stifle any further rant about Penelope. 'I called the only costume hire place in the area, and they told me they only have one Grim Reaper outfit, but it wasn't back yet because it was being cleaned.'

Grandad nodded. 'Impressive.' Rex could tell Amy appreciated the compliment by the way she lowered her head slightly and stifled a smile.

'Of course, it could be just a coincidence.' Amy's smile faded quickly. Grandad let it sink in while Amy went through it in her mind.

Rex jumped in. 'Yeah, maybe, but put it all together — the cloak, Nick, Garrett mouthing off in town — you have to admit it's possible.'

'Oh, I agree,' said Grandad. 'Highly likely even. Probably not enough to get the police excited though.'

Rex and Amy nodded in reluctant agreement.

'You'll need more,' said Grandad. 'But,' he paused. 'Be extremely careful. If what you say is true'—he again held up his hand as Rex and Amy both were about to defend their position—'then we're dealing with some very dangerous people. And if Nick is involved, possibly the law as well.'

Rex and Amy fell quiet.

'Now,' continued Grandad. 'I asked Mrs Birch to place a few cameras in the caves we know about.' Amy nearly spat some wine over the table as she sipped it. 'I know, I know. She doesn't look like the sort for cloak and dagger stuff, but trust me, she knows her stuff. And I needed to be up here to help her get the placement right and tune the frequencies. They're, ah, not strictly legal, so keep quiet about them, hmm?' Rex and Amy nodded. 'We should have some useful video by now, but ...' he stood. 'That will have to wait until I get you home, young lady.'

'Oh. Right,' said Amy. 'I forgot about that. Thank you for cooking Grandad, it was delicious.'

'You are very welcome. Come on then. Rex can clean up while I'm gone, and then he better get reading that diary.'

'You two are getting along alright?' asked Grandad, as he and Amy drove down the hill away from the hotel.

'Yeah, I like Rex,' said Amy. Unused to having wine, its warmth had spread through her body and made her quite relaxed with Grandad. 'Actually'—she glanced at Grandad, who had his eyes on the road ahead—'I think I like him a lot.' She hoped Grandad would get what she meant without her having to explain.

Grandad smiled knowingly. 'I know you do.' He glanced at Amy, who was beginning to regret opening up to him. 'Don't worry, your secret's safe with me.' Amy relaxed.

'Do you think he knows?' she asked.

'He hasn't got a clue,' replied Grandad with a chuckle. Amy fell quiet for a while. She was not really expecting this information. 'Don't worry, he'll wake up eventually. He might be a smart kid, but he's a bit clueless with girls. Most boys are, although they'll never tell you that.'

Grandad pulled the car into the driveway of Amy's house. 'Here we are.'

Amy got out of the car and turned. 'Thanks again for dinner and the lift ... and everything.'

'Not a problem,' said Grandad. 'Have a good night. See you soon.' Amy closed the car door and waved before heading up the path to the front door of her house.

Grandad waited until she was inside before backing the car out and headed to the police station to hand in the grenade.

Only a few of the hidden lights were on in the hotel foyer. The remaining guests had all retired to their rooms, Rex's parents were in the private wing relaxing, and Rex had done as Grandad suggested and gone to his room to read more of Limbick's diary. The only sound was the steady ticking of the grandfather clock and the distant sound of surf beating the cliffs of the bluff. Even if anyone had been in the foyer, they probably would not have noticed a black-clad figure slip in from the carpark lift corridor. Making no sound, the shadowy body paused to scan the foyer before quickly and deliberately heading for the security room door. There was a beep and a click that sounded loud in the otherwise quiet space. The figure looked around to confirm nobody had come to investigate, then pushed the door open silently and slipped inside, quickly closing the door behind them.

Inside, the image covered walls showed deserted scenes from in and around the hotel. Some were cycling through different positions, and others were scanning scenes from left to right and back again. The intruder watched for a moment to make sure all was quiet then turned attention to the monitors on the desk, nudging computer mice to bring them to life. Most of them displayed a login screen, but one showed a green tinged grainy view of a sandy floored cave, framed by thick wooden pylons and beams. Bingo! Turning to the rack of equipment, the intruder examined each of the units within, crouching down to read the labels of the ones near the floor. None of them were of interest. The figure stood again and noticed one unit placed on top of the cabinet. Examining the front of the unit carefully the intruder saw a steady red pilot light and an LCD display on one side of the front panel showing '008:37:26' counting the seconds upwards, and the flat rectangular outline of a DVD drawer. The intruder pressed the button beside the drawer to open it. Thin black gloves withdrew a blank disc from a hidden pocket, placed it in the tray and pushed until the tray swallowed the disk. Turning back to the screen, the intruder waited until a control menu popped up over the view of the cave. Manipulating the mouse, the intruder clicked the stop recording button, then entered '16:47' into the time search field. The view blinked and became much lighter, the green tinge disappearing with the extra light. Fast-forwarding at high speed, the intruder waited until some figures could be seen in the cave, skipped back until just before they arrived, then went forward again, watching the scene as figures flickered about. When the view returned to an empty cave, the intruder entered start and end times and hit the 'Write to Disc' button. The unit on the rack whirred into life, a whining sound rising in pitch as the disc got up to speed. Before long, the process was finished and the disc drawer once again opened, presenting the intruder with a copy of the video. Before retrieving the disk, the intruder moved the mouse pointer to the 'Delete Selected Segment' button and clicked. The intruder retrieved the disc and slipped unseen out of the room.

CHAPTER 26

The following Monday, Rex, Amy and Scott met during their lunch break and headed down to the foreshore where Rex's dad had set up a marquee for promoting the hotel, not far from the marina.

'Why here? He expecting to get cops and ambos to stay?' asked Scott, pointing across the road at the local police and ambulance stations.

'It's where the tourist buses come in,' replied Rex. 'Not too many locals are going to want to stay in the hotel anyway, especially when they know it isn't really haunted.'

'Looks like the locals are curious anyway,' said Amy.

A throng of people, obviously not tourists, was milling around the marquee. Some were watching the promotional video playing on a big flat screen on one side and others were picking up pamphlets and flipping through them. Some just came to see if there were any free promotional pens or fridge magnets.

The three said their hellos to Rex's dad and Grandad, who was helping, and found a spot on the grass nearby to eat their lunches. They'd just finished when Scott called their attention. 'Uh oh. Here it comes.' He pointed to someone approaching from across the road. 'Garrett.'

They watched him approach the display, a sneer on his face and clenched fists held stiffly by his side.

'When are you going to sell the place?' Garrett shouted over the heads of the surrounding people, who whipped around to see what the fuss was. Getting no answer, he continued. 'Business can't be too good if you're resorting to advertising on the street and, I hear you're losing staff. Sounds like a dump to me.'

A few of the locals shook their heads at him and walked away, but one or two asked Roy directly. 'Are you selling?'

Roy stepped out from under the marquee and held his hands up to quieten the crowd. 'I'm not selling the hotel; you can be assured of that. Mr Garrett just wants to get his hands on it, but I'm happy to inform him that it would not be my decision anyway. So, he's wasting his time.'

Garrett's face turned a deep red colour and took a step forward. 'How many more bodies is it going to take before you go broke? And anyway, I don't need to buy it, I already own it! My Great Grandfather ...'

BOOM!

Everyone ducked down and swiveled in the direction of the loud blast.

'That sounded like a bomb!' Someone in the crowd shouted. The blast came from the direction of the marina, echoing back from buildings and the hills behind town. A small cloud of black smoke rose from under the pier. Rex, Amy and Scott were on their feet instantly and, along with half the crowd, ran toward the marina. Scott was worried that the Saint Helena might have exploded, others worried that Scales might have exploded.

Before they reached the old pier, Charlie ran out from underneath. 'Get an ambulance. There's someone hurt! Get the police too.'

'They're already here,' someone said. 'Must have heard it from the station.' The police made it across the road from the station first with the ambos following, slowed down by all the equipment they were carrying.

A few of the crowd made to go past Charlie to see what had happened, but Charlie held his arms wide to block them. 'Don't go there, it might not be safe.' They halted and tried to peer into the dark beneath the pier. One of them again tried to slip past, but Charlie grabbed him. 'Mate, seriously?' He shook his head slowly as he said, 'You don't want to see that. Let the professionals do their job.' He dragged the man out of the way of the two policemen who pushed past and ducked under the pier to investigate. One emerged a minute later looking like he might throw up, and gave the ambulance crew the okay to go in. Charlie told them, 'It's Mrs Birch ... I think. She's pretty messed up.' They ducked under the pier with their equipment and out of sight. Nearly all the police in Lenzie Bay had arrived from the station across the road and started moving people back from the area and clearing a path for the ambulance now emerging from its garage.

After a few minutes the policemen under the pier emerged. One of them walked away from the crowd pulling out his phone, while the other climbed up off of the beach and had a word with a few of the other officers. In response, the police started moving people even further back from the pier. The crowd re-formed where the marina met the foreshore. Garrett pushed his way to the front of the crowd. He launched back into his tirade, directing it at Roy and Grandad. 'I bloody told you!'

'Boil your head, Garrett!' Someone in the crowd shouted back. 'Yeah, get lost!' shouted another.

Garrett turned, searching for the culprits before two burly policemen intervened and escorted Garrett away from the hostile crowd.

An air ambulance was called for Mrs Birch, fueling pensive speculation among the remaining group. Rex, Amy and Scott pushed through the crowd to find Roy and Grandad. Rex racked his brain, trying to remember if he'd seen other hand grenades in the crate. Did he miss one? Could he have prevented this? Worried looks passed between them all in silence while they waited for any news. Amy seemed to sense what Rex was thinking and put a hand on his shoulder in a sort of half hug.

It seemed like hours to the worried onlookers before the rhythmic whumping of helicopter blades alerted everyone to the arrival of the air ambulance helicopter. It curved through the air across the bay to touch down in a space cleared by police. The whine of jet engines lowered in pitch as a rescue crew sprang into action, taking a spinal board and racing down to beneath the pier. Another twenty minutes later they emerged carrying a body wrapped in silver blankets and strapped to the board, leads from monitors trailing to equipment slung over the shoulders of the crew.

The onlookers held their breath as the figure was carried past them to the waiting helicopter. A small inflatable tent held a thermal sheet away from her head so her face was completely hidden. A woman in the group gasped and raised a hand to her mouth.

'Oh no,' said Amy directing a worried look at Rex. 'She's not dead, is she?'

Rex was too choked up to answer. Tears brimming in his eyes, all he could do was shake his head, slowly. Every time Rex had encountered Mrs Birch, she had helped him, and now there was nothing he could do to help her.

'We've got to catch the bastards who did this,' said Scott voicing what everyone around them was thinking. Several of them nodded in agreement, and maybe a tinge of anger that such violence had disturbed the peace in Lenzie Bay.

The crew loaded their precious cargo into the helicopter and closed the doors after them as the jet engines built up power. The rescue helicopter lifted carefully off the ground, turned in place and edged out over the shoreline, slowly gaining height before tilting forward to gain speed.

The crowd dissipated, returning to businesses and homes. Roy said to Rex, 'You three had better get back to school. We'll pack up now. I don't think it's a good time for us to be promoting anything.' They all turned to head back to the display tent.

Rex allowed the others to go ahead while he walked with Grandad. 'Do you think she'll be alright?' asked Rex, fighting off thoughts of the unimaginable. Grandad glanced down at Rex and Rex thought he saw a flicker of fear cross Grandad's face.

'I hope so, Rex. She's survived worse, but ...' He finished by putting an arm over Rex's shoulder and giving him a reassuring hug as they walked on.

Near the tent, they were met by the police sergeant. 'Mr Roux?' he asked, talking to Grandad. 'I think we need to have a chat. Can you come with us?'

Grandad nodded, patted Rex on the back urging him to catch up with Amy and Scott and headed across the road with the sergeant.

On the way back to school, they filled Scott in about the events of the Saturday. When they arrived, it was already the afternoon break, so they slipped in through the gates unnoticed by the patrolling teachers.

Amy asked, 'Do you think Grandad had anything to do with this?' Rex shot her a look, but Amy quickly went on. 'The hand grenade I mean, not that he did anything.'

'I doubt it,' said Rex. 'He seems to know what he's doing. He wouldn't leave one lying around, and he did say he was going to take it to the police.'

'Yeah. Maybe the cops just put two and two together and got five,' said Scott. 'But maybe we shouldn't mention to anyone that you had lobster last night. Just in case. It wouldn't look good, even if Grandad did get them from my dad.'

This was news to Amy. 'He did?'

'Yeah, well, via Mrs Birch. She picked them up from Dad yesterday afternoon, I saw them together looking them over. She must have given them to Grandad. How were they anyway? They looked a bit dodgy to me. No wait, let me guess ... Lobster Thermidor.' Scott watched Rex and Amy's amazement that he knew what they had for dinner.

'How did you know?' asked Amy.

'He does it every year. Dunno why. It's delicious though.'

They arrived at the lockers. Penelope was already there retrieving books for the next lesson.

'I heard your grandfather got arrested,' said Penelope. She closed her locker door. 'He'll get off though. With all the cameras at the hotel, I'm sure he'll turn up on one of them.' She gave an insincere smile, more like a grimace, and flounced off looking pleased with herself.

Rex was sure he heard Amy mutter 'bitch' under her breath as she opened her locker.

'She's got a point though,' said Rex. 'Grandad was setting up cameras yesterday, remember? I bet he even got whoever killed Mrs Birch on camera.'

'But,' said Scott. 'Didn't you say the new cameras were not entirely legal? He can't tell the police about them.'

'Oh, come on,' said Amy slamming her locker door. 'We've only got *her* word he was arrested. Anyway, he was with us when it happened, and we were with him most of last night. When was he supposed to set up a bomb to kill someone he liked?' She rolled her eyes and walked off to class leaving Rex with Scott.

'Wouldn't hurt to have a look at the recordings anyway,' said Scott. 'And I don't think my dad will mind if I come after school and help you go through them.'

'Thanks,' said Rex. They headed off after Amy.

After school, Rex and Scott were in the security room at the hotel. As Grandad was still being interviewed by the police, Rex showed Scott how to use the surveillance camera software and they went to work. They found the vision of the cave and rewound to the start. The time stamp showed it started not long after Mrs Birch was driven into town. Fast forwarding through, the view of the cave entrance under the old pier remained the same except for the changes in light. Scott saw some movement on the ground and stopped to rewind.

'Check it out,' said Scott. 'Here comes last night's dinner.' They both watched as a lonely lobster struggled through the sand from the mouth of the cave. 'No wonder they looked dodgy. How far in did you say you found them?'

'About fifty metres. No more than a hundred. It's hard to tell.'

Scott fast forwarded again watch the light fade and the occasional blur of another lobster making its getaway. The scene flashed and went green.

'Woah!' Scott hit the pause button. 'What just happened?' He hit the rewind button, stopped again when the scene brightened and hit play. 'It jumps! Look at the time stamp.' He rewound again and showed the transition from day to night to Rex.

'Someone's deleted something,' said Rex. 'They could only do that from here.'

'Grandad wouldn't. Would he? Nah. He wouldn't.'

'Let's check the camera for outside this room,' said Rex and he turned to another monitor. He found the feed for the camera outside the security room. Entering the time of twenty minutes before the cave camera came back on, he started fast forwarding from that point. It showed a view of the outside of the security room door from above and behind. Sure enough, a dark figure approached the door. Rex slowed the feed down to normal and they both watched the intruder enter the code.

'Who the hell is that?' asked Scott.

'I don't know, but it looks like a woman. She must have erased the recording.' Rex fast forwarded again. They watched the black shadow slip out of the door about fifteen minutes later.

'Not Penelope, surely,' said Scott.

'Can't tell from this angle, but I can't see her doing anything like this.'

'Keep going. See if your Grandad is on there.' Rex sped up the feed again and sure enough, Grandad entered the room another fifteen minutes later.

'That must be after he dropped Amy off. So that's it then. We've got proof he was here,' said Rex.

The door to the security room opened and Grandad walked in.

'Grandad! You're back!' said Rex.

'Yep. Video evidence saves the day.' He drew up a swivel chair and sat down on it backwards, leaning on the back rest. 'Ah, I see you've been going through the feeds. Did you get Penelope to drop off the disk of the cave camera anonymously?'

'What? No,' said Rex. 'We only just found it.'

'And a big section of it has been erased,' added Scott.

'Hmmm. Interesting,' said Grandad. 'Well, the funny thing is, Penelope turned up at the police station after school and handed in a disk. She said she found it.'

'Let me guess,' said Scott. 'A feed from the cave camera from about a quarter to five to just after nine o'clock?'

Grandad nodded. 'Not only that,' he said, 'but it shows Garrett talking to two men. One skinny bent guy, and one short and fat guy. Poachers. I've seen them around before, but I never thought they'd do anything like this. Then it showed those men taking some heavy bags out of the cave and, setting up a trip wire hooked up to ...' he looked inquisitively at Rex and Scott in turn to let them finish off the sentence.

'A hand grenade,' they said in unison.

'Correct,' said Grandad. 'Now, let's look further on and see if it shows Mrs Birch.'

Rex fast forwarded until the screen went blank, then backed it up and hit the play button.

The scene steadied on the cave entrance. Sunlight was penetrating through the cracks in the pier deck above casting bright, angled stripes on the sand below. There was something on the wall of the entrance to the cave that was hard to make out. It was down near the ground. Grandad leaned over to take the controls and enlarge the image. There was a grenade with a length of braided fishing line tied to the safety pin and stretching across the cave entrance a few inches above the sand.

'Uh oh,' said Grandad. Struggling into view was a desperate looking lobster, dragging most of its legs behind it. He zoomed out again just in time to see Mrs Birch approach the cave entrance. Getting caught up, the lobster dragged the trip wire, straining forward against it. The pin pulled out of the grenade allowing the firing lever to spring up. Mrs Birch stopped suddenly as she heard the metallic click. The three observers watched as she looked for the source of the sound, found it and began to turn to jump back out of the way. There was a bright flash. The view spun and went dark to be replaced with the words, 'Signal Lost'.

They sat staring at the screen for a moment.

'Brutal,' said Scott. He cut the video to get rid of the words none of them wanted to believe.

Rex and Scott sat back in their seats. Grandad pushed himself away from the desk. All three of them wondering what happened after the camera went blank.

Rex picked up on what Grandad said before. 'Hang on. Did you say Penelope handed in the video?'

'Yes. Why?' asked Grandad.

'Have a look at this,' said Rex. He leaned over, brought up the feed from the camera outside the security room and replayed the video of the black shadow sneaking in and out of the room.

'It's not Penelope if that's what you're thinking,' said Grandad. 'This woman is taller. Older, too, judging by the way she moves.'

He rolled his chair over to another monitor and logged in. 'I need to change the entry code on this door. Someone must have watched it being entered.' He punched in some numbers. 'One seven nine four zero seven two seven. Got that?' He looked around at them to make sure, then hit the enter key. 'Right, I think we're done here. Dinner time,' said Grandad.

Scott looked at his watch. 'Oh, is that the time? ... uh ... gotta go. See you tomorrow.'

He was halfway out the door before Grandad called out, 'Thanks Scott.' The door clicked shut behind him. 'We better get ready too. I'm starving.'

Grandad crossed to the door. He was about to open it when there was a chirp from his pocket. He stopped, and from his pocket withdrew a bulky looking mobile phone that Rex had never seen before. He held it to his ear. Rex could only hear Grandad's side of the conversation.

'Yep ... Right ... Yep ... Got it. Thanks for letting me know.' He hung up, opened the door and held it for Rex to exit. 'See what Antonio has cooked up would you? I don't feel like cooking tonight.'

CHAPTER 27

Rex had just finished breakfast in the kitchen the next morning and was about to cross the hotel lobby to go to school when Nelson Garrett shoved his way through the front doors. Nick, Penelope and two sheriffs followed close behind. Tom entered behind them and lay down in the sunlight coming through the door, watching attentively. Roy and Sylvie looked up from the reception desk and came out from behind the counter to see what they wanted.

'Got something for you, McGregor,' said Garrett brusquely. 'I want you out of here by nightfall.' He shoved a folded piece of paper in front of Roy's face. Roy took the paper without saying a word and unfolded it while Garrett rocked back on his heels looking smug.

Sylvie leaned in to see what the paper was. 'A warrant for eviction? Pfffft! Not a chance.' She returned to the reception desk shaking her head. Rex passed her as he approached the group.

Roy read the paper carefully and slowly while Garrett grew increasingly impatient.

'You seem to have made a mistake,' said Roy.

'There's no mistake! I want you out by nightfall and these two'—he indicated the sheriffs—'are here to make sure you go.'

'This is dated next month,' said Roy with a matter-of-fact voice. He turned the paper around and held it up to Garrett's face. Garrett snatched the paper from Roy's hand, read it with eyes looking like they were going to pop out of his increasingly reddening face.

Garrett spun around to Nick. 'You bloody idiot! The date's wrong.'

Nick took the paper, glanced at it before scrunching it in his hands. He turned to Penelope who had her mouth tightly shut to stifle a laugh. 'This is your doing! You deliberately got the dates wrong to make us look like fools!'

Penelope's face changed from laughter to indignation in a millisecond. 'I cut and pasted it off the email you sent *him*,' she jabbed a finger at Garrett. 'It's not my fault you got your months mixed up with your days. You're supposed to be the lawyer, you should have checked it. You should also have checked out that so-called deed he gave you.'

'What about the deed?' asked Nick. 'There's nothing wrong with it.'

'Then why is it dated 1898 when the original grant of land wasn't until 1920? The Torrens system was in place by then, so there couldn't possibly be a deed.' She turned to Rex. 'It's a fake.' She turned to one of the sheriffs. 'Look it up on the internet.'

The sheriff pulled out a tablet and began searching.

'Don't listen to her,' said Garrett, shouting now. He took a step towards Penelope to lean over her. 'She can't even get the right change for dry-cleaning!' Spit flew from his mouth narrowly missing Penelope, who cringed back in revulsion.

The other sheriff stepped forward between them, arms ready to grab Garrett if he made another move toward Penelope. Penelope backed away and found herself standing with Rex and his father, facing Nick and Garrett.

The sheriff with the tablet looked up to ask Nick for the deed. Nick reluctantly slid it out of a manilla folder and handed it over. The sheriff took it, checked the date and handed it back. 'She's right. It's a fake. We're done here. Mr Garrett, we'll be speaking to you later about this.' He looked at the other sheriff and crooked his head at the door. The two of them left, leaving Garrett and Nick staring after them, fuming.

'I think it's time you both left,' said Roy to Garrett and Nick.

Garrett slapped Nick's arm roughly as he turned and stormed out, aiming an ineffective kick at Tom who growled in return. Nick made to follow when Rex spoke up. 'Oh, one more thing.'

Nick stopped, not quite turning all the way back.

'You're fired,' said Rex.

'You can't fire me,' said Nick with a sneer as he faced them front on.

'He can, and he has,' said Roy. 'I'll expect all materials you have related to this business to be delivered here tomorrow morning. Now get out of here before I call the police and have you removed.'

Nick skulked out without another word, giving Tom a wide berth at the door.

'Now, you two,' Roy said to Rex and Penelope with a smile. 'I think you have earned a lift into school. Come on.' He headed for the carpark lift. Rex and Penelope following with grins breaking out.

CHAPTER 28

As Rex and Penelope entered the school gates together, Rex spotted Scott and Amy talking to each other near the entrance to the main building.

'I'll catch you later,' said Rex. Penelope smiled and headed for the side entrance closer to the lockers.

As Rex approached, Amy broke off what she was saying to Scott.

'What's *she* doing getting a lift with you?' she asked, not hiding her contempt for Penelope.

'It's been an interesting morning,' said Rex.

'Oh?' said Amy. 'Do tell.' She didn't look happy.

'Dad just told me that hotel bookings are up and all the staff that left have come back; Garrett tried to have us all evicted from the hotel; I fired Nick and, ah, what else ...' Scott and Amy's mouths fell open and their eyes widened. '... Oh, yeah. Penelope screwed up Garrett's plans, saving us from being evicted, and told me Scales is up for sale,' Rex finished with a grin. 'Interesting enough?'

'Scales is up for sale?' asked Scott.

'Yep. Garrett is going to try to buy it.'

'Hang on, hang on, hang on ... Penelope what?' asked Amy, a puzzled look on her face.

'Garrett had a deed for the hotel property, but Penelope pointed out it was a fake.'

Amy just stood there, dumbfounded.

Rex continued. 'She said that Garrett's trying to keep the Scales auction quiet so he can buy it himself. He doesn't want any bidders, so he's going to get his assistant, Beryl, to pretend to be on the phone to a bidder.'

'Why is she telling you this?' asked Scott.

'She's fed up with Garrett and Nick treating her like dirt and, I think she might have seen that security video, although she never said so.'

'You didn't tell her about you-know-what, did you?' asked Amy.

'No. I don't think that would be a good idea,' said Rex. Amy looked relieved.

'When is this auction?' asked Scott. 'Because if Garrett gets his hands on Scales, you can bet he's going to be digging around. Literally.'

'Sunday morning at Scales,' said Rex. 'And you're right. We can't let him get away with it. We need a plan.'

'We also need to go inside, we're late,' said Amy.

'Come and stay at the hotel on Friday night?' Rex asked, as they moved off quickly towards the other entrance to avoid going past Mrs M's office.

'Good idea,' said Amy.

'Yeah,' agreed Scott. 'And we should tell as many people as we can about the auction. We need witnesses. The whole town will turn up.'

'Did you really fire Nick?' asked Amy as they disappeared inside.

Rex, Scott and Amy made plans for the auction over dinner in the hotel dining room on Friday evening. The starter was a small quiche made with spinach and Roquefort cheese with a crust that melted in the mouth, followed by a medallion of lamb topped with tapenade, served with crispy roasted potatoes, and steamed beans. Dessert was lemon meringue pie drizzled with a tangy lemon sauce.

'That was amazing,' said Scott. He leaned back in his seat and stifling a small burp.

'What is Roquefort anyway,' asked Amy.

'Blue cheese,' replied Rex. 'From France.'

'Oh.' Amy seemed surprised. 'I'm not usually a fan of blue cheese, but that quiche was delicious.'

'My mouth is watering all over again,' said Scott.

'You can have more if you want,' said Rex.

'Uh uh, I'm full,' said Amy.

'Yeah, me too,' agreed Scott. 'What are we doing tonight?'

'We're going to send a robot into the base to start mapping it,' said Rex.

'You bought one and had it delivered, or did you just happen to have one lying around?' asked Amy sarcastically.

'No, of course not,' replied Rex. 'Grandad had one. He used it when we first bought the place to speed up the remodeling.'

Amy scoffed. 'Convenient.'

'Wait until you see what it can do. I tried mapping by hand during the week, but it was taking ages and I kept messing it up. Then I thought of the robot and gave up. I left the lift running so the robot can use it go up and down.'

'Can it open doors?'

'No, but it will give us a basic idea of where everything is and save us a heap of time walking around getting lost.'

Amy agreed, still not convinced Rex had just magically found the very tool they needed.

'We'll set it free in the tunnels tonight and see what it has in the morning,' said Rex.

'What about the lift? Won't it fall down the shaft?' asked Amy.

'We can control it remotely for a while and teach it what to do. It has cameras and everything,' said Rex. 'But first'—he folded his napkin in preparation to leave the table—'we're going to take a look at Grandad's latest attraction.'

Rex led Amy and Scott to the second level of the old part of the hotel.

'This was just finished today,' he said, leading them down the soft carpeted corridor. He stopped in the middle of the corridor and turned to face them.

'Notice anything?' he asked.

'No, why?' Amy looked around the empty corridor. Then she saw the wall beside them. 'Eeeuwwwww!' The surface was covered in oozing green slimy gel that was slowly dripping down the wall. 'What is that?'

'Snot!' said Scott. He started chuckling at his own joke. 'It's a snot wall.' He reached out a finger and wiped a dollop of squishy green muck onto his finger. 'Did you have a sneezing fit?'

'Gross,' said Amy looking revolted.

'Yeah, it's not snot but I wouldn't eat if I were you,' said Rex. 'Grandad made me taste some of it.' He shuddered and made a face. 'Disgusting.'

Scott tried to wipe the snot back onto the wall but ended up getting more on his finger instead. He pulled out a handkerchief and wiped it off on that. 'Acts like snot, too,' he said.

'Late at night, it's lit by special lights that make it glow. Looks really cool.'

As they began to walk back towards their usual rooms, Scott said, 'Hey, you know that speaking tube we found near our rooms? Did you find any more?'

'I did actually. I think there might be at least two on every floor. They're in the service cupboards.' Rex pulled out his service key and opened the nearest service door between guest rooms. He reached in and found the light switch. The light flickered on, creating shadows from the plumbing. 'Yeah, here's one. Check it out.'

He squeezed past some more modern ventilation ducts to get to the speaking tube, Scott and Amy following behind. This tube still had labels on the circular junction tap where the pipes joined after rising through the floor.

'Look, this one goes to the kitchen,' said Scott, pointing to one of the labels. 'Let's see if it works.'

He turned the lever to face the label marked *Kitchen* and plucked the plug out of the tube. They all listened quietly. Distant sounds of cutlery and muted conversations came echoing through the tube.

Rex whispered. 'I don't think that's the kitchen, I think it's the dining room. We moved the kitchen to make the dining room bigger.'

Scott whispered back. 'Are you thinking what I'm thinking?' A cheeky smile broke out on his face.

'I think I am,' replied Rex. 'After you.'

Scott cupped his hands around the flared opening, leaned in close and made a ghostly 'Woooooooooo!' He had to stop because he was starting to laugh.

Rex took over. 'Uuuuurrrrrrrrghhhhhhhh!' He dissolved into a fit of silent laughter.

Amy pushed her way in and took the stopper from Scott and replaced it in the tube. 'Stop,' she said. 'You shouldn't be doing that, you'll scare the life out of them.'

'Yeah, that's the whole idea,' said Rex, still laughing.

'Spoilsport,' said Scott. 'Let's listen and see if they heard.'

Amy reluctantly removed the stopper again. They leaned in close. The sounds of the dining room had changed, with less cutlery sounds and more talking.

'It came from over here, I think,' came a muffled voice.

'Leave it John, it might be real.' A woman's voice this time.

Scott started to say 'Jooooooohn!' but Amy shoved the stopper back in and broke out into a laugh.

'Come on, let's go before John has a heart attack.'

They headed back to Rex's room, making ghostly noises, and laughing all the way.

Rex and Scott carried the mapping robot around the outside of the hotel to the kitchen back door while Amy distracted Grandad in the security room. Minutes later, Amy opened the door to the kitchen from the inside and let them in.

'Quick. Antonio's greeting diners after *someone* asked to give him their compliments,' she said with a wink.

Lugging the robot into the cool room was tricky, but Amy went ahead and opened the doors to the base for them. They set it down in the dark corridor and breathed a sigh of relief. Rex turned a heavy switch on the side of the robot, then pressed a button on top of the control panel. The robot came to life, standing up taller on its articulated legs and testing its wheel motion and sensors. After a few seconds it became motionless with just a light blinking on top.

'I think it's broken,' said Scott.

'It's programmed to stop moving if it detects people to stop the mapping being screwed up,' said Rex. 'If we hide around the corner, we might see it start off.'

They retreated to the side corridor and poked the heads around the corner just in time to see the robot cast a flat beam of violet light that scanned quickly up and down the entire interior of the corridor. As soon as the beam touched their faces it shut off again and the blinking light on top of the robot began flashing.

'Let's go.'

Amy re-locked the doors and they all carefully retreated from the kitchen, heading for Rex's room.

By the time they got there and Rex had switched on his monitor, the robot had already mapped the corridor down to the big door near the pier. Rex manipulated the three-dimensional image, zooming in and out to show Scott where he and Amy had gone before Mrs Birch was blown up.

'This thing works fast,' said Amy approvingly.

'Yeah, and the best thing is, we don't have to ride in that lift contraption,' said Scott.

'Woah, wait. What's it doing now?' said Amy. The camera image showed the tunnel walls streaming past faster than someone could run.

'Oh yeah, Grandad made some modifications. Bigger batteries, faster motor and stuff. When it knows it's in a dead end, it backtracks at high speed because it already knows where it's going and how fast it can go,' said Rex. The image slowed down to walking pace. 'Look, see? It's back at the kitchen entrance.'

The 3D image showed the corridor growing as the map-bot made its way along. The three of them sat watching it for a while, transfixed.

'Have you noticed the closed doors all have those little black panels next to them?' asked Scott.

Rex leaned in as the map-bot rolled past another door, then another.

'Yeah, well spotted.' He brought up a complicated panel for controlling the robot and froze the image on one of the doors. Manipulating the mouse, he drew a line around one of the black panels, pressed a few keys and closed the panel again. He zoomed out of the ever-growing image to reveal little red dots at every doorway.

'You're right. Nearly every door has one,' said Rex.

'Hey, zoom back in, quick,' said Amy. 'Here comes the lift.'

The robot approached the lift as Rex pulled a game controller out of a drawer and plugged it in. The lift cars scrolled lazily past the openings in the shaft wall leaving darkness in between each car.

'Crikey, that looks dangerous,' said Scott.

'Shouldn't it be stopping?' said Amy in an anxious voice.

Rex was pressing buttons on the controller frantically. On the screen, a little box appeared on the bottom — 'Setting up your device, this may take a minute'.

'Uh oh,' said Rex.

They watched helplessly as the robot approached the opening where cars were going down. Between each car, yawning gaps left the shaft open for anyone or anything to fall down. Still the robot kept going. The edge of the shaft got closer and closer when suddenly, a wall appeared from above, sliding down the view until the floor of a car could be seen coming down to floor level. The robot slowed briefly then quickly sped up, driving safely onto the platform.

'Your device is now ready' said another little box on the screen.

'About time,' said Rex quickly pressing the stop button on the controller. The robot stopped moving, showing the wall on the other side of the car sliding steadily upwards. Scott and Amy relaxed in their seats. Rex used the controller joystick to slowly turn the robot around. In the image, a room slid up into view while the 3D image bloomed a room into existence.

'I reckon just leave it there to go all the way around,' said Scott. Rex nodded and put the controller down. Rooms grew out from the shaft as the robot passed them. When the car reached the end of its journey, it shifted to the right and began creating another shaft parallel to the other, this time heading up. Each room it passed became more detailed on the second pass.

Once the whole trip had been mapped, Rex took up the controller again and guided the robot off the platform just as it reached the floor of a room.

'Okay, now it knows how to do it, let's see what happens,' he said. He pressed another button on the controller and put it back on the desk. The robot started moving again. It approached a closed door like the one Rex and Amy first opened and halted.

'What's it doing?' asked Amy.

Rex brought the control panel back up. He pointed to a number next to a label marked GPU that was rapidly changing between fifty and eighty. 'Dunno. Thinking?'

The number dropped to the twenties and the robot moved again. It turned side-on to the sliding door and moved itself close. Rising on its wheeled legs, the robot slowly backed against the door lever. The image shuddered briefly before the robot slowly moved backwards taking the door with it.

'It learned how to open doors. I don't believe it.' said Amy.

The robot lowered itself to normal position and swung into the now open doorway and continued its mission.

'That is definitely cool,' said Scott, impressed.

'Yeah. By tomorrow we'll know how big this place is,' said Rex. 'We'll check it out for real tomorrow, but now I have to show you the diary.'

In the morning the kitchen was way too busy for Rex, Scott and Amy to get into the base via the cool room unseen, so they headed up the hill to enter from the top. Once inside with headlamps and torches blazing, Rex pulled out sheaves of paper and handed one each to Scott and Amy.

'Maps,' he explained. He leafed through a few pages until he found a photograph taken from the map-bot's camera. 'I think we should head here.'

The photo showed a door with the words *Trompe and Generator* in big red letters on it.

'If we get the power on, we might be able to open the other doors,' said Rex.

Scott was looking at the pages of maps, flipping between pages. 'That's way, way deep,' he said looking at the long shafts of the lift well. 'Do we have to use that thing?' he pointed at the lift.

'Yep,' said Amy with a grin. She grabbed one of Scott's arms and Rex grabbed the other. 'Come on.'

Scott was marched over to the lift where they waited for a car to come into the opening.

'Big step,' said Amy as though she was talking to a child.

Once on the car, Scott quickly went for the handrail and gave it the white-knuckle treatment as the car descended to the lower levels.

When the *Level 0 approaching* sign scrolled past, Scott said 'This is us, right?'

'Nope, not yet,' said Rex. 'Minus three for us.' Scott watched the ground floor level roll past and became visibly more anxious.

'Relax,' said Rex. You've seen the map-bot do this. Nothing's going to happen.' Scott did not seem very reassured.

The *Basement 3* sign rolled past and the opening to the floor came into view.

'This is us. Jump out whenever you're ready.' Scott didn't wait and ducked down to leap out before the ceiling was even at waist height. He underestimated the height of the room though, and dropped nearly two metres. He landed hard and went down on one knee, holding his arms out to steady himself, his head lowered ready to tuck in for a roll that wasn't needed. Rex and Amy waited until the floor was nearly level and casually stepped off into the room.

'Nice hero landing, mate,' said Rex. 'Impressive.'

'You'll get used to it,' said Amy. She slapped him on the back as she walked past him, heading for the door. 'This way.'

Rex helped a sheepish Scott to his feet and the two of them followed Amy.

'This ceiling is taller than the others, and look'—Amy pointed to two large pipes emerging from the corridor ceiling that then turned a gentle curve to run horizontally along one wall—'they must go to the Trompe.'

Moving along the corridor, their footsteps were accompanied by the muted hiss and gurgle of water running through the pipes. They arrived at a steel wall with a solid steel door set into it. A complicated array of pipes and levers surrounded the door that was painted with yellow and black diagonal stripes. A sign next to the door, just like in the photo, said *Trompe and Generator.* Scott walked forward and grabbed a lever that had a label saying *Open.*

'I hope this works,' he said. 'Opening these things manually is a pain.' He pulled the lever sideways towards the door. There was a loud hiss of compressed air then the door started sliding out of the way with a mechanical whirring sound. 'Wait for the floor plate to drop down, then go through,' he said. As the door came to its fully open position, a hinged plate leaning against the door from the floor was lowered flat over the tracks of the door mechanism. Scott continued to hold the lever down. 'Right, go through now.'

Rex and Amy went through quickly. Scott followed while keeping his hand on the lever. He grabbed a similar lever on the other side of the door frame and held it down as he went though. Only then did he release the lever.

'Ok. This might get a bit loud. Depends if it's the fast close type or not,' said Scott. He put one finger in his ear and waited for Rex and Amy to block theirs. Scott reached out to a stubby lever marked, *Emergency Close — Stand Clear,* and activated it. As soon as he did, he quickly blocked his other ear and the door slammed shut with a very loud BANG!

Unblocking their ears, the loud sound of the door slamming echoed back from the network of corridors.

'Does it have to do that every time?' asked Amy.

'No, normally it closes the same speed as it opens. I just wanted to test the emergency close,' said Scott with a grin. Scott looked over Rex and Amy's shoulders and his eyes opened wide. 'Woah! Check it out.'

Rex and Amy spun around to see a massive steel sphere two stories high and nearly touching the ceiling. This room was double the height of the corridor they came in from. A door set high in the wall connected to the top third of the sphere with a steel gantry which circled around and continued to a door on the other side of the room. The big pipes from the corridor were suspended underneath. A ladder ran down the wall by the first door to floor level, where one of the pipes entered the sphere. The other pipe entered the sphere above its equator, curving gently to join straight on. Near the top of the sphere, other small pipes came out and branched off in different directions. The largest of these stretched across to the wall opposite the door they just entered, turned to follow the wall down before it turned again and went through the wall. The three of them stood there for a minute taking it all in, becoming conscious of the sound of rumbling water.

'So, this is the Trompe, eh?' said Scott.

Rex went over to where the largest of the top pipes entered the wall. There was a large valve just above the curve and a gauge sticking out at right angles. 'This gauge goes up to four hundred psi. It's air pressure,' he said. 'This is a giant, water-powered compressor.' He turned to Amy and Scott, who came over to see what he was looking at.

'Two hundred and fifty it says now. Crikey, no wonder it's locked up in a separate room.'

'It must power the generator,' said Amy. She pointed at the other door in the room, identical to the one they had just entered. A sign next to the door said *Generator*. 'Shall I?' she reached up to the 'open' lever.

'Go for it,' said Scott. 'Just keep your hand on the lever as you go through after us. It's a safety thing.'

Amy pulled the lever. There was a short hiss, then nothing.

'Hmmm, no pressure,' said Scott. He took over from Amy and tried again, but this time there wasn't even a hiss. 'We'll have to pump it manually,' he said. 'Wait, what? There's no handle.' There was a hole and label where a handle would normally attach. 'Now what?'

'There must be valve around here somewhere,' said Rex. He followed the wall around behind the trompe, emerging on the other side. He played his head lamp and torch over the wall. 'Over here,' he called out.

Scott and Amy came closer, each using their torches to light up the wall. There were dozens of individually labeled valves leading off from a large tube running horizontally across the wall.

'Here! I found it,' said Rex. One of the tubes was labeled *Pressure Doors* and branched left and right. There was a valve on each side of the branch.

'The left hand one is closed,' said Scott. Rex took hold of the valve lever and tried to turn it, but it wouldn't budge. They all tried to prise the handle into the open position, but it was frozen solid.

'Now what?' said Amy.

'I supposed we just check out the rest of the base and see if there are any other doors we can get through,' Rex said with a shrug of his shoulders.

They passed back through the first door and headed back towards the lift.

CHAPTER 29

Sunday morning, Rex, Scott and Amy emerged from underneath the *Dissa-pier* into bright sunlight and clear skies. They made their way up to Scales where a large crowd was gathering for the auction, much to Garrett's visible disgust. Keeping to their plan, Scott headed off through the crowd to spread the word that Garrett would keep upping the reserve so he was the last bidder, then buy Scales himself at a cheaper price. He'd use fake bidders so nobody could tell it was him bidding. Rex and Amy headed for the table where bidders could register. Beryl was keeping a watchful eye over the table, so Amy distracted her asking questions about the contract of sale and wanting to know the reserve price. Beryl was getting quite irritated and didn't realise Amy was steadily turning her away from the table. Rex saw his chance and quickly added his name to the bidder list, took a photo of it, and stuffed a paddle with his bidder number under his jacket. Amy finally ran out of distractions and Beryl turned back to the table to find Rex leaning over the table.

'What are you doing?' said Beryl.

Rex plucked a business card with Beryl's name and phone number from a little stand and held it up for Beryl to see. 'Just getting a card. That ok?' he said with raised eyebrows. Beryl harrumphed and shooed him away with a flap of her hands.

Rex and Amy melted back into the crowd.

'Here, look at this,' he said to Amy. He showed her the photo of the bidder list on his phone. 'Any names familiar on that?'

Amy took the phone, zoomed in on the names and slowly scrolled them up.

'This one,' she said. 'He died a few years ago. Seriously, how thick is Garrett thinking nobody would remember?'

Rex took the phone back and scrolled across to the number, then compared it to Beryl's business card.

'Gotcha,' he said, and held the phone and card so Amy could see.

Amy smiled. 'Phase two, then,' she said. Rex nodded.

They both headed in opposite directions in the crowd seeking out anyone with a bidding number.

Ten o'clock arrived. Garrett, wearing a shirt in a particularly dreadful shade of pink and shiny suit pants, banged a roll of paper on his palm to get the crowds attention.

'Ladies and Gentlemen, we'll start in just a few minutes,' he called out. 'If you could all move in a bit closer that would be appreciated, as we are having technical difficulties with our P.A. system today.'

Penelope scoffed loudly from the edge of the crowd earning her a filthy look from Garrett. She glared back in defiance. The crowd shuffled forward a few paces.

'Right, well, ah, thank you all for coming out on this beautiful morning. I must say I am surprised at the sudden late interest, but anyway ... I'm sure you all know what a wonderful institution Scales is, set on five acres of prime beachfront with beautiful views and close proximity to the town centre. The bar and restaurant behind me has steady business with plenty of scope for expansion or development.'

A wave of grumbles swept over the crowd of mainly locals who would rather leave the pub as it was.

'Would someone give me a starting bid, please?'

The crowd fell silent. Not even a seagull squawked.

'Anyone?' Garrett paced back and forth around the area in front of the table.

A voice from the back of the crowd called out, 'What's the reserve?'

Garrett withered a little before gathering his defences. 'I'll let you know the property is on the market when the bidding reaches reserve. So come on. Someone start me off.'

The silence from the crowd continued for a while.

'Anyone? Come on, I'm sure you've all got better things to do than waste time here. Start me off. Any bid at all.'

'Ten dollars!' came a call from the crowd.

Garrett was well rehearsed for moments such as this. 'Well thank you for your bid, but I'm afraid we'll need a bit more than that.'

'Why did you ask then?' came the retort. 'Stop muckin' about and make a vendor bid.'

'Ah ha ha, very good.' Garrett's mouth was smiling, but his eyes gave him away.

'Alright then, I will offer a vendor bid of one million five hundred thousand.' Garrett paused, thinking that ought to shut them up.

'Do I see one six?' He spread his arms, inviting bids.

A suited man in the crowd nodded and flashed a number.

Garrett pointed with his roll of paper.

'One six I have; do I have one seven. One seven anyone.' There was no reply. 'One ... seven.' Garrett spread the words out and glared in Beryl's direction.

Beryl had her phone held to her ear talking quietly to someone on the other end of the line. She flashed up a bidding number.

'Thank you. Phone bidder at one seven. Do I have one eight? One eight anyone?'

More silence.

A different suited man called out. 'Two million,' and held up his number.

'Thank you, sir. New bidder at two million. Do I have two, two?' Garrett again looked towards Beryl. She flashed up her number.

'Two million two on the phone. Back with you sir.' The second man shook his head. 'Alright then, the bid is two point two million, looking for two, four.'

Another call from the back, with a number held over the heads of the crowd. 'Two point five!'

'Thank you at the back, now asking for two point eight.' Again, Garrett looked to Beryl who obliged by flashing her number.

'Two, eight on the phone. Anyone further bids?' Garrett scanned the crowd daring anyone else to bid.

'If there are no further bids, I will pass the property in. The highest bidder will have the first right to negotiate with the vendor. Any further bids? Looking for two million nine hundred thousand.'

Rex stepped out from behind another man standing at the front of the crowd and held up his sign.

Garrett had already launched into his well-practiced auctioneer speech before he realised who the bidder was. 'Two nine I have! Two nine from ... aah ... I'm not sure we can accept your bid young man, and I will warn you that disrupting an auction is an offence.' Garrett's fake smile was slipping into a scowl, and he was starting to get red in the face again.

Someone else in the crowd yelled out. 'Too late Garrett, you already accepted it, and he has every right to bid. Get on with it, we're not even at reserve yet!'

The crowd broke out into chuckles and murmurs of agreement.

'All ... right then. Two point nine million it is to the young man.' He scowled at Rex. 'Do I see three million anywhere?' Garrett didn't even bother looking at Beryl this time, he just aimed his roll of paper at her. Beryl flipped up her number and without even seeing it, Garrett continued. 'Three million on the phone!' He gloated at Rex. The move didn't go unnoticed by the crowd who grumbled and shook heads.

'Anyone for three point five?' Garrett looked mockingly at Rex.

Rex smiled and held up his number and called out. 'Four!'

The crowd gasped. Garrett spluttered. 'Four?' He was visibly fuming now. 'Four it is,' he said through gritted teeth.

'Phone bidder?' Garrett looked at Beryl, who again held up her number.

'Thank you. The bid is five million. Any advance on five?'

Rex shook his head. Garrett scanned the other bidders, who all shook their heads as well.

'Right then, if there are no further bids, I will pass the property in to the phone bidder. Last chance. Any advance on five million dollars?'

Rex took out his phone, tapped the screen and held the phone to his ear. A few seconds later the phone against Beryl's ear blared out a long, loud ring. She jumped and nearly dropped the phone.

The crowd was outraged — calls of 'You're a charlatan Garrett!' and 'Dirty thieving scum!' could be heard.

Garrett was livid. He glared at Beryl with a face so purple it clashed with his shirt.

'Alright! Alright!' He tried to calm the crowd down flapping his hands. The outrage continued for another minute before Garrett was able to make himself heard. 'Alright, I will pass the property in to the last bidder before my assistant obviously lost connection with her phone bidder.'

Jeers from the crowd. They were having none of Garrett's obviously fake excuses.

'That bidder was the young man in front at four million dollars, and he damn well better be able to cough it up if it's accepted. The property is passed in. Thanks for coming.' He turned to Beryl and hoiked his thumb at Rex. 'You handle this.' He stumped off inside the pub to escape the crowd.

Rex followed him into Scales, accompanied by a pensive Beryl. Just inside the door Garrett turned and grabbed Rex by the jacket. He leaned down and breathed foul breath over Rex's face.

'You better be able to come up with a deposit you little hooligan or I'll throttle you!' He pushed Rex towards Beryl. 'Sort it out with her. I've got better things to do.' He pushed through the door and walked out leaving Rex shaken but satisfied.

CHAPTER 30

By the time Rex emerged from Scales most of the crowd had gone home to lunch. Scott and Amy were sitting by the side of the boat ramp amongst tufts of spiky coastal grasses. Seeing him coming, they slid back down to the path and hurried up to meet him, dusting sand off as they came.

'How did it go?' asked Amy.

'Did you really buy it for four million?' asked Scott.

'How come Garrett stormed out?'

'Does this mean you get a staff discount?'

Rex held his hands up against the barrage. 'Alright, alright, settle down.' He gestured for them to follow him away from the entrance of Scales and some curious locals who were edging closer to hear any news. They walked down to the *Dissa*.

'Well?' asked Amy when they reached the wooden deck of the pier.

'I did buy it, yes,' said Rex.

'Whoa! Really? Four million bucks!' Scott was impressed.

'No, no, it wasn't four million. Nowhere near. Actually, it ended up being surprisingly cheap.' Amy and Scott remained silent, waiting for the price. 'One point two million.'

Amy's jaw dropped. 'But that's — that's way below what other bidders were offering.'

'Yeah, I know, and I wouldn't go advertising that around either, but there's a reason.'

'I can't see why Garrett would let it go for cheaper than he could have,' said Scott. 'Money hungry git.'

'Yeah, but he has a habit of treating his employees like dirt, and Beryl has had enough now too. Garrett threatened me just before he stormed off and Beryl didn't take too kindly to that. She told me Garrett was in bed with some Chinese investors. She's had to deal with them on the phone and they're the nasty kind that don't take no for an answer. Anyway, while we were in there, she rang the vendors and explained the situation. The vendors didn't want to sell to the Chinese, so they agreed to let me have it below the asking price just so the Chinese couldn't get it.'

'Who were the owners?' asked Amy.

'Some investment group. She never mentioned them by name, but the voice on the end sounded very posh English. Beryl was ultra-nice to them.'

Scott and Amy digested that information for a moment.

'I reckon Beryl's going to get fired now for sure. Garrett will go nuts,' said Scott.

Rex nodded. 'Yep, that's what Beryl said too. She seemed kind of relieved. That's why she told me more about Garrett's Chinese mates. They've been promising him buckets of cash if he could pull the deal off.'

'And we just stopped him,' said Amy.

'We did, yeah.' Rex looked quite proud. 'This time anyway. Beryl told me he's trying to buy up as much property for them as he can get. Once they've got enough, they can start forcing locals out and take over the entire town. They've done it before apparently. It takes years, but they have deep pockets and know who to bribe.'

'Hang on, how come you got all this out of Beryl?' said Scott.

Rex smiled. 'I told her we knew she stole the security footage. She didn't admit it, but she didn't deny it either.'

'Wow,' said Amy. 'Beryl's sneakier than I thought.'

'Yeah, she sure is. She's going to tell Garrett that the vendors withdrew from the sale. She's going to handle the paperwork herself, but once Garrett finds out, she reckons he'll start evicting tenants in revenge.'

'Then we need to get rid of Garrett,' Amy said.

'What?' said Scott, surprised at Amy. 'You mean'—he held a finger up to his throat and slashed it across—'make him disappear?'

'No, you idiot! Get him out of town. Put him out of business.'

'What did you have in mind?' asked Rex.

Amy thought for a moment. 'We need to cut him off.' Scott brought his finger up to his throat again, grinning. Amy ignored him and went on. 'We need to get the town on our side.'

'Easy,' said Scott. 'They already hate Garrett.' He turned to Rex. 'You should have heard what some of them were saying after he left.' He turned to Amy. 'If you did mean, you know.' He did the finger thing again. 'There are plenty of people who'd do it for free.'

Rex intervened. 'I don't think we need to go that far.'

'You sure? They're all pretty upset that Scales is being sold.'

Rex thought for a moment. 'We need to reassure them. Tell them Scales is in safe hands. Tell them to be wary and warn them of what Garrett's doing.'

'We could send out flyers in people's letterboxes,' suggested Amy. 'That way Garrett would be kept in the dark about what we're doing for as long as possible.'

'Good idea. And I think we know someone who can get them printed pretty quickly.' Rex looked at Scott and Amy, expectantly.

'Not Penelope,' said Amy.

'Nope. Beryl. She gets flyers printed all the time.'

The days following the auction, Rex, Scott and Amy spent their time after school delivering flyers to every letterbox and business in town. By the end of the week, it was apparent the whole town was responding. Everywhere Garrett went he was given excuses like, 'No, sorry, we're out of fish,' and 'Sorry, the coffee machine's broken'. When Garrett marched into The Breakers Milk Bar demanding coffee, he finally got the message.

'What do mean there's no coffee?' It was more a bark than a question.

Mrs Reynard replied in a calm voice. 'Oh, we have coffee alright, just not for you. You're not welcome here anymore *Mister* Garrett, so you can just turn yourself around and get out.'

Garrett was speechless for a change. His head turned a dangerous shade of purple and the veins on his forehead stood out like they were going to pop. Mrs Reynard just stood there with a calm smile on her face, daring him to say something.

Garrett spun around and stormed out, slapping the fly screen flaps so hard they whacked the shop window. Mrs Reynard calmly went back to cutting sandwiches for the lunchtime rush. Even the skies opened up to dump rain on Garrett as he stumped back to his office. He entered, slamming the door against the wall.

'Beryl! Make me a coffee! A strong one!' Beryl went into the back room to make coffee while Garrett ranted on from the front office.

'Bloody whole town's run out of coffee, apparently.' He tapped aggressively on his computer keyboard, nearly bashing the keys through the desk. 'Oh, for crying out loud, another one! That's nearly every property in town.'

Beryl returned from the back room carrying a delicate teacup for herself and a big mug of black coffee that's she'd made extra strong for Garrett. 'Hmmmm?'

'They've all withdrawn from sale.' He started shuffling things around on his desk. 'Where are those rental brochures? They were supposed to be here two days ago.'

'They're at the printer,' Beryl responded. 'They won't deliver from so far away.'

'What do you mean? They're only down the bloody street, they could walk them here.'

'No, our local printer was busy, so I had to get them done by the other one. You'll have to drive there and get them.' Garrett was starting to fume again. 'It's only half an hour away,' said Beryl.

'Well, you better get going, then,' said Garrett in a condescending voice.

'I can't go, my car is in for a service, and I can't drive your manual shift car.'

Beryl sipped her tea to hide a smile.

Garrett glared at Beryl, fuming. He snatched up his keys and a binder marked 'Rentals' from the desk, glared at her and stormed out without another word.

Beryl calmly sat down at her desk, picked up the phone handset, and started dialing.

In Rex's hotel room, Rex, Scott and Amy were reading on-line reviews of the hotel.

'Hey look! We get a mention. This one says, 'Some guests reported hearing moaning and wailing in the walls.'' They all laughed at the memory of making spooky noises through the speaking tubes. Rex's phone rang. He reached over absent-mindedly and held it to his ear. Scott and Amy could hear someone talking for a minute.

'Right, thanks. Bye.' Rex hung up the phone. 'That was Beryl.'

'Beryl? What did she want?' asked Scott.

'She thinks Garrett's twigged to what's going on. She sent him out of town to get brochures of the rentals so she could copy the rental list for us, but he took it with him. She said he looks like he's about to pop a blood vessel.'

'He's getting suspicious,' agreed Amy. 'We're going to have to get the list ourselves.'

'The library might be able to help us,' said Scott, holding up his access card. 'We can search for past rental advertisements.'

'Good idea,' said Rex.

'That won't get us any new ones though. Not if he's only just got brochures printed,' said Amy.

'We should have written them down when we were delivering the flyers,' said Scott. 'We'll have to ride every street in town again, and if this rain keeps up, we'll be soaked.'

Rex opened a new window on the screen and brought up a feed from the hotel's weather radar. A wide band of blue was moving in from the sea with a clear patch following.

'It will stop soon, for a while anyway. Enough time to ride through the streets. There can't be that many of Garrett's rental signs, can there?'

'Probably not,' said Amy. 'People have been leaving them empty rather than have Garrett handle them.'

'Let's go then,' said Rex. 'By the time we get down to the bikes, the rain will have stopped. We'll have about an hour before the next band of rain moves in.'

Rex, Scott and Amy rode into town, stopping at the library. It didn't take long for the smart searching capabilities of the back-room computers to come up with a list of past rentals. But there was no information about any for the past few days.

Outside the library, they prepared the next stage of their plan.

'Let's start at the back of town, farthest away from school. That way if we don't finish, we can get the rest after school tomorrow,' said Rex.

'Yeah, good idea,' said Scott. 'Plus, that's the highest point in town so it will be all downhill.'

They cycled their way along slick and muddy streets, standing on the pedals to climb the steeper part at the back of town where the hills rose towards the hinterland. They reached their splitting up point. There was a rundown weatherboard home with one of Garrett's rental signs zip-tied to the low, chain-link front fence. The house looked like it had seen better days, with walls painted pea green and peeling badly. The best that could be said about it was its thriving garden. The front veranda was guarded by a moat of blue hydrangeas, and the side fence was completely hidden by brightly coloured dahlias.

Amy took her smartphone out to take a photo of the house and rental sign.

'Hey, Rex, look,' Scott said. 'Snot walls!' He began to laugh. 'An entire house, made of snot!'

'Shhhh, there might be someone in there,' said Amy.

Rex took out a map of the town, divided into sections with coloured highlighters. 'Everyone know where they're going?' Scott and Amy leaned in to check the map.

'Yep, same as before,' said Scott.

'Got it,' replied Amy.

'Okay. We'll meet up here before we split up again.' Rex indicated a point where the road from the neighboring town entered Lenzie Bay.

The three of them cycled off down different streets in search of Garrett's rental signs.

At the rendezvous point, Rex and Scott stopped outside another of Garrett's rentals and waited for Amy. They saw her speed around the nearest corner. She leaned over so far the bike's pedals scraped the road. She rode up on to the footpath at next door's driveway to avoid a massive puddle and pulled up beside them out of breath.

'You want to be careful leaning over like that in the wet,' said Scott. 'I nearly went over a few times the streets are that slippery.'

Amy ignored him. 'I've just seen Penelope delivering junk mail,' she said, catching her breath. 'I think she spotted me and started following me, so I had to double back a few times. I lost her, but we better get moving.'

'Why would she follow you?' asked Rex.

'I don't know, do I? She's mental. I still don't trust her.'

'Right. I'll just take a photo of this place,' said Rex. He pulled out his phone and walked along the path to the sign.

Scott and Amy were about to remount ready to ride away when, from the road out of town came a small car moving quickly, its tiny engine revving hard. It was Garrett's branded company car, a purple faced Garrett stuffed in behind the wheel. Garrett saw the three of them beside the road with Rex holding a camera up taking a photo. The car changed course and aimed for them. Scott and Amy tried to push their bikes away, but it was too late. Garrett aimed the car at the puddle and plowed through, sending up a huge wash as the tiny wheels aquaplaned in the deep water. The wave splashed over Scott and Amy, drenching them from head to toe. As the car roared off into town, Rex turned to see Scott and Amy standing beside dropped bikes, their arms held out from their bodies and dripping with muddy water.

Rex tried not to laugh, but the look on his face gave him away. 'I think we better call it quits today. We'll go back to the hotel, and you can dry off in the kitchen by the ovens.'

After they dried off, Scott and Amy were preparing to go home at the front of the hotel by the bike rack.

'That's still not all the rentals though,' said Amy. 'I know there's another one closer to town, but I can't remember exactly what number it is. I can go past on the way home and let you know.'

'Yeah, I could probably do a bit more on the way home as well,' said Scott. 'Now that we're not soaking wet.'

'Alright,' agreed Rex. 'Just be careful. Garrett sounds like he's on the warpath, and Penelope's probably still hanging around. We don't want her finding out what we're up to. Like you said Amy, I'm not sure we can trust her yet.'

'Looks like the rain's moving in again, too,' said Amy.

CHAPTER 31

After driving through the puddle, Garrett switched on the windscreen wipers to clear the muddy water. He looked in the rear-view mirror and saw those kids that messed everything up at the auction staring after him, dripping wet. He chuckled to himself for the first time in weeks; since that McGregor boy had turned up in fact. He thought back. Yes, everything was connected to him. And now, here he was taking photos of his rental property. They're planning something. First, he had to deal with that woman who called herself his assistant for sending him to the next town to get printing. They'd finished the job days ago and wanted more work. Every printer was desperate for work, including the Lenzie Bay printers, and Beryl bloody knew it! She must have set him up to get rid of him. He swung into a carpark outside his shop, stopping at an angle with a screech of tyres.

Garrett again pushed the door of his shop open so hard it bashed the adjacent wall, this time narrowly missing a woman who was talking to Beryl. He ignored the customer, dumped the brown paper wrapped stack of brochures on the reception counter and barked to Beryl. 'I want a word with you. Back room. Now!'

Beryl followed Garrett out of the reception area leaving the customer gaping.

As soon as the door shut, Garrett launched into a tirade. 'You and those bloody kids have been plotting against me, haven't you! First, I find out you let that McGregor brat get Scales for less than what I could have got it for, then you send me on a bloody goose chase to get rid of me!' He was inches from Beryl's face, foul breath and spittle causing her to recoil. 'I bet you were going to give them the rental list as well, hmmm?'

Back in reception the customer listened intently, straining to make out Garrett's muffled shouts. Every now and then Garrett would go quiet for a few seconds before starting up again, each rant louder than the one before.

Soon there were footsteps and the door to the back rooms was pulled open abruptly.

'You're fired!' Garrett shrieked. 'Get out!'

Beryl walked through the door shrinking away from Garrett and went to her desk. She calmly picked up her teacup and put it in her handbag, reached under the desk and took up a large shopping bag already filled with her things from the office. She stepped out from the reception desk and walked to the front door without even looking at Garrett. The customer opened the door for her, and Beryl passed through without a backwards glance. The woman threw Garrett a filthy look before walking out herself. The door began slowly closing until Garrett pushed it shut with a slam. He pushed his fuchsia flushed face up to the door glass for a moment before pulling back and flipping a sign from 'Open' to 'Closed'.

A few hours later, Garrett emerged from the shop carrying a heavy duffle bag, dumped it in the back seat of his car and went back into the shop. After a minute, the lights inside went out. He came out again carrying another bag, dragging the door shut behind him. He locked it and hurried to his car, opening the door, and throwing the bag onto the passenger seat before squeezing himself behind the wheel. He gunned the engine and leapt out of the car space causing someone approaching from behind to brake suddenly and blast their horn in protest.

Garrett didn't even notice. He was on a mission. Those bloody kids wouldn't be causing him any more trouble after today. He drove to the last place he saw them and traversed the streets, searching. It took him ten minutes before he saw one in the distance. He slowed down to a normal pace and drove quietly up behind the girl. It was Penelope; not that other girl who hangs around with the McGregor brat. Well, she was probably in cahoots with them as well after that stunt she pulled at the hotel.

He drove past her and pulled over. She hadn't noticed him. He grabbed something out of the bag beside him and got out. Penelope looked surprised to see him.

'Penelope!' He finally got her name right. 'I've got a job for you.' He kept talking as he approached her, putting on his best real estate agent's smile to keep her distracted. 'I need a new receptionist. Big pay rise for you.'

By the time Penelope realised what he was talking about he was in front of her.

'I'm not interested,' she said, turning away from him. Garrett pounced, whipping a large mail sack out from behind his back and pulling it over Penelope's head, dragging it down her body to trap her arms and pulling the ropes shut tight around her. Grabbing her around the middle, he lifted her on to his shoulder. Penelope's screams were muffled by the bag, her legs flailing in the air as she tried to struggle loose.

Garrett threw her into the back seat of his car and tied her legs with another length of rope. Looking around to make sure nobody was watching, he got in behind the wheel and took off, heading to the back of town.

Amy and Scott resumed their search for more rentals a few streets from where they were soaked by Garrett. They were about to go across an intersecting street when Amy spotted Garrett's car. 'I don't believe it! Here he comes again!'

Garrett's car raced past nearly hitting them.

'Did you see that?' asked Scott. 'It looked like tied up legs.'

'It did look like legs. Struggling legs. But whose?' asked Amy.

Scott shook his head, slowly. 'Aww, he's gone mental now,' he said with trepidation.

'We've got to follow him. Come on!' She turned and pedaled after Garrett's car, Scott close behind her. The long street curved uphill, making it even harder to keep up. They watched Garrett turn at the end of the street and drive out of view. Scott and Amy pedaled as fast as they could up the street to see where he was taking his captive. Someone was in trouble, and Garrett was clearly unhinged.

By the time Scott and Amy reached the top of the street, Garrett was gone. They hurtled along searching for signs of him, eventually reaching the end of the street where it turned and headed straight back into town down the hill. They pulled up, out of breath.

'We lost him,' Scott said between breaths.

'He must have pulled in somewhere, or else why would he come up here? There's no way out of town from here.' said Amy. She craned her neck around to see behind her. 'Look! That house for rent, it's one of Garrett's.' She cycled back to the front of the house. 'It's the one we first found, remember?'

'Who could forget that green monstrosity?'

Amy was off her bike and headed up the path to the front door.

'Wait!' said Scott. 'What are you doing? He might be in there.'

Amy turned, waiting for Scott to catch up. 'There's no car in the driveway, and look. The front door is open. It wasn't this morning. He probably dumped whoever it was in there and took off.'

'We should call the...' Scott began, but Amy was already up the steps and on the veranda.

She hesitated and turned back. Scott thought she was seeing sense, but instead she said, 'Go around the back and check it out in case he runs.'

Scott figured there was no stopping her, so he turned and ran around the corner and up the concrete driveway.

Amy crept up to the door and slowly pushed it open. Inside was a long dark hallway with a few closed doors along the length. The only light was from the now open doorway and was quickly swallowed by the dingy interior.

'Hello? Anybody there?' called Amy.

There was a thump from inside, followed by a muffled shout. Amy stepped inside quietly, listening. 'Hello?' she said again. More thumps, from behind the door on the left. Amy carefully turned the high-set old fashioned doorknob and slowly pushed the door open. A faint smell of cats wafted out of the darkness while Amy let her eyes adjust. She took a step into the room on threadbare carpet. In the corner of the room there was something moving. 'Hello?' Amy called again.

'MMMMmmmmmm! MMmmmMMMM!' came the muffled reply.

Amy took another step inside and could make out something struggling in the corner. It was the legs in a bag! She moved towards the bag but before she could take another step, she was grabbed from behind and lifted off her feet.

'Gotcha!'

Amy struggled; twisting and thrashing her feet to try and break free. 'Let. Me. Go!'

Her attacker did just that and threw her into the corner on top of the struggling legs. Before she could regain her feet, a heavy bag was pulled over her head, blocking out all light. Amy lashed out with her hands trying to grab at whoever it was. She found a face and dug her fingernails in.

'Arrrrrghh! You little bitch!'

Amy recognised that voice. Garrett!

'You've torn my face open!'

'Get off me you creep!' Amy shouted.

'Shut up, or I'll shut you up!'

'HEEEEELLLLP!' screamed Amy at the top of her lungs.

Garrett raised his fist and brought it down on the top of the bag, connecting with Amy's face inside. The bag went limp. Garrett pushed her into the corner with the other bag.

'Get off her!' Garrett spun around to see Scott coming at him through the door.

Scott swung a fist at him. Garrett ducked underneath and dived forward, connecting with Scott's stomach and knocking the wind out of him. Scott was driven backwards off his feet and thumped down on the floor, banging the back of his head. He went limp.

Garrett stood and stretched his back out, aching from the effort of subduing the three teenagers. In the corner, Penelope was still moving, struggling to take rasping breaths. Garrett smiled to himself and knelt down to tie up Amy's legs before moving on to tie up Scott's unconscious body.

He left the room, closed the front door from the inside and went out the back door into the garage. He got back in his tiny car, thumbed the remote to open the garage door and backed out of the driveway.

CHAPTER 32

Rex awoke early the next day and was ready for school in time for a decent breakfast. He used the main stairs and was heading for the dining room when his mother called out from reception, a phone still to her ear.

'Rex? Did Amy stay here last night?'

'No, why?' He walked over to reception, wondering why anyone would even think that she would.

'It's her mum on the phone. Amy didn't come home last night. Are you sure she didn't stay?'

'Of course I am. She rode back into town about five o'clock yesterday with Scott.'

Sylvie spoke a few words on the phone and said she'd call back. She rang off and started dialing.

'Hello, Charlie ... Yes, that's why I'm calling ... Hang on.' She spoke now to Rex. 'Scott didn't stay either?' Rex knew she was just being sure and shook his head in reply.

'Charlie? No, he didn't stay here. He went into town with Amy about five o'clock yesterday.' She listened for a second. 'Yes, do that. I'll call Amy's mother and let her know.' She hung up.

'Scott didn't come home either. You don't think they went off together, do you?'

'No!' said Rex, a little more emphatically than he expected. They wouldn't. No, of course not. 'They were going to look for more of Garrett's rental properties.' A horrible thought popped into Rex's head.

'Mum? I think we need to call the police.' Sylvie's eyebrows raised, like she was expecting Rex to confess to something he shouldn't have been doing. 'No, listen. Garrett saw us yesterday. He drove his car at us and went through a big puddle soaking us. He's nearly run me off the road before that as well. And he's probably mad about us stopping him getting his hands on Scales.'

Sylvie nodded in agreement. 'Yes, you're right. The police should know about this. Go and find Grandad. I'll call Amy's mum back and then the police.'

Breakfast forgotten, Rex first tried the security room — no Grandad. Rex paused to look at the security monitors. There he was, checking the hotel bicycles just outside the main door. He left the room, passing his mother talking on the phone as he headed for the front door.

Shortly after Rex and Sylvie filled Grandad in with what was happening, Grandad had the hotel meeting room set up with extra phones and a whiteboard. On the left of the board was a list of people to call, on the right was Scott and Amy's names under the heading 'Missing'. Below that, a timeline that started from when Garrett drove at Rex, Scott and Amy yesterday until now.

Rex was talking to Mrs Mansfield on the phone explaining why he, Amy and Scott were not at school.

Sylvie was finishing up a call. 'Gracie Reynard says she hasn't seen them or Garrett — which is expected since she banned him yesterday — but Beryl is there having breakfast, which is *un*-expected. She'll ask if Beryl knows anything and get back to us.'

Grandad put a tick next to Mrs Reynard's name and added a note — 'calling back about Beryl'.

Rex finished his phone call as well. 'Mrs M is going to ask around but wondered if we knew where Penelope was. She hasn't turned up for school today either.' Grandad wrote Penelope's name on the board underneath Amy and Scott.

'I hope she hasn't gone missing as well,' Grandad said.

The door opened and Roy entered with two police officers behind him.

'Syd? Superintendents Buijs and Whitmore would like a word.'

'Certainly. Come in gentlemen, take a seat.' While they were sitting, Sylvie's phone rang. She answered and moved it down the far end of the table so as not to interrupt.

'Thanks, Syd. We came to ask if you could help us, but I see you've already started,' said Buijs, indicating the whiteboard. 'We can fill in some of the gaps for you. Garrett's missing. He hasn't been seen since yesterday and his office is closed. We haven't tracked down his assistant yet.'

Sylvie looked up, still on the phone. 'Excuse me gentlemen, we've found Beryl. She's at The Breakers Milk Bar. Garrett fired her at about four o'clock yesterday and she hasn't seen him since. Beryl says Garrett was extremely agitated.' She went back to talking as Grandad put a tick against Beryl's name and added Garrett to the timeline, just after the note about him driving at Rex, Scott and Amy.

Superintendent Whitmore pointed to the board. 'Penelope Greenwood's missing as well?'

Rex answered, 'She hasn't turned up at school. She loves school, and ...' Rex paused, unsure if he should be a part of this. He looked at his dad who nodded for him to go on. 'Garrett isn't happy with Penelope either. She was doing some work for him, but he treated her so badly she quit. She's helping us now. Garrett might have gone after her as well.'

Supt Whitmore made a note. 'Looks like we'll have to contact Penelope's parents, too.'

'Right, well we know about Garrett's ambitions, but what's he got against you four?' asked Supt Buijs.

'We stopped him buying Scales. He set up a bogus auction, and we out ...' Rex paused. He was about to say 'outbid him' but decided not to mention anything about buying Scales. 'We outsmarted him, exposing the fake bidder. He was furious and actually threatened me afterwards.'

The two Superintendents looked at each other with worried, grim faces.

'Okay well I think it's best if you don't leave the hotel for now. Not until we find Garrett anyway,' said Supt Buijs. 'We'll head back to the station.'

They stood ready to leave as Sylvie finished her call.

'I've asked my friend, Vivienne, to pick up Amy's mother and bring her here if that's alright?' she said. 'Scott's father is on his way here as well. We'll let you know if we hear anything.' Sylvie showed the officers out.

Missing:

Amy Gardiner
Scott Lawson
Penelope Greenwood

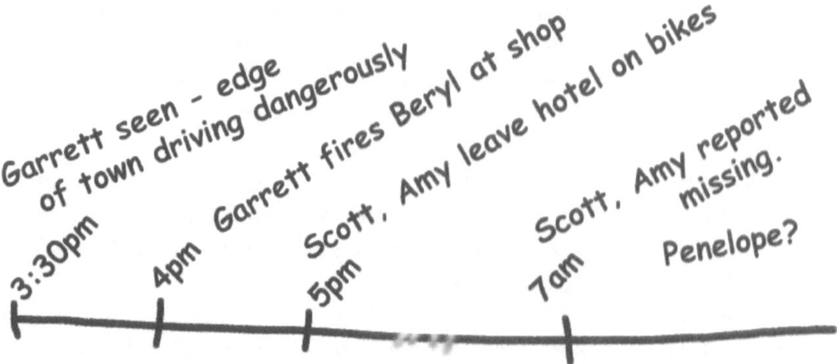

After the police left, Grandad sent Rex to the dining room to get some breakfast and bring back a pot of coffee.

Rex dished himself up some scrambled eggs, a grilled tomato and some beans. Somehow it didn't feel like a bacon sort of day. The sky outside the wide dining room windows was darkening with ominous clouds, threatening a storm. Amy was missing, Scott was missing, and now it looked like Penelope was missing as well. By the way the police reacted, they seemed to believe Rex about Garrett. Even Mum and Dad were taking him seriously at last. He sat at a table and picked at his food, worrying about where they could be. They weren't at the library when he called to see if they'd gone there. He even called Scales. They were nowhere to be found. All he wanted to do now was get on his bike and try to find them, storm or no storm. All these phone calls were just making him worry more. Eventually he gave up on food with only half his plate finished.

Taking a full jug of coffee and a stack of mugs nestled between one arm and his body, he backed out through the dining room doors.

'Let me help you with that,' said a voice behind him. He turned, letting the door close behind him. It was Beryl.

'I need to see your grandfather,' said Beryl. She took the mugs from Rex's arm.

'Right,' said Rex, his voice steeped in suspicion. He remembered the last time Beryl was at the hotel.

Beryl seemed to sense what he was thinking. 'And I'm sorry about the security video ... and Mrs Birch. I had no idea he was going to go that far.'

Rex was sceptical but remembered she had given the video to Penelope to give to the police. 'I hear you got fired,' said Rex. 'Sorry to hear that.'

'Humph, don't be. Best thing that's happened to me in years. Well, that and seeing his face when he figured out you'd bought Scales.' She smiled, and to Rex she now seemed like an entirely different person.

'This way,' Rex said, and led her to the meeting room.

When Rex entered, Grandad was gazing at the whiteboard twiddling a marker in his fingers. He glanced over his shoulder and saw Beryl Hoopell following.

He turned. 'Back again, Miss Hoopell?'

Beryl's face fell into guilt.

'It's alright,' said Grandad. 'We're moving on, and I think you've since redeemed yourself.' he looked at Rex, who nodded.

Beryl relaxed. 'Thank you,' she said. 'It hasn't been easy since the auction. He's been watching me like a hawk. I knew my time was short.'

She looked into the distance, remembering. 'I even had all my stuff packed up ready.'

Grandad regarded her for a moment and softened. 'Have a seat and some coffee and tell us all about it.' He sat down opposite her while Rex poured.

'He came in yesterday afternoon, furious. I know he's usually ranting about one thing or another, but this time he was exponentially worse.

'He took me into the back room and yelled at me for a good ten minutes.' Her face wrinkled, remembering Garrett's foul breath.

'Did you notice him doing anything unusual in the office between the auction and yesterday?' asked Grandad.

Beryl thought back. 'He was locked in his office more than usual. I just figured he was talking to his investors. He was always in a worse mood after talking to them. He wouldn't let me in there. He kept the door locked when he wasn't in there, even when he went out for coffee.

'I did get one peek in there though. I told him I heard a noise from out the back.' Beryl smiled at her own cleverness. 'He must have thought it was someone snooping because he bolted out to check. I only got a glance, but he had some big heavy bags in his office. I couldn't see what was in them. Something long?'

'Were they stacked on top of each other?'

Beryl tilted her head, thinking. 'No. Now you mention it, they were all laid out on the floor.'

Grandad waited, but Beryl seemed to have finished.

Rex prompted, 'So ... you said you had to see Grandad. Ah ... why?'

'Oh, yes. Well, when Gracie told me about your friends going missing, I started thinking. If Garrett has taken them, he'll have put them in one of his vacant rentals.' She looked away remembering something. 'I couldn't get hold of the list; he took it with him to the printers.' She looked back at Rex. 'Like I said, he was suspicious. Paranoid even. When he fired me, he started ranting on about you, and said something about 'snotty kids deserve a snotty house', but I can't think of what house he's talking about.'

It took Rex a moment for it to register. Snotty kids deserve ...

'A snotty house!' said Rex. 'I think I know which one!' He jumped up and called behind him as he raced from the room. 'I'll get the address, it's in my room.'

Rex ran up the stairs taking two and three steps at a time, pelted down the corridor and slammed into his room. Rummaging in his backpack, he pulled out the notebook with rental addresses on it. The snot house was the first one on the list. He dialled the meeting room, Grandad answered as soon as it started ringing.

'Got it?' asked Grandad.

'Yeah. Thirty-nine Edge Street. Get the cops, I'll meet you there.' Before Grandad could remind him that he shouldn't be leaving the hotel Rex had slammed the phone down, was out of his room, and headed back down through reception. Rex didn't even wait for Grandad as he ran through the lobby and out the front door to the bike rack. He grabbed the first bike and was out the hotel grounds before Grandad was even off the phone to the police.

Ten minutes later he was pumping the pedals as he climbed the hill to the back of town, following the same route as the day before. He rounded the corner and saw it. The ugly green snot house. He rode in the front gate and jumped off the bike letting it crash into the grass. At the top of the steps of the veranda, he had to stop and catch his breath for a moment.

He banged on the front door. 'Amy! Are you in there?' He couldn't hear anything he was breathing so heavily. 'Scott! Penelope!' *Bang bang bang*! Not hearing anything, he moved to the front window. Thick curtains meant he couldn't see in, so he rapped on the glass and cupped his hands to his mouth and shouted, 'Amy! Scott! It's Rex!'

Thump, thump, thump, came the reply.

'Hang on, I'm coming in.' He moved back to the front door. There was no doorknob, just a heavy lock. Rex launched himself at the door and crashed into it with a thud. It didn't budge. He tried a few more times without success.

'I'll try the back!' he shouted and took off around the house and down the driveway to find the back door. It was the same. Heavy and locked. Rex tried leaning back and kicking it, but it wasn't moving.

From the front of the house, he heard a siren and the sound of cars screeching to a stop. He ran back to the front to see Grandad's SUV in the driveway and a police car pulled up behind. Grandad was out of his car first with the police not far behind.

'They're in there, I heard them!' shouted Rex. 'Hurry!'

Grandad crashed into the front door. There was a crack of splintering wood as the door frame started to give way. He leaned back and raised a heavily booted foot and slammed it into the door.

The door smashed open and banged against the wall. Splinters of wood and the remains of the heavy door latch flew down the hallway. Rex tried to follow one of the policemen up the stairs, but the second policeman held him back. Inside, more banging sounds as doors were thrown open.

Grandad shouted, 'They're here!'

Soon after, the other policeman emerged back into the hallway from the back of the house. 'Clear!'

Rex pushed past into the hallway. Through the doorway to the left, Rex saw Grandad sweep the heavy curtains open flooding the room with light. Grandad went to the legs that were struggling the most and started cutting rope with a knife drawn from a scabbard strapped to his belt.

Rex dived for the first bag he saw and tore open the ropes freeing up arms. He helped lift the heavy sack over shoulders to come face to face with Amy. Her hair was all over the place from struggling, dried blood all over the left side of her face. Grandad freed up Scott and was cutting the rope around Amy's legs before moving on to Penelope.

Amy struggled to her feet and threw her arms around Rex and hugged him close. Rex wrapped his arms around Amy and steadied her, keeping her from falling. Behind Rex, Scott clambered to his feet to find Amy and Rex embracing and swaying gently, their eyes closed. He went to help Penelope who was now free but struggling to breathe. He helped lift her to her feet with Grandad on the other side of her, and they helped her out of the room and outside.

Supt Buijs coughed gently. 'Right-oh you two, there'll be time for that later.' Rex and Amy broke their embrace, tears rolling down Amy's face leaving dark bloody tracks. 'Let's get you checked out at the hospital, eh?' he said gently.

Amy nodded and allowed the Superintendent to guide her outside. Rex followed wiping tears of relief and happiness from his face.

He emerged outside to find Grandad helping Penelope into the back of the police car. Scott came back to Rex and Amy. He held out his hand to Rex, but Rex ignored it and drew him into a brief hug. They broke apart.

'How did you find us?' asked Scott.

Rex looked around at the ghastly green walls. 'It was the snot house,' he said. 'Garrett gave the clue away when he fired Beryl.'

'Did you get him? Garrett?' asked Amy.

'No. He's gone to ground. Nobody's seen him since yesterday. What happened?'

'We saw Garrett drive past with some legs struggling in a bag, so we followed him,' said Scott.

'Garret drew us into a trap using Penelope as bait,' added Amy. 'He got me from behind.'

'Yeah, I tried to knock him out, but he was too quick for me,' said Scott. He reached up and rubbed the back of his head where he hit it when he was knocked to the ground. 'He rushed me, but I don't really remember what happened after that. When I woke up, I couldn't move or see anything.'

'Eventually we figured out it was Penelope,' said Amy. 'She has asthma and was really struggling to breathe in that bag.'

'Yeah, but Amy calmed her down a bit,' said Scott. 'Said you'd come to help.' He took his hand from the back of his head to check for blood, and added, 'She's brilliant.'

'Yeah, she is,' agreed Rex.

Amy smiled at Rex, and Rex at Amy. Scott looked back and forth at each of them. He started to smile himself, but his head gave a twinge of pain and he winced instead.

'I got him!' said Amy, remembering. 'I scratched him on the face.' She held up a hand and examined her fingernails.

Supt Buijs stepped over and held Amy's wrist steady as he had a close look. 'Right. Try not to touch anything with that hand. Hang on and I'll get an evidence bag.' He went to the car and came back with a white paper bag which he placed over Amy's hand. 'We'll get a sample of that at the hospital too,' he said. 'Um, he didn't ... you know?'

'No, nothing like that. Once he'd tied us up, he left. I think.' A dull throb in her temple started up again where Garrett hit her.

'And you definitely saw it was Garrett?'

'I did,' answered Scott. 'And I saw him hit Amy.'

'Right. Well, you both need to be checked out. Sounds like you might have concussion. Amy, could you ride with us please?'

'Yeah, sure,' replied Amy. She waved her bagged hand at Rex and Scott like a sock puppet and was led to the police car as a ripple of thunder rumbled across the sky in the distance.

Grandad came over to Scott and Rex. 'You alright, Scott?'

'Yeah, I think so,' replied Scott. 'Hungry though.'

Grandad chuckled. 'I'm not surprised, but you might have to wait a bit longer while the doc checks you out, okay?'

Scott nodded, and instantly regretted moving his head.

'Come on then, we're following the police to the hospital.'

Later that evening, everyone was at the hotel. Scott's dad couldn't go out in the Saint Helena because of the violent storm rolling in from the ocean, so he agreed with Scott that a giant-sized meal would be the best medicine for a hungry sore head. Amy's parents arrived with Amy soon after at her insistence. Even Penelope was there. She wanted to thank Rex and Grandad in person, so once she was cleared from hospital, she was brought to the hotel by the same policemen that helped rescue her. The police showed her to the meeting room where Rex, Amy and Scott were giving statements to Supt Whitmore.

'Come in,' said the Superintendent. 'I can take your statement now if you like. Would you like an adult with you?'

'No. Thank you,' said Penelope. 'But can everyone else stay?'

'Of course, of course.'

Scott pulled a seat back for Penelope to sit at the large shiny table with them.

'Whenever you're ready, Penelope. Take your time.' Supt Whitmore had a pen at the ready.

Penelope looked around at everyone at the table as though she never imagined she would be sitting with these three, in the same situation, in such a lovely room. Scott was absent mindedly rubbing the back of his head. Rex and Amy waited passively, some strips of adhesive tapes holding a cut together on the side of Amy's forehead.

'First, I want to thank all of you. I don't know what would have happened if you hadn't seen me.'

Rex, Scott and Amy smiled encouragingly. Amy leaned forward and filled a glass of water and pushed it across the table to Penelope.

Penelope gave a nervous smile and went on.

'I was out delivering promotional stuff. You know, junk mail? A car pulled up and Mr Garrett got out. He said he had a job for me. I told him I wasn't interested and turned away. That's when he pulled something over my head. My arms were trapped. Then he lifted me up and threw me in his car. I struggled but I couldn't reach the knots on the bag. I tried to kick the window out but all I did was stir up the dust in the bag ... I started having trouble breathing. My inhaler was still in the bag with the pamphlets, not that I could have used it anyway. I told Garrett I needed it. He just told me to shut up. After a while the car stopped, and he dragged me out and carried me somewhere that smelled of cats and threw me down. Next thing I hear is Amy, but I was too weak to call out very loud. Then someone fell on me, and I heard Scott tackling Garrett ... there was a thump, and everything went quiet. Garrett must have been tying you two up.' She looked at Scott and Amy in turn. 'Everything was quiet for a while then, but eventually I heard Scott and Amy stirring. We tried to undo the knots, but couldn't do anything one handed, so we just had to wait. Ages later we heard Rex banging on the door, and then ... well, you know the rest.'

Supt Whitmore took another minute to finish writing. He put the pen down and looked up. 'Thank you, Penelope. We'll get this typed up for you and you can come into the station any time in the next few days to sign it.' He became serious. 'Now, you four, I can't stress this enough. We still haven't found Garrett, and there's no telling what he will do next. We believe he has weapons, and we know he's already used them. Please. Don't leave the hotel. You are far safer here with all the security cameras than anywhere else in town. Understood?'

They all nodded.

'Good.' He turned to Penelope. 'Right then, Penelope. Mrs McGregor has agreed to take care of you for the time being.' Rex, Scott and Amy all looked up at this, wondering what was going on.

Supt Whitmore smiled and said to Penelope, 'Shall I tell them or ...'

'No, let me,' said Penelope.

'Alright then. I'll let you four catch up, and I'll see you all in the next few days.' He stood from the table and left the room, closing the door behind him.

'You're staying here?' asked Scott.

Penelope nodded. A sad look came over her face. 'The police rang my foster parents. They hadn't even noticed I was missing.' She shook her head in disbelief.

Amy was indignant. 'How can they not know you were missing? What kind of people are they? Wait ... what?' Amy paused. 'You said, foster parents?'

Penelope nodded slowly. 'My real parents died when I was six. I went to live with my grandma, but she had cancer and, well ... I ended up in the foster system.'

'I'm so sorry,' said Amy. 'I had no idea, and I've been ...' Amy looked ashamed and sympathetic all at once.

'It's alright, really,' said Penelope. 'I'm kind of used to it.'

Rex asked, 'They really didn't notice you were gone?'

'No, well you see, I have nine foster brothers and sisters. I think they do it for the money and leave us kids to fend for ourselves most of the time. That's why I was out delivering; for money to buy books. Anyway, it suits me that they leave me alone. Some of the other foster parents I've had haven't been so ... hands-off, shall we say. The police were so furious with my parents they reported them. I have no other relatives, so the police said they knew of someone else in town who might be able to take me in. So ...'

'Us?' asked Rex.

'No, not you.' Penelope smiled. 'I'm not sure you'd like me as a sister. Your mum said I could stay here while everything is sorted out.'

There was a knock at the door. Sylvie poked her head in. 'We're having dinner soon, in the first floor dining room. Meet you there in a few minutes?'

'Great, I'm starving,' said Scott. He was out of his seat and through the door before it swung closed again.

'Come on,' said Rex to Penelope. 'We'll show you around.'

He let Penelope go out the door before him. Amy held him back, and whispered, 'We're not showing her everything are we?'

Rex glanced at Penelope to make sure she hadn't heard and shook his head. Amy seemed relieved and let go of his arm. She scooted forward to walk with Penelope.

'It's up the stairs,' she said, leading the way. 'Come on.'

CHAPTER 33

When they entered the room Penelope stopped for a moment to take it all in. Rex nearly bumped into her.

'What's up?' he asked.

'Nothing, I ... I just didn't expect a dining room to be this big,' said Penelope.

'Yeah, well ... dining room, slash function room,' replied Rex, matter-of-factly. 'But yeah, it is big.'

Penelope took in the size of the room. It was tall, with ornate gilded mouldings that extended around the entire room, framing frescos of individual scenes high up in the centre of each wall. At each end of the room were large picture windows with views of the trees on the hill above the hotel at one end, and a view over the point at the other. The storm had come in with distant bursts of lighting and was showering the window with rain. She lowered her gaze to the table. It was long and covered with plates, cutlery and glassware, all lined up like a royal banquet. To the side was a buffet, with steaming bain-maries holding delicious looking and smelling food. Penelope had never seen anything like it.

'Do you do this often?' she asked Rex.

'What? No. No way. The guest dining room was nearly booked out, so Antonio set us up in here. This is actually the first time we're using it.' Rex looked around himself. Amy's parents were seated, chatting to Scott's dad over plates of steaming *boeuf bourguignon, cassoulet* and a bowl of soup with a grilled cheese crouton floating on top. Scott was still loading his plate up with roast beef and potatoes.

Sylvie saw them and came over. 'Welcome, Penelope. Come and get something to eat. I'll show you what we have.' She led Penelope away to the buffet and handed her a plate.

'Do you think she'll be your sister?' Amy nudged Rex in the ribs with a cheeky grin.

'What? No way.' Rex paused, letting the thought sink in. 'Cripes, I hope not.'

Amy laughed. 'I'm kidding. Come on, I'm starving. I only had a sandwich at the hospital, and it was *awful.*' She took Rex by the arm, and they went over to the buffet.

Thirty minutes later, everyone was seated and almost finished their meal. Scott was leaning back in his seat rubbing his belly from eating too much. Seated around the table was Charlie, also leaning back and rubbing his belly, Amy's mum and dad, Roy and Sylvie with Penelope and Vivienne, Mrs Reynard chatting to Mrs Mansfield and Miss Lally, Amy beside Rex, and Grandad talking quietly with Beryl while slipping an occasional small scrap to a grateful Tom under the table. Vivienne gazed over at Rex sitting with Amy and smiled. Rex returned the smile, remembering their last conversation. One of the wait staff came in to clear plates and top up everyone's wine.

'Rex?' asked Amy. Rex turned to her. 'Who is looking after all the security cameras? I mean, everybody is here. So, who's keeping a look out?'

'Grandad told me he's set all the perimeter cameras to alert his phone if there's any movement. And he set the camera up again down at the pier entrance. Garrett would have to be nuts if he thinks he can get in here.'

'Yeah, that's what worries me. Garrett clearly *is* nuts, and the police don't seem to be able to find him.'

'That's why we're here. We have something better.'

'What?'

Rex motioned for her to look at the end of the table. 'Not what, who. We have Grandad.'

'What do you mean?'

'Well, have you noticed that the police always seem to seek him out? That they let him do things that nobody else seems to be able to get away with? I mean, walking into the police station with a live hand grenade and not being locked up instantly has got to be some kind of superpower, don't you think?'

Amy reached up to the tape on her head and lightly scratched around the area, thinking. 'Yeah, and where does he get all this technical gear from anyway? I've looked some of it up on the internet and it is *seriously* serious stuff.'

Rex nodded. 'I think he's got a lot more contacts with his old forces buddies than he lets on. In fact,'—Rex reached over to gently take Amy's hand away from her face to stop her scratching—'it wouldn't surprise me if he knew about this whole thing.'

'Yeah, he never batted an eyelid when we gave him that hand grenade,' said Amy.

'Shhh,' said Rex. Grandad was standing up with a glass in his hand. He rang the side of it with a spoon. Everyone fell silent. He replaced the glass on the table and spread his hands out wide.

'Well, what can I say? One hell of a day, eh?' A murmur of agreement replied.

'Everyone here, in one way or another, has helped us today. We know for sure that the recent unfortunate events are the work of one man, and finally ... finally, the police are actively searching for him. We know they do their best, but sometimes it takes people like us to notice things that are not right, to try to correct them, and to persevere in the face of adversity.' Grandad looked around the room, pausing his gaze on Rex, Amy and Scott. 'On a happier note, our newest investor'—Grandad glanced at Rex and gave him a wink—'has pulled off an extremely canny acquisition, adding the Scales pub to the hotels assets.' Grandad picked up his glass. Everybody at the table reached for their own glasses.

'To our friends and family!' He raised his glass.

The sound of glasses touching others rang around the table as everybody toasted with those nearest to them. Grandad took his seat again as another waiter entered the room carrying a phone. He approached Grandad and whispered in his ear. Grandad took the phone and answered.

Rex sensed something was wrong and sure enough, Grandad stood, no longer looking jovial and relaxed. He motioned for everyone to be quiet while he listened. A few moments later he took the phone from his ear and ended the call.

'That was Garrett. It seems he hasn't given up after all. He demanded we all leave immediately — something we most certainly will *not* do. He said he's arranged a demonstration to interrupt our lovely dinner.' Grandad looked up through the windows looking out over the hill, narrowing his eyes to peer into the dark.

'It might be wise for us to vacate this room.'

Rex whipped his head around to look out the window just in time to see a streak of flame arc across from the hill to the old unrenovated buildings at the back of the hotel. Flames burst over the roof of the structure and plumed towards the stormy sky. If not for the steady rain, the flames would have spread and consumed the roof, but the fuel was quickly diluted, and the flames petered out to darkness again.

Then there was a CRACK! A glass on the table shattered followed by the whine of a bullet spinning off the surface of the table. Rex looked to the huge picture window and saw a small bullet hole.

Grandad roared, 'Everybody out! NOW!'

Seats were thrown backwards as everyone went for the door. Grandad made sure everyone was out before following them out and closing the door. 'Rex, Scott, Amy, get to the security room and keep watch. I'll be there shortly. Roy? Better get the guests in the dining room into the conference room, they'll be safest there. We'll get the rest later when we figure out what he's up to.' Everyone started moving down the stairs, Rex, Amy and Scott in the lead. Tom bolted for the door and pushed his way outside. They made it to the security room in less than a minute. Once inside, they drew seats up to the desk and wriggled mouses to bring the monitors to life. They scanned the walls covered with scenes of the hotel. The external views lit by infrared light showed nothing in the grainy images.

'Is there a master switch for lights somewhere?' asked Amy.

Rex searched the console. 'Got it!' He jabbed a button with his finger. All the monitors burst into colour but still, there was nobody outside.

'He must be up the hill,' said Scott. 'That's the only way he could have known we were having dinner.'

Rex found the control for the camera on the tower of the hotel and manipulated the joystick to turn the camera toward the hill, scanning it for signs of Garrett.

'There!' said Amy. 'Back a bit ... there.' There was someone moving across the face of the hill, heading around towards the gates.

Scott peered at the monitor, craning his neck forward and squinting. 'What's he got? It looks like ...'

'A bike wheel,' said Rex.

'What the hell is he going to do with that? I told you he was nuts,' said Amy.

Rex panned the camera along, following Garrett's progress. He disappeared from view behind some trees, but Rex kept panning, hopeful Garrett would reappear on the other side. He didn't. The trees cleared a little and were replaced by a power pole. A large metal pipe was clamped to the side of the pole from the ground to the top where it sprouting thick cables that attached to overhead lines stretching away from the hotel back into town.

'He's going for the power,' said Rex.

A shower of sparks burst out on the wires near the pole. Everything on the outside monitors went dark, back to showing grainy night vision scenes. The internal monitors showed emergency lights casting feeble light.

'How come this all works still?' asked Scott.

'All the security stuff is backed up with batteries,' said Rex.

The door behind them beeped and opened. It was Grandad.

'Right, you three, grab torches. This power is only going to last about ten minutes. After that we'll be blind. Go to the conference room with the others,' directed Grandad. He went to a large metal cabinet in the back corner of the room.

'What are you going to do?' asked Rex. Grandad didn't seem like he was coming with them.

Grandad opened the cabinet door and pulled out a helmet with high-tech looking optics on top and a shimmery visor. 'I'm going to try and get the power back on. Then I'm going to stop Garrett.'

'Garrett's done something to the power line. Up the top of the pole,' said Amy.

'And I think there's another way to get power,' said Rex.

'If you go out there, we'll be sitting ducks,' said Scott, then added, 'Can I come?'

Grandad smiled momentarily. 'No, I don't think so. Charlie would never forgive me.' He looked around at the three, considering.

After a moment, he said, 'You don't happen to know what 'Trompe' is, by any chance? Some sort of power source? There's something on the switchboard marked 'Trompe Power".

'Yes!' said Rex. 'That's what I'm telling you. We found it. It powers a generator, but we couldn't get the door open.'

'Right then.' Grandad turned back to the cabinet and pulled out some two-way radios. They looked much more professional that the ones Rex had. He handed one to each of them. 'Keep these with you at all times.' He went back in the cabinet and pulled out some torches. 'These are very powerful, so don't look into the beam. You can dial back the power with these buttons.' He held one up and demonstrated before handing them over.

'Let's go, then. Show me this generator.'

CHAPTER 34

Rex led the way to the kitchen with Grandad, Amy and Scott following close behind.

They went in through the cool room, through the heavy door behind and made their way to the lift. Even Scott didn't hesitate to jump in the first car that came down. They followed the water pipes again to the trompe room pressure door and Scott pulled the lever to slide the door aside. They went through and Scott closed the door behind them.

Grandad paused a second, playing his torch over the huge sphere of the trompe. 'I've heard rumors, but I never thought it was true,' he said to himself.

'Over here,' called Rex. Grandad came over to the wall where high pressure air was distributed out by the branching tubes. Rex tugged again on the valve handle for the other pressure door. 'I can't budge it.'

Grandad gave it an experimental heave, but it didn't move for him either. 'Looks like it might have rusted a bit.' He turned and started playing his torch around the floor, looking under the Trompe sphere. 'There! Get me that bit of pipe.' He pointed to a metre long length of iron pipe that had rolled under the sphere. Scott dived under the sphere between the heavy steel posts that held it up. When his body could go no further, he reached under and dragged out the pipe, poking it out for Grandad to grab. Amy helped Scott up while Grandad went back to the valve. He first tapped the sides of the valve with the heavy pipe, then slid it over the handle and used the extra length as a lever to slowly open the valve. There was a soft hiss as the generator door reached pressure. Amy crossed to the generator room door and pulled the handle. The door slid open and they all went through.

Inside was a large cylindrical machine mounted on a heavy cast-iron base. An old, enameled sign with the words 'Alternator Running' hung from the roof above it next to a bare, red coloured globe. Rex was reminded of a steam museum exhibit. Thick cables came out of a box at one end of the machine and curved up to a steel cable duct that went out through a hole in the wall. At the

193

end closest to the trompe, there was a circular array of stubby cylinders capped with domes arranged around the central axis of the generator. A flexible steel-cased hose led from the centre of each dome to join up with the air pipe from the trompe. Where the pipe came out of the wall, there was a gauge and a valve marked 'Engine Air'. Grandad reached up and slowly pulled the lever of the valve.

There was a hiss as the air lines filled. The smaller cylinders started making little mechanical hissing sounds. The sound of something spinning up to speed could be heard, and the light above the machine glowed into life casting red light around the room, building in intensity. The overhead fluorescent tube lights flashed and blinked into life. All four of their faces broke into smiles. The door keypad on the opposite side of the room gave a loud beep and Rex rushed to try the door. It was locked.

Rex, Amy, Scott and Grandad crowded around the door. The keypad had an old, segmented vacuum fluorescent display that read 'Enter Code'.

Grandad asked, 'What's the key?'

Rex, Scott and Amy said the same thing at once: 'Perseverance!'

Rex followed the little letters on the keypad and punched in the equivalent numbers.

The display went blank and beeped, returning to display 'Enter Code'.

'Wait, let me try something else,' said Rex.

He started punching in numbers that, to the others, seemed totally random. He hit the hash key. The red light turned green, and the door lock clicked.

'What was that?' asked Grandad.

'It was 'Perseverance', but I used the same cipher Limbick used to encode his diary.'

'Huh! Well done,' said Grandad. 'In we go then.'

They moved into the next room through a heavy door that closed solidly behind them. The room was brightly lit, with an ancient looking switchboard against one wall and, incongruously, a modern looking panel with a dozen of what looked like automatic teller machines with the display replaced by red and green buttons and a crank handle at the bottom. They were all sticking out from the cabinet. The old switch board had an angled desk with knobs all over it, and above on the vertical panel were big round meters and dangerous looking knife switches that Rex had only seen before in cartoons. On the wall behind them was a coat rack with full length rubber suits hanging from them, and a shelf with thick rubber gloves.

'What are the suits for?' asked Amy.

'No idea,' said Rex. 'But I've seen these before.' He pointed to the modern cabinets. 'In a movie. They're circuit breakers.'

Scott moved along the panel reading the labels above each one. 'They're all in Russian. Who built this place? Here, this one! It's in English — 'Homestead'.'

'Good!' said Grandad. 'I'll go back to the hotel and turn on the trompe switch. Are you alright to sort that out Rex?'

'Yep, go for it.'

'I'll let you know when I'm there,' said Grandad, waggling his two-way radio. 'Stay in touch.' He went back out the door to the generator.

'What do we do now?' asked Scott.

'We need to get these units wound back in,' said Amy. 'They were probably drawn out to make sure they didn't clash with the mains supply.'

'Since when did you become an electrical engineer?' asked Scott, impressed, nonetheless.

'Dad works at the mine, he showed me once.'

Amy grabbed the crank handle and gave the panel a push. It slid in a short way, then she started winding the handle. The whole unit started moving slowly into the cabinet. When it was flush with the faceplate of the cabinet, Rex reached up and pressed the 'Close' button. Nothing happened.

'You need to arm the spring first.' Amy teased a handle from the face of the unit and stood back. 'Pull that down until you hear a loud clunk. Then it's armed.'

Rex grabbed the handle and pulled down. The handle was stiff and clicked several times with each pull. After nine pulls, there was a loud clunk and an indicator on the panel turned yellow.

'That's it,' said Amy. 'Now press the 'Close' button.'

Rex used his thumb to press down hard on the big green button. There was another loud clunk and a green indicator marked 'Open' turned bright red.

'What now?' asked Rex.

'Now we wait for Grandad.'

Scott started winding the next circuit breaker into its panel. 'Come on, we might as well get these powered up as well.'

Rex and Amy both moved to circuit breakers and started winding them in.

'We'll arm them, but don't switch them on yet,' said Amy.

After a few minutes of winding and pumping the charge handles, all the breakers were ready to be closed.

'We don't know what these things do'—said Amy—'but we're here to activate the base, aren't we?'

'Exactly,' agreed Rex. 'Here goes.' He thumbed the next breaker's close button in the line. Nothing seemed to happen.

Amy pressed the next one. Again nothing. They moved down the line closing each breaker, wondering what function the strange characters on the labels described.

'Last one,' said Scott. He reached up and thumbed the green button.

A loud klaxon sounded making them all jump with fright. A bright red light set into the top of the old control panel started flashing.

'Arrrgh! Let's get out of here!' Scott shouted over the noise.

Amy crossed over to the old panel and pressed down on a knob. The flashing red light stopped, and the room fell silent.

'Or ... we could just turn the alarm off,' said Amy.

'What was that?' asked Rex.

'Dunno,' said Amy. 'The panel just says 'Power'. We turned it back on, so it could just be letting everyone know?'

'Well, hopefully not everyone,' said Rex.

The radio gave a short burst of static. It was Grandad on the radio.

'The power is back on. Well done you three. Very well done. No sign of Garrett yet. Hopefully we've scared him off. Come back upstairs when you're ready.'

Rex keyed the radio and replied, 'Will do. See you soon.' He clipped the radio back onto his jeans.

'Come on,' he said, and started heading to the generator door.

'Hang on,' said Scott. 'Look. There might be a quicker way.' He pointed to another door in the control room. There was a list on it under the heading 'Access to:'. The first thing listed underneath was 'Homestead'.

'Well spotted,' said Rex. 'Let's go.'

CHAPTER 35

A bare concrete corridor led away from the electrical room behind them.

Scott pointed. 'Down there. A lift.'

They ignored the other doors leading off from the corridor and went straight to the lift. The doors were not like normal lift doors. There was a short leather strap attached near the lip of the upper door and above it a small glass window with wire embedded in it. Next to the strap, a handle that looked like it matched up to a recess in the top of the doorframe.

'They must open vertically,' said Amy.

Rex pushed up on the handle, but the doors didn't open, they just moved in and out slightly.

'Hang on,' said Scott. He went to the side of the lift and pressed an unmarked button.

From the lift well came the sound of a powerful electric motor starting. The doors moved outwards a little with the pressure of the lift approaching. It seemed like ages until light could be seen rising through the window, then the motor wound down and clunked to a stop. Rex shoved on the handle again and nearly toppled into the lift well as the counter-weighted doors slid open; the lower door going into the gap between the lift and the floor, the upper one sliding up leaving just the leather strap to re-close it.

It was a big lift. The floor had slabs of scarred and scratched wood covering it, and the rear wall was missing allowing the lift to be entered from both sides. They stepped inside and found the control panel on the side wall with German writing on it. Above it was an enameled white sign with a bright red border — *Aufzug im Brandfall nicht benutzen.* Small, black chunky buttons spaced out horizontally, numbered zero to five gave no indication of what floor they were on.

Scott pressed the button marked '5'. It stayed pressed in and nothing happened. Rex reached up and grabbed the leather strap, pulling it down to close the doors. As soon as they were closed, the lift motor whined up to speed and the lift started descending. Like the paternoster, exposed concrete walls slowly moved upwards.

'Had to be the wrong way, didn't it,' said Scott rolling his eyes.

They waited patiently until the lift reached the lowest floor and the motor slowed to a stop. Rex slid the doors open and they stepped out into a wide corridor that ran past the lift. It was lit by caged fluorescent tubes, some of them blinking. A pair of steel rails was set into the floor. To the right of them on the opposite side of the corridor was a door with 'DC Power Switchboard' in black letters.

'Hey look,' said Rex. 'There might be more breakers in there. Let's check it out.'

Scott pulled the leather strap to close the lift door and joined Rex and Amy at the door. Rex tried the same code he used for the other electrical room. The door beeped and clicked.

'It worked!' Rex pushed the door open.

They walked into a dark, warm room that hummed with electricity. On one side of the room was another old switchboard, a sign on top said *DC Distribution*. Opposite, large steel cages with huge octopus shaped glass globes emitted a strange bluish-purple light. Thick wires running from somewhere behind the switchboard attached to the ends of steel rods sticking out of odd-shaped glass tubes that attached to the bottom of the globes. Inside, dancing arcs of light fired from the rods to pools of silvery liquid at the bottom of the globes.

'Why do I feel like I need sunglasses?' asked Amy. She shielded her eyes from the arc light.

They turned to the switchboard.

Scott leaned forward read the labels above some of the big knife switches. 'Hg rectifiers ... Sleeping Beauties ... Degaussing Loop,' he shook his head. 'What kind of a base is this exactly?'

'Not sure,' replied Rex. 'But my eyes are starting to hurt. Let's get out of here.'

They exited the room and continued down the corridor.

'Do you think we can train the map-bot to enter that code in?' asked Scott.

Rex laughed. 'Ha ha, yeah. We'll attach a blown-up rubber glove to an arm and move it backwards and forwards to press buttons.'

'Didn't some guy called Malcolm do that in a movie?' asked Amy.

'Yeah, the one about trams and robbing banks,' said Rex.

They reached the end of the corridor where it widened out to accommodate some lockers. The rail tracks went under two big doors marked with huge letters *L.D.*

Rex rattled the locked doors. In each door there was a window like the one in the lift door. Rex peered through trying to see beyond, but it was completely dark. Scott went over to the lockers and started opening them. 'Nothing in that one,' he called out, and went to check the next one. Rex went to the keypad mounted on the door frame and entered in the same numbers as earlier. The light went green, and latches clicked open. Rex pushed the doors open. The light spilling from the corridor showed a wide concrete area stretching away before them into gloomy darkness. The steel rail tracks from the corridor led away to join other tracks. Rex and Amy moved cautiously through the doors. Something felt different. There was the salty smell of seawater, and it was much colder. The sounds of Scott opening and closing lockers echoed around. Amy found a heavy metal switch beside the door and pushed the lever up. There was a clunk in the distance as a light high above them gave a flash of light before going dim again, followed by another clunk as a light beside it burst into life, followed by another, and another all in a line. Lights continued to fire into life in turn, slowly building in intensity until the whole area was brilliantly lit. Rex and Amy stood there gaping at the sight.

Scott finished banging about. 'Just empty boxes in the lockers,' he said as he joined them. He too stopped, his jaw falling open.

'Holy ...' said Rex.

'How did ... what?' said Amy.

'What the ...' said Scott. 'If you think I can fly that thing, you're crazy.'

'Where did it come from?' asked Amy.

'And how did a sea plane end up in a secret base under a hotel?' said Rex.

The three of them stood taking in the enormous space. It must have been more than three hundred metres long and about half as wide. There was a pit running up most of the length of the floor with cleats and bollards spaced along its edge. The sounds of water lapping against the edges of the pit and floats of the plane drew them closer. To the left, a wheeled crane sat on tracks running parallel to the dock. A boom on the crane stretched over and down into the dark, undulating water. From the base of the crane, an articulated arm plugged into a port in the floor of the dock where a steel mesh section of floor hinged open. To the right, the plane was tethered to the side of the dock by long steel lattice beams that held it in a fixed position away from the edge. On the side and wings of the plane, a large red spot with a white outline was painted.

'I think we've found the base,' said Rex, quietly.

'You can say that again,' said Amy.

'No wonder we have to keep it secret,' said Scott. 'That's a Japanese war plane. It looks old, too. Like the real thing.' He started to walk towards the plane to look closer.

In the corridor behind them, the sound of the lift starting up made them turn around and run back to it. Through the small window in the door, the light of the lift disappeared up the lift shaft.

'No one else knows about this place,' said Amy. 'It must be ...'

'Garrett!' finished Rex and Scott.

'He can't find out about this,' said Amy, frantically. 'Get the doors!'

They ran back to the end of the corridor. Amy pulled the loading dock light switch lever and joined Scott and Rex to close the wide double doors, swinging them back into place where they locked shut.

'We can hide the doors with the lockers,' Scott said.

'Good idea,' replied Rex. The three dragged, shoved and pushed all the lockers to cover the door space completely.

'What about the tracks?' asked Amy. 'If Garrett sees them, he'll know they must go somewhere.'

'Boxes!' said Scott. He opened one of the lockers, pulled out some empty boxes and stacked them so they leaned against the lockers, covering the tracks.

They all stepped back.

'Hopefully he'll think it's a dead end,' said Scott.

'Looks good,' said Rex.

Behind them, the sound of the lift motor stopped. They walked quickly back to the lift, listening for more activity. They heard the lift door opening and slamming shut again. The lift motor started again.

'He's coming,' said Amy.

'We need to find some stairs,' said Rex. 'We'll lure him away from that end.' Rex indicated the lockers and boxes. 'Come on!'

CHAPTER 36

They ran down the corridor, away from the lockers. At the end, the corridor made a turn with more doors on the left and right. The first door they came to was a large double door. They pushed both sides open easily, swinging them back to reveal darkness.

They all flicked on torches revealing rows and rows of high shelves stretching into the distance, most of them empty but for a few boxes left behind when the place was cleared out.

'It's a warehouse. There's got to be another door in here,' said Rex. 'We can lure him in and go out the other end. Amy, see if you can find a light switch for the corridor.' Rex grabbed a box from a shelf and ripped off some cardboard. He folded it up and wedged it under one of the double doors, leaving the other one to close slowly by itself.

The lift motor whined to a halt. The door clattered open. Garrett stepped out of the lift. He spotted Amy and started towards her. Amy found the switch and plunged the corridor into darkness. While Garrett fumbled in the darkness, Amy ducked back into the warehouse.

'Garrett's coming. He saw me,' said Amy.

'Let's go,' whispered Scott.

They walked quickly but quietly through the rows of shelves, heading away from the wedged open door.

About halfway along the rows, they heard a noise and spun around. It was just the door finally closing against the jam, but before they could relax a voice called out.

'I know you're in here,' Garrett yelled into the darkness. 'You're not getting away from me this time!'

Rex, Scott and Amy turned and ran, headed for the end of the aisle. Overhead lights flickered into life, flooding the shelves with light.

'Now I've got you, you little bastards!'

BANG!

A cardboard box on a shelf next to Amy jumped and tumbled to the floor.

Amy squealed and ducked.

Rex turned and aimed his powerful torch directly at Garrett's face, now adorned with four deep scratches running from temple to chin. He recoiled from the light, temporarily blinded.

'This way!' said Rex. They darted between two rows of shelves to get out of the line of fire.

'The guy's a raving looney,' said Scott, as they reached the end of the row and headed for a door near the back corner.

Another BANG! A bullet pinged off a nearby shelf and ricocheted away.

They made it to the door and shoved through. Scott slapped a light switch on his way through the door, killing the lights in the warehouse, then slammed the door shut again.

Behind the door, another BANG followed by Garrett yelling, 'Come back here!'

'Not bloody likely,' said Scott to himself as he ran after Rex and Amy.

They burst through another door.

'How many corridors does this place have?' asked Amy.

'Too many,' said Rex. 'And I didn't bring the map.' He looked left and right. 'I think we're close to the paternoster. This way!'

They ran up the corridor following Rex.

'I hope you're right. I can hear him coming,' said Scott.

Just as the door from the warehouse opened, Rex shouted, 'In here!'

He slid a door open and sure enough at the back of a room past a maze of crates and timber, the lift stood vacant and lifeless.

BANG! They jumped through the door just as a chip of concrete on the wall exploded above them.

They darted around crates and long lengths of wood strewn around the room, trying to find a path to the lift. A sign above the control lever said, *Level -5*.

'I don't like to mention it, but these crates have 'Explosives' written on them!' said Scott with a worried voice. 'If he lets off another one, we'll all get blown out the top of the hill.'

They made it to the ascending side of the lift. Scott and Amy jumped in and grabbed the hand holds while Rex turned the lever to 'running' and jumped in after them. The car started ascending slowly. They saw Garrett storm through the door just as the lift went up and safely away.

Rex whispered instructions. 'We'll go up a few floors then get off and go back down again, as quietly as we can. He'll think we're going all the way up.'

The car approached the next floor. Scott made to get off, but Amy held him back. 'Not this one ... too soon,' she whispered.

The floor sunk out of sight as they heard Garrett clamber into another car below them.

The floors scrolled past them slowly but steadily.

At one floor Rex whispered, 'Look, the Trompe floor. We can't let him off there or he might find his way into the hotel.' Their torches showed the big pipes going through the wall to the corridor. 'He's two cars below, so we need to go up higher.'

Rex watched the floors go past intently, vaguely remembering the sequence before the long ascension to the bunker.

Rex mouthed *next floor* at Scott and Amy, and they readied themselves for a quiet exit. The floor came into view and they each got a foot ready to step off. Stepping soundlessly out of the car, they quickly went across to the downside and slipped into the next car.

They listened to see if Garrett heard them as his car slid past them unseen. They could hear him grumbling to himself in frustration.

After he'd passed Scott whispered, 'Did you know there were levels below zero?'

Rex nodded and whispered back, 'Yeah, but the map-bot didn't get that far yet. Probably couldn't get past the boxes.'

They arrived back at floor minus five and stepped off. Rex turned the lever to 'Stop' and the lift slowed to a halt, then quickly turned the lever to 'Out of service' so Garrett couldn't operate it.

Through the lift shaft they heard Garrett cursing. 'Little bastards, I'm coming for you!' A door slammed open and the sound of boots on metal stairs echoed down the shaft ... and from somewhere else.

'Uh oh,' said Amy. She swung her torch around to cast light into the corner of the room. 'I forgot about the stairs.'

'Let's go!' Rex yelled.

Rex and Amy used boxes like vaulting horses while Scott opted to get up on them and use them like steppingstones. In their haste, the long lengths of propped up wood started toppling like dominoes, clattering down around them and making the boxes even more difficult to negotiate. By the sound of the boots in the stairwell, Garrett was getting closer.

Scott leapt over the end of a length of wood to make it to the doorway but tripped and fell heavily, sprawling over the floor and rolling into the corridor. Rex and Amy caught up and hoisted him to his feet by his armpits, helping him along until he regained his balance. Behind them, boxes and wood were being thrown about as Garrett struggled through the room.

They made it to the door that led to the warehouse. Amy tugged on the handle, but it didn't open.

'Rex! The code, quick!' she said urgently.

Rex moved to the keypad and started entering numbers. Garrett burst out of the lift room and fired at them again. The bullet pinged off the steel doorframe and ricocheted away, whining as it spun further down the corridor.

'I've got you now!' Garrett yelled. He raised the rifle again, aiming more carefully this time.

Click!

Nothing happened. Garrett pulled back the bolt and the action latched open.

Empty.

'Ghaah!' He lurched towards the three waiting at the door.

Rex finished entering the code and the door unlocked. He yanked it open. They all dived inside to safety. Garrett threw the rifle towards them sliding it in between the door and the frame, jamming the door open.

Rex, Amy and Scott bolted as fast as they could towards the warehouse door, Scott favouring his ankle. He'd only just caught up to Rex and Amy after Rex had entered the code and opened the warehouse door.

'Not so fast, you little ...' Whatever Garrett said next was drowned out by another loud bang.

The three looked around. Garrett was in the corridor doorway aiming a pistol at them and reaching for the rifle on the floor.

'Run!' yelled Rex. 'Back to the lift!'

They ran towards the central aisle that led to the big doors at the other end of the warehouse.

Rex glanced behind them. 'He's jammed the door open again!'

He stopped to run back, but Amy grabbed him. 'No! Leave it! He'll catch you.'

Rex ran on behind Amy, Scott limping and half skipping ahead. Rex grabbed every box he ran past and flung it onto the floor behind, hoping to slow Garrett down. They had to get back to the lift before Garrett.

Garrett burst through the warehouse door. There was a crash and a bang as Garrett tripped over boxes. He went down, accidently firing a wild shot that hit the shelving, well wide of the three running up the main aisle. He recovered quickly and was in the main aisle behind them just as they came to the main doors. They made it through and headed for the lift, Garrett pounding through the warehouse behind them. He was getting closer.

The lift doors were still open. *Thank goodness*, thought Rex. They all dived into the lift, Scott rolling on the floor gripping his ankle. Amy stabbed at the leftmost button repeatedly as Garrett got closer and closer. Rex was exposed as he reached up to grab the leather strap. He hauled down on it.

Garrett got his arm through the gap and fired off a shot that hit the back wall of the lift well and embedded itself there. He stuck another arm in trying to grab at Rex, then pushed his face up to the gap. 'Here's Johnny!' Garrett roared, his face a scarred contorted snarl peering through the smoke from the shot.

Rex chopped Garrett's arm causing him to recoil in pain, and banged the doors closed on the hand holding the pistol. The pistol fell to the floor. Garrett howled, yanking his arm out and allowing the doors to close.

Immediately the lift started moving, locking the doors shut. Garrett raged on the other side. He thumped the doors, yelling incoherently.

The lift ascended away from him to safety. Rex and Amy slumped to the floor beside Scott, exhausted.

The echoing sounds of Garrett still howling and thumping the doors below decreased as the lift climbed higher, walls and doors scrolling past the two open sides.

Rex's ears were still recovering from the loud gunshot at close quarters. It was nearly a shout when he asked Amy 'Are you alright?' He coughed with the smoke from the gun.

Amy nodded and turned to Scott. Scott was untying his laces to remove his running shoe. 'I think it's alright,' he said, probing his ankle gingerly. 'It's not swelling up or anything, just a bit sore.'

The ringing in Rex's ears was subsiding as he rubbed his ear holes with fingers.

Garrett gave one last heavy thump on the doors and a roar of frustration, then went quiet.

'Do you think he'll come after us again?' he asked the other two.

'Yes, but he can only use this lift if we close the doors when we get out,' said Amy.

They arrived at another floor and slowed to a stop. Rex made to open the doors on the side they entered from, but they wouldn't open.

'Uh oh. Now what?' Rex looked around the edges of the door to see if there were any obstructions.

There was a clatter behind them. They all turned their heads to see the doors on the other side of the lift sliding apart into the ceiling and floor.

It was Grandad and Tom.

'Tom led me down here and I heard shots. Everyone alright?'

'We're fine,' replied Rex. 'Scott sprained his ankle,' he added, as Grandad looked at Scott.

Grandad nodded and stepped into the lift and picked up the handgun. He removed the magazine, pocketed it, then racked the slide, expertly catching the ejected live round in his hand.

'Do you know if he has any more firearms?' asked Grandad as he placed the pistol on the floor outside the lift.

'He has a rifle, but it will take him time to get it and reload,' said Rex.

'Where is he now?'

'He was trying to get into the lift down the bottom, but it sounds like he's gone.'

'The doors don't have keypad locks?'

'Yes, but the way we came they were only on the other side. There's nothing stopping him going back to some stairs, and he could jam the doors open to get back. That's how he nearly caught us.'

Amy and Rex stepped out of the lift into a small room lined with empty shelves. Scott hopped out while pulling his shoe back on.

'Where are we?' Amy asked.

'Just off the storeroom. It was too small for what we wanted so we built more storage racks in the main room just out there and forgot about this room.' Grandad indicated the door opposite the lift doors. 'I didn't notice there was a lift in here since it was blocked by shelves. But when I heard shots and shouting, I came in here and found it. It took me a while to take enough shelves down to get at the door.'

'Hey look at this,' said Rex. 'There's a control panel here.' The others came over to look.

'Looks like we can control everything the lift does,' said Grandad. He flicked a switch from 'Auto' to 'Manual Control'. 'It even tells you when someone is in it.' He pointed to a light marked 'Occupied' that was dim. Scott put his leg inside the lift and put weight on the floor. The light glowed brightly.

'Cool,' said Rex. 'If we can get Garrett back in the lift, we can trap him inside until the police come and get him.'

'But even if he does get in the lift, we can't make him close the doors,' said Amy.

Rex examined the panel. 'Yes, I think we can. Hang on ...' He turned a knob marked 'Doors' from 'Manual' to 'Close'. Beside them, the lift doors closed quickly. Rex turned the knob further to 'Open' and the doors slid open again. 'There's an 'Auto' setting as well. That must open the doors automatically at whatever floor the lift stops at.'

'We can't let Garrett get out on the generator floor,' said Amy. 'He'll cut the power again.'

'Right,' said Grandad. 'Close the doors and send the lift down again. We'll put the doors on 'Manual' at the bottom and hope Garrett gets in. When he does, we'll take control and bring the lift up. We just need him to get back in that lift.'

'Wait!' said Scott. He unclipped his two-way radio and set it down just inside the lift door.

'Good thinking,' said Grandad. 'If he's not too far away, he might come back to the lift. Send it down.'

Rex closed the doors and pressed the button marked '5'. The lift sank out of sight. Lights indicated the lift was travelling down and what floor it was at. It reached the bottom and Rex switched the doors to 'Manual'.

'Amy? Would you like to do the honors?' asked Grandad.

Amy unclipped her radio and held it up near her mouth. 'Help!' she said into the microphone. 'Help us! He's been shot! We give up! Help us!'

Scott placed his ear to the lift door. They waited.

After a few tense minutes, Scott shook his head. 'Nothing. He must be going back up the stairs.'

'Any suggestions?' asked Grandad.

'The speaking tubes?' Rex suggested. 'There might be some that connect down there.'

'There are,' said Grandad. 'Follow me.'

Grandad opened the door and ushered Rex, Amy and Scott out, locking the door from the outside.

CHAPTER 37

Grandad led them up to the ground floor to a door marked 'Utilities' and used his keycard to let them in. Inside was a short corridor with other doors leading off one side. He took them past one marked 'Electricity', another marked 'Water Control' and into a door marked 'Communications'. Inside, racks of modern equipment stood with blinking lights and whirring fans.

'This is where all the telephones and cameras are connected,' said Grandad. 'But we want the next room.' He went to the end of the room and squeezed through a gap between the last rack and the wall. The others followed and found Grandad using a key to unlock a door that was not marked. He reached inside, flicked a switch on with a loud click, and motioned for them to come inside.

The room was about three metres square lit by four naked bulbs, one on each of the walls. Below them, the walls were lined with thick speaking tubes rising from the floor, each with a flared ends facing into the room. Some were like the one Rex, Amy and Scott found in the service room with a selector for choosing what room they connected to. Fading labels marked the destinations.

'It's like a switchboard,' said Amy.

'It connects to everywhere in the base,' said Scott, reading some of the labels.

'Good,' said Grandad. 'You three see if you can locate Garrett and lure him back to the lift. I'll go back to the storeroom ready to bring him up when he gets in the lift.' He left the room leaving them to peer at labels.

They spread out and scanned up and down the rows of labels.

'Got it!' said Rex. 'Paternoster minus five to five.'

'And here's the warehouse,' said Scott. 'North, south, west and East.'

'Try them all,' said Amy.

Rex and Scott yanked out bungs and placed their ears to the openings. Every now and then, they'd turn the selector knob and listen again. It was Rex who found Garrett first. He waved at the others to get their attention. 'He's on the trompe floor,' whispered Rex. Amy motioned for him to replace the bug.

'Tell him you've got his gun now and you're coming to get him,' said Amy.

'What? He'll just run,' said Rex.

'No. No, he won't. He's not thinking right, and he thinks he's smarter than everyone else. He'll come looking for you.' Rex looked doubtful. 'Trust me. If it doesn't work, we'll tell him you've run out of bullets.'

Rex nodded and pulled out the bung again.

He put his mouth to the mouthpiece and shouted, 'Hey Garrett!' Rex turned his head to listen. 'He's stopped moving,' he whispered to Amy and Scott.

Again, he shouted, 'Hey Garrett! Not so good without your pistol are you! Now I'm the hunter, and you are my prey!'

'Bit melodramatic, mate?' whispered Scott. Rex nearly laughed out aloud and turned back to the mouthpiece.

Rex shouted into the mouthpiece like a kid playing chasie. 'Ready or not, here I come!'

There was a loud bang from the tube followed by, 'How do you like that, smart-alec? Think you can outrun me this time? THINK AGAIN!'

'Uh oh,' said Rex into the tube.

'Yeah, you better 'Uh Oh' ya little brat. I'm going to blow your brains out!'

Amy intervened, whispering. 'He took the bait! Switch floors to draw him down again.'

Rex turned the selector knob to minus one. 'You've got to catch me first boofhead!' Rex listened again. 'He's gone down the stairs,' he whispered, and selected the next floor down. 'Run, run, run, as fast as you can!' Rex taunted.

'Bastard!' yelled Garrett, thundering down the stairs.

Rex dialled the next floor. 'You can't catch me, I'm the guy who bought Scales for less than you were going to pay!' Another floor, and 'Come on beetroot brain, keep up!'

Amy scanned more labels, found the warehouse access corridor, and plucked the bung out.

Rex replaced his bung. 'He's at the bottom.'

Amy went into action. 'No don't close the door, Rex. Give the silly old git a chance!' She listened at the tube, then replaced the bung. 'He's coming. Over to you, Scott.'

Scott listened at the warehouse tube, turning the selector through each compass position. 'Got him,' he whispered. He turned to the tube and shouted, 'Come on, Rex! Stop taunting him and help me carry this gold to the lift.' He listened again and heard Garrett coming to the back door of the warehouse. He switched from North to South and again shouted into the tube. 'You'll never catch us alive, Garrett! Haa, ha ha ha haaaa!' He listened again, then replaced the bung. 'He fell for it. He's heading for the lift.'

Amy raised the two-way radio to her mouth. 'Quick you guys! Through the lift. He'll never know there's a door on the other side.' She lowered the radio. 'Uh oh. I forgot. There isn't a door on the other side down there.'

'Yeah, but he won't remember that,' said Rex. Amy bit her lower lip, hoping he was right.

Scott was listening to the warehouse tube again. 'I think he bought it. He's in the lift.'

The radio hissed to life. 'You little brats think you're clever, don't you! I'll see you soon ... What?' They heard the doors shut before Garrett cut the transmission.

'We got him!' Scott yelled.

'Come on, let's get down to the storeroom,' said Rex.

On their way back to the storeroom, Rex, Amy and Scott met the police coming in the main entrance. It was Supt Whitmore wearing a ballistic vest and helmet followed by two big policemen geared up with full-on battle armor and automatic rifles.

'Rex! We couldn't get through the gate until now. What's happening?' asked Supt Whitmore.

'Garrett attacked us and chased us three through the ... ah ... corridors of the hotel,' said Rex, not wanting to let on about the base beneath their feet.

Amy caught on. 'He was shooting at us, but we trapped him in a lift.'

'Where is he now?'

'We'll take you to him,' said Rex. 'Follow us.' They led the police down to the storeroom. Rex led them to the small storeroom door and knocked. Grandad opened the door a crack, peering through to see who was there. He motioned them all in and closed the door. Tom growled at the lift doors.

'Start the lift, Rex,' said Grandad. Rex hit the button marked '1' on the horizontal row of floor buttons. The lift whined into action.

The radio burst into life again. 'Right, you bastards! I'll shoot each of you and then I'm going to go through the entire hotel and shoot every last one of you. I'll save that bloody dog until last!'

'Charming,' said one of the policemen. He checked his rifle to make sure a round was chambered.

Rex smiled at Amy and Scott, happy that the police heard Garrett's threats. Amy smiled back and watched the lift door window. Suddenly her eyes opened wide as she realised everyone would see the lift coming up, not down. She looked at Rex, pleading for him to read her thoughts, but Rex just looked confused. Amy stepped closer to Rex and looked at the panel. She found what she hoped was there and flicked a switch marked 'Light'.

The radio came to life again. 'Think you're smart don'tcha! I've got a torch you know. I'm not scared of the dark, but you should be!'

Whitmore held out his hand to Rex indicating for him to hand over the radio. He took it and keyed the transmit button. 'Mr. Garrett, this is the police. We know you are armed. If you make one move, we will use deadly force to stop you.'

The lift motor slowed and stopped as the lift reached them. Amy turned the light on again.

Whitmore motioned everyone back and the two policemen took up positions on either side of the door. He looked through the window and saw Garrett's scarred face looking back, his eyes taking in the two heavily armed policemen.

'Move back from the door, put your weapon down and interlace your fingers behind your head.' Whitmore watched as Garrett complied. 'Now turn around. Remain still. Any move you make will be treated as an act of aggression.'

Whitmore watched Garrett slowly turn around, then motioned for Rex to open the door. The doors slid open and a burly policemen stepped in and slapped cuffs on one of Garrett's wrists and dragged him to the floor, pulling his other arm behind his back to secure him with the cuffs.

Garrett complained. 'Get off me! I'll bloody get you for this! I own this place. It's mine. Let me go so I can wring your necks!' He was hauled to his feet and marched out of the room by the policemen, cursing incoherently all the way. Tom followed, growling at Garrett.

'You'll want us to give statements again, I suppose,' said Rex to Supt Whitmore.

'All in due time, Rex,' he replied. 'Grandad will help you get your stories straight first. We wouldn't want people knowing any more than they need to, would we? I'll see you all tomorrow.' He gave a salute to them all and followed his officers with the prisoner.

CHAPTER 38

Grandad ushered the three out of the lift room and locked the door. As he handed Rex the key he said, 'You'll be needing this. Down there is your operation. I need to speak to the police and sort out the mains power. You three ...' He looked at each of them in turn. 'Well done. The base is in good hands. Let's keep it that way, hmmm?'

Rex, Amy and Scott broke out into grins as Grandad turned to go upstairs. He stopped and turned back. 'While I'm keeping the police busy, you might want to find how Garrett got in. I thought I saw something on the carpark camera.' He winked and left.

Each of the friends checked in with their parents to assure them they were alright. Strangely, emerging from a room where a psychotic killer had been arrested and dragged out wasn't questioned.

They met upstairs by the carpark lift. Amy pressed the call button, then thought the better of it. 'You know what? I think I've had enough of these things for one day. Let's take the stairs.'

They emerged from the stairwell into the carpark.

'Look!' Rex pointed to the back wall.

'Another lift door!' said Amy. 'That's how he got in.' They approached where the wall had been torn apart just enough to expose the call button and give access to the door.

'We'll need to cover this up before the police find it,' said Scott. He looked around for something large enough.

'In the sports cupboard. There's a tarp,' said Rex. They went to the cupboard and hauled out the tarp, again knocking over the tennis balls which bounced away into the carpark. 'Scott, grab that ladder. I'll get a hammer and nails.' They went into action, and soon had the tarp hanging over the hole Garrett smashed into the wall.

As they replaced the ladder and hammer, Amy asked, 'How did he know it was there, anyway?'

Rex thought back. 'I did catch Shifty Nick sneaking around down here one day.'

'He was probably casing the joint,' said Scott.

They headed back up the stairs, where they met Vivienne. 'Rexxy, there you are. Come upstairs to the dining room. Grandad's got some news for us all.'

Back in the dining room, the broken glass on the table had been cleared away and the room was crowded with family and guests. Grandad saw them come in, and again rang a glass to get everyone's attention.

'Ladies and gentlemen, if I could have your attention, please?' Everyone quietened to listen.

'First of all, everyone is safe and unharmed. The man who attacked the hotel tonight, Nelson Garrett, is in custody and in the face of overwhelming evidence, has already confessed to what he did. He will not be seeing the light of day for the rest of his miserable life.'

The room erupted in cheers and raised glasses. Grandad settled them down again.

'Particular thanks must be given to three young men and women who managed to trap Garrett after he made it into the hotel. And I must say'— Grandad turned to Rex, Amy and Scott—'that luring him into the air conditioning ducts was a stroke of genius.' He winked at them. 'Rex, Scott, Amy, the hotel is now safe, Scales is safe and now thanks to you three, the entire town of Lenzie Bay is safe!' More cheers erupted. 'Garrett is charged with numerous offences ...' He pulled a list out of his jacket pocket. 'Arms trafficking.' A murmur of surprise went around the room. 'The serious assaults on Mr Limbick and Mrs Birch — both of whom are recovering well — kidnapping, and murder. The police will also be investigating his real estate dealings.' He put the list away and picked up a glass. 'So please, raise your glasses ... Amy, Rex and Scott, we will always rest easy knowing you are looking out for us. Amy, Rex and Scott!' Everyone raised their glasses and toasted, while the three beamed at each other.

When the cheers and applause died down, Grandad called out. 'Please, help yourself to food and drink, and enjoy yourselves!'

The three friends were crowded as everyone came to shake hands and hug them.

Rex, Scott, Amy and Penelope were excused from school the next day. It was a Friday, so they had the whole weekend to recover from their ordeal. Yesterday's storm passed overnight giving way to a warm, sunny day. After a leisurely breakfast, they wandered about the hotel grounds and watched as the police combed the hill above the hotel to make sure Garrett hadn't left any nasty surprises. Penelope filled the three of them in about what Garrett was like, and Rex retold the story of how he managed to be kicked out of his last school. They arrived at the place where the lady of the lake threw her sword into the lawn. Rex ducked inside to get the sword and brought it out to them to demonstrate how it was held in place. He aimed the sword at a gap in the lawn and slowly lowered it down. The magnetic forces took over and pulled the sword from Rex's hands, pulling it deep into the grass.

'That is so cool,' said Penelope. She looked up at Rex. 'There never was any more treasure, was there? When you were talking in The Breakers?' Rex shook his head. 'No, I didn't think so. I made the mistake of telling Garrett, though.' Penelope looked worried. 'What if this is all my fault?'

'No. Garrett was already off his rocker before then. He threatened me after he killed the cook.'

Penelope accepted this with a nod. She looked at each of them. 'I never thought that helping Garrett would end up this way. I'm sorry for that.' She looked down at her feet.

Amy spoke to her, gently. 'Penny? I don't think any of us, no one, really, blames you for any of this.' A tear rolled down her face. 'I'm sorry I was so nasty to you.'

Rex and Scott looked at each other, surprised to hear Amy being nice to Penelope.

'Come on, then. Hug it out,' Scott said to them, motioning them to get together. Amy and Penelope both laughed and leaned in for an awkward hug.

'Right then, let's get lunch,' said Scott, clapping his hands together. 'I'm starving, and I have to help Dad on the boat tonight. Got to get some vittals in me.' He strode off towards the dining room, leaving the others to follow.

'Did you find new foster parents?' Amy asked Penelope as they ambled after Scott.

'Yeah, I think so,' she replied. 'You know Rex's mum's friend, Vivienne? We were talking last night. She had a rough childhood as well, apparently, so ...' She shrugged. 'She's going to think about it and let me know tomorrow.'

'Cool,' said Rex. 'I like Vivienne. She'd be great to live with.'

Scott stuck his head out of the dining room doors. 'Oi, you lot! Hurry up! There's roast pork and it's going fast!' He pulled his head in again.

'I really don't know where he puts it all,' said Amy.

Later, Rex went with Grandad into town to pick up some fish from Charlie, and fresh vegetables Mrs Reynard had picked from her own garden. On the drive back up to the hotel Rex was deep in thought. Grandad asked, 'Something on your mind?'

Rex wondered how much he should say to Grandad. He opted for a question instead.

'You know your way around guns, don't you, Grandad?'

Grandad nodded. 'Yep,' he said. 'You do remember I was in the services? Well, it comes with the territory.'

'Yeah, but'—Rex faltered—'you still have some?'

Grandad looked over at Rex, not sure where this was going. 'I do, yes.'

Rex pondered for a moment. 'You know about the base, right?'

Grandad smiled. 'I do, yes. But you're wondering how much I know?'

'Well, yeah,' said Rex.

'I know it's there. I know you've been charged with reactivating it.' This was news to Rex, who looked at Grandad in surprise. 'I knew about the door in the cool room, too, but I never could get through those gates. And, I know that what happens inside that base is not my job.' He checked to see if Rex understood what he meant. Rex looked confused. 'I don't know however, exactly what is *inside* the base ... other than what you showed me, of course. I reckon I could hazard a guess, but as I said. Not my job.'

Rex nodded his understanding. 'Do the police know? They never asked us for statements, and ... well ... it seemed like they didn't want to know.'

Grandad nodded. 'Some do, some don't. The same goes for a lot of people in this town. You met a few of the ones that do last night.' Grandad let that sink in for a bit.

Rex was taken aback. 'You mean Mrs Reynard ... and my teachers ... Scott's Dad?'

Grandad smiled.

'Why didn't you tell me? Why didn't anyone tell me?'

'For the same reason you haven't told Penelope.' Grandad turned to Rex. 'You haven't, have you?'

'No ... we don't really know her, but you know me.'

'Of course I know you, but I didn't know how you'd react, how you felt about what you've been asked to do ... It wasn't meant to be you that got that phone call, Rex.'

'You know about that?'

'Yes. I organised it, but it was supposed to go to our friend Superintendent Whitmore.' Grandad glanced at Rex. 'I bet that explains a few things.'

Rex's mind was reeling.

'Not really, no,' he said indignantly. 'I got kicked out of school! Was that you as well?'

'No, that was just coincidence, but we saw that you seemed interested in finding out more, so a decision was made to let you run with it. And as I said, I know you and I knew you'd be up for it, but others didn't. They needed to see you step up to the task and take it on. It had to be your decision.'

Rex lapsed into thought. The whole town knew about the base. Mr Limbick was testing him.

'Was Garrett in on it as well?'

'What? Oh, hell no! He was identified as a threat years ago. We even had Beryl Hoopell go work for him to keep an eye on him. We actually thought she'd turned on us at one stage, but she did what had to be done.'

Rex gaped. 'The library?'

'Yep. All part of the Excalibur network.' Grandad smiled at Rex. 'Didn't Limbick tell you that you'd have resources at your disposal? Anything you need, just ask.'

'Unbelievable,' said Rex.

Grandad chuckled. 'Yep. And that's the way we like it. There are bigger threats to us than Garrett, Rex. You've read Limbick's diary? That's just the start. Corrupt governments, global criminal networks ... some very, *very* nasty and evil people live in this world, Rex. We may not be able to stop everything, but we stop what we can, and we can't show our hand. Everything has to be done in secret. And that, Rex, is why I don't know what's in the base. I don't need to know.'

Rex nodded, still stunned at what he just learned.

'Do I report to you?'

'Me? No, not me. Limbick is your man. I'll help you as much as I can, but as I say, I can't be a part of whatever you get up to. I understand he's got some training lined up for you, but I don't know any details.'

The car pulled into the underground carpark of the hotel. Rex hadn't even realised they'd arrived.

'Right then, you can help me get ready for dinner. We're having a more intimate affair tonight. Just our family and Amy's and Scott's.'

'What about Penelope?'

'She's going to Vivienne's for the night to see how they get along. So, you can talk relatively freely at dinner. Just don't mention anything inside the base, alright?'

'Got it,' said Rex. 'And, Grandad?'

'Yes, mate?'

'Thanks. For being honest I mean.'

Grandad slapped Rex on the back, and they unloaded the car.

An amazing red sky sunset and an unseasonably warm breeze spilled over the hills behind Lenzie Bay as if to repay the town for the past few days. Rex waited outside the front doors of the hotel with Tom for Amy and Scott to arrive. After the interrupted celebration of the previous night, Rex's mum and dad suggested a quiet family meal with Amy, Scott and their parents, and rooms for the night. Rex couldn't wait to tell Amy and Scott what Grandad had told him. A magpie flew down to the lawn area leading around to the dining room for an evening forage and gave a short carolling greeting to Rex. Tom looked around, sniffed, yawned and slumped down for a snooze.

Two cars entered the gates and pulled up at the doors. Rex watched Amy get out the first car, while Scott jumped out of the other one.

'Hiya,' said Amy to Rex.

'Hi,' replied Rex. Amy was wearing a retro summer floral print dress that flared out from her waist. Her wavy blonde hair was tied back with a white ribbon, exposing blue sapphire earrings that were the same shade of blue as her eyes. 'You look great,' said Rex. Amy smiled in appreciation.

'Cheers, thanks, mate,' said Scott, approaching behind Amy.

'They're going to park in the carpark,' said Amy, swinging to make her dress flare out as the cars started moving away.

'Right,' said Rex, not really listening.

'What's new?' asked Scott.

Rex suddenly registered Scott was there, and remembered he had something to tell them. 'Well, you'll never guess what Grandad told me today,' he said.

'Umm, let's see,' said Scott, holding a finger up to his temple and closing his eyes in concentration. 'Yes ... yes ... It's coming ... wait ... Got it!' He opened his eyes again. 'Our parents are all secret agents and the whole town knows about the base.'

Rex's jaw dropped. He looked at Amy, who was smiling widely.

'Mum and Dad told me earlier,' said Amy. She looked at Scott. 'Same?'

'Yep,' confirmed Scott. 'But it wasn't really a surprise. Not when you think about it.'

'Yeah, I suppose, but still ...' said Rex.

'I know,' said Amy. 'I couldn't speak for about half an hour, which is a bit of a record I'll admit, but after I thought about it, yeah. It all made sense.'

'Hey,' said Scott. 'Do your parents know you know?'

'I don't know if they know I know, you know?' said Rex smiling.

'Yeah, I know. Well, then. You know what?'

'What?'

'Since they don't know that you know, and we do know that we know, we should pretend that we don't know,' finished Scott.

'Hmmmm, I don't know,' said Rex slowly.

'Oh, give it a rest you two,' said Amy. 'Grandad will have told them he told you.'

'Yeah, you're probably right,' said Rex.

'I know,' said Amy, smiling. 'So, who's hungry? What's Grandad cooking up tonight?'

'Fish and chips, he told me,' said Rex. 'But I suspect it's a bit more elaborate than that.'

Rex, Amy and Scott arrived at the family dining room just as Amy and Scott's parents were going in. The parents exchanged handshakes and kisses, then turned their attention to Rex, Amy and Scott. Grandad distributed slender glasses of French Champagne while pleasantries were exchanged.

Grandad disappeared into the kitchen and returned shortly after. 'Canape?' He held a plate covered with various snack sized nibbles. 'We've got spicy Swiss dumplings, smoked salmon and avocado, cornichons, olives, *Bündnerfleisch* ... Try something.' Amy didn't wait for the others and picked a dumpling and smoked salmon before the others had even decided what to try.

Soon, Sylvie was inviting them all to sit while Grandad poured more Champagne. Rex was at the end of the table with Amy on his left and Scott on his right.

'Something smells good, Syd,' said Charlie. 'Fish and chips again?' he asked with a grin.

'How did you guess?' replied Grandad. 'But first, a starter.' He went back to the kitchen and returned with a large plate covered in slices of tomato, fresh basil and raw mozzarella, drizzled with balsamic vinegar, olive oil and sprinkled with black pepper. He dished a small amount onto everyone's plate before taking a seat himself at the head of the table and raising a glass.

'Welcome!' he said. The adults gave each other knowing looks and they all turned to Rex, Scott and Amy and raised their glasses.

After they all sipped and lowered their glasses again, Rex said, 'Thank you. And, yes, we do know what's going on ... sort of. Grandad told me earlier.'

Sylvie answered. 'We're sorry we couldn't tell you, Rex.'

Roy continued. 'We thought it would be better if you found the base yourself. I wasn't convinced, but as it turned out, you proved beyond a doubt you've earned your title.'

'Title?' said Rex, surprised. 'What title?'

'Well,' replied Roy. 'We didn't think, considering what you've achieved and done over the past few days, that Corporal was worthy enough. So ...'

'Private?' asked Rex.

'Well, we don't actually use ranks most of the time, but it helps to establish a hierarchy. We decided that something more fitting be bestowed upon you, Captain Rex.'

Scott nearly spat Champagne over the table. He recovered and turned to Rex. 'Captain Rex. Has a ring to it, don't you think?'

Roy continued. 'And you two can think of yourselves as Commander.' Rex, Amy and Scott beamed at each other.

'Now eat! Please,' prompted Grandad. 'I'll get the main course ready.'

Soon, Grandad was back with plates expertly layered on his arm. He lay a plate before Amy and announced, '*Sole Meunière*, and *Rösti*. My favourite version of Fish and Chips.' On the plate was a whole fish with parsley and flaked almonds drizzled with clarified butter. To the side was a portion of crispy potato *Rösti* and a generous wedge of fresh lemon.

'Looks delicious,' said Amy.

'Simple food is often the tastiest,' said Grandad, before distributing plates to everyone else.

It wasn't long before Grandad was again serving dessert. Tonight's was a piece of *Bündner Nusstorte* dusted with sugar, a dollop of cream and a raspberry sauce in a little pot to drizzle on top. They all tucked in and were soon sitting back in their chairs, full and happily satisfied. Scott went to the kitchen for seconds while Rex and Amy dabbed the cream from their mouths. As they replaced the napkin on their laps, their hands touched briefly under the table and withdrew in surprise. Neither of them gave anyone else any indication it had happened, but they both sought each other's hands again, this time holding firmly. Scott returned from the kitchen and started tucking into his extra piece of cake. With his mouth full he looked up to see Amy and Rex smiling broadly.

'What?' he said, around a mouthful of cake.

'Nothing,' replied Amy. Scott shrugged and returned to his plate.

Rex turned to Grandad. 'Thanks, Grandad, that was excellent. Everything is.'

'You are most welcome,' replied Grandad graciously. 'And now'—he raised his glass—'I would like to make a toast.'

He waited while everyone else retrieved glasses from the table.

'To Rex, Scott and Amy. May all your missions be successful.' Everyone tinged glasses and sipped.

'Thanks,' said Rex. 'I'm not really sure what we do next, though. There's so much to learn, and …' He glanced at Amy and Scott. 'I'm not sure any of us know enough to be doing any sort of mission.'

'Ah, that reminds me,' said Roy. 'I understand you've been given some access cards at the library?' Rex nodded. 'Well, they also work on any other things to do with the base. You know, locks et cetera, so keep them safe. Also, they will carry any orders you might receive. I understand Mr Limbick has arranged some training for you all, so when you are done here you can check that out. I dropped off a card reader in your room earlier, Rex. Once you plug it in your computer, you will be able to use your cards to access the secure areas you need to. You will still have to go to school, but you'll have plenty of time to do the training.'

CHAPTER 39

As they were returning to their rooms after dinner, Scott said, 'You know what? We should check that our cards work.'

'Yeah let's,' said Amy. 'Was there really a floating plane down there or did I just dream it?'

'We definitely need to check,' said Rex.

They turned back, headed down to the storeroom and took the lift to the bottom floor. They emerged from the lift and headed straight for the lockers at the end of the corridor. After clearing away the boxes and pushing the lockers back to their original location, Rex tried his card on the keypad. It immediately beeped and the light went green. The door locks clicked. Scott pushed the doors open. Rex switched the big light switch. Again, the lights clunked into action and lit up the huge area in sequence.

Amy gulped. 'It's still there.'

They walked in, closer to the plane. It bobbed gently on the calm surface of inky black water.

'Looks cold,' said Rex.

They approached the edge of the dock and walked along to the mobile crane sitting in rail tracks that led off to huge doors at the end of the room. There was a small control panel mounted on its side. Scott read the labels of the four buttons.

'Connect, Retract, Lower and Raise,' he read. He turned to Amy and Rex. 'What's it going to raise? The Kracken?'

They all laughed. Amy said, 'Go on then, press it. Raise the Kracken!'

Scott reached out and pressed the button marked 'Raise'.

Nothing happened.

'Some Kracken,' said Rex.

They looked around, expecting to see the crane move at least.

'Uh oh,' said Scott. He pointed to the water. It was becoming more turbulent, swirling around.

A shape formed into view beneath the surface, growing clearer. Now the crane was tilting back, exposing more of its long metal girders. The surface of the water was broken by a long pole rising vertically, followed by a large, long metal shape. It projected out of the water, towering above them until half the length of water surface erupted in wash. The huge craft settled as water washed from its decks. The three friends stood there agape before a huge submarine. The crane boom stretched over the water to the sub where it attached to a port in the deck. The seaplane was now positioned on a long ramp on the sub that extended to the bow. On the side of the submarine conning tower, painted with big white letters was 'I-418'.

Underneath was a Japanese flag.

'Somehow I don't think that's a Kracken,' said Scott with a mix of awe and trepidation in his voice.

'That's one hell of a secret,' said Amy.

'I think I've got a fair idea of what kind of missions we'll be doing,' said Rex, quietly.

'You can say that again,' answered Amy.

Scott sighed. 'I hate boats. Planes? Good. Boats? Especially boats that go under water ... not so much.'

'I think I know why they made you Captain, Rex,' said Amy.

They stood for a long time, taking it all in and realising the enormity of the task ahead of them.

Rex broke the silence. 'Well, you two. We can't stay here all night. Let's go back up and find out what our mission is.'

Amy and Scott looked at each other, then replied with a hearty, 'Aye, aye, Captain!'

ABOUT THE AUTHOR

R.M. Ruxton is an I.T. Specialist based in Brisbane. This is his first novel.

Guvf cntr vagragvbanyyl yrsg oynax.

www.ingramcontent.com/pod-product-compliance
Lightning Source LLC
Chambersburg PA
CBHW030934210726
48290CB00007B/2180